Searching

for

Persephone

Peter + Tracey,

~~Hope~~ you enjoy
reading this!

978-1-7781749-0-2 (paperback)
978-1-7781749-2-6 (hardcover)
978-1-7781749-1-9 (e-book)

Publisher: Melikos Publishing
www.melikospublishing.com

Book Design: S. M. Perkins Carr
Cover Design: S. M. Perkins Carr and A.S. Carr
Cover Photo ©2022 Lichon Photography

Printed and bound in Canada with First Choice Books, Victoria, BC.

This is a work of fiction. While it references existing locations, institutions, and global events, the characters and their lives are wholly imaginary. Any resemblance to actual persons, living or dead, or actual personal events is purely coincidental.

Searching

for

Persephone

~a novel~

S. M. Perkins Carr

Part One

Prelude

Persephone and Violet were stuck. Their backs against a tall hedgerow, they watched a sizable herd of Cornish cows encircle them, closing in slowly and somehow menacingly. Violet's mind raced, retracing all the decisions that had brought them to this moment and wondering where it had all gone wrong. They'd decided to visit Cornwall to connect with their ancestral roots; they'd chosen to go for a long walk to see the ancient Men-an-Tol stones; they'd asked a local farmer for directions and followed the path he'd pointed to (his words were rendered unintelligible to them by his thick rural Cornish accent); and finally, they'd decided to cross this particular field, the only visible route in the right direction.

"Shit! What do we do?" Violet looked over to Persephone for guidance, but Persephone shrugged.

"I have no idea. You're the vegetarian animal lover. Can't you charm them like you do with cats, or

1

something?" Persephone's dark wavy hair bounced on her shoulders as she turned from Violet back to the brown beasts.

"They're not just over-sized cats, Persephone. I never even met a cow before," replied Violet impatiently.

"Well, you're about to meet a whole lot of them."

"I don't *want* to meet them! They're freaking huge, and not very friendly!"

At that moment, one cow bared its large flat teeth and let out a sound somewhere between a growl and a groan.

Violet screamed. "That cow wants to kill us! Do something!" Her blue eyes were wide with panic as she turned to Persephone, who stood calmly beside her, looking pensive.

"Calm down. They're just cows."

Violet breathed deeply and tried to collect herself. "Nice cows?" she offered, somewhat unconvincingly. "I don't eat you. Please don't kill me."

"Jesus Christ, Violet." Persephone rolled her eyes and shook her head. "Is that the best you can do?"

The towering bovines were closing in, now only several feet away from the two young women. Violet closed her eyes and pressed herself harder against the hedgerow, almost resigned to her fate of death by farm animals. The newspaper headlines appeared in her mind: "Two Canadian tourists trampled to death by cows in Cornwall." She wondered if their was an afterlife, and hoped vehemently that the great beyond included rivers and oceans she could swim in.

At that moment, however, Persephone began to sing, quietly yet confidently.

"Hello cows, hello,
Hello cows, hello."

Violet opened her eyes slowly, to see the cows had stopped in their tracks and were now regarding Persephone with what appeared to be a mix of confusion and curiosity.

"Hello cows, it's music time,
It's good to see you today."

It was the song Persephone used at the start of her music therapy sessions with children. Realizing with relief that she might not die today after all, Violet joined in as they repeated the simple song. Persephone waved her hands in time to the music, as if conducting an invisible orchestra, and began to step forward. Apparently hypnotized, the cows slowly parted for her, and Violet followed close behind.

They moved cautiously across the field in this way until they'd nearly reached the other side, when Violet was startled by the sound of hooves beating on the ground. Turning, she saw a single cow running towards her, apparently not impressed by the song or the conducting. Violet had no time to think, but having already decided that today was not the day she would die, her body seemed to find a solution on its own. "Shhhh," she said, waving her hand in a circular motion. The cow stopped suddenly, regarding Violet suspiciously, giving the two young women just enough time to escape through a nearby gap in the hedgerow. Relief flooded Violet's body and mind.

Persephone adjusted her black-rimmed glasses and looked over at her friend. "I really think you should consider eating those things."

Violet was bent over with her hands resting on her knees, her heart still racing. She took several deep breaths before replying, "I thought they'd be nicer in person."

Persephone laughed, and Violet sat down on the damp ground, dissolving into tearful giggles, awash in a mix of emotions.

"I actually thought they might kill us." Violet smiled as she wiped a tear from her eye.

"It would have almost been worth it, just for the irony of a vegetarian being killed by a herbivore."

Violet laughed until her stomach hurt, and Persephone helped her back up on to her feet.

"Come on, we survived. Let's go find those crazy neolithic stones."

Chapter 1

Crete, May 2019

Κρήτη, Μάιος 2019

Violet's feet dragged as she stepped off the plane in Chania, exhausted and dazed from the long series of flights. She was ten time zones from home, and, she thought, quite possibly in an entirely different universe. Travelling had never sat well with her; she always had the sense that her body wasn't really built to move so swiftly through space, and the unnaturalness of it drained her completely. On top of this, airports tended to fill her with dread; all the passport control and customs officers checking up on everyone, the line-ups at security which made her palms sweat even though she had absolutely nothing to hide. In these places she felt that at any point, something completely out of her control could happen and things could all go terribly wrong.

But thankfully this airport was small and unassuming. Violet breezed through passport control, though she couldn't remember what she'd actually said to the customs officer, who smiled and seemed to be genuinely pleased to welcome her to Greece. Mostly Violet just wanted to have a shower and sleep and wasn't too bothered about which country these two things happened in.

She always half-expected her suitcase not to turn up, especially after three connecting flights, but as if by miracle, it appeared on the carousel, taunting her with its arrival.

"See! I told you I'd get here, Violet."

"Shut up!" said Violet aloud before she realized she was talking to her purple suitcase. "I need to sleep," she thought. Except this also came out as words, and just as she was beginning to doubt her sanity, turning around slowly with her belligerent suitcase, Violet was swept up in the arms of a large Greek woman who spoke excitedly in a mix of Greek and English that Violet would soon dub *Greeklish*. She smiled politely while her addled brain struggled to process fragments of her aunt's words.

"Vee-o-lettaaaa! Welcome! I kept telling your *mitera*[1] to send you. Why you take so long to visit? Never mind, we are so happy you're here. How was your flight? Is very long, no? You must be hungry, I have *spanakopita* in the car for you, then we feed you properly at the taverna, yes? You look skinny, they not feed you in Canada? Your *Theios Kostas*[2] is very excited to see you too. We'll take care of you, you don't worry about anything, OK? You remember Angelos, your cousin, you met him when you were ten and we came to visit. Your *yiayia* and *pappous*[3] are so excited to finally meet you. You'll see, Sfinari Bay is very special, a good place to rest."

1 Mother
2 Uncle Kostas
3 Grandma and grandpa

6

The monologue continued, and Violet mumbled the occasional short response but mostly *Theia Maria*[4] chatted incessantly, seemingly without pausing for breath. This suited Violet just fine, as she was not in the mood to make conversation. In fact, she hadn't spoken much at all over the previous eight months, and she now found herself wondering if her vocal chords would one day cease to function properly if she continued in her silence. She wasn't really worried though; Violet was fairly certain she'd have very little to say over the course of the coming months and years. Certainly she'd never have as much to say as her garrulous aunt.

It was over an hour's drive to Sfinari and Violet must have nodded off at some point. She was jolted awake as the car came to a stop by the family taverna, with *Theia Maria's* chatter still continuing. Had she stopped at any point on the drive? Violet wasn't sure.

"Here, you see? Our *Paradise Taverna* is there, the beach just here. *Poli oraia*.[5] Paradise, yes?"

Violet opened her car door, and stumbled out slowly, certain that *Theia Maria* was exaggerating. But as she took in the scene before her, she felt that peculiar pang across her chest that one feels when faced with a certain otherworldly and unexpected beauty. It had been a long time since she'd felt anything at all, and the sensation caught her off guard.

Nestled in a sheltered bay, a beautiful grey pebbly beach bordered with tamarisk trees and Aleppo pines lay

4 Aunt Maria
5 Very beautiful

before her. Rustic sun umbrellas made from grass, and simple wooden lounge chairs lined the section of the beach in front of the taverna. Just behind the pine trees, nearer the taverna, sat several inviting little tables. A bright blue and red sign over the patio area read, *"Paradise Fish Taverna."*

It was not an upscale place, there were no luxury upholstered chairs or leather-bound menus, no grain of pretense to be found. Rather, it possessed an earthy charm and an indefinable allure.

The turquoise Mediterranean Sea (or the Sea of Crete, as she would soon learn the locals called it) glistened and beckoned through the trees in the intense golden light of the early evening. The air was warm, with a gentle salty breeze coming in from the sea, mingling with the scent of freshly-cooked fish, lemon and herbs coming from the taverna. Violet had the feeling she'd travelled backwards in time at least fifty years, or perhaps, she thought, this place existed outside of time entirely.

Theia Maria was too busy chatting (now mostly in Greek) to notice Violet's stunned response, or perhaps she noticed and continued talking, as she couldn't bear even the slightest possibility of silence, and Violet was clearly not in the mood to talk. Before she knew it, her suitcase was taken away by *Theios Kosta*, who gave her a warm but comparatively understated welcome.

"Welcome," he said gently as he hugged her and then disappeared with her purple suitcase.

"Where is he taking it?" she wondered, but before she could ask, she was whisked over to a table by the sea.

Violet's grandparents, whom she'd never met, stood up from the table, exclaiming excitedly in Greek and approaching her with open arms. She was enveloped in a sea of embraces and chatter that she couldn't understand as her *yiayia* held Violet's face in her hands and inspected it rather closely. They knew their granddaughter didn't speak Greek but they couldn't stop the flow of words in their emotional state. Violet smiled and tried not to look too confused. Fortunately, her cousin Angelo joined them and translated what he could.

"*Yiayia* says you look like a pale version of your mother."

It wasn't the first time Violet had heard this, but she smiled anyway, trying to share in the excitement as best she could in her current state.

As she sat down at the table, a wave of exhaustion washed over Violet and she managed to interject a brief sentence into the Greek chatter. "*Theia Maria*, I'm very tired—"

Her aunt nodded knowingly. "*Nai.*[6] Yes. Eat first and then sleep. You sleep better on a full stomach." She disappeared into the kitchen, leaving Violet nodding at the table.

The food appeared in waves that reminded Violet of a stomach flu in reverse. Just when she thought there couldn't possibly be more food, another course appeared and she had no choice but to eat. Thankfully Violet's mother had informed her sister Maria that Violet didn't eat meat, but the fact that she didn't eat fish either seemed

---

6 Yes

to have been lost in translation somewhere. She looked down at the whole *skaros*[7] on her plate, its unseeing eye gazing up at her accusingly, and pondered whether this was a battle worth fighting.

"My Angelos caught that fish this morning just for you! Your mother said you no eat meat, but I said it's OK, we are fish people!" *Theia Maria* smiled proudly and Violet knew she didn't have the heart to disappoint her. She consoled herself with the thought that it was at least wild-caught and sustainably sourced.

Surprisingly, even through her exhausted hazy mind, Violet could tell the food she was being force-fed was more flavourful than anything she'd consumed in her nearly twenty-five years of existence. She found herself devouring the *skaros* and wondered who this person was, sitting at the table hoovering fresh fish into her mouth like she hadn't eaten in months. In fact, she'd eaten very little since the preceding August and would have found it impossible to describe a single meal she'd had since then. Until now.

Following the fish, (which had followed bread, *choriatiki*,[8] and *dolmades*,[9] there were several rounds of vegetarian dishes (to make up for the lack of meat, which *Theia Maria* kept reiterating): *boureki*,[10] *yemistes piperies*,[11] *briam*,[12] *avronies*,[13] and finally some syrupy sweet halva[14]

---

[7] Parrotfish

[8] Greek salad

[9] Rice and herbs wrapped in vine leaves, cooked in lemon juice

[10] Roasted vegetables with cheese

[11] Stuffed peppers

[12] Roasted vegetables with pureed tomato

[13] Wild asparagus

[14] A sticky cake made with semolina, honey, cinnamon, and cloves

for dessert. By now, Violet was becoming genuinely concerned that her stomach might actually burst, and withdessert served, she hoped desperately that she could now finally excuse herself and go to bed.

But just then, *Theios Kosta* emerged from the kitchen with a bottle of *rakomelo*[15] and some glasses. "Good for...digest," he offered. His English wasn't quite as good as his wife's, but he patted his stomach and Violet nodded.

She didn't really feel like drinking, and she'd already been forced to sip some local red wine, but at this point she was resigned to doing whatever she had to do in order to finally get some sleep. She drank the *rakomelo* down easily, with unexpected enjoyment. It reminded her of cough syrup from her childhood, the sickly-sweet kind she used to beg her mother for more than just a teaspoon of.

Her uncle smiled. "You like?"

"*Nai,*" replied Violet, surprised that this was her honest answer, and also that she'd spoken one of the few Greek words she knew.

"You speak Greek soon!" her uncle said, beaming quietly.

Theia Maria had disappeared into the kitchen and Violet took the opportunity to ask her uncle if she might get some sleep.

"Yes yes. Is....long travel," he managed to say with some effort. "Come, I show you." he gestured for her to follow him.

Next to the taverna was an unassuming two-storey building with six rooms, usually only used during the

---

[15] Honey raki

high season. They didn't advertise, as they were quite happy for it to be a word-of-mouth endeavour, and they preferred having some idea of the sorts of people who stayed there. Occasionally an adventurous tourist would wander in, eat at the taverna and inquire about the rooms, but for the most part, it was only frequented by a smattering of distant relations and visiting friends.

Theios Kosta proudly took Violet to the upper floor and opened the door to the room nearest the sea. "Best room," he said, smiling.

It was modest, but impeccably clean, and the Mediterranean sunlight streamed in through windows on three sides, painting everything a certain shade of glowing golden-yellow. The cream-coloured curtains had been pulled aside, and they moved lazily in the warm breeze that came in through the open windows. Through one window, Violet could see the azure sea sparkling through the dark pine trees. There was a small kitchenette with a sink, a kettle, a hotplate and a small fridge, and on the opposite wall, a single bed with a bedside table and a dresser at the end. A small shower room sat at the back.

"Thank you," said Violet. "It's perfect."

Her uncle smiled. "You need anything, you call." He pointed to a business card on the bedside table. Violet noticed her purple suitcase had already been placed beside the bed. "If you change thoughts, and you want...stay with us? You call," said *Theios Kosta,* looking rather serious.

Violet had been reluctant to leave her home. She had agreed to the visit on the condition that she have her own place for the duration of her stay. Her mother had warned her this could come across as rude, as family always stayed in the family house, but Violet refused to budge. She needed her space and her privacy and she didn't want to feel she was imposing. The rooms were empty in May anyway, and they were only ever half-full even at the best of times, so Maria and Kosta had no reason to turn down the request. Any possibility of being offended was mitigated by their knowledge of what Violet had endured, and a desire to care for their only niece.

"Thank you," said Violet to her uncle, her eyelids beginning to droop and fall over her eyes.

"You sleep well," nodded *Theios Kosta*, and left quietly.

There was no question of a shower at this point. Violet simply laid down on the bed and slept for nearly fifteen hours.

Chapter 2

Persephone and Violet had initially been drawn together by a mutual dislike of the game of red rover being played by their first grade classmates at recess. Always one of the smallest in her class, Violet found she was inevitably the weak link where the opposing team would choose to break through, as well as the most likely to be called over by the other team; her small body was easily deflected as she tried to force herself past the linked hands much larger than hers. She tended not to try very hard in either case. It hurt too much when she did, and she could never get through her opponents anyway. She found the whole thing decidedly unpleasant and couldn't understand the appeal of it to her peers. Persephone, on the other hand, simply preferred to read.

So, when Violet drifted away from the group that day, she found Persephone sitting on the steps by the school doors, reading a book.

"What are you reading?" asked Violet, leaning over her classmate, trying to peer at the pages.

"You wouldn't like it," replied Persephone without looking up.

"How do you know?" asked Violet.

"It's a grown-up book about Greek myths," said Persephone, briefly peering up at Violet, certain she would lose interest and leave her to read in peace.

"Oh *I* know Greek myths. My mom is Greek. Is your mom Greek?" Violet sat down beside Persephone and tried to sound out a word, any word, on the page. But the writing was small and the words were long. The truth was that even Persephone, though a precocious reader, could only read about half the text, but there were pictures too, and she was enjoying decoding the stories.

"No. My mom says she's from the universe," said Persephone. "But my dad says she's from Kiss-tilano." Persephone wouldn't learn to pronounce 'Kitsilano' correctly for another six months or so.

"Where's the universe?" asked Violet, intrigued.

"I'm not sure. I think it's sort of everywhere. The book says the universe came from...chaaa-os." Persephone sounded out the words phonetically, with mixed results. "Then, there was dark and light. And then–" she paused as she flipped through pages at the beginning of the book to jog her memory. "Oh yeah. There was earth and ocean and sky, which is also called Oo-ran-us." She glanced at Violet and as she appeared to still be listening, Persephone continued. "Then, there were some crazy gods called Titans. They did lots of weird things. Kron-os was one of them. He ate all his kids, except one."

"Ew! Why did he do that?"

"Cause he was *scared* of them. But then they came back up out of his stomach, and they were fine."

"Ewww!"

"And then they killed him."

Violet screwed her face up in disgust. "OK, that's very gross and very weird, and a little bit sad."

"Yeah. But I thought you already knew the Greek myths?" asked Persephone, slightly accusatorily.

"My mom never told me that one."

"She probly thought it was too scary for you."

"Yeah."

"See, I told you you wouldn't like it." Persephone looked at Violet and shook her head.

"I do like it!" countered Violet. "Tell me another one."

Their friendship grew from that point on, and by the end of the school year the two had become inseparable. Violet's parents, Anna and Martin, were increasingly aware that Persephone's home life was somewhat lacking in stability, and were happy to help nurture and support their daughter's friend. They began to consider her almost a second daughter, or at least an adopted niece. And if Anna had ever worried about not providing Violet with a sibling, her mind was put at ease when she watched the two of them together on their frequent play-dates, absorbed in their own shared world, sisters in all but their bloodlines.

Chapter 3

Crete, May 2019

Κρήτη, Μάιος 2019

Waking up from her long sleep, Violet wasn't sure if she'd only slept a few hours or an entire night. The sun was bathing the room once more in its distinctly Mediterranean glow, but she felt unexpectedly well-rested, so she judged she must have slept all night and woken up the following day.

Her cellphone battery had died hours ago and Violet wasn't in the habit of wearing a wristwatch. The thought of trying to dig out her phone charger from somewhere in her purple suitcase filled her with dread. And in any case, Violet was enjoying the sense of unusual freedom that comes with not knowing or needing to know what time it is; she had nowhere to be, no appointments to keep, no one relying on her for anything.

Taking a long shower, she was struck by the sense that she was washing away remnants of the life she'd temporarily left behind. Remnants that didn't belong to her anymore. She had resisted her mother's idea to send her here; movement had felt nearly impossible within her comfortable puddle of grief and angst. But now she was here, she understood (though she wasn't quite ready to admit it out loud) that her mother had probably been right.

She tied her light brown hair up into a quick ponytail, not attempting to tidy it. Her hair was somewhere between wavy and curly and annoyingly uncooperative when she tried to style it, and besides, she wasn't looking to impress anyone today. As she pulled on her favourite denim shorts and a loose-fitting tank top, Violet became aware of another sensation she hadn't felt in a long time: hunger. "Damn that's annoying," she said aloud to herself. She didn't dare go down to the taverna, as she wasn't quite ready to be drawn back into the real world of schedules and socializing, and she hadn't had the chance to stock her small fridge and cupboards.

Violet decided to ignore her hunger for now and go for a walk, but as she opened the door to her room, she smiled to see a large box of food waiting for. Having grown up with a Greek mother, she had some sense of the importance of food in this culture, but she still hadn't quite anticipated just how much she'd be fed by her family. Nonetheless, she was grateful for this particular offering, and took it down to the beach, heading to her left away from the *Paradise Taverna*, not wanting to be seen by anyone just yet. In her worn-out state the day before, she hadn't noticed there was a second taverna in this direction. The sign over the door read simply *Sfinari Beach Taverna*. Violet wondered vaguely who owned it and whether they were friends or competitors, but was much more concerned with consuming the Cretan delicacies in the box she carried. Sitting down under a large tamarisk tree, she began to eat a glorious bowl of yogurt topped with honey and fruit. Again, the intense flavour of the simple food surprised her. Biting into the *dakos*[16] she was sure this must be the first time she'd eaten real tomatoes. And the various cheeses here certainly bore no resemblance to the cheese found in the grocery stores back home in Vancouver. Even the expensive feta her mother used to buy from the Greek deli was no match for the rich creamy textures that presented themselves here. There were also a few *dolmades,* which she was fairly certain were not a traditional breakfast food, but by now she understood that her family wanted to ensure she consumed as much food as was humanly possible while she was here.

She was pondering whether to eat the *dolmades* or save them for later when a large ginger and white tomcat appeared next to her and mewed loudly, looking up at her with large sorrowful eyes. Violet threw it a bit of rusk, which it licked, then looked back up at her and mewed again as if to say, "Haven't you got anything better than that?"

"Sorry kitty, I'm a vegetarian," said Violet, shrugging. "And these tomatoes are way too good to give away." Another cat appeared, this one slightly smaller with black and white patches. It ate the rejected rusk, then mewed wistfully at her.

"You know, once you feed them, they'll never leave you alone." Violet turned around quickly. The words had

---

[16] Tomatoes and mizithra cheese on rusk

been spoken in an unmistakably American accent and she half-expected to see a blonde, blue-eyed movie star behind her. Instead she was presented with a tall olive-skinned stranger, probably a few years older than her, and looking much more Greek than he sounded. He stood with his head cocked to one side, his mouth curled into a teasing smile.

"You don't sound Greek," Violet blurted out awkwardly. It was all she could think of to say, as her brain was simply repeating the phrase, "I hope I'm not related to him." Sfinari was a small village and her grandparents both came from large local families, so she knew she had plenty of second and third cousins in the area.

"You don't *look* Greek," he shot back.

"I'm only half-Greek. What's your excuse?"

He ignored her question. "Which half of you is Greek?"

"Dammit," thought Violet, "this is not what I need." But out loud she said, "Well it must be my bottom half. It's definitely not my head cause my tongue sure can't speak Greek." Inwardly she wondered how on earth she was so effortlessly flirting with this dark-haired stranger. She nibbled carefully on a *dolma*, attemping to make it look sensual rather than messy.

"Your tongue would get used to it if you practiced."

Violet's mind raced. Hearing him talk about her tongue was sending her thoughts in all sorts of directions that she had no wish to explore until she'd ascertained for sure that they weren't relatives.

But somehow she collected herself and replied, "Like you practiced your American accent?" Violet was taken aback by her own playfulness and wondered if indeed there was something in the food that was making her act like someone else entirely. She had the feeling she was suddenly the heroine in a cheesy Hollywood romantic comedy, churning out impossibly witty lines, sure to win the heart of the handsome leading man.

"I come by my accent honestly," he said, still grinning. "I grew up in northern California. What's your excuse for being so pale?"

Violet gave him an exaggerated glare and then raised her eyebrows as she replied, "Excuse me, but I think you'll find this is a lily-white complexion, much sought-after by the British upper class in Victorian times."

He smiled, "Yes, and much-maligned by English tourists burning in the Mediterranean sun. You should wear a hat."

"Thanks 'Dad', but I'm in the shade and it's only early May," shot Violet, feeling annoyed at his impudence but also not wanting the conversation to end.

"OK, whatever you say. But don't worry about the cats, we give them plenty of leftovers from the taverna."

"You work for my aunt and uncle?" said Violet, hoping this didn't sound as if she was fishing for information on whether or not they were related.

"No, my family runs the other taverna." He pointed to the *Sfinari Beach Taverna* behind them. "And no offence, but our *dolmades* are much tastier than yours."

"I very much doubt that," said Violet, eating the last one. "You'll have to prove it."

"OK, I'll bring you some later. You like honey?"

"Sure," shrugged Violet, "it's OK."

"OK?" he shook his head incredulously. "You've never tasted honey from Crete have you?"

"Of course I have. I just had some on my yogurt actually. Tasted pretty much like all the other honey I've ever had," said Violet, tilting her head coquettishly, intentionally baiting him as she sensed this was a weighted topic for him. The honey, of course, had been far superior to any honey she'd tried back home, but she wasn't about to admit it.

"Well," replied the stranger, "the honey they sell in the stores in America is usually mixed with corn syrup and barley malt." He shook his head in disgust. "I'll bring you some of my honey, and you tell me if it tastes like all your American honey."

"Whoa, whoa, whoa!" Violet, waved her hands melodramatically. "That's *Canadian* honey, OK? If you grew up in America then I'm sure you must have heard something about the big cold country just north of you?" Violet didn't pause to allow him to reply. "And by the way, I've only been awake on this island for a total of two hours and I've been basically force-fed the whole time. You're all a bit obsessed with food you know."

"Food is how we communicate here." He smiled.

"So, I just met you and you've promised me soggy vine leaves, rice, and bee spit. What are you communicating exactly?"

At that moment, a voice called from the nearby taverna in Greek.

"I have to go. But technically it's more like bee vomit. It was nice meeting you, Violet."

He turned and walked back to the taverna, saying something in Greek to a woman Violet presumed was his mother.

Violet noted that he knew her name, though she hadn't told him. Sfinari was a small place with few secrets between locals and clearly word of her arrival had spread.

"That is so inconvenient," she agonized out loud after he'd vanished.

Not for the first or last time, Violet desperately wished Persephone was around to help her navigate life's unexpected turns. But then, if Perse had still been alive, Violet most likely wouldn't be here now, on a sizable island in the Mediterranean with relatives she hadn't met since she was a child, trying not to entertain thoughts of a romance she was sure she was in no state to pursue.

She thought back to Persephone's scathing appraisal of the one man she'd called her boyfriend for eight months. There had been other dates of course, but most of them didn't hold her interest for long, the conversations stilted and the goodnight kisses awkward. But James had stuck around. Persephone, however, had been brutally honest in expressing her views on him.

"Well, if you want to be with someone who is undeniably inferior to you intellectually, James is a great choice."

Violet smiled at the memory, though her best friend's disapproval had been upsetting to her back then. She'd thought she loved him at the time, but looking back on it now, she was sure she'd only been in love with the idea of being in love. He'd made her laugh, he was pleasant company and easy on the eyes. Surely that was enough?

But increasingly, she'd found herself drawn to other friends and activities, not finding time in her schedule to see him. He'd eventually taken the hint and they'd gone their separate ways.

Violet sighed, and standing up, she decided to follow the path that went behind the tamarisk trees and up the headland to the left. She still had no idea what time it was, and no desire to check just yet. She certainly wasn't ready to be enveloped by her well-meaning *theia* once more. She promised herself she'd head to the taverna after her walk and be sociable then.

As she wandered down the path, three stray cats followed her hopefully, including the ginger and white tomcat, who stayed particularly close to her. Violet was aware of a strange mix of emotions brewing in her mind and heart as she ascended the gentle slope. For the first time since that day in August, she dared to feel a certain lightness. Her feet moved willingly underneath her, even quickly, encouraging her along the trail, while before they'd only dragged and felt impossibly heavy.

Breathing in the fresh sea air mingled with the scent of pine and wildflowers, Violet wondered if she was actually feeling happiness again, or at least a hint of it. It was glorious and liberating. But underneath this, a layer of guilt festered and filled her mind with questions. How could she possibly feel happy after what had happened? What right did she have to feel content? If she *was* happy, did that mean she'd forgotten her friend? Did it mean she'd never really cared for her? Violet knew this layer of feelings didn't make any sense. She knew that Persephone, ever practical, would have wanted her to be happy. But knowing that didn't put her confused conscience to rest. And beneath the guilt, however beautiful this place and however content she might feel in moments, the pain still sat like a stifling weight within her chest, very real and very raw.

"Persephone would have loved this place," she thought to herself, as she wound up the path through a patch of carob trees that gave way to towering thistles as tall as she was (which she'd later learn were wild artichokes). Giant bumblebees and honeybees crawled on the purple flowers and huge grasshoppers skipped over the path. The only sounds were the sea, the gentle breeze, and the soft buzz of bees.

Persephone had always loved nature, and had often extolled the virtues of forest therapies and garden therapies alongside other creative therapies such as her own. They'd talked about living together somewhere on BC's Sunshine Coast one day, where they'd have their dream jobs and an affectionate cat or two. Of course, Persephone knew exactly what her dream job was, while Violet would shrug in those conversations and jokingly say that her dream was to figure out what her dream was.

The path straightened, then came to an end near the top of the headland and Violet scrambled over some rocks to get as high as she could. From the top, she could see over to another smaller beach on the other side of the headland, also pebbly and completely empty. A small abandoned cottage sat nestled to one side, white paint peeling off the stone walls. Violet wondered how many of these amazing beaches this island held hidden.

Having grown up on the coast, she was used to finding secret beaches, but in Vancouver they tended to be tucked away behind large upper-class houses, squeezed in and often overlooked by wealthy homeowners. And while there were certainly beautiful pieces of coastline and wild places around her hometown, (including her favourite spot on the Capilano River), there was, she was sure, an entirely different quality to these Cretan shores. The land felt soaked in ancient stories and events; she had the sense that the earth here shared all its secrets with whoever stumbled across it, enmeshing the history of the humans and the land. In Canada, despite the natural beauty of the forests and coast, she'd always felt that she was a guest on the land, and it would only reveal its secrets in certain consecrated moments of its own choosing.

"Maybe I'm in an alternate universe," said Violet out loud, as she sat down to take in the views, remembering Persephone trying to explain the multiverse theory to her. She breathed deeply and tried to reconcile where she now found herself with where she'd come from, but her mind struggled to connect the two disparate worlds. Instead, her thoughts wandered off to another day by the sea in yet another part of the world.

Chapter 4

Near Penzance, Cornwall, October 2017

Violet and Persephone had walked a long way from Penzance. They'd visited Madron Well and the Men-an-Tol stones, and fended off some dangerous cows. They sat down for a much-needed rest and to take in the views from the ruins of an old tin mine overlooking the hamlet of Morvah and beyond that, the Atlantic Ocean. It was a windy day, with high white clouds that filtered out only a small amount of the autumn sunlight.

Persephone took out her vintage film camera and snapped a black and white photo of Violet sitting on the wall, silhouetted with the light behind her, her hair blowing in the atmospheric wind.

Though she wasn't keen on photos of herself, Violet still had a print of that photo at home on her mirror. When she looked at it, she felt she could see herself through Persephone's eyes. Frozen in that moment she could almost pretend she was a mythical creature descended from the Piskies, part of the landscape around her. But in reality she was (at that time) a recently graduated twenty-three-year-old with no idea what career path to choose, or how to fit in to the baffling society she found herself in, which seemed to expect so much of her but offer limited guidance on how to achieve those lofty aims.

Persephone, on the other hand, was an unusual mix of creativity and practicality. Where Violet had studied psychology simply because it interested her, Persephone had thought carefully about her future after graduation. Wanting to make good use of her grandmother's trust fund that had paid for her studies, she researched carefully and decided to undertake a music therapy degree. This meant she was essentially trained for a job, whereas Violet felt she had learned a lot of interesting information but was left with no idea of how or where to apply it. She had no interest in becoming a counsellor or psychologist; she'd just followed her natural curiosity about people and what made them tick. It had seemed like a good idea at the time, but since graduating, she'd often wished she'd had Persephone's forethought.

Persephone was unusually grounded, which she always said was despite her parents, rather than because of them. Her mother was, by Perse's own definition, "a crazy, well-meaning new-age hippie," who seemed to think her maternal role was essentially over once she'd given birth to her daughter. Of course she'd ensured in her own slightly detached way that her daughter was fed and clothed, and had introduced her to the practice of yoga from a young age. Persephone vaguely enjoyed the movements and stretching as a child, but admitted she hadn't fully appreciated what it was about until, as a teenager, she'd attended a yoga workshop led by a teacher who was also a physiotherapist. This particular teacher had explained the benefits of yoga for the mind and body in physiological terms, which Persephone had found surprisingly sensible. Certainly this language bore little relation to the phrases she'd heard from her mother, which tended to be along the lines of, "Turn your attention to your kidneys," or, "Become one with the room." As Persephone approached adolescence, sentences such as these increasingly caused her to roll her eyes so far into the back of her head she was sure she glimpsed her so-called "third eye."

Her father, born in Canada, but of Cornish origins, was a reclusive researcher who studied Paleolithic cave art. He had obtained a PhD but decided that the politics and bureaucracy of academia were not for him. Despite this, he found freelance work with various museums and cultural organizations, and published papers and books on the subject. He was, in fact, highly revered within his own esoteric circles.

While he wasn't exactly sure how to be a father, he had always doted on Persephone and perhaps because of this, she always felt loved as she grew up, despite being largely left to her own devices. She developed a striking ability from a young age to be "self-contained," able to entertain herself for hours with a box of crayons or a blob of play-dough.

There was an old piano in the small apartment that Persephone had always enjoyed playing, and it was her grandmother who had witnessed her picking out the melody to "Camborne Hill," a Cornish folk song she'd often sung to her. Seeing this, she paid for Persephone to take weekly lessons with a local teacher, first on piano and then on guitar. Her grandmother ensured she was taken to her classes every week, as neither parent could have managed this regular commitment. Persephone often said that her mother gave birth to her, her father gave her love, and her grandmother raised her. It was an unusual combination, but fortunately it seemed to have worked out well for Perse.

At the old tin mine, Persephone put down her camera and took out a small book of Cornish folklore she'd bought in Penzance a few days earlier.

"It says there's a Piskie that guards the Men-an-Tol stones. I didn't see one, did you?" she asked Violet jokingly.

They'd come here via the ancient circular stone which Violet had commented looked like they were trying to work out how to make a doughnut but didn't have quite the right materials. They'd laughed, and crawled through the stone, which they felt obliged to do, despite neither of them really believing it would "cure all ailments" as the booklet stated.

Violet smiled. "Of course I saw the Piskie, he was hopping all over you! Couldn't you feel him on your back?"

"You're definitely lying cause it says here he's a good Piskie, who undoes the work of the naughty ones. A good Piskie would *not* have been jumping all over me!"

"Well maybe he was annoyed that you were crawling through when you have no ailments to speak of. Save the healing powers for the rest of us mere mortals!" Violet was half-joking, but as with many jokes there was a kernel of truth in her assertion that Persephone did appear to have everything sorted, and there was a small part of Violet that couldn't help resenting her just a little for this at times.

"I have many ailments," replied Persephone. "I just happen to know how to manage most of them, most of the time."

"All of the time," said Violet rolling her eyes.

"That's not true," shot back Persephone. "Who would I have cried to about all my internship struggles if you hadn't been around?"

It was true that Persephone had had some difficulties during her internship, struggling to navigate growing tensions with her supervisor. It had been an unusual situation for Perse, who tended to get along easily with most people, though she was rather particular about who she'd choose to spend time with, having little patience with fools and idiots. Violet had always thought that her supervisor was in fact, inferior to Persephone in her talents and intelligence, and this had led her mentor to feel increasingly insecure in her role as she watched Persephone's skill and confidence grow. Persephone had said she felt they were just mismatched, and was unusually defensive when Violet had suggested her theory to her. It was the only time Violet had felt she'd perhaps had a better understanding of an interpersonal relationship than her best friend.

"Ooh it says that a changeling was once passed through the stone and the healthy infant was restored," offered Persephone, looking up and raising her eyebrows.

"Oh maybe I'm a changeling and I've come through the stone doughnut as a real person again. Maybe my life will sort itself out now!"

"You are a real person, Vi." Persephone was the only person who she'd let shorten her name to "Vi" as she thought it sounded like "vile" and reminded her of words like "violence."

Violet sighed. She'd been struggling since graduation with finding her feet in the world. She'd somehow vaguely assumed that she would be welcomed into the adult working world as a new graduate, and that some sort of fulfilling work would present itself to her. Only it hadn't. And beyond this, Violet realized that she had no idea what her idea of fulfilling work actually was, which made looking for it a rather challenging proposition. Sometimes she felt as if the world she was born into wasn't the one she truly belonged in, so the idea of being a changeling somehow resonated.

Violet's father was from Cornwall and had told her stories of the Piskies from a young age. She'd been particularly frightened of the changeling stories, fearing that one night she'd be abducted by naughty fairy-folk. Her father had assured her this would never happen for a number of reasons, including the fact that no one had ever seen a single Piskie anywhere in Canada. Violet had argued that Canadian Piskies might be very good at hiding, or they might have recently come over on a plane or a boat, but her father had said someone would always spot a Piskie eventually, and they were not good travellers so they'd never make it this far anyway.

"Do you think the Piskies used to actually exist?" mused Violet, changing the subject from her wayward life.

Persephone looked at her. "Do you?"

"Way to reflect back the question, Miss therapist," joked Violet. "You know I'm not one of your clients."

"Am I not allowed to genuinely want to know what you think?" teased Persephone. Reflecting back questions was a common tool of her trade. "Come on, what do you think?"

"Well, I'd sort of like to think they did. It's strange the way people not that long ago spoke about seeing them, about knowing they were around...and now you sound like a crazy person if you even entertain the possibility."

Persephone gave a wry smile. "People not that long ago also spoke about amazing miracles happening, being cured of paralysis by spring water at that well we passed by."

"Exactly!" said Violet earnestly. "It's like people had a whole different experience of the world. I mean, maybe none of those things happened, but people really believed that they did. So, either the way the world operates changed drastically, or our perceptions changed completely."

Persephone furrowed her brow slightly and looked out towards the sea, "Well, we know that our perceptions develop as a result of our experiences. So, you know, for example, we're born with eyes that function but our brains have to learn to interpret the light they perceive. Babies aren't born with depth perception. They have to learn that things that are farther away appear smaller, and they learn that as they explore the world around them, right?"

Violet nodded. Infant and child development had been one of her favourite subjects during her degree studies.

"So," continued Persephone, getting more animated and starting to talk with her hands, "if, when we learn to see, no one around us can see Piskies, would we develop or maintain the ability to perceive them with our eyes, even if they were there? If we pointed at them and our parents said 'What's that? There's nothing there,' maybe we'd just learn to filter out those perceptions. And maybe if our parents or grandparents talked to us about the Piskies, and saw them as well, maybe, just maybe we'd grow up being able to see them."

"Ooh I like your theory!" Violet's eyes lit up. She loved the way Persephone could mingle logic and fantasy. Violet could grasp both, but rarely connected them in the way Perse could. "So, we've sort of trained ourselves not to see them anymore?"

"Something like that," said Persephone, still thinking.

After a short pause, Violet continued, "But what caused the shift? Why did people stop seeing them in the first place?"

Persephone shrugged and looked back down at her folklore booklet. "The book says the Piskies disappeared when Christianity was brought here. The monks had no room in their teachings for the Piskies and people felt they had to choose between the new Church, or their old folklore. I guess most people chose the Church. It says the Piskies disappeared when no one believed in them anymore."

"That's so sad," said Violet, shaking her head. She had a sudden thought. "Is it a bit like Schrödinger's cat?"[17]

Persephone tilted her head "Dead and alive at the same time? You mean in the sense that it's our observing of things that sort of forces it to choose a reality? Piskies here or Piskies not here?"

"Something like that," mumbled Violet, not at all confident in her grasp of quantum physics, though she'd always been drawn to Persephone's descriptions of it. It seemed to mingle magic and science into a deliciously tantalizing soup of thoughts and questions, and Persephone's enthusiasm was often contagious.

Persephone smiled and her eyes came alive suddenly. "Ooh that reminds me of something I read recently. They talked about the slit experiment—double-slit I think it was called. Did I tell you about that one yet?"

"I don't think so."

"So," said Persephone, "they sent a light, a laser beam, through two slits, and you know, it makes a pattern of stripes, caused by wave interference. Which makes sense cause light is waves. But then someone realized that light was also made of particles. And *then*—" Persephone was now smiling broadly and gesticulating wildly as she continued, "they measured where the photons went.

---

[17] Schrödinger's cat is a thought experiment devised by physicist Erwin Schrödinger in 1935, demonstrating that, when its fate is linked to a random subatomic event, a hypothetical cat in a box can be both dead and alive simultaneously, as long as the box is not opened and the cat is not observed.

Photons are the light particles. I mean, they actually checked which slit the particles of light went through, and when they did that, the light didn't create the interference pattern you'd expect with waves! It behaved as if it was made *only* of particles!"

Violet looked at her friend, slightly puzzled, though she thought she'd managed to grasp the general gist of the short lecture.

"So what you're saying," recounted Violet slowly, "is that, a bit like with Schrödinger's cat, our perceptions can somehow change reality? Or maybe even define it? Or at least, make something that was two things, decide on one thing?"

"Yeah! Amazing, right?" exclaimed Persephone.

"So, if the Piskies both exist and don't exist, when we perceived them, they existed, and now that we don't see them, they've stopped existing."

"Maybe," said Persephone shrugging.

Violet knew that her friend wasn't the type to believe in Piskies, as much as she might want to. She'd often told Violet that she liked having a companion who believed in the things she couldn't quite convince herself of.

"That's really sad," said Violet pensively. "I wonder if we could bring the Piskies back."

"I don't think it's up to us," replied Persephone, ever practical. "I think it would require a seismic shift in the way society views the world. I guess when we took on Christianity, we lost the folklore, and when we took on science, we lost religion." She paused and sighed. "Shame we always have to choose one. Surely they could co-exist." She looked back down at the booklet. "The book says the

Piskies shrunk down smaller and smaller until they disappeared."

"What a way to go. Poor little Piskies," mused Violet as she gazed back out at the Atlantic.

Chapter 5

Crete, May 2019

Κρήτη, Μάιος 2019

Violet was jolted out of her reverie on the headland by the sound of loud panicked voices down in the bay she'd come from. She stood up quickly, and looking down the hill, saw her cousin Angelo running toward the headland and yelling. The strained voices of her *theia* and *theios* also rose up through the air but Violet couldn't make out what they were saying. Wondering what on earth was happening, she began making her way back down the hill, slowly realizing that Angelo was shouting her name in his thick Greek accent.

"Vee-o-lettaa! Vee-o-lettaa!"

Unsure what what possible disaster her relatives were trying to save her from, Violet began to run down the slope, calling, "I'm here, I'm here! I'm coming!" She met a very out-of-breath Angelo about half-way down (he could swim for hours but running was clearly not his type of exercise) who yelled back down the hill something in Greek.

"Angelo, what's going on?" Violet was somewhat distressed.

"We couldn't find you," he gasped. "My mother was worried." He panted, trying to catch his breath. He had an excellent grasp of English, learned from American sitcoms and Hollywood movies, but his accent was thick and not always easy to understand.

"I only went for a walk," said Violet. "I didn't think I was gone that long?"

"It's OK," replied Angelo, the rhythm of his breath finally beginning to slow. "My mother just...worries a lot."

"But what did she think?" sputtered a confused Violet. "Where could I have gone? Did she think I went and drowned myself in the sea or something?"

Angelo looked away and frowned slightly. "She just feels responsible for you. Your mother called and said you weren't answering your phone. She asked where you were and my mother couldn't find you. She panicked."

"I'll say," said Violet.

They walked slowly down the hill and as she calmed down and processed what had happened, Violet offered an apology, "I'm sorry if I worried everyone."

Angelo waved his hand as if swatting a fly. "Don't worry, it's not your fault. We're glad you're OK."

"Of course I'm OK," thought Violet to herself, bewildered by the whole fiasco. She knew her *theia* was an intense and often larger-than-life character, but the panic did seem disproportionate, even for her.

They continued to walk in silence. Angelo took after his father and was a quiet and kind soul who chose his words carefully. He was a calming presence, easy to be around and generally not easily flustered, except for today of course.

As they walked back down to the bay, Violet's curiosity got the best of her and she couldn't help asking about the *Sfinari Beach Taverna*. "Who runs it?" She tried to sound casual.

Angelo frowned and looked away again. "The Sfakianakis," he said simply.

Even for Angelo, this seemed a short response.

"Are they friends? Relatives?" pressed Violet.

Angelo shrugged. "Friends." He paused and then added, "but we don't talk to them much."

Violet waited, sensing there was more, but not wanting to push Angelo too much.

"Did your mother never tell you anything about them?" he asked.

"No," said Violet. "Why would she?"

Angelo looked at her. "Well, she grew up here, they were good family friends. I thought she might have mentioned them."

Violet shook her head. "She talked about this place. A lot. But I don't remember her mentioning another taverna or the family who ran it."

They were approaching the Sfakianakis' taverna now and Angelo put his finger to his lips. "We should keep our voices down. We can talk more later. Don't bring it up with my mother, she doesn't like to talk about it so much."

Violet nodded, desperate to know more. But it was clear now was not the time. She realized with a sigh that she had to now rejoin the scheduled adult world.

At the *Paradise Fish Taverna*, her aunt and uncle were preparing lunch. A table of four adventurous tourists sat at one of the tables by the sea. *Theia Maria* embraced her niece as if she'd come back from the dead, talking in *Greeklish* once again. Violet caught a few phrases.

"So so worried...your *mitera*, she worry...*tragodia*[18]..."

"I'm sorry if I worried you," offered Violet, "I only went for a short walk."

Theia Maria wasn't angry, but underneath her relief there was still a lingering fear. "Don't go in the sea unless Angelo is with you," she stipulated sternly, wagging her finger.

Violet felt like a reprimanded ten-year-old, a mixture of confusion and annoyance rising up inside her. She planned on spending a lot of time in the sea, and certainly didn't need a lifeguard. But before she could react outwardly, Angelo said something gently in Greek to his mother and Maria sighed and returned to the kitchen.

Angelo turned to his cousin. "Don't worry, the bay is safe. Just avoid the rocks over that side." He pointed over toward the headland she'd walked up earlier. "You can swim right?"

"Oh yes," said Violet, raising her eyebrows. Sometimes she felt more comfortable in the water than on the land. Water, she found, was soft and forgiving, molding itself to whatever entered into it, or whatever it came up against, whereas the land was hard and slow to change. Violet had always felt safe in the water. Her mother had made sure she'd learned to swim from a very young age, taking lessons and completing all the levels

---

[18] tragedy

through the years. Though the Pacific Ocean around her hometown was cold even in the height of summer, Violet still swam regularly. There had also been plenty of summer days out to nearby lakes with clear inviting waters, and of course the local swimming pool, where she'd taken her swimming lessons as a child. As a teenager she and Persephone had found a secret swimming spot on the Capilano River, down a steep narrow path and tucked away in the trees. It had been one of their favourite haunts through the years, but Violet hadn't been there since the previous August.

Angelo smiled and gestured for her to sit down. "We'll bring out lunch in a minute."

"Can I help?" she asked, but Angelo was already gone. "Here we go again," thought Violet. It couldn't have been more than two hours since she'd she'd eaten the food left outside her door. Still, she knew better than to try and refuse food here.

Violet turned and watched the group of tourists. Two couples, sipping fresh orange juice, spoke quietly in German. They looked out at the view, smiling and seeming relaxed. Violet wondered what had led them here, and how they'd found this out-of-the-way place. She envied how at ease they appeared, like they'd never felt pain or grief.

Violet was sure that since she'd lost Persephone she carried around a visible aura of emptiness, that everyone who saw her must have sensed that she was incomplete. Everyone else, it seemed to her, was content and absorbed in their own fulfilling lives. For eight months, she'd felt isolated from the rest of humanity, as if time had stopped for her, but no one else had noticed; and so clocks kept ticking, trains and buses came and went, people went to work, ate and slept, as if the world hadn't collapsed that day. She felt she'd become a mere observer of her surroundings, separated from everything and everyone by an invisible barrier of grief.

Violet sighed. At least here, she had some moments of feeling alive again. She thought back to her brief flirtation this morning and couldn't help smiling a little. Maybe it was OK to feel something again, a little crush, a bit of excitement. Maybe the door to the living breathing world was opening just a crack. She resolved to call her mother after lunch and tell her she was going to be alright.

Chapter 6

Anna

'Αννα

Anna Christina Daskalaki left Crete the day after her eighteenth birthday, on August 13, 1991, determined to never return. She had grown up in the small village of Sfinari, and had travelled little. She simply wanted to be as far away from the sea as possible. Beyond that, she didn't mind where she ended up.

Her parents had resigned themselves to her leaving, but were nonetheless certain she would be back. Who would move away from such a beautiful place? She would go abroad, have some adventures, find herself, get homesick, and return and marry a nice Greek boy. They were sure of it. So they contacted relatives in Toronto, and arranged for Anna to stay with them while she found her feet.

There was no sea or ocean near Toronto, Anna had checked in the atlas. There was a lake, but she thought she'd be able to tolerate that. Lakes were smaller and calmer, just large puddles of water really. Anna had only seen ponds and it was difficult to get a sense of scale from the atlas pages.

When her relatives took her for a day out on the shores of Lake Ontario, Anna gasped at the sight of it. It stretched out before her as far as she could see in all directions, looking every bit like the sea. Thankfully it was a calm summer day; had it been windy with whitecaps, as often happened, it might have been too much for her. Her relatives seemed proud of the size of this lake; they told her enthusiastically that it even had tides. Tides. The sea Anna had left behind didn't have any tides to speak of. How was it that this lake moved to the whims of the moon but the Mediterranean was oblivious? She asked, but no one was sure.

Anna later checked this at the local library and found that both her sea and the giant lake had very small tides, only a matter of centimetres. The Mediterranean, she learned, had such small tides due to its very narrow connection to the Atlantic, making it impossible for the water to rush in and out fast enough. The Great Lakes, on the other hand, had small tides proportionate to their size. Although "great" as lakes, and appearing to stretch out forever, they were small compared to the oceans and seas of the world, and their tides reflected this. Anna wondered at the fact that something could be both small and large at the same time. A large lake, but a small body of water as far as the moon was concerned.

Anna didn't wish to inconvenience her kind relatives for too long and was determined to find her own way in Toronto. While she only held a high school diploma, she had a sharp mind and a strong independent spirit, as well as a sound grasp of English. As a teenager with plans to leave the island, she'd had the forethought to put extra effort into her English lessons at school. All this led her to find work in a small jeweller's in Toronto, and she soon discovered she enjoyed the interactions with customers, and the rows of shiny trinkets, watches and accessories always made her feel like she was in a treasure trove. She discovered she also was good with her hands and was soon trained up by the owners to do basic repairs. Anna learned quickly, was reliable, and charmed all the customers. Within six months, she had been promoted to assistant manager, and managed to rent herself a small studio flat in the suburb of Etobicoke. Anna was ecstatic. She had a job she enjoyed and her own little place, which was all she'd ever wanted. And the sea was nowhere to be seen.

In the back of her mind, however, Anna knew there was a time limit on her dream. She'd obtained a two-year temporary working visa but there wasn't an option to renew it. Without close relatives in the country who could sponsor her, there weren't many ways a Greek citizen could settle permanently in Canada at that time. She knew that marriage could offer her a route into the country, but she didn't give the idea more than the occasional wistful passing thought. She'd dated little in her lifetime, so the idea of a husband seemed entirely abstract and more than a little premature. Worst case scenario, she thought, she could return to Greece and live in the mountains in the north.

Unprepared for the harshness of the eastern Canadian winter, Anna had somehow bundled up and borne it with the resilience and adaptability of a true Cretan. At first, the snow had been exciting. Anna had mostly only seen snow on far-away mountaintops; it fell in Sfinari once or twice when she was a child, but had only ever left a thin dusting on the ground, like icing sugar, which then disappeared quickly. In her new homeland, however, it piled up several feet deep in places and she had to learn to walk into it and through it. She watched, fascinated, as children built snowman sculptures out of it just like she'd seen in the movies.

By February, however, the novelty had worn off. The slushy snow that remained became an unwelcome remnant of the fresh white winter she'd been welcomed into. Anna found herself wondering if spring would ever come to this frozen world.

But spring did come, and with Easter, Anna felt the first pang of homesickness. She didn't want to admit it, but though she remained happy in her new life, there was an aching empty spot that had previously been filled by her parents and her sister. They kept in touch with letters and phone calls, and up until Easter, Anna had been too excited about her new life to really miss anything from home.

Her relatives had her over for a very Greek Easter celebration, complete with spit-roast lamb in their backyard, with what appeared to be the entire Greek population of Toronto present. Anna felt overwhelmed and couldn't help remembering Easters at home, which were so similar yet so different. Not for the first time, she was aware of the juxtaposition of cultures she was straddling. Roasting a lamb outside your house in Crete on

Orthodox Easter Sunday would have been entirely ordinary. Here, she could see neighbours peering through windows, doubtless wondering what on earth was going on next door, and probably checking whether the local bylaws prohibited roasting a lamb over a fire in one's backyard. She was reminded of Lake Ontario being so large for a lake, but not large enough for tides. So much depended on context.

Still, Anna felt compelled to continue on her path and as spring arrived and the earth warmed she began to feel a new sense of being at home here. Summer came, and she was almost resigned to staying one more year and then returning to Greece and living in a mountain village, perhaps somewhere near Thessaloniki. Fate, however, had other plans for Anna, and the day Martin Morcomb walked into the jeweller's, everything changed for both of them.

Chapter 7

Martin

Martin's watch battery stopped working one Sunday in July, which was rather annoying as he didn't like to go anywhere on a Sunday, but he liked even less not having a functioning watch. After glancing at his wrist several times and being none the wiser about the time, he decided to set out and see if he might find a jeweller's that was open. He had been walking towards the mall, figuring that would be his best bet, when he noticed the small shop tucked away in a plaza between a sushi restaurant and a store selling birdseed and feeders. He shrugged and went in.

Anna was inspecting a ring someone had dropped off earlier to be cleaned and appraised. In the moment before she looked up to greet him, he saw her serious furrowed brow and concentrated look, as if her dark eyes were delving into the very molecules of the ring and existing in this tiny world for that one moment. Then she looked up with her broad and welcoming smile and he felt the same eyes delve into his soul.

"Good morning. How can I help you today?"

Martin was momentarily speechless and stood for what seemed like an eternity, trying to find his voice. "I came in to have my watch battery changed. But now I'd like to buy an engagement ring and ask you to marry me."

It was a bold move and certainly it could have backfired. A pretty and slender young woman with long dark hair and deep brown eyes, Anna had of course had her share of flirtatious customers, who she was generally polite but firm with. Martin, however, was different. She was taken with his ginger hair, his unfashionable beard, his unusual accent and the mix of earnestness and light-heartedness in his voice, as if he understood that life was both deadly serious and a splendid joke at the same time, and that both aspects needed to be honoured.

Anna laughed at his opening remark. "Well, I can definitely change your watch battery for you. The second one, I think you should wait a bit."

Relieved that he'd been asked to wait and not turned down outright, Martin smiled and stepped forward to hand her his watch. While Anna dutifully opened up the watch and skillfully replaced the tiny battery, Martin playfully asked her which ring she'd like.

Anna laughed quietly again, and shook her head slightly, not taking her attention off of the watch.

"I know," said Martin, "This one here!"

Anna looked up briefly and scowled, though she couldn't see exactly which ring he was pointing at.

"No diamonds," she said, her face serious. "Everyone has a diamond. So ironic that everyone wants one because they're rare, but then they're not rare at all because they're on everyone's fingers."

"Alright. So in the parallel universe where I ask you to marry me and you say yes, what ring would you want me to put on your finger?"

Anna had replaced the battery and closed up the watch carefully. She looked up and held the watch out for him.

Anna did have a favourite ring in the shop, but it wasn't in the section with the other engagement rings. It was a small vintage ring, with a cornflower sapphire in the middle and six tiny pearls around it. The colours reminded her of Greece, while the style belonged in an old Hollywood movie.

"I can't sell you a ring today, it wouldn't be right. But if you take me out for dinner, I might tell you which one is my favourite."

Martin was seven years and two months older than Anna, and had grown up in Penzance, Cornwall, which Anna soon learned was in South West England. His father was a fisherman, and Martin witnessed first-hand the decline of the local fishing industry and its replacement with tourism in the region. As a young boy, he'd expected to be a fisherman like his father, but by his late teens, this was looking decidedly unlikely. His father stopped speaking about handing down his boat and his skills, and eventually stopped fishing altogether.

His parents then opened a small bed and breakfast, converting part of their already compact house into a self-contained suite, which made their own space even more cramped. Still, they were adaptable and resilient, and his mother continued knitting traditional fisherman's jumpers, selling them in local shops for much less than they were worth, because that was all people would pay.

Martin always had the sense that his parents were content with each other and could weather any storm together. His father, he knew, had been devastated when he'd had to sell his boat and give up his fishing, but he refused to dwell on it. "Onward and upward," he used to say.

So it wasn't entirely surprising that Martin chose to study Environmental Sciences at the University of Exeter's Penryn Campus, and wrote his undergraduate dissertation on the effects of over-fishing in the waters around Cornwall. His university education had been free, something he'd always felt grateful for. He qualified for some small maintenance grants, and his parents did what they could to support him. He graduated with First Class Honours and a desire to learn more about marine ecosystems.

On a family holiday to Mull in Scotland, celebrating his graduation, Martin became enamoured with the puffins on a boat tour to the island of Lunga. He was immediately taken with their charm and beauty, and was sure there was something of the Piskies about them. They seemed to belong to a mythical world where birds were dreamed up by artists and had no fear of humans. At the time, puffin populations were healthy and growing, but Martin, with great prescience, worried about the effects that over-fishing might have on these charismatic creatures.

Keen to learn more and ensure the continued safety of his feathered friends, he looked into nearby universities where he might pursue further research studies. With his strong grades, he had no trouble being accepted to his course of choice, and he completed a Master's degree and PhD in quick succession at the University of Glasgow, barely pausing for breath, as his studies were the very life-force that sustained him.

Having completed his degrees, Martin found himself in Toronto for the summer, staying with an old friend from his undergraduate days in Penryn. He'd always wanted to see the Great Lakes, having heard about these bodies of fresh water big enough to fool a person into thinking they were staring out to sea when they stood on their shores. So when he was invited to stay with his friend for the summer months, helping to catalog data from his studies on the Great Lakes, Martin hadn't thought twice about taking up the offer. However, Toronto was only a stopgap for him; he'd accepted a postdoctoral research position at the University of British Columbia studying the hooded merganser, and was moving to Vancouver in September.

Martin explained all this to Anna over their first dinner together. Anna laughed at the irony of it all. She'd come here to escape the sea, and yet here she was, having dinner with a man whose father was a fisherman and who studied seabirds and was about to move to another coastal city. Some women might have simply run away, but Anna could sense that her future was tied inextricably to this pale Cornishman, whose last name literally translated to "valley leading to the sea." She supposed it was the universe's way of making her face her demons.

Anna didn't have much time to decide whether she'd accompany Martin to Vancouver. She thought about staying in Toronto and going for visits to Vancouver, but air travel was expensive and Anna was not one to do things by half-measures. She pretended to think it over for a month or so, as she didn't want Martin thinking she was overly keen. In the meantime he brought her flowers every Sunday, and they went for long walks and picnics in the parks.

As they sat on the shores of Lake Ontario one warm sunny afternoon, Martin recounted stories of Cornish folklore to an amused Anna, who had never heard of Piskies and assumed he simply couldn't pronounce the word "pixies."

"No, the pixies are in Devon," he explained.

"Are you sure the Cornish people just couldn't pronounce 'pixie' the right way?" teased Anna.

Martin was quick to retort, "I think what you mean is that the Devon people couldn't pronounce 'Piskie' the right way." He winked playfully, enjoying Anna's musical laughter. "Do you have any small folk back in Greece?"

"Well, we don't have any Piskies or pixies, but we do have the cave nymphs." Anna paused, unsure how much of her home country's myths Martin wanted to hear.

"Go on," he urged.

"Well, they live in caves and usually work with the bees, or in some myths they are bees. They fed Zeus with Cretan honey when he was an infant and had to be hidden in a cave. The Greek word for them is *Melissae,* which also means honeybee."

"Right. And why was baby Zeus in a cave?"

"So his father, Kronos, wouldn't eat him, of course."

It was Martin's turn to laugh and he nearly choked on his ginger ale.

"What's so funny?" asked Anna, pretending to be offended. "Kronos had eaten his previous five children, so it seemed likely he'd eat the sixth! He was very jealous and thought his children would steal his kingdom from him, probably because he'd stolen his kingdom from his own father. So, would you have left Zeus in his hands?"

Martin took a moment to recover. "Jesus. I thought Cornish folklore was weird but you have us beat I'd say."

Anna smiled, cognizant again of the way the myths sounded out of their context on her home island. She'd never questioned them growing up, they were part of the shared culture and collective memory. But out here, they were out of place and time and felt like orphaned children. She knew she couldn't possibly explain this to Martin, she wasn't sure she had the words to even explain it to herself. Still, she wanted this new land to be her home and she wanted to share her life with Martin and to know all about the myths and stories of his land.

"Will you take me to Cornwall one day?" she asked.

"Of course," he said, smiling. "But first you have to come with me to Vancouver."

Anna was silent, a soft smile playing on her lips as she looked from Martin down to the grass, feigning shyness. Later that night, however, she agreed to go with him. They'd only known each other two months, but sometimes a soul recognizes another soul and time has no meaning in those meetings.

And so Anna found herself once again by the coast, and was slightly horrified to discover that even Martin's university was placed firmly beside the ocean. In fact, in Vancouver, the Salish Sea seemed to greet her at every turn. It seemed that every downhill road and path led to an inlet or a coastline.

Strangely, however, she didn't find this as off-putting as she would have thought. The cold and open Pacific Ocean seemed to be a completely different proposition from the gentle Cretan Sea. Indeed Lake Ontario had more in common with the Mediterranean than this vast expanse of highly tidal waters, whose fingers snaked into the city, becoming rivers.

Anna eventually came to feel that it was a mostly benevolent goddess, who would protect her if she showed it the respect it deserved, though it still maintained the possibility of turning on her if she mis-stepped. She regarded it with caution, but not terror.

Early the following year, Anna and Martin were married in a small ceremony that Anna only told her family about afterwards. She knew this would cause chaos and consternation at home. They would have accepted a pale non-Greek for their daughter if she so chose, and they could have even accepted her living thousands of miles away (though this was a harder pill to swallow). But what was unthinkable was that she would get married with only two witnesses in a city hall. No Orthodox Church ceremony, no family, no festivities, no huge feast with drinking, music, dancing. A wedding was not something the Greeks did on a small scale, and Anna's mother at first didn't believe her daughter when she called to share the news. When Elena realized her strong-spirited youngest child wasn't joking, she let out a loud wail and the phone fell to the ground. Anna could hear muffled voices, asking her mother what was happening, and Elena simply cried and wailed. Anna hung up the phone, not wanting to hear any more.

She hadn't wished to upset her family, but the thought of flying back to Crete and planning a large wedding was even more unappealing. Besides, Martin couldn't have left until the summer and then her visa would have expired. It was all too complicated. And the truth was, though she missed her family, Anna wasn't ready to return to Crete, and she wouldn't be for many years.

When Violet was born a year later, Anna resolved that her daughter would not share her fear of the sea. She took her to the local swimming pools from a young age and enrolled her in swimming lessons as soon as she could. Violet took to the water so naturally, her mother used to tease her and call her a water nymph.

Less frequently they took family trips to the ocean, and Violet paddled in the chilly waves, Anna watching her carefully, confident that her daughter was a strong swimmer and there were no rocks on the sandy beaches of Jericho and Spanish Banks. The North Shore Mountains, often still snow-capped well into the summer, rose up on the other side of the inlet and Anna always had the sensation they were watching over her, keeping herself and her daughter safe. They were different to her mountains back in Crete; here many of them were covered entirely in tall evergreens, but on the highest peaks, these grew thinner and then disappeared entirely towards the summits, giving way to jagged rocky shapes that resembled a frozen windswept sea.

Anna reflected that a mountain range is in fact, a very slow-moving ocean made of rock, the waves moving so slowly that we see them as stationary. She felt calmed by their near-stillness, and by their combination of the new and the familiar. *Gaia,* the earth goddess, would protect her here, she was sure.

Martin eventually got a tenured post at the university and they moved into a small house on the suburban mountainside in North Vancouver. It was further from the university, but Martin was easygoing and made the best of the commute, and Anna felt safe being high above the ocean.

They'd planned on having one or two more children, but it wasn't to be. Anna had had a difficult childbirth with Violet, following an unremarkable pregnancy, and she wondered if her body had simply opted out. Still, she had no desire to be prodded by a doctor, and to undergo long and difficult fertility treatments, so Anna and Martin decided to let things be. Besides, the three of them were happy as they were.

And so Violet grew up with two loving parents, telling her stories about magical seaside lands called Cornwall and Crete.

Chapter 8

Crete, May 2019

Κρήτη, Μάιος 2019

In the two days that followed her arrival, Violet was swept up by her aunt and given an enthusiastic tour of Western Crete, with Maria's lively chatter as the soundtrack. In every town, she seemed to know someone who ran a taverna and they hardly ever paid for a meal. "We feed them when they come to Sfinari," she explained. "Old friends."

The village of Sfinari up above the taverna was sleepy and small. The one main road boasted several restaurants, most of them not yet open for the season. There was a mini market, and several hotels and villas for tourists, nestled in with the locals' houses.

Violet enjoyed the picturesque drive along the old coast road towards Chania, the roadside dotted with wildflowers in red, purple and yellow, framing the sea behind them. Her grandparents joined them on that day, speaking cheerfully in Greek, often looking at Violet for a response, as if they half-expected her to understand the language simply because she was their grand-daughter. Maria did her best to remember to translate.

It was a little overwhelming, but Violet could feel how excited they all were to have her there, and to show her around their little pocket of the island. Their enthusiastic care coupled with the beautiful scenery made her feel unexpectedly safe and comfortable. She didn't talk much, but took in all the sights as best she could, still struggling through jet lag.

Chania itself Violet found incredibly charming, with its colourful shops and cafes, and the pretty harbour. Still quiet, it was just waking up for the tourist season. A buzz of anticipation filled the air as stores and restaurants prepared to re-open after the winter.

Early on the second day, Maria drove Violet down to Elafonissi Beach. It was a popular spot, and with good reason. "It will get very busy here soon," said Maria, gesturing at the long sandy spit that stretched across the impossibly turquoise water. It was only 7:30am, on May 5th. "I bring you here before it's full of people. So many people. By 8:30, even early May, people everywhere." She gestured with her hand, sweeping across the scenic beach.

They walked down the long expanse of white-pink sand, admiring the sea that lapped gently on the shores on either side of the promontory. The finger of land grew narrower, looking like it might disappear into the sea, and indeed they briefly waded through the shallow waters before the land rose up again and blossomed out into another wider section with the same soft pale sand. Scrubby vegetation and rocky sections lay scattered across the small island.

"This part, the island, is much quieter," explained *Theia Maria.* "You know, Elafonissi means 'island of deer', but there are no deer on Crete so, we don't know why it was named that."

"Were there ever deer here?" asked Violet, surprised to find she had a question to ask and the space to ask it.

"I don't think so, but who knows."

Maria seemed content to leave the issue there, but Violet continued to silently wonder what had inspired the name. She imagined deer roaming the soft sands, nibbling on the sparse plants, wading through the shallow waters. She turned to look behind them, where the high rugged hills rose up from the sea, carrying a sense of ageless mystery and a rich history Violet somehow felt in her bones.

"I can see why this would be a popular spot," said Violet, eyeing the sea and wishing she'd brought her bathing suit.

"Yes. Too popular. But I thought you should see. Is very beautiful, no?"

"*Nai,*" said Violet, smiling, still watching the imaginary deer wander along the sandy island.

Violet was less impressed by Falassarna, the long sandy beach thirty minutes north of Sfinari. Another popular spot for tourists and locals alike, it also boasted a rich history as an ancient port. But after Elafonissi, it looked like a dull nondescript stretch of grey sand to Violet, the kind where you had to pay for chairs and sit too close to the people around you, but without the unusual striking beauty of Elafonissi. There was a rocky section just north of the main beach, with a grove of pine trees behind it that Violet found a little more inviting, but it still didn't compare to either this morning's stunning location, or the quiet bay she was staying in. She couldn't put her finger on it, but Sfinari Beach seemed to hold a special magic that she didn't feel elsewhere, however beautiful the surroundings.

"I think Sfinari is much more beautiful," commented Violet.

"Yes, of course Sfinari is better, we know that, but we don't tell too many people." Her aunt smiled mischievously.

After a visit to Kissamos, where they'd waited out a sudden rainfall in a cafe, sipping tea and nibbling on sweet bougatsa,[19] Maria took Violet for a drive through the mountains. The sun had re-emerged, and all the olive trees and wildflowers shimmered in the sun, as if covered in tiny diamonds. The eerie, dream-like beauty filled Violet with an unexpected calmness as she gazed out the window. Even Maria paused her chatter momentarily and fell silent.

They had dinner that evening in Kaliviani, at a charming restaurant on a hill with views of the sea. For dessert, they were served a mouth-watering *portokalopita,* an orange-flavoured pastry dessert. Violet's mother had made it at home before, but it tasted different here, so much richer.

"Made with the local oranges," explained Maria.

Violet tried to pay for the meal but her aunt shook her head.

---

[19]A dessert made with phyllo pastry filled with custard, dusted with cinnamon and icing sugar.

"You pay when we come to Canada," she said firmly.

It was wonderful and exhausting at the same time. *Theia Maria* had never been able to tolerate a moment's silence, and Violet found that by the time she'd formulated a response, her aunt had usually moved on to the next topic of her monologue.

Violet's gratitude for her *theia's* hospitality wrestled with her desire for space and silence, so she was more than a little relieved when her aunt said she needed to get back to the taverna. Maria was satisfied that she'd given Violet a sense of her surroundings and a warm welcome, and now, she knew, it was time to stand back a little.

"Angelo will be around, and you can still ask us if you need anything. And of course, we feed you! OK?"

"Nai, vevaia!"[20] She had picked up a few Greek phrases in her recent tours.

Her aunt clapped her hands with glee. "We make you Greek before you leave us, yes?"

A slow smile crept over Violet's lips. "I'm already half-Greek *Theia Maria.*"

"*Nai,* yes, we work on the other half." Maria said this with such earnestness, Violet wondered if she was actually serious.

---

[20] Yes, of course!

Chapter 9

The next morning, still groggy with jet lag, Violet woke up very early to a clear sky and the sea still as a mill-pond. She'd been dying to go for a swim, but besides the fact that her aunt had whisked her around for two days, everyone kept telling her the sea was still too cold. She doubted it was anywhere near as cold as the Pacific Ocean (which she'd been known to swim in in May) and was resolved to have at least a quick dip.

Bathing suit on and towel in tow, Violet slipped out of her room, past the row of pines and the tamarisks, and down to the sea. Dipping a toe in cautiously, she couldn't help but giggle. "This is *not* cold," she said quietly out loud, running excitedly into the water on the smooth small pebbles that mingled with sand. It stayed shallow for a few metres and then the sea floor suddenly dropped away and Violet was quickly submerged, to her surprise and delight. She came up for air and then dove down under the waves, feeling the clear clean waters envelop her. She opened her eyes underwater, taking in the shades of blurry brown and grey pebbles and a few tiny fish swimming away from her. She surfaced and swam along the shoreline, then back underwater. She thought gleefully that she could stay in this water all day. She dove under the waves again and swam out toward the open sea. She couldn't understand why anyone feared water. It was her safest and happiest place.

Back on the shore after a long swim, Violet heard Angelo calling to her from the taverna. He'd just returned from his early morning fishing trip.

"*Kalimera!*[21] Did you get in? No wetsuit?" he asked in disbelief.

Violet smiled and shook her head. "You Greeks. That water is *not* cold. It was beautiful! You should feel what the Pacific is like in May!"

Angelo shivered theatrically and disappeared into the taverna.

Violet laid out on her towel. The sun hadn't yet warmed the air and the land, but by Canadian standards, it was just warm enough to sunbathe, and she wanted to enjoy a bit of the morning air before going inside and changing.

A moment later, she heard another voice behind her.

"Did you go swimming?"

Violet knew before she turned around who it was, though she hadn't yet been able to glean his name. Unsure whether she felt more excited or anxious about seeing him again, she sat up and turned quickly to face him.

---

[21] Good morning!

"Yes. I went swimming. And it's not cold. You're all crazy." She raised her eyebrows, challenging him to respond.

"Crazy is in the eyes of the beholder," he said, walking closer. "We all think you tourists are the crazy ones, getting in the water at the start of May."

"Well, just to put this into context, the ocean where I live is at least ten degrees cooler than this, even in August."

He frowned. "Does that make this sea warm?" He sat down beside her and Violet tried to suppress the inevitable but annoying butterflies that began to stir in her chest.

"Yes," said Violet matter-of-factly. "To me, it does."

"And to me, it does not."

"That's fine, I like having the water to myself." They looked at each other for a moment, and Violet noted his dark, nearly black eyes.

They both looked away.

"I brought you those dolmades and honey I promised." He handed over an unexpectedly large jar of golden viscous liquid and an equally large box of stuffed vine leaves.

"Whoa," said Violet, "Is this your *small* jar of honey?" It appeared to be about a kilogram. She had no idea how she would consume this amount of honey before she left Greece.

"Yes," he smiled "that, in Crete, is a small jar of honey. I honestly didn't have a smaller one, and if I did, it would have felt insulting to give you so little."

"Yeah, I suppose that wouldn't have been the food-based communication you were hoping for," teased Violet, cocking her head slightly and hoping her wet wavy hair didn't look entirely awful.

He gave a wry smile and looked away.

"Is it your honey?" probed Violet.

"No, it's the bees' honey." He turned and smiled broadly, showing slight dimples on both sides. "But they agreed to let me take it and give it to you."

"How very generous of them. Thank you, bees."

He looked at her for a moment, a slight smile still on his lips. "You tell me what you think, of the honey and the dolmades too."

"Sure. But I won't lie, and if my aunt and uncle's dolmades are better, I won't hold back."

"Are you always so cheeky?"

"Ooh a British word, spoken by a Greek-American. How cultured!"

"Are you going for another swim?" he asked, ignoring her teasing.

Violet hadn't planned on it, but suddenly it seemed like a good idea. "Ooh maybe, the water's just *so* warm and inviting. You wanna come?"

"I thought you said you didn't want to share the sea."

"I don't, but I feel that not inviting you would be rude in light of the giant jar of bee spit and box of dolmades you've brought me."

"Bee vomit," he corrected her, smiling broadly.

"Race you to the sea!" And Violet was off.

Dimitri, she'd later learn he was called, followed behind her, kicking off his sandals. He ran in to the water in his shorts and t-shirt, not wanting to be out-raced by a petite pale half-Greek tourist. Violet was already swimming across the waves, laughing, as Dimitri swore loudly in Greek, splashing his way in with little dignity and no grace at all.

"Gamoto!" [22] he yelled, physically and mentally unprepared for this impromptu swim.

"You have to put your head under or it doesn't count!" joked Violet.

"What? Christ, Violet, you didn't tell me that!"

"You didn't ask! Dunk or it doesn't count!"

Dimitri held his breath and dunked his head, re-emerging out of breath and shivering. Violet laughed playfully.

"How the hell do you look so comfortable? I can't feel my hands!"

"I don't *look* comfortable, I *am* comfortable," replied Violet, diving under the waves.

Dimitri swam back to shore, unable to tolerate the cold any longer.

Violet resurfaced and saw him clambering quickly over the beach trembling with cold. He had no towel and she suddenly felt a little sorry for him.

"You can use my towel!" she yelled from the waves.

Dimitri waved his hand out to one side, swatting away her suggestion.

"You're trouble," he said, and disappeared into his taverna, presumably to dry himself off with a tea towel.

"Oh dear," said Violet quietly but out loud, floating

---

[22] Fuck!

lazily on her back. "I'm not sure I made such a good impression. Probably just as well."

Back in her little room, showered and dressed, Violet made herself a cup of tea. The daughter of a Cornishman, she was usually picky about her tea, but here she found she had to settle for an insipid weak variety. There was only one type of black tea available in the local shop and no matter how long it brewed, it never seemed to darken properly. She wasn't sure if it was the tea itself, or something about the water. She sighed and popped one of Dimitri's dolmades into her mouth as she waited for the tea to brew (or not brew). "Dammit," she thought to herself. "He's right, these are better than ours. They must have secret herbs."

Now curious about the honey, Violet opened the jar and snuck a little taste. "Holy shit," she said out loud. She scooped a full teaspoon into her mouth and closed her eyes, savouring it. It wasn't just sweet. Underneath the sweetness there were flavoured layers of fresh earthy herbs that made her think of mountain meadows full of purple wildflowers. The aftertaste was dark and mellow, like a pine forest. Violet had never tasted anything like it. "It's going to be very annoying if he keeps being right about things," she mumbled to herself, spooning a generous dose into her pale tea. "At least this might just make the tea drinkable."

Violet wondered why they weren't serving this honey on her breakfast yogurt at her family's taverna. She thought back to the cryptic conversation she'd had with

Angelo and wondered if she'd ever get the chance to ask him about it again.

Chapter 10

Jet lag does strange things to one's body and that night it woke Violet up at 2am with a grumbling stomach. She tossed and turned for what felt like hours, and finally gave up on sleep. She got up, switched on a lamp, and nibbled a dolma from her little fridge. She could hear Persephone's practical voice in her head telling her not to eat, that the best way to combat jet lag was to follow the meal schedule of the current time zone. But Violet was too hungry to listen. She glanced out the window at the darkness outside, and wondered what the stars were like here.

Throwing on a jacket and grabbing her phone to use as a flashlight, she opened her door and ventured out into the coastal night. The air was cool and fresh and she could hear the waves lapping at the pebbly shore. Walking along the row of tamarisks and pine trees she inhaled their scent, which seemed stronger in the darkness. She wandered toward the *Paradise Taverna* and out onto the beach, settling on one of the lounge chairs. She chose one that wasn't quite under a sun umbrella to allow a view of the night sky. Turning off her flashlight, she looked up and waited for her eyes to adjust to the blackness that surrounded her.

The stars began to appear gradually, like a painting being created before her eyes. After a few minutes, Violet was sure she could see stars shining in every square inch of the sky; there didn't seem to be any darkness at all, only light. The sky, like the sea that morning, seemed to envelop her as if it was a dark sequinned blanket. To her left, rising above the headland like a white river from the sky, was the milky way.

She remembered her mother telling her that the Greek word for galaxy, *"galaxias,"* came from *"gala,"* meaning "milk." Looking at it now, pale and flowing against the dark moonless sky, she understood why ancient people had made this connection. She'd seen it before of course. There were plenty of dark skies in Canada outside of the cities. But she'd never seen it look so vivid, as if she could simply walk up the headland and touch it.

At some point Violet fell asleep under the velvety cloak of the night sky. She dreamed the sky was an ocean, and she was rowing through it in a small boat. The air was warm and still, and the boat moved easily with each effortless row. The stars floated around her in the water and above her, and somehow she knew these were souls who had departed this world, watching over her and protecting her. She tried to focus on each star individually, searching for the one that might be Persephone, but when she looked directly at them, they seemed to dissolve into the sea or the air in which they hung. But as long as she kept rowing ahead, she could sense them all around her, and she knew she was completely and entirely safe.

Violet woke up as the sun rose behind her, hearing beautiful otherworldly music for a moment in that mysterious place between sleeping and waking. The music faded into the dawn chorus, hundreds of songbirds filling the air with their melodic calls announcing the new day. As she lay listening, Violet realized this had been the first dream she'd had since Persephone had passed away, or at least the first one she could remember.

Someone had put a light blanket over her at some point and she wondered who had seen her. As far as she knew, no one lived down here in the bay; all the houses were up the hill in the village. Perhaps one of her family members had come down to check something at the taverna late last night? It seemed odd, but then everyone here did seem to want to look after her, and at least they hadn't woken her. The clock on her phone read 6:15am. A good time for a swim of course.

There was no breeze and the sea lay quiet and almost waveless once more. As Violet swam, she thought about her dream and found she still carried the sensation of complete calmness within her. She dove under the waves and imagined the stars shining all around her in the blue. Surfacing, she looked up at the clear sky and reminded herself that the stars and the milky way still filled the space above her and around her, temporarily bleached out by the much brighter light of the nearest star. "How strange to think that light can obscure so many things, when we're so used to it illuminating everything," she thought to herself as she floated on the waves.

Wandering slowly back to her towel feeling pensive, Violet was startled by Dimitri's voice.

"Hey, how'd you sleep?"

"Oh you know, a jet-lagged sleep." She shrugged. "You're up early."

"I'm going to check on my bees. You wanna come meet them?"

"Umm I suppose I could clear my very busy schedule," Violet joked. "Can you give me five minutes to change?"

"Of course, I'll grab you a beekeeper's jacket. Meet you back here?"

A few minutes later Violet found herself walking with Dimitri towards the hives carrying an awkward white coat with a large netted hood.

"You should put it on now, you're burning already."

"Oh come on, it's not even 7am. And you're just jealous of my lily-white complexion."

"I don't think a lily-white complexion would suit me," grinned Dimitri.

It was true that Violet had burned slightly in the first few days, but she hoped it didn't show as she didn't want him to know he'd been right.

They walked through a grove of pine and cypress trees.

"You know, the whole western half of the island used to be covered in cypress forest," said Dimitri, pointing to a small cypress tree.

"Really? So what happened to it?"

"They got cut down a long time ago. The wood was very good quality and in high demand. The Venetian navy was made almost entirely of Cretan cypress."

Violet thought to herself how strange it was that this land that felt so wild to her had in fact been altered so drastically by humans. Of course, she'd noted the large olive groves that dominated the landscape, but even those looked ancient, some of the trees with huge gnarled trunks like fossilized faces. She tried to imagine the landscape covered in forests of cypress, but couldn't quite picture it. She thought of the sky, full of invisible stars, and wondered if the trees from the past were still here as well, tucked away and invisible to the naked eye.

"Was the cypress wood as good as the honey?" mused Violet.

"So you liked it?" He smiled confidently.

"It actually makes the tea here almost drinkable, which I didn't think anything could do. So thank you for that."

"The coffee is much better here. Have you tried it?"

"Coffee? Oh no, it would go against the Cornish half of my upbringing to abandon tea-drinking," said Violet with mock seriousness. "And besides, now I can basically drink your honey with a bit of tea in the mornings, I think things will improve."

Dimitri smiled. "So, it didn't taste like the honey you bought in the grocery stores in Canada then?"

"Yeah yeah, you were right," said Violet, surrendering. "I expected it to be sweet, but it kind of has layers of flavours. I felt like I could almost see fields of wildflowers every time I tasted it. And then pine forests."

"Did you?"

Violet suddenly worried that what she'd just said sounded much weirder out loud than it had in her head. "Sort of." She shrugged, feeling suddenly a little sheepish.

He glanced at her as they walked. "What kind of flowers?"

Violet wasn't sure if he was teasing her. "Small purple ones," she said quietly.

Dimitri slowed his pace and turned to look at Violet. "It's thyme honey, from my hives up in the mountains." He paused. "The flowers are actually purple. And I mixed in a bit of pine honey, from here."

Violet felt his dark eyes on her and had the sense that he could somehow read her unspoken thoughts, which was exhilarating and terrifying at the same time. "Oh," was all she could say. "That's weird," she added lamely.

"Maybe not," replied Dimitri. "The thing with honey is, it's a sort of snapshot of the bees' surroundings at that time. The flowers and plants of course, but also the weather, the geography, everything in the environment. The honey is like a record. So, it's not that weird to be able to taste the flowers the bees were foraging on. Maybe you're a honey super-taster."

Violet smiled as they walked slightly uphill towards the hives, the twelve colourful wooden boxes now visible nestled on a small flat section on the hillside. The air began to buzz with the thrum of bees and Violet was sure she smelled a subtle hint of honey. The trees had thinned out, giving way to rockier terrain, but a few small carob trees provided a little shade and shelter for the bees.

Dimitri pointed proudly at his hives and increased his pace slightly. "You know, we were the first in Europe to keep bees. We learned from the Egyptians in ancient times." He paused and as they moved closer he added, "You should put your jacket on now. I mean, not just because of the sun." He smiled, showing his dimples, and helped Violet ensure it was zipped up and secured. He couldn't help but be amused at how large it was on her. "I'm sorry I only have one size," he apologized. Violet was only five foot three and had her mother's slender build. The jacket swam around her and hung from her limbs like a tent.

"I don't feel like this is very flattering for my small but perfectly formed body type," she replied, laughing a little self-consciously, feeling like a munchkin in an adult-sized space suit.

Dimitri laughed and added, "Maybe not your best look, but I'd rather you were safe." He handed her a pair of latex gloves. "If you want to hold the frames, you should wear these. And just remember to move slowly."

Violet suddenly felt nervous. She hadn't expected to hold any frames, and all the precautions seemed to imply a high level of risk. She wondered vaguely if he was getting even for the uncomfortable swim she'd instigated the previous day. "Are they friendly bees?" she asked, trying to cover up her trepidation with playfulness.

"Don't worry, we're safe. I know the bees well. It's a very calm morning, they have lots of food this time of year, they'll be chilled. I'm just being extra cautious. I'd feel really bad if you got stung."

Violet watched as Dimitri lit the smoker, an odd-looking contraption that resembled a tin can with a small bellows on its side and a crooked cone on the top. He then carefully took the lid off the first hive and placed it upside down on the ground beside it. He used only a little smoke on the top of the hive; too much would reduce the quality of the honey, he explained. His movements remained slow and methodical as he removed the super on top of the brood box and placed it on the upturned lid.

"What's in that box?" asked Violet curiously.

"Your favourite honey," he answered wryly, not looking up, as he applied just a little more smoke and removed what looked like a wire rack from the top of the the second box.

"Don't we need to inspect the honey?" asked Violet hopefully.

"Not right now," he replied. "It's a little early for harvesting and I don't want to disturb the bees more than I have to."

Dimitri continued his careful manipulations, using a metal tool to shift the first frame, a simple board devoid of bees, which he removed and leaned carefully against the hive. He then shifted the second frame and pulled it out gently, the comb a light brown colour and nearly covered in bees, all moving about as if they knew exactly what their business was, not seeming greatly perturbed by being removed from their hive. He shook the frame gently, dropping a number of bees into the hive to expose more of the comb beneath. Dimitri observed it closely and appeared lost in thought for several minutes.

"What are you checking for?" asked Violet quietly.

"Mostly just making sure the queen is laying well, that the brood looks healthy, and they're not overcrowded." He glanced over at her. "Do you want to hold this one and have a closer look?" He held out the frame. "Look, they're very relaxed. Just move slowly and take deep breaths and you'll be fine."

Violet didn't want to hold the frame at all, but she also didn't want Dimitri thinking she was scared of the bees, so she nodded and stepped forward slowly.

"I promise you're safe, I've explained to the bees you're a friend."

Violet giggled nervously. "I didn't hear you say anything."

"Bees don't communicate with language. They feel energy, movement and smells. They know my smell and I told them what they need to know."

Violet took the screen gingerly, trying to pretend a confidence she definitely didn't feel. She looked closely at the bees through the mesh hood. They did indeed seem calm, shuffling around a little here and there, flapping their wings, greeting other bees by rubbing their antennae together. The sight reminded her of an aerial view of a crowded train station, with people moving and shifting, standing, waiting, talking, walking, all seeming to know when to move and where to go.

Dimitri pointed to the comb cells, visible here and there under the moving bees. "You can see the larvae in the cells, I'm checking that the laying pattern looks consistent and the larvae look healthy, which they do."

Violet nodded.

"There are worker bees and drones," he explained, anxious to share the fascinating world of his bees with Violet. "The workers are all females and they do pretty much everything, foraging and cleaning the hive. The drone bees are just for mating with queens."

"Really?" Violet felt calmer now that the bees hadn't shown any signs of wanting to attack her. "So if you're born a honeybee, your job is either to prepare food and maintain the hive, or mate?"

"Or to lay eggs and eat royal jelly, but only if you're the queen."

"So is that what traditional gender roles are based on here? You know, the females cook and keep house, and the males just hang around getting their lady pregnant."

"Ouch! Is that your perception of Greek values?"

Violet laughed. "Well, not entirely, but how many women in places like this have fulfilling careers?" She handed the screen carefully back to Dimitri.

"It depends what you mean by fulfilling. Gender roles might be a little out of date here, especially in small villages like this one. But I wouldn't say North American culture is perfect either. And anyway, you'll be pleased to know that the drone bees get kicked out and left to die in the fall." He paused, but Violet was still formulating a sympathetic response to the unfortunate drones when he asked, "So what's your fulfilling career?"

The question could have come off as offensive but his tone was one of curiosity. Violet was more than a little annoyed that she didn't have a good answer for him. She thought briefly about pretending she was a counsellor or an accountant, but she knew she wouldn't be able to keep up the charade for long, and she wasn't really cut out for lying. She sighed.

"I'm still looking for it."

"Is it hiding?" he teased.

"Yes, obviously, or I would have found it by now."

Dimitri had returned the frame to the hive and gingerly pulled out the next one. He continued to skillfully inspect the hive as they talked, keeping his eyes on the bees. Two stray cats had wandered over and sat looking at Violet, near enough to keep an eye on her, but still a safe distance from the bees. She recognized the large ginger and white tomcat from her first morning on the beach.

"I studied psychology," offered Violet, hoping it might redeem her intellect in his eyes. She looked over at the cats, wishing she had something to feed them.

"Psychology? You must be good at reading people."

"I'm not bad, but Persephone was always better at that." Violet hadn't meant to mention her friend, but her name had slipped out before she could stop it. She took a deep breath, hoping Dimitri wouldn't ask too many questions, but knowing he would.

"Persephone? That's an unusual name. Is she Greek?"

"No. She's...I mean, she was Canadian." It still felt strange talking about Perse in the past tense, but Violet felt oddly compelled to continue. "She was part Cornish, like me, but her mom was a bit of a free-thinking new-age type who was really into Greek mythology. She told her she'd named her Persephone so she'd be perfectly balanced. You know, summer and winter, light and dark."

Dimitri was quiet for a moment. "And was she?"

"Yeah...I think so." Violet was glad for the mesh hat, as her eyes had welled up with tears.

She hadn't expected to be talking about Persephone with someone she barely knew, but it felt unexpectedly cathartic. The ginger tomcat braved the bees and moved closer. He rubbed up against her legs and sat down very near her feet, looking up at her.

Dimitri didn't speak for a short time, closing up the first hive and opening another with the same unhurried and mindful movements. He reminded Violet of Persephone's mother doing slow flow yoga in her living room.

"Is that why you came here?" he asked quietly, still focused on his bees, removing the first frame from the second hive.

"Because of Persephone?" Violet knew what he was asking but wanted to avoid it or at least delay answering properly.

"Because you lost someone and needed a place to heal."

"Yes. My mom thought it would be a good idea." Violet hoped her emotion wasn't evident to Dimitiri through her beekeeper's hat. She'd never had much of a poker face and a few tears had escaped her eyes and trickled down her cheeks. She realized she hadn't cried in a long time. She'd sobbed uncontrollably in the days immediately following the event, and then her emotions had seemed to hibernate for months while she tried to process what had happened.

Dimitri was silent for a few minutes, checking each frame with the attention of a doting father and the grace of a dancer executing a well-known routine.

"You know, the ancient Greeks thought that bees were made from the corpses of oxen."

Violet was silent. What a strange thing to say.

"They thought they didn't reproduce sexually at all, that they came into being out of death. If you wanted more bees, you had to kill a bull."

"Did it work?" Violet managed to ask.

"It must have, cause they kept doing it." She could hear the smile in his voice.

"Have you tried it?" Violet was regaining her composure.

"Not yet. Maybe tomorrow."

Violet couldn't help but smile.

Dimitri continued checking each frame in silence for some time. Violet tried to think of something to say that wasn't about Persephone or dead bulls. The ginger and white cat blinked up at her.

"You know, my middle name means honeybee," she offered.

"Melissa?" He pronounced it the Greek way, the way her mother did, emphasizing the first syllable.

"Yeah."

"Ah, well that explains your honey-deciphering abilities." He smiled. "So you're a flower and a honeybee. A good combination."

"Yeah well, you'd think I'd be more together with such a harmonious name."

"Are you not together?"

Violet shrugged, "I don't *feel* together most of the time." She didn't want the conversation to go back to her grieving, so she went on. "I mean, some people seem to know what they want to do in life, and they go for it, and everything seems to fall into place for them. I've just never been sure what I want, and even if I had an idea, I wouldn't know how to make it happen."

Dimitri didn't respond straight away and Violet wondered if he'd been listening or if he had become absorbed in his bees.

"Sometimes having too many options can make us paralyzed." He paused. He was on bee time now, everything slowed down. He was still inspecting the frames in the second hive carefully and occasionally glancing up at Violet as he spoke, pausing after each sentence. "I found that when I went back to America for a bit, when I was twenty. I worked a few different jobs, and I thought about starting up my own business, you know, just something small, maybe setting up some hives there. But every option seemed really complicated, and expensive. I felt like it would be such a huge investment of my time and energy and money that I needed to be two hundred percent sure of whatever choice I made." He shook his head. "So I couldn't make a choice in the end. It was just overwhelming." He paused again, replacing the last frame in the hive, then placing the queen excluder, the super, and finally the lid back on top, closing it up. Moving on to the next one, painted bright pink, he spoke again.

"You know, when I first got there, I went into the closest grocery store, just to get a few basic things. It was a huge store. I wandered around for about twenty minutes trying to find the canned tomatoes and when I did find them, there was maybe half an aisle of different types of canned tomatoes! What on earth does anyone need that much choice in canned tomatoes for?" He looked over at Violet, who was listening quietly. "I felt like that sort of summed up America. Or at least affluent America." He shrugged, though the movement was difficult to see through his beekeeper's jacket.

Violet was stunned and relieved that someone other than her had been similarly scuppered by the plethora of options in life. Maybe, she thought, she was just in the wrong place. Maybe it wasn't her that was broken after all. The ginger and white cat had moved off a little and sat licking his paws on the rocks to her right.

"So, what's it like here?" she asked thoughtfully. "Fewer choices? And is that somehow more freeing?"

"You know, I think it is. At least for some people."

"Do you think it would be better if we were more like the bees, and just did the jobs we were born into?"

"I don't know if I'd go that far," he frowned a little under his mesh hat. "I think people need more choices than bees. But having a 'hive' helps, you know, a community where you have to, or want to, figure out how you fit in and how you can be helpful and comfortable. There are maybe fewer choices, but they're easier to execute, and everyone helps you."

"So, you have a good hive here?" asked Violet hopefully.

"Well, I'll admit that sometimes the Sfinari hive feels a little on the small side. You know, there are only just over one hundred people in the village." Dimitri paused, replacing one frame and removing another. "Still, for me, I much prefer this to a big city."

He continued his silent slow choreography, scrutinizing the bees, the comb, and the larvae. Violet watched him, so at ease in his movements and his thoughts, and pondered where or what her ideal "hive" might be. It certainly didn't feel like Vancouver. Even her suburban neighbourhood in North Vancouver didn't feel like a community she could be a part of. She sighed audibly.

Dimitri replaced the last frame and closed up the third hive. There were nine more he'd planned on checking this particular morning, but they could wait until tomorrow. He led Violet away from the hives and they removed their jackets. It was still early.

"I take it you don't need to rush off?" asked Dimitri, as he scribbled a few notes in a small notebook, recording what he'd seen in the hives he'd checked.

"Not just yet."

Violet's tears had dried, but without the mesh hat, she was sure the evidence of them remained and she avoided meeting his gaze.

"Have you been over to Platanakia beach?" he pointed over across the headland they were part-way up.

Violet shook her head. I think I saw it, when I walked over there," she pointed down the cape towards the sea. "I couldn't see a way down to it."

"It's easier from this end. Come on, I'll show you."

They left their jackets and Dimitri's equipment tucked into the trees by the hives, and she followed him over the headland and down the other side, toward the empty beach with the abandoned cottage she'd seen on her first full day on the island. The terrain turned rocky and they scrambled downhill. The ginger tom followed them briefly and then sat on the rocks, regarding them curiously. Dimitri led her across a narrow ledge to the mouth of a small cave that looked out over the bay.

"Welcome to my cave," he announced, turning around to face Violet as he sat down in the entrance and gestured for her to do the same. From the cave they could see the gentle morning light bathing the sea, still with barely a ripple on it.

"Do you come here often?" said Violet before she realized she'd accidentally used the most clichéd pickup line in history.

Dimitri laughed. "Not often enough. But when I do come here, I always leave feeling better about things."

Violet nodded. It was a peaceful spot with beautiful views, near to the tavernas but out of sight. She could see how it would be an ideal place to escape to. Anxious to avoid any further questions from Dimitri about her past, Violet asked him about his upbringing in the States.

"My parents moved to California after they got married, so that's where I was born. But my mother never really settled there. We came back here when I was twelve, in 1999."

Violet quickly did the math in her head. He was seven years older than her, the same as the age difference between her parents.

"We were all here together for about four years, until my dad left again, when I was sixteen. So, when I was twenty, I went back to America for a bit, like I mentioned earlier." He paused briefly. "I thought I might stay, but it was...disappointing. You know, I told you about the tomatoes." He smiled. "But also, it just wasn't how I remembered it. So, I ended up back here."

Violet had a million questions in her head in response to this brief summary of his life, but didn't want to probe too much.

"Why did they leave in the first place? It's so beautiful here." She thought this was a relatively safe question to ask.

Dimitri frowned a little and looked out at the sea. "Something happened when my dad was young. He got blamed for something. I don't know if it was his fault. Anyway, he didn't feel welcome here, so he thought it would be better to start a new life somewhere else." He paused. "Your mom grew up here, right?"

"Yes. Angelo said she would have known your family, but she never mentioned them, which I thought was strange."

Dimitri looked at her and seemed to be trying to figure something out. "Did Angelo say anything else?"

"Just not to ask my aunt about it. And that our families were sort of friends, but they don't talk much or something."

Dimitri nodded almost imperceptibly, then was quiet for a long time, looking out over the small bay. Violet wondered what he was thinking and eventually decided to break the silence.

"You said America wasn't how you remembered it. Was it just the tomatoes, and the options?"

He sat thinking for a moment before he answered. "You know how you sometimes have a memory of something or someone, a really great memory, but when you go back to that place or that person, it's not like you remember at all. And you find yourself questioning which reality was true? I remember California being *so* great growing up. Beautiful sandy beaches, we had a nice little house, typical American dream with a picket fence, you know?" He turned to her and smiled. "I had lots of school friends. We used to go out to the beach, the whole family, and eat ice cream. So American right? I didn't want to leave. I was devastated when my parents told me we were moving to Crete. I'd never been here, my friends were all there. I couldn't understand why we had to leave. But my mother was the one who insisted. She missed this place a lot, and she also thought they should be helping my dad's parents with the taverna as they were getting older. My dad had two older brothers but they'd both left as well, moved to Athens."

He stopped and hesitated briefly, deciding whether or not to say more. "Later, years later, I found out the real reason we left America was that my dad was having an affair. My mother found out and tried to leave him, but he convinced her they could start again back home, he promised to be faithful. So, we came back here and I, well, I got used to it I guess. But I don't think I appreciated this place then. It wasn't much fun for a teenager, not a lot to do, you know. I missed California." He was silent for a moment. "But that was when my dad started keeping bees, during the four years he lived here with us, and he taught me about beekeeping before he left. He'd learned from his dad, years ago when he was young."

Violet smiled. She wanted to ask why his father had left the second time but decided against it. She worried that the more he shared, the more he'd expect her to share, and she needed more time. She opted again for what she thought was a safer question.

"Are they your dad's bees, the ones you have over there?"

Dimitri gave a short dry laugh and shook his head. "His bees turned on him before he left. They swarmed and left and never came back."

"Does that happen?"

"Sometimes. The bees don't tolerate their keeper being unfaithful to his wife, or her husband," he added. "It seems he didn't keep his promise to my mother."

"Is that really true? I mean, about the bees?"

He shrugged. "I saw it happen. And my bees have never done that."

"Well you don't have a wife to be unfaithful to, do you?"

"Not yet." He smiled and turned to Violet. "Like your fulfilling career, my beautiful wife seems to be hiding."

Chapter 11

Penzance, Cownwall, October 2017

"What about him?" asked Violet playfully, gesturing with her head towards the waiter who had just brought their wine. They were sitting in a small pub with dark wood-panelled walls, waiting for their dinner, exhausted after their long walk to Morvah. They'd managed to call a taxi from a payphone and had thankfully made it back to Penzance; there had been no cellphone signal and no sign telling when a bus might arrive at the stop.

Persephone tilted her head and assessed the young man from across the room. He was a little older than her, average height, with light brown hair and grey eyes, not unpleasant to look at. "I'd give him ten minutes to see if he could keep my attention."

"So you'd date a waiter?" teased Violet.

Persephone was notoriously picky when it came to men. Her confidence and strong features often attracted them to her, but she mostly unceremoniously thwarted any attempts to kindle a romance. Occasionally she'd accept an invitation to dinner or coffee, but there was rarely a second date. There was always something on the first meeting that turned her off. Over the years, she'd compiled an interesting list of dating faux-pas: he grabbed my chin when he kissed me; he ordered for me; he thought Schrödinger's cat was a mobile grooming service; he wants five kids, that's at least four too many; he said I reminded him of his mother and he seemed to think that was a good thing.

Recently, however, she'd been on a record five dates with a graduate student, a pianist she'd met in an improvisation workshop. Violet thought he was fantastically attractive, with dark curly hair and blue eyes. He was passionate about all types of music, but especially the classical and romantic eras, and was doing a master's degree in piano performance. The pair seemed well-matched, and Violet was sure that Persephone had finally found a partner. She alternated between feeling fabulously happy for her friend and ever so slightly jealous, though she wasn't sure if she was envious of Perse or her boyfriend. But then, just before their trip, Persephone had broken it off with him too.

"So you'd date a waiter, but Adam wasn't good enough for you?" Violet reiterated.

"First of all," replied Persephone, "I wouldn't judge a person based on their job. Our waiter over there could be, I don't know, a stained glass apprentice, or an archaeology student. Secondly, I don't want to talk about Adam." She sat back in her seat and folded her arms and then, as an afterthought leaned forward again and added, "And thirdly, we can't all be content with a 'James.' You know I have high standards, and Adam didn't live up to them. That's all." She took a sip of red wine.

Violet ignored the remark about her ex; she had no desire to go down that road again, and she was desperate to know what had happened with Adam. Narrowing her eyes, she looked carefully at her friend across the table. Persephone's gaze darted around the room, taking in any and every point that was not Violet, successfully avoiding any hint of eye contact.

"OK, if I guess right will you tell me?"

Persephone sighed and glanced over at the waiter once more, accidentally catching his eye. He smiled and she shifted in her seat, uncomfortable in every way.

Violet didn't wait for a response. "Did he kiss with his mouth really wide open? Like this?" She opened her mouth and wiggled her tongue around in the air. It didn't take much wine to make her lose her inhibitions and she'd already taken a few sips on an empty stomach.

Persephone groaned and giggled at the same time. "Jesus Christ, put your tongue away you weirdo. No he did not kiss like that. He was a very good kisser, I'll have you know."

"OK, did he have really sweaty hands, and at dinner, he kept breaking up the rolls with his hands and handing you the pieces and all you could think of was his gross sweat all over the bread?"

"Where the hell do you come up with this stuff?"

"Oh I didn't make that up. Happened to me once. I can't remember his name now. Josh? John? Alex maybe. I'm pretty sure he was gay anyway. Oh wait, *I* know! I know why you dumped poor sexy Adam! He's very religious and he's saving himself for marriage and you couldn't possibly be with someone who worships God instead of quantum physics, and who thinks that sex is a wedding gift from God, or something." Violet was rambling, but she stopped talking abruptly as Persephone frowned at the table. "Oh my God, that's *it!* He's religious??" Violet's voice had risen and her accusation rung through the quiet pub.

"Shhh!" said Persephone, glancing once again at the waiter. "We don't need the whole restaurant to hear!" She looked around and leaned back in her seat. "Look, it wasn't just that he was religious. I mean, he kinda was, but I was OK with that. He didn't try and convert me or anything, and he wasn't 'saving himself for marriage,' as you put it. We just didn't have...the same views on things."

"On *what* things?" Violet tried to keep her voice low, but her patience was waning.

Persephone sighed loudly, defeated. "Fine, I'll tell you, but you have to promise not to judge me, or him."

"Judge you? Judge him? Wow, Persephone, Queen of the Underworld, what *did* you do to the poor man?"

Persephone took a sip of her wine, and looked over to her left towards a dark window. "Well, the thing was...it sort of became clear—"

"For the love of God, *what?*" sputtered an exasperated Violet, while jet lag, wine, and suspense brewed an increasingly unpleasant mix in her body.

Persephone paused dramatically, raised her eyebrows and looked at Violet for several seconds before declaring flatly, "He was a Tory."

Violet burst into a fit of laughter so loud, the whole pub turned to look at the pair. Persephone sat with her head in her hand, embarrassment slowly giving way to amusement as she began to giggle as well.

Chapter 12

Vancouver, 2016

Violet had taken a series of jobs after graduation, thinking each one would be a temporary stopgap on the way to figuring out her career. She worked for a charity briefly, answering calls on a mental health crisis line. She'd thought it would be fulfilling to help people, and her psychology degree was certainly relevant. But after two weeks of training, Violet was so upset by the way the callers were viewed and treated, she began to feel physically ill.

One lonely man in his sixties, struggling through a lifetime of addiction and mental health difficulties, used to call nearly every day. Violet listened to several of his calls, along with two other trainees, while her manager, Sarah, spoke to him. She used the same lines every time, from the list in the training manual: "What caused you to reach out today?" and "I'm hearing that you're feeling depressed today." Violet thought she sounded like a robot. Her two fellow trainees nodded sagely and in the discussion that followed, they both remarked on how expertly Sarah had used the approved lines. Violet was silent.

They were taught to assess the situation and whether the person was in immediate danger of harming themselves or someone else. If they weren't, they were to end the call as quickly as possible without being rude. They didn't have the time or resources to formulate long-term plans for every caller. If they judged the crisis was indeed imminent, they were instructed to call the police, even if the caller had explicitly asked that the police not be called.

None of this sat right with Violet. Of course, she understood their job was to manage crises and prevent harm, but she felt the callers were treated with pity rather than empathy, and the lack of respect and transparency bothered her.

The lonely man in his sixties just kept calling, was listened to briefly, assessed as non-crisis, and with the ending of the call, he was sent back to his isolated existence in his tiny apartment, where he doubtless called another line, or signed up to another waiting list for support services he'd perhaps never be able to access.

But it was at the end of the second week when Violet knew beyond a doubt that she couldn't continue in her role. A caller with schizophrenia expressed that she feared her call was being listened to by a large group of people. Violet looked around the room where herself and two other trainees were listening. Surely they should leave.

"I'm hearing that you're feeling worried," chimed Sarah, not seeming bothered that the woman's paranoia was in fact, based in reality. Violet looked in desperation at the other new recruits. They all looked serious, brows furrowed, listening intently. No one else seemed unsettled by the situation. Sarah's voice continued in its unnatural tuneful recitation of lines that hinted at compassion but rang hollow underneath.

Violet tried not to listen. After all, she had no right to; the caller clearly didn't want anyone else hearing what she had to say. And didn't this struggling woman have the right to have that very basic wish respected? Why was everyone seemingly oblivious to the truth of the woman's fears? Violet closed her eyes and bit her lip.

Following the call and subsequent discussion, she said she felt unwell (which was entirely true) and texted Persephone, asking her to meet her at their favourite spot on the river.

Persephone found Violet perched on a rock on the riverbank, her knees hugged into her chest as she watched a kingfisher fish from a nearby tree.

"What happened?" asked Persephone as she apprached and gave her friend a long hug.

Violet shook her head. "It was so horrible, but I'm not supposed to tell anyone anything. I signed a confidentiality agreement."

"We'll just call it supervision," Persephone said matter-of-factly. "I'm nearly qualified now, and I understand confidentiality. I'm probably the safest person for you to tell. And I think you're going to explode if you don't tell someone."

Violet sighed and recounted the phone call to her friend. Persephone listened, increasingly concerned as Violet's story unfolded, but still calm and philosophical.

"Wow, that's fascinating in a really disturbing way. I'm hearing that you were upset by this," she added cheekily.

Violet brought her forehead down into the palms of her hands. "Please don't start talking like that, I can't even deal with that as a joke right now."

"OK, OK, it was just meant to cheer you up a bit." Persephone sighed. "So, no one could see that the thing she was supposedly paranoid about, the thing she feared, was in fact happening? Didn't someone mention it when you had the discussion afterward?"

"No, they all just said how well Sarah had handled the call, and had helped to deescalate her anxiety, or something like that."

"So, what did you say?"

"Nothing. What the fuck could I have said? I felt like I identified more with the caller than with the people around me. Maybe I have schizophrenia?"

Persephone laughed despite herself. "Violet, as your very best friend who has known you since you were six, and as a nearly certified music therapist, I promise you, you're not schizophrenic. What you are is naturally empathetic, and more tuned in to the people around you, and their feelings, than most people are. And that's a gift, but it's also a curse."

"I don't want the gift or the curse."

"OK, well I don't think the universe takes returns, but I'll check their policy."

Violet looked across the river at the cedars. It was September and the air was just starting to turn cool.

"What if people with schizophrenia are actually a bit like me though? I mean, tuned in to something that the rest of us can't see? That woman knew, I mean, she *knew* there was more than one person listening to her. And yes, maybe she was just paranoid and she would have felt that way even if no one else had been listening. But what if she wasn't? What if people with mental illness, especially hallucinations and paranoia, are actually either hyper-aware, or maybe experiencing a different plane, a different, I don't know, a parallel universe or something?"

"Whoa, that's a big question." Persephone sat and thought for a moment in silence. "I don't think we can ever know that for sure." She paused and looked over at the two pale logs forming a "v." "I mean...we all believe what our minds tell us. That's our only real window into reality." Persephone frowned just slightly and shifted her gaze up into the tops of the cedars across the river. "I don't think my mom experienced the world the same way you or I do, and I definitely don't think people with autism experience the world in the same way either. And, you know, who's to say which version of reality is true? Which plane, which parallel universe, which bundle of perceptions is the 'right' one? It almost doesn't make sense to ask that question. It's all just...impressions from our senses. But—" she turned to Violet and seemed to finally find the certainty she'd been looking for, "that's why I think we need to value everyone's experiences the same way we value our own. Everyone's world, the way they perceive it, is valid and, in a sense, true. It's their own truth, their own world."

Violet sat and pondered her friend's words in silence for several minutes, as they both watched the water catch the sunlight and meander slowly downstream. She mulled over the multiple ways in which her day had been experienced: by herself, by the caller, by her manager and by her fellow trainees. She imagined what Sarah must have thought of her, as she sat quietly in the discussions with so little to say compared to the other trainees, and then when she suddenly took ill and went home. She probably thought she wasn't the right fit for the job, and certainly Violet couldn't disagree with that.

Eventually Violet sighed. "So what should I do?"

"About what? The job or the multiple realities experienced by people with schizophrenia and autism?"

Violet half-smiled. "About the job."

"Run for the hills."

"Really?"

"Yeah. Look, I'm sure they do some good work there and have helped people who were really in crisis. There's not nearly enough funding for mental health, so in some ways, I understand why it's flawed. But it really doesn't sound like the right fit for you."

So Violet went back to helping her mother in the jewelry store she'd set up years ago in Lynn Valley, with the help of her former employers in Toronto. She didn't mind the work. Like her mother, she enjoyed interacting with customers, though she felt she lacked her mother's grace and quiet confidence. And she certainly didn't have the patience for the repairs. She could just about change a watch battery, but it took her twice as long as her mother, and this just reinforced her feelings of inadequacy. As long as she was working for her mom, Violet felt she hadn't really found her own path.

Persephone had once suggested that Violet write a novel. Violet had laughed. She'd been known to write poetry, which only Persephone had been allowed to read, but she'd never even written a short story, so the thought of writing a novel seemed absurd. But Persephone had pointed out that a writer needs to be psychologically astute, to create believable characters. "I bet you'd write a great book. I'd read it."

"Thanks Perse, maybe I'll write it for you one day."

"Excellent. Can't wait."

Violet continued to drift, taking some part-time work as an administrator at the university where her dad worked. She discovered that spreadsheets, once she got the hang of them, were endlessly pleasing. She felt that if she could just get her whole life into a spreadsheet and type in the right formula, it would spit out the elusive answer to her happiness.

Persephone, on the other hand, found two part-time jobs within a few months of completing her internship. She worked with children on the autism spectrum one day a week, which she always said was her favourite day. Persephone was endlessly fascinated and often amused by the way these children saw the world. She was able to watch her clients respond and learn and grow through her part-crafted and part-improvised sessions with them, something that gave her endless joy. It was a job where she had to constantly think on her feet and be prepared for anything from flying instruments aimed at her head, to elaborate role-playing, to moments of exquisite beauty and exhilarating breakthroughs. Sometimes a child that had never spoken would say their first word in her session. Sometimes parents cried with joy, suddenly seeing the potential in their child that Persephone saw in every one of them.

She also worked part-time in a long-term care setting and after six months, impressed with the effects of her work on the residents, they increased her hours to two days per week.

Violet wasn't prone to jealousy as such, and she was happy for her friend, but the better Persephone's career went, the more she felt the lack of her own meaningful work as a gaping hole opening up beneath her. She had the sinking feeling that things were easy for everyone around her, their lives falling effortlessly into place, while for her, everything was a struggle and the puzzle pieces the universe presented to her never quite fit together.

Persephone and her mother had both assured her that these things sometimes take time and there was no rush. She was still young, after all.

"What do you want to do?" asked Persephone one rainy November afternoon as they sat mulling things over in the sunroom in Violet's family home. They both loved the sound of the rain on the glass and on days like this they called it the "rain room." "I mean, forget about money for a second and forget about your degree. If someone said they'd give you whatever money you needed to do whatever you wanted with your life, what would you do?"

Violet felt terrified at the seemingly endless options this scenario presented her with. She shook her head, feeling lost. "I...guess I'd...buy a little house on the Sunshine coast, and a cat."

Persephone blinked. "That's it?"

"What's wrong with that?"

Persephone tilted her head and raised her eyebrows. "Whoa, dream big, Violet!" she teased.

"Well, what would *you* do?" Violet turned the question around, feeling a little sheepish.

Persephone didn't need time to think. "I'd start a non-profit providing creative therapies to people who need them, free of charge. And we'd expand to having craft groups, gardening therapy, forest therapy, music lessons, artist residencies. We'd have centres throughout Canada and eventually the world."

Violet's jaw dropped. She hadn't realized other people had dreams that big. "I think I forgot to dream."

"I'll say," replied Persephone.

So Violet tried to dream but found herself awash in a vast sea of options, all with their own merits but none of them feeling like they were really *her* dreams. She kept moving through life like a piece of driftwood in the currents, hoping the universe would offer her an answer one day soon. But so far, it had been silent.

Chapter 13

Crete, May 2019

Κρήτη, Μάιος 2019

Violet didn't see Dimitri for the next two days. She glimpsed him helping at the taverna, and waved, but didn't want to disturb him while he was working. Her days were filled with swimming and walking, and some evenings she called her mother. Anna was relieved that her daughter was beginning to sound like herself again.

"I told you it was beautiful," said Anna over the phone one evening (it was morning in Vancouver).

"It is. But, so, why did you leave, Mom?"

Anna was silent for a moment. "Well, I wanted to find my own path. And, you know I had a younger brother who passed away when I was young. I needed to get away from where that happened."

Violet mulled this over. "You said he was sick, right?"

"Yes," replied Anna. Her mother had never offered further information on her brother, and Violet had always sensed this was the one thing her mother found difficult to talk about, so she didn't ask any more about the illness.

"Hey Mom, did you know the Sfakianakis family? The ones who run the taverna next door?"

"Yes, we knew them. We knew everyone in the village."

"Yes, I know, Mom, but their taverna was right next door. I remember you mentioned lots of family members and other families in the village, but not them."

"I didn't realize I hadn't," offered Anna. Violet was silent. "Violet, is something bothering you?"

"Not bothering me, it's just, something seems a bit odd. Angelo said something about not being very good friends with them anymore, and told me not to ask *Theia Maria* about them. I thought you might know something."

"We were always friends. Maybe something happened after I left that I don't know about?"

"Maybe," said Violet, vaguely satisfied for now.

Anna changed the subject. "Are you wearing sunscreen?"

"Yes, Mom, SPF 50, I promise."

"And a hat? You know you have your father's skin."

"Believe me, I know, Mom. My pale skin gets mentioned at least three times a day here. And yes, I'm wearing my hat. I'm gonna go now. It's a nice evening for a swim."

"OK, I love you, Violet."

"Love you too, Mom. Say hi to Dad for me."

Violet had always been baffled that although she was the one with two well-adapted and nurturing parents, somehow Persephone was the one who appeared better prepared for adult life, and had seemed to sail through unimpeded. She wondered if in fact her parents had been so attentive she hadn't had the opportunity to develop her own resilience or autonomy.

Chapter 14

Sandra, Harmony, and Unity

Persephone's mother had always been a distant floating sort of figure in the background of her life. Born to an upper-middle class family in Vancouver, she grew up in a big house in Kitsilano and spent summers at the family cottage on Saltspring Island. As a teenager, when her peers became interested in boys and makeup, Sandra developed a fascination with Eastern philosophy. She began to practice yoga obsessively and spent hours meditating in her room. Her parents assumed it was a phase, but if it was, it was one she never outgrew.

At sixteen, she stopped responding to "Sandra" and demanded everyone call her "Harmony" from now on. She then became interested in Greek mythology and briefly adopted the name "Aphrodite," but it didn't stick. She went back to being "Harmony" and memorized all the Greek myths in between rounds of meditating and yoga. She refused to go to university, much to her parents' dismay. Her two older siblings, incidentally, hadn't displayed any of this unusual behaviour and were dutifully studying the conventional subjects of engineering and chemistry. But Sandra (or Harmony) asked instead to undertake a two-year yoga, meditation and enlightenment training in Hawaii. Her parents, used to throwing money at problems, consented. They had no idea what else to do.

So Harmony went to find enlightenment and came back saying she was now called "Unity." "Because, beyond harmony, we find unity. Namaste," she declared to her baffled parents when they picked her up from the airport.

Unsure what to do next, Sandra, Harmony, and Unity meditated for several weeks in the dark. Eventually she had a vision of a cave painting of a bison, which she was sure was located in Spain. She told her parents that the universe had spoken and she must go to Spain to find the bison on the cave wall. Again, her parents consented as again, they had no idea what else to do.

Unity flew into Madrid and wandered around with a small phrasebook and a picture of a bison, asking about ancient cave drawings as best she could. Eventually someone directed her to Altamira, in the north. She took a train and then hitch-hiked, and it was there she stumbled across Richard Drummond, a quiet and studious young man doing postdoctoral research on Paleolithic cave art.

The two were an unlikely pair. Bespectacled, skinny and socially awkward, Richard wasn't used to being noticed by women, so Unity's attentions were at first flattering and quickly became all-consuming.

When Unity fell pregnant only a month later, he did the honorable thing and asked her to marry him, but she laughed and said they didn't need those sorts of silly papers. They were fine just as they were.

Persephone was born in San Sebastian, Spain on a cool day in November 1994. Richard let Unity choose the name of course. He mostly let Unity do what she wanted, as there was no stopping her in any case.

"Isn't Persephone the goddess of the underworld?" ventured Richard quietly, less sure of the name than was his free-thinking partner.

"Yes, for half the year, and for the other half, she's the goddess of the spring. So, you know, she'll be perfectly balanced."

Richard shrugged. "Can I choose her middle name?"

"I don't see why not."

"Elizabeth?"

"Elizabeth," repeated Unity. "Yes, that's a good strong name. Persephone Elizabeth McCullough-Drummond."

Richard didn't dare question the double-barrelled last name. He was just relieved that his daughter would have another name to use if she was later bullied for being named after a Greek goddess.

Once Richard had finished his term in Spain, the two packed up for Vancouver. Unity had already overstayed her three-month visitor limit by seven months and five days, and Richard's visa was linked to his research. Originally from Edmonton, Richard had begun to enjoy living by the sea, so he was happy to follow Unity back to her hometown on the temperate west coast. His mother, who had been born in Cornwall but had spent most of her life in Alberta, joined them there two years later, selling her house in Edmonton and buying a small townhome near her son's family. She had understood from the phone calls that Richard's partner was as unusual as his research interests, and sensed correctly that they might need some practical help bringing up their daughter.

Life continued in their little family unit in this way until just after Persephone turned sixteen, when Unity went on a trip to Bali and apparently forgot to return. Violet was greatly perplexed by the way in which Perse and her Dad took this in their stride.

"The thing is," Persephone said, "she wasn't really *here,* anyway. I mean, she was sort of always on her way out, heading somewhere else on an astral plane we can't see."

"How's your Dad doing?"

Persephone shrugged. "He's sad she's gone I guess, but I think he's OK. He told me he was surprised she stayed as long as she did. He sort of always expected her to leave. He said he thought I was the only reason she stayed for so many years."

Violet frowned. "But come on Perse! Aren't you angry? Sad? Upset? Don't you feel abandoned or miss her, or feel anything most people would feel? I mean, I know she was weird, Perse, no offense, but seriously, *what the actual fuck?"* demanded Violet. She didn't swear often, but when she did, she really meant it.

"No," said Persephone honestly. She sighed. "You knew my mom. 'Weird' is the understatement of the millennium. I don't hold her to the same moral standards I hold the mere mortals in my life." She raised one half of her mouth in a wry smile. "If my mom abandoned me, she essentially did that the moment I was born, or maybe when she stopped breastfeeding me. She was never really a mom to me. If my grandmother had disappeared to Bali, then yes, I'd feel all the things you listed and more."

It wasn't that Persephone was unfeeling. It was that she'd genuinely never bonded with her mother, and was fairly certain that no one ever had. Certainly, her father had fallen in love with her in his own way, but he'd always had the sense he was only borrowing her from another parallel universe.

When her grandmother passed away suddenly two years later, Persephone, to Violet's relief, exhibited all the emotions one would expect from a person who lost someone close to them. Perse sang her favourite Cornish folk song, "The White Rose," at the funeral and managed to hold it together until the very end of the song, her voice only cracking slightly as she sang the final verse:

Now I am alone, my sweet darling,
I walk through the garden and weep,
But spring will return with your presence
Oh lily white rose, mine to keep

Strumming the final chord on her guitar, she dissolved into tears and Violet had gently helped her return to her seat.

"I didn't get a chance to say goodbye to her," Persephone cried later. "I just wish I'd known. I don't even think I ever told her how much she meant to me, how much I appreciated what she did for me. She basically raised me and I never said thank you. And she was the one who organised all my music lessons. I wouldn't be studying music therapy at all if it weren't for her."

"She knew all that," said Violet quietly.

Persephone shook her head. "I just wish I'd known, that last time we talked, that that would be our last conversation."

"I know," said Violet, hugging her friend close and wishing she could make her stop hurting.

Chapter 15

Crete, May 2019

Κρήτη, Μάιος 2019

As she swam once more in the early morning, Violet thought back on Persephone mourning the loss of her grandmother and wondered if she'd been a supportive enough friend. Until Perse had died, Violet had never experienced that kind of loss, and she now felt she'd completely underestimated the depth of Persephone's emotions.

She wished now that she could ask her friend how she ever got over losing her grandmother, or if, indeed, she ever did. The vast abyss that Persephone's departure had opened up for Violet didn't seem like it would ever close again. She was feeling alive again, it was true, but she also felt an emptiness in the space Persephone had inhabited in her heart. She still had occasional lapses where she forgot for a fleeting moment what had happened and thought, "I must tell Perse that!" only to remember suddenly and painfully that she couldn't tell her best friend anything ever again.

Her mother had bought her a book on grieving and Violet had flipped through bits of it back in Vancouver. It said there were five stages: denial, anger, bargaining, depression, and acceptance. Violet thought she'd gone through the first two in a matter of hours, found no room at all for bargaining, and sunk into a deep depression for eight months. Here, perhaps she was finally crossing the threshold over to acceptance. But it didn't mean the hurt was gone. Sometimes Violet missed her friend so intensely, she half-expected the strength of her wanting to bring Persephone back. Maybe that was her bargaining. "Oh God, I can't even mourn in the right order," thought Violet. "So typical."

She'd been in Crete a week now and had got into the routine of her morning swim, breakfast, walking, lunch, siesta (which she rarely took, usually going for a second swim instead) and walking or reading under the pine trees until dinner, then usually swimming again around sunset. She tried not to think about Dimitri, which of course meant that she constantly thought about him. For all her knowledge of psychology, Violet had very little control over the workings of her mind, a fact that she was painfully aware of and constantly frustrated by.

That afternoon after her second swim, Violet saw Angelo and waved hello. She hadn't seen him without her aunt and uncle around since her first full day on the island when she'd inadvertently caused chaos by going for a walk.

"Yia su!" [23] he greeted her in Greek.

---

[23] Hello!

"Yia su." replied Violet. *"Ti kanis?"* [24]

"Kalla." [25] He was a man of few words.

"Do you not take siesta?"

"I usually do. But I'm not tired today. Thought I'd help get things ready for dinner at the taverna."

"Or maybe go for a swim?" teased Violet.

"Noooo, another month at least before I'll get in that water." He sat down next to his cousin.

Violet tried not to sound overly eager, but couldn't wait long to ask him about Dimitri's family.

"Hey, Angelo, remember you said something about the Sfakianakis that first day I was here?"

"Did I?"

"Yes," said Violet, slightly annoyed that no one seemed to remember what they had or hadn't told her about this family. "You told me our families were...friends, but didn't talk much or something. And you said not to ask your mom about it. You said we could talk more later."

Angelo adjusted his seated position and looked visibly uncomfortable.

"I don't know if it's my place to tell you."

"Tell me what?" Violet was getting a little exasperated with the tidbits of information she was being drip-fed.

"I feel like your mother should tell you about that."

"I asked her and she said she didn't know anything."

"Really?" Angelo turned and looked at Violet, surprised.

---

[24] How are you?

[25] Good

"Yes." Violet had a strange sinking feeling. She had no reason not to believe her mother, she trusted her entirely. But something wasn't adding up.

Angelo sat thinking for a few minutes. "I don't want to hide anything from you, it just doesn't feel right for me to tell you the whole story. It's not my story."

"So whose is it?" demanded Violet.

"Your mother's," he said quickly.

Violet frowned, but she could see Angelo was sincere.

"And my mother's too, sort of, but I know she won't talk about it," added Angelo.

"Well, is there anything I should know? I mean, do I need to be wary of them?"

"Wary?" It wasn't a word Angelo had heard much in American sitcoms.

"I mean, can I trust them?" asked Violet.

Angelo smiled slowly. "Oh....If you're asking about Dimitris, he's a good guy and he's nothing to do with what happened."

"Thank you," said Violet, relieved at least, but still confused.

"I'm sorry I can't be more helpful," added Angelo. "Some things are just difficult for people to talk about."

Violet understood that all too well. She sighed.

"I'm gonna go inside and have a bit of a siesta after all," she said as she stood up to leave.

Angelo stood up too. "Violet—"

She turned to face him. "I just wanted to say, I'm sorry about what happened to your friend."

Violet managed to nod and walked back to her room.

Of course Angelo knew what had happened. Her mother would have told his mother, who would have told everyone. Dimitri probably knew as well. Maybe that's why he hadn't asked many questions. Or maybe he didn't know because, for reasons unknown to her, these two families were the only two in Sfinari who barely spoke. Violet wished she had some honey raki in her room.

She laid down on her bed intending just to relax briefly and mull things over, but she must have indeed dozed off at some point as she woke up to a knock on her door. Rubbing her eyes, Violet stood up gingerly, unsure how long she'd slept. She was still battling the tail-end of her jet lag, which didn't help her disoriented state. Eyes half open, she opened her door, expecting to see her aunt or uncle summoning her to a meal, but instead she saw Dimitri.

Seeing her state, he apologized for waking her. "I didn't think you took siestas."

"I don't," said Violet, wishing she'd at least brushed her wet frizzy hair before answering the door. "It was an accident."

Dimitri laughed. "An accidental siesta?"

"Yes, haven't you ever had that happen?"

He shook his head, smiling. "I brought you some *kalitsounia* we had left over." He held out a box of the sweet cheese pastries.

"Ooh another food communication," teased Violet, now fully awake and hoping her wit would outweigh her disheveled appearance.

Dimitri smiled. "I was thinking, I know your aunt showed you around a bit, but if you have some time tomorrow, I have the day off and there are some beautiful places you should see while you're here. You wanna go for a drive?"

"Sure." Violet hoped she didn't sound overly eager.

"Great. I'll come get you at eight? Get an early start?"

Violet nodded and hoped she didn't look as excited as she felt.

Chapter 16

Violet didn't want to appear eager by being ready early, but also didn't want to seem flaky by being late, so had decided she'd just sit under the tamarisk trees at 7:55am and look relaxed, like she was ready but not waiting.

She had already had her usual morning swim. There was a slight breeze today and small waves were breaking on the shore. Underwater, Violet had heard the soothing sound of the pebbles being gently pulled by the waves and marveled that this was a sound she'd never heard before in all her years of swimming. Despite her excitement about the day, or perhaps because of the trepidation that accompanied it, she had been reluctant to leave the embrace of the sea this morning.

She heard a car pull up behind her and stood up. It was exactly 8am. Dimitri waved through the window and Violet walked over to the car.

"You're on time. That's not very Greek!" she joked.

"Ah, but I'm an American-Greek hybrid and I know better than to keep a Canadian woman waiting." He grinned. "Besides, we have a busy day ahead of us!"

"Where are we going?"

"Wouldn't you like to know." He raised his eyebrows and began to pull away, up toward the main road in Sfinari.

"Oh, I just remembered, I better text my aunt and let her know I'm with you today. I don't want them freaking out like they did the day after I got here."

Violet took out her phone and began to type.

"What happened that day?"

"I went for a walk and for some reason everyone thought I was dead." said Violet, suddenly wishing she hadn't mentioned death.

"That seems odd," said Dimitri.

Violet shrugged, "It was odd. And then my aunt said something about not swimming in the sea. Angelo told me it was OK, but it did put me off a bit."

Dimitri was uncharacteristically quiet.

Violet sent the text message and tried to think of something to fill the silence. "Are we going to Knossos?" She knew it was many hours' drive away and not likely but didn't know what else to guess.

"No, nothing that clichéd."

"Is it clichéd? I thought it was an amazing archaeological site?"

"Depends what you mean by amazing. If you mean crowded, overpriced, restored in controversial ways, and excavated by a foreign man who mistook a beekeeper's storage room for the 'snake cult room'—and that wasn't the worst of his mistakes—then yes, it's amazing."

"Oh wow, so many aspects of Cretan culture and politics I don't know about. I didn't know you were such a history buff, Mr. grew-up-in-America."

Violet's phone beeped and she looked down at the message.

"I'm half-joking," he clarified, "Knossos is worth seeing. One day. But there are a million archaeological sites all over this island. You could dig anywhere and find ancient buildings and cities. Knossos is just the most excavated and studied. And marketed."

He glanced at Violet, who appeared distracted, frowning at her phone. "What's wrong?" he asked.

"I just got a weird message from my aunt, asking if my mother knows I'm spending time with you." She turned to Dimitri, who also frowned. "Dimitri, someone has got to tell me what's going on. What happened between our families? My mother says she doesn't know, Angelo says she does know, and she should tell me, and neither of them are liars, but someone is lying! What is the freaking deal here?" Violet's voice had risen a little and she immediately regretted this slight loss of composure in front of Dimitri. He watched the road, frowning.

"Violet, I have to agree with Angelo, your mother should be the one to tell you."

"Ugh! But she *won't!*" Violet tried to reign in her emotions. "I asked her specifically, she literally said she knew nothing. My mother's never lied to me before." She sighed. "I'm sorry, it's all just a bit confusing. Anyway,

Angelo said you were nothing to do with anything, so why would my mother care if I'm spending time with you?"

Dimitri thought for a moment. "Some people blame a whole family if one person does something wrong."

Violet was tired of these mysterious hints and where she would normally have let things lie, she couldn't help but ask one more question.

"Is it to do with your father?"

Dimitri breathed in slowly and glanced at Violet. "I can tell you that it is, but I can't tell you anything else. And it's not because I don't want to, or I don't think you deserve to know. It just wouldn't be right for me to tell you."

Violet was frustrated, but she could see she'd pushed Dimitri as far as he would go.

"OK, sorry," said Violet, resigned to the fact that she wouldn't find out anything more today.

"For what?"

"Just for getting upset, making you uncomfortable."

"You don't need to be sorry, and I've been much more uncomfortable before and somehow survived."

Violet laughed and relaxed in her seat. She put her phone away and didn't reply to her aunt's message.

They drove north on the winding main highway, then turned off to the right.

"I'm going to take you the mountain route," he smiled. The road twisted and turned up and around the mountains, the olive groves giving way to open fields. Sweeping views of the sea opened up before them, then disappeared, only to reappear, slightly altered with the next turn. Gentle yellow chamomile, blood-red poppies and small white daisies lined the roadside and stretched out into the fields. Spiny broom covered the hillsides in vibrant golden blooms. Violet stared out the car window, trying to absorb the beauty of the colourful landscape, wishing she could bottle all the sights, scents and sensations.

After about twenty minutes, Dimitri turned down an unmarked dirt road to the right.

"Where are we going?"

"Almost there," he replied, savouring the surprise.

Dimitri pulled over amid the wildflowers, and got out of the car without a word of explanation.

Violet looked out over the high fields surrounding her and as she got out of the small white car, she had the sensation that she'd been here before, though she knew she hadn't. Turning toward Dimitri, she could just make out the eight hives behind him, nestled in a small fenced-off area with a few shrubs around the edges.

"Oh, are these your mountain bees?" asked Violet, smiling, though she couldn't see the little purple flowers she'd tasted in the honey.

"Yes," smiled Dimitri. "But the thyme won't bloom until next month. It's too bad you'll miss it." He paused. "Is this what you saw when you tried my honey?"

Violet giggled nervously, still slightly embarrassed about her strange vision of purple thyme.

"Yes, I think so actually. But with the purple flowers of course."

"Do you often have...those sorts of things?" he asked curiously.

"Not really. I mean, occasionally I have dreams that turn out to be oddly prophetic. Persephone and I used to dream communicate a lot." She was aware this time, of choosing to mention Persephone, grateful that the ice had been broken on the topic.

"Dream communicate?"

"Yeah, you know, I'd dream something, like I was on a long walk, trying to read an old paper map but it kept ripping, and changing every time I looked at it. And Perse would tell me the next day that her satnav stopped working on her drive home the night before, and she literally had to pull in to a gas station and ask for directions, like it was 1982. And I had no idea. Or sometimes we'd have very similar dreams in the same night." Violet shrugged, unsure what Dimitri would make of this confession.

"The world is a strange place." He paused and looked over at his hives. "You know, the night my grandmother died, I had a dream. It was about an old lady, she didn't look like my *yiayia,* but we seemed to know each other very well in the dream. And she was crying, and she just kept telling me I was going to be OK. I kept asking 'What? What's wrong? What's going to be OK?' But she just kept saying, don't worry, you'll be OK."

"Were you close with her? Your grandmother?"

"Yes, once we moved back here."

"I'm sorry you lost her," said Violet quietly. "Was it recent?"

"About five years ago," he said.

"Do you still miss her?"

"Of course." They were leaning on the side of the car. He looked at her, perhaps surmising whether grieving was a topic she wanted to broach.

"I still miss her, but it's funny, you know, I still hear her voice in my head all the time. I mean, I don't really *hear* it, but you know, I'll be thinking about whether or not to do something and I'll hear her saying 'Don't be a fool, Dimitri. Of course you should do this!' It's like I've sort of got an internal version of her that still gives me advice, whether I want it or not." He smiled.

Violet looked down and smiled a little as well. She still heard Perse's voice in her head all the time too. She was terrified that one day it might stop.

"Do you think you'll always have that? Your internal *yiayia?*" she asked quietly.

He nodded. "If I know my grandmother at all, she's definitely never going to leave me alone." He turned to her and smiled. "Come on, honeybee, this was only our first stop."

Back in the car, they drove back to the road they'd turned off, and continued north, toward the sea along a mountain ridge, passing through a few sleepy hamlets. Small shrines were dotted along the winding road, boxes made of various materials perched atop a stand. Some were quite ornate, decorated like miniature churches. Violet strained to see inside them as they drove past. Most contained a burning lamp, a bottle of something, and photos she couldn't quite make out. There were also often flowers and other small objects.

"What are all these little shrines about?" Violet asked Dimitri. She'd noticed them on her drive with her aunt, but hadn't had a chance to ask about them.

"They're called *kandilakia.* Or sometimes we call them *ekklisakia,* which means 'tiny churches.' They're set up where people have had accidents on the road, either because they survived and it's a sort of offering of gratitude, or—" he hesitated, not really wanting to bring up death once again. Not seeing any way around it, however, he continued, "sometimes people didn't survive and their family puts a shrine up in their memory."

Violet sat mulling this over. "But there are *a lot* of them," she said quietly, suddenly feeling vulnerable sitting in a small ten-year-old car with a man she barely knew.

"We do have a lot of accidents on Crete, partly because," he waved at the meandering road, now descending through tight turns, "you know, the roads have to wind up and down through the mountains, but also, people often don't drive so well, they don't wear seatbelts, they drive when they've been drinking, and they just go too fast." He glanced at Violet, who was watching the road intently and trying to suppress an urge to hit an imaginary brake pedal at her feet.

"Don't worry," Dimitri smiled reassuringly, "I know these roads well, and I promise I haven't had anything to drink this morning."

Violet laughed. "Not even a shot of *raki?*"

"Not even a shot of *raki.*" He grinned as he watched the meandering road in front of them.

To Violet's relief, they soon rejoined the main road and headed briefly east, then back south. Violet had given up trying to orientate herself on the winding roads. The sea seemed to be on all sides, the road constantly twisted, and her sense of direction had never been strong.

"This sure isn't a grid system is it?" she joked.

Dimitri laughed.

After about twenty minutes, they pulled into the small village of Polyrrhenia.

"Stop number two," said Dimitri getting out of the car.

They wandered through the narrow streets and walkways of the village, a charming patchwork of stone buildings, half-ruined walls, Roman aqueducts, and ancient dwellings cut into the rocks. Wildflowers and garden flowers seemed to mingle along the stone walls and along the edges of the streets, overflowing out of neatly kept gardens. Apricots, nearly ripe, hung from trees they passed. Violet was sure they'd walked straight into the Garden of Eden. She wondered how a country so rich in produce could be so economically poor. She accidentally voiced the question out loud and Dimitri answered thoughtfully.

"I'm not an expert on these things, but I think there are a lot of factors. Lots of corruption and mismanagement by the government, lots of political unrest. And there's the geography of course; we don't have the space for giant fields of monoculture like they do in America. But beyond all that, I just don't think we're really suited to capitalism."

"How so?" pressed Violet as they strolled slowly between stone houses.

"Well, I'm going to generalize here, but we're not really consumers, not like Americans. We're more interested in being self-sufficient than mass-producing, and besides the geographical issues I think there's a cultural difference, especially on the islands and in rural areas. Most people in Crete still make their own olive oil, and yes of course, some people produce it on a larger scale and sell it, as a business, only after they've kept the best for themselves and their families." He paused and grinned, showing his dimples. "But, you know, we want to *enjoy* our food, we want to know where it comes from. We enjoy producing the ingredients, preparing food, and sharing it with friends over conversation. We don't want to go to a fast food drive-through and scoff down a bunch of shitty salty processed food." He lowered the edges of his mouth in disgust.

"It's kind of the opposite of the American dream. People in America, they seem to think they can consume life like a super-sized happy meal, and then they wonder why they're not happy, so they order another one. They're always looking for the next thing, the next job, the next promotion, the next...girlfriend. And they just end up on this endless treadmill, climbing an imaginary ladder up to an imaginary dream that someone told them would make them happy."

Violet was silent, mulling this over.

"Maybe they all just got lost in the canned tomato aisle and they didn't know what else to do."

Dimitri laughed.

"So, are you happy here? With your bees and the taverna?" asked Violet.

"You know, when you say it like that, I feel my American side wanting to justify why that's enough for me to be happy. There are other things I'd like one day, maybe a family. But yes, overall, I feel content here."

"I don't think you have to justify that at all," said Violet. "It sounds very refreshing to me."

A small gift shop had appeared on their right, on the edge of the town. Dimitri slowed his pace and nodded towards the shop. "If you want to buy a souvenir, or something to take back to your family, this is the place," he said as they entered.

As they passed through the door, the shop owner's eyes lit up as he greeted Dimitri *"Yia su Dimitri! Ti kanis?* It's been awhile."

"Of course they know each other," thought Violet, amused. Dimitri explained that the shop owner, Niko, was also a beekeeper, and they often shared tips and helped each other catch swarms. "There's a beekeeping code," he explained to Violet. "We all help each other out."

Violet smiled. "You're in the same hive."

Dimitri grinned and nodded.

The shop was a treasure trove of handmade wooden objects and Violet didn't know where to look first. The scent of warm olive wood hung in the air, and every wall and every surface was adorned with works of art, both practical and decorative. There were salad servers and bowls, tiny jewelry boxes, huge wooden chests, hanging ornaments, and decorative sculptures almost as tall as

Violet, all made from the richly toned wood of olive trees.

As she looked around, stunned, Dimitri introduced her to his friend Niko. Niko looked like a caricature of an older Greek man, with grey whispy hair, a strong nose, and an unkempt beard, but a kind and smiling face underneath.

"Yia su," Violet said shyly, feeling painfully aware of her foreign accent and feeling she should be able to do better as a half-Greek. Niko said something in Greek and smiled mischievously. Violet could only smile back.

"He says you are the most beautiful thing in the shop, except for maybe the sculpture of the siren he just completed."

Violet laughed. In another context, she might have found this mildly offensive, but she could tell Niko was from a different era and there was no sense in trying to bridge the gap between his well-meaning joke and the subtleties of modern feminism. It would have been like trying to teach a goat to fly by explaining the principles of aerodynamics.

"I thought sirens were like mermaids?" Violet asked as she inspected the graceful wooden sculpture. It was a woman's head and winged torso playing a lyre, with the legs of a bird. It measured about a foot and a half tall and was so expertly carved that Violet half-expected the feathers of the wings to be soft to the touch.

"Yes, that's what they eventually turned into in later myths, but the early sirens were half-bird, half-woman," explained Dimitri.

"Really? Well, she's very intriguing," replied Violet, running her fingers across the wings and down the feminine back that transformed seamlessly into the tail of a bird.

Violet turned to examine the other wooden treasures surrounding her while the two men chatted in Greek. She found a small box she thought her mother would like and then found herself wondering for a brief moment what she should bring back for Persephone, before being hit once again with the agonizing realization that her friend was no longer alive. She wondered when those moments would stop. The waves of almost physical pain that accompanied them were horrendous, and difficult to hide when they happened in public.

She closed her eyes for a moment, waiting for the feeling to pass. Opening them again, she sighed and looked over the jewelry. Her attention was caught by some necklaces made with small perfectly round beads of olive wood. Violet didn't wear much jewelry, but she liked the simple design and the natural tones of the wood. She decided to treat herself and walked over to the checkout.

Dimitri and Niko had been looking at some wooden bowls and chopping boards. Seeming to have made a decision, Dimitri brought a smooth honey-coloured salad bowl over to the checkout. "For my sister," he explained. "Her name day's coming up. Did you find something?"

Violet held out the items she'd chosen. "I thought I'd get these."

Dimitri paid for his bowl, but when Violet tried to pay for her gifts, she was waved away.

"Did you pay for my things?" she asked Dimitri, a little annoyed.

"Yes, I thought I'd treat you."

Violet was still holding out her credit card but Niko refused to take it. She looked from one man to the other, feeling foolish and perhaps disproportionately exasperated. Maybe it was the wave of grief she was recovering from, or maybe it was the feeling that she'd been left out of a whole conversation, but Violet was decidedly annoyed.

Seeing her consternation, Dimitri apologized. "I'm sorry, look, I'll let you buy us a snack at the cafe, then we'll be even," he offered.

Violet sighed. She knew he only meant it as a nice gesture, but she felt like a child. She thanked Niko, trying to be polite.

Outside, Dimitri was apologetic once more. "I'm sorry if I upset you. I should have asked you."

"Yes, you should have," said Violet. "I wouldn't have minded you paying, I minded you not asking me."

"I know, I'm sorry, I think I forgot you don't understand Greek."

Violet shook her head, "If I find out you know the cafe owner and he or she doesn't charge us, you'll be in real trouble." She couldn't stay properly mad at him for long.

Leaving the little village, they climbed up a hillside strewn with wildflowers in yellow, white and purple. Ruins of an ancient metropolis dotted the landscape, though many were half-hidden by the long grass and flora. Violet read an information board that described the vast ancient city, the centre of a huge city-state that covered the whole western half of the island. One of its ports had been in Falassarna, the vast sandy beach her aunt had taken her to.

"I know there isn't much left of the ruins now, but I wanted to show you the views," said Dimitri. "Look, we can walk to the chapel and then carry on up to the acropolis if you want." He pointed up the steep hillside. "The views will be worth it and then you can treat us to a snack on the way back down, and I promise I won't even offer to pay." He held up his hands in surrender.

Violet had given up trying to stay annoyed. She half-smiled and shook her head, pretending she was still just a little angry, and began the steep ascent.

From the top of the hill, looking north, Violet could see the sea melting into the sky, both impossibly blue. She felt as if she was floating at the top of the world, looking down on a landscape so stunning it surely must have been the creation of a master artist. She took a few photos on her phone but found they did the scene no justice at all.

"Can you see Sfinari from here?" asked Violet, squinting over to the west.

"Nope. But it's over there somewhere."

"Like the stars," said Violet, though she hadn't meant to voice the thought.

"The stars?" asked Dimitri.

He was standing quite close to her and Violet felt his arm brush hers.

"Oh, I was looking at the stars the other night, and the milky way. It was amazing, just hanging over the headland, you must have seen it?"

Dimitri nodded. "Yes, but for the best views of the milky way, we should go to the south coast sometime."

Violet smiled, liking the thought of another trip with Dimitri. "It's just, I know it's really obvious on one level. We all know the sky is full of stars all the time, but when we can only see the sun, it's easy to forget about them. And even the way we talk about the stars 'coming out' at night, as if they weren't there before but then just step out into the sky when it gets dark. It just made me think, we trust our senses a lot, but they're kind of limited aren't they?"

Dimitri nodded. "Bees can see things we can't."

"Really?"

"Yeah, they can see ultraviolet light. A lot of flowers have markings that guide the bees to the nectar, but they're on the UV spectrum, so we can't see them. They can also sense the electric charge of flowers. It changes after a bee lands on it, so if a bee detects that negative charge, they'll skip that flower, cause they know it's already been pollinated."

"Wow," said Violet, genuinely intrigued. "I had no idea the world would look so different to a bee." Before he could answer, Violet remembered something. "Hey, did you put that blanket on me the night I fell asleep outside?"

"Definitely not," he said, his mischievous grin giving him away.

"How did you even see me?" Violet wasn't sure if it was creepy or romantic.

"I sometimes don't sleep so well," he admitted. "I walk along the beach at night a lot. It's very peaceful."

"It was. Very peaceful," agreed Violet, wondering how long he'd watched her without her knowing. She realized he must live closer to the tavernas than she'd thought. "Do you live down by the beach? I thought everyone lived up in the village."

"My mother lives up in the village, and I spend winters with her there. But I wanted to have my own space, and be nearer the bees for the summers, so a few years ago I fixed up an old cottage, behind the tavernas."

"Really? I thought I'd walked around the whole area and I didn't see a cottage."

"It's sort of uphill a bit, further back than you probably went, tucked in the trees. I'll show you later."

Violet thought of Dimitri sleeping so near to her little room and was sure that she blushed.

They ambled slowly back down the hill and stopped at the cafe, where Dimitri dutifully allowed Violet to pay for two *kries sokolates*[26] and *sfakianopites*.[27] They both agreed the pastries were delicious, but would have been better topped with Dimitri's thyme honey.

They walked back through the village to Dimitri's car.

"How are you feeling?" he asked her as they got in.

"Pretty good after that *sfano…kiapita?*" she ventured, giggling as she knew she'd got it wrong.

"Sfakianopita," he corrected her, laughing.

"I'm a rubbish half-Greek," joked Violet.

"You just need a bit of training," he joked back. "Are you up for a bit of a drive? I want to take you to one of my favourite places, but it's about an hour's drive from

---

[26] Cold chocolate drinks
[27] Cheese-filled pastries topped with honey, nuts, and cinnamon

here, and then of course we have to get back. Is that too far?"

"Hey, in Canada, we drive an hour every day just to get to work, so I think I'll manage."

"In the snow, right?" he teased, knowing full well that the west coast remained temperate into Vancouver.

"Yes, in the snow. Obviously. And when I say drive, I mean drive a team of sled dogs, of course."

Dimitri laughed as he pulled away.

Just over an hour later, they pulled up to a small dusty parking lot with a tiny wooden ticket booth that appeared to have landed there by accident. A large faded sign read "Aptera."

"Ooh another ancient site?" asked Violet as they both got out of the car, relieved to stretch their legs.

"The best ancient site in western Crete, at least I think so. I found it by accident when I was a teenager. I used to drive around a lot, cause, you know, there wasn't much else to do, and after my dad left, it was...sort of my therapy, to just drive and see where I ended up. But anyway, one day I saw the brown sign and thought I'd have a look."

The brown signs denoting ancient Minoan and Mycenaean sites were certainly plentiful, and Violet had become aware that the whole island could have been an archaeological site, if it had not had a current resident population.

Dimitri was careful to ask Violet if she'd mind terribly if he paid the four euros for their entry fee. Violet laughed. "Are you sure you can stretch to that?"

"Just about," he smiled, handing over the money to the young man in the ticket booth, who appeared to have been asleep when they arrived.

The large site stretched out on the high plain dotted with grey stone walls and remnants of ancient buildings, the lower walls half-enveloped by the long grass and tall wildflowers, but other walls still standing tall after thousands of years. The land was mostly green, with yellow-brown patches foreshadowing the dry summer months. A soft breeze breathed through the grass. A twelfth-century monastery stood silent and undamaged among the ruins.

Violet read some of the information boards and marveled at the long history of the site, inhabited since the fourteenth century BCE. She tried to grasp this breadth of time in her mind but found it disorienting. Still, she felt that the earth beneath her and the ruins around her held memories of all the people, all the civilizations, the conquests, the layers of time that had unfolded here.

The city, Dimitri told her in a hushed voice, had been inhabited until it was destroyed by an earthquake in the seventh century. Violet wondered to herself what that sort of destruction must have been like to experience, and reflected that her own tragedy certainly paled in comparison. She heard a warbler singing behind her in a grove of trees, the sound floating through the still silent air. She was sure that time must have stopped momentarily, such was the feeling of complete tranquility where they stood.

They wandered through the ruins quietly, whispering instead of talking, not wanting to disturb the quiet calmness of the land. Dimitri led her to the Roman cisterns, huge water tanks sat in the hillside like gaping stone mouths, nearly ten metres high. They still held water, though time and neglect had turned it murky and green.

Standing in the entrance to one of the tanks, the air was refreshingly cool out of the sun and near the water. There were no barriers and it was possible to wander inside, along a narrow ledge above the water, though Violet didn't dare venture in far. This was not water she wanted to swim in.

"How is it so peaceful here?" whispered Violet, her quiet voice amplified in the structure, bouncing off the water and the curved ceilings.

Dimitri shrugged and smiled.

They stood in silence for a few moments, taking in the shadows and reflections playing on the edge of the water, and the shape of the high vaulted ceilings. Violet's thoughts returned to the earthquake that had destroyed the city after so many years. Had any of its citizens survived? What must it feel like to live through something like that and lose so much?

"Hey, Violet, can I ask you something?"

"Sure."

"What happened to your friend?"

Violet took a deep breath. She hadn't expected him to ask that particular question, at least not just yet. She didn't answer.

"You don't have to tell me if you don't want to," he added, sensing she'd tensed.

Violet closed her eyes for a moment. She wasn't sure she could answer. "She was...attacked. Randomly. She was stabbed." It sounded like someone else's voice. Violet was sure it wasn't her own. She'd never said it out loud to anyone and the words felt dry and hoarse in her mouth. She still couldn't bring herself to say that Persephone had been murdered, the word felt too harsh, too much like something on a sensationalist crime drama rather than real life.

Dimitri gasped audibly, searching for words. Violet stared blankly down into the standing water.

"I'm so sorry, Violet."

They were still speaking in hushed tones and the acoustics gave their voices a strange quality, as if they were coming from inside the cistern.

"She was just going into the library to pick up some books she had on hold. It was...so strange. Not a rough area, not even night time. Three other people were injured. She was the only one who died." Violet paused briefly, wondering whether she would say the sentence that followed. "I was just with her, right before it happened. I left in a hurry to catch my bus home."

Violet felt oddly numb as she spoke the words. She hadn't said any of this out loud before. Her words seemed to draw the events into very sharp focus, transforming them from a nightmare she'd run from into a reality that had followed her even here, in this timeless ancient place. Her legs felt weak and she lowered herself to sit on the cold floor, taking a deep breath.

Dimitri sat down beside her.

"I don't know what to say. I'm so so sorry."

Violet hugged her knees into her chest and looked down into the darkened water. She wondered what was hiding in the murk that she couldn't see. She stared until her vision began to blur and she remembered to blink again. Dimitri was sitting very close to her, not quite touching her.

Time had no meaning in the cisterns and neither were sure how long they sat in silence before Dimitri asked gently, "When did it happen?"

"Last August, just a few days after my birthday. She'd just taken me out for a birthday lunch and we'd walked to the library together after."

Dimitri was silent, not sure there were words in any language that would form a suitable reply.

Violet was surprised to find herself continuing. "The thing is, besides just losing her, which would have been hard enough on its own, I can't help but feel...if she hadn't been taking me out that day, she probably wouldn't have been at the library at that time. And maybe if I'd not been so worried about catching my bus—" Violet's voice trailed off.

"Violet, you know it's not your fault. You know that right?" He spoke gently, in hushed tones.

Violet nodded, "Yes, in so many ways, yes. And I can hear Persephone in my head telling me I'm being an idiot to even consider blaming myself. But the thing is, there's another voice in my head that says I'd be a terrible person if I didn't feel a little bit guilty about it. I mean, logically, if it weren't for me, it wouldn't have happened. If I don't acknowledge that, doesn't that make me very—" Violet shook her head, "just a bad, selfish person?" She paused. "How does anyone ever figure out what to feel?" she added.

Dimitri sat in silence for a moment. "First of all, you are definitely not a bad person, Violet. You've been through something horrible, so it's understandable you don't know what to feel. I don't think I'd be coping anywhere near as well as you. Secondly, what you said might be true, but you also don't know what might have happened in Persephone's life if you hadn't met, or if you hadn't met up that day. Her life could have been very different. She could have died years before, or she could have ended up at the library at the same time, and the same thing might have still happened to her."

"Or she could have lived to be an old lady and done amazing things," Violet added.

"Maybe." He shrugged. "But the point is, it's not up to us to choose how things play out. We can never know how each of our decisions will affect everything."

"So how does anyone decide anything? If so much rides on every simple little decision, how do normal people not second-guess everything they do?"

Dimitri shrugged, "I guess we need to have a certain amount of trust, in ourselves, and in...God, or the universe or however you want to think of it."

Violet thought for a moment. "Persephone used to talk about the multiple universe theory. I didn't understand it fully, but it was something about a whole new universe being created every time anyone chooses something, or with every different random thing that happens. So, for example, if you throw a dice, that creates six different universes, each with the dice landing on a different number. And that's just one event." Violet shook her head. "So, with all the various things that happen, and choices we all make, that means you somehow end up with an infinite number of universes with all these different realities."

"She sounds very clever."

"She was. Much cleverer than me. I found the theory paralyzing. I didn't even want to think about it, but she found it *so* exciting." Violet smiled. It was both difficult and comforting to reminisce about her friend. "She was going to write a book one day, a non-fiction book," Violet continued. "She was figuring out exactly what it was going to be about, but she said it would be about creativity and process, and the nature of reality, and how we can somehow use that understanding to find happiness and balance." Violet paused and glanced at Dimitri, checking if perhaps he was tired of listening and she should stop talking.

"Go on," Dimitri encouraged her.

"She loved her work, her music therapy, and she was so talented. She knew what she wanted and she just sort of, got on with stuff. I used to think everything came easily to her. But now I think she was just really good at knowing which path to take when. I just, I couldn't even choose a path."

"I couldn't even choose a can of tomatoes."

Violet laughed despite herself, then dissolved into heavy tears. Her muscles softened and Dimitri put his arm gently around her. Violet could hear her sobs echoing back through the cistern and felt oddly comforted by the sense that someone else was sobbing back to her. Just an echo, of course, but in the moment she was sure that the ancient city was crying with her, and who's to say it wasn't.

A bee-eater flew quickly past them, just outside the tunnel opening where they sat, so close that they both flinched. Violet turned to look at Dimitri and saw a tear falling down his cheek before he could wipe it away.

"Oh God, I'm so sorry, I didn't mean to make you cry."

"Jesus, Violet, you definitely don't need to be sorry." He wiped away his tears and offered her a tissue from his pocket.

Violet restrained herself from apologizing for apologizing. Persephone had always told her she apologized too much, though she admitted she was guilty of the same at times.

They sat in silence and Violet wasn't sure if only a few minutes had passed or an hour. Time had ceased to have any meaning. Eventually Dimitri stood up slowly, and helped Violet to her feet.

"Come on, honeybee, there's a theatre with amazing views I want you to see, if you're feeling OK?"

Violet nodded, feeling drained but unexpectedly lighter.

He held her hand as they walked over to the recently excavated theatre. An impressive semi-circle of stepped seating surrounded a large stage. They looked out over the green hills and out to the bay of Souda, with the White Mountains, still snow-capped, behind them to the South.

"You alright?" he asked gently.

She nodded and resisted the urge to apologize once again.

Violet was acutely aware of Dimitri holding her hand, and, as usual, her mind was divided. She both wanted him to keep holding it, and to let go. She also wanted to kiss him and at the same time was terrified he might kiss her. Violet thought about the two universes stretching out before her: one in which she kissed him and one in which she didn't. There were only two options: kiss or don't kiss, and she still felt paralyzed. Violet wondered how on earth she'd ever navigate adulthood if she was always like this.

She let go of Dimitri's hand and sat down in a shady spot on the top step of the theatre seating. He followed and sat down beside her, leaving a little more space between them.

"You know, Aptera means 'wingless'. In Greek mythology, this is the place the sirens lost a singing contest to the muses. The muses, when they won, plucked out the sirens' feathers, and made themselves crowns out of them. The sirens were so humiliated they threw themselves into the sea, and became the islands in the bay down there." He pointed down to the Bay of Souda.

Violet frowned. "Well that's a cheery tale," she answered a little sarcastically, unsure if this story was meant to be somehow helpful, or if he was just trying to distract her.

"It's interesting that your friend's name was Persephone. The sirens were her companions. Do you know why they sang?"

"I thought it was to lure the sailors into the rocks?"

"Yes, eventually." He paused briefly. "But actually they first started singing in order to find Persephone."

Violet looked straight ahead, not able to meet his gaze.

"They were so distraught at losing her, they begged Demeter, Persephone's mother, to give them wings so they could find her more easily."

"And did they find her?"

"No, not in time anyway. It was Zeus who found her eventually. I guess the wings weren't as useful as they'd hoped, as she was underground, after all. In some versions of the myth, Demeter doesn't give them wings, but she curses them when they don't find her."

Violet sat mulling this over. She'd been familiar with other parts of the myth, in which Persephone is abducted by Hades. Demeter, her mother, searches for her and convinces Zeus to help rescue her. Persephone is found, but is only allowed to live above ground for half the year, as Hades had tricked her into eating the fruit of the underworld: pomegranate seeds. But Violet hadn't known about the muses. Funny also that her friend's mother was the opposite of Demeter, leaving her instead of trying to find her. A warbler sang somewhere in the trees behind them. Something clicked in Violet's mind.

"Hey, Dimitri, is your name linked to Demeter?"

"Yes, it means follower of Demeter, the goddess of agriculture. So I'm sort of a man of the earth." He smiled and turned to Violet, who sat silently, still not meeting his gaze. She was unsure how much of what she was thinking to say out loud.

"So, should I ask you for wings? Or not bother because they're not going to work anyway and I'll end up throwing myself into the sea?" She turned to him and half-smiled.

"The sirens were also known as sea-nymphs, so I suppose that would make you a sort of siren," he smiled.

Violet laughed. "Well, I have no intention of luring anyone into the rocks."

"Neither did the sirens. They were just searching for Persephone," grinned Dimitri.

Both were silent for a few moments.

"Well," said Dimitri, "It's spring, so, maybe Persephone is already here."

Violet smiled a little and willed her eyes not to well up again. "Maybe she is."

Dimitri smiled back at Violet, catching her eye briefly.

"Are you hungry? I have some food in the car."

"Of course you do," laughed Violet. "The whole trunk is probably full of dolmades."

"Pretty much," said Dimitri, departing to get the picnic. "I'll be right back."

They ate quietly in the shade, chatting over the delicious *chortopita*,[28] *kalitsounia,* and of course Dimitri's mother's famous dolmades.

Feeling she'd shared enough to ask Dimitri a tough question, and eager to move the spotlight off of herself, Violet asked boldly, "Do you ever miss your dad?"

Dimitri tried to laugh but found instead only a dry breathy exhalation. "No," he said initially. After a pause, he continued, "When I was a kid, I thought my dad was

[28]Local wild greens and mizithra cheese in phyllo pastry

147

great, he was always so much fun. I thought my mom was the, what's the word…spoilsport. She always seemed to be angry, yelling at him and, at the time, I blamed her for driving him away. But when I went back to America as an adult, my dad had a girlfriend who looked not much older than me. I know age doesn't always matter," he looked at Violet who suddenly felt very conscious of the seven-year age difference between them. "But," he continued, "I didn't like the way he treated her, or the way he talked about her when she wasn't there. And then I found out he had another girlfriend as well." He shook his head.

"I think he thought I'd be proud to have a dad who had such a way with women, but I was disgusted. I was so disappointed in him. I couldn't understand how he could have raised me to be one way, but then act completely different. That wasn't how I'd want my sisters to be treated." He paused and shook his head again, more vehemently this time.

"I realized that my dad might have been a good dad to me when I was young, but he definitely wasn't a good husband to my mother. It's strange, you know, when you suddenly see someone completely differently, and then nothing you remember makes any sense anymore." He looked down at the *chortopita* in the cardboard box he held.

"So, no, I don't miss the version of my dad I saw when I was twenty, but yeah, maybe I sometimes miss the version of my dad I remember from my childhood."

Violet half-smiled, feeling guilty for having two functional, in-love parents.

"What about your parents?" asked Dimitri as if he'd read her thoughts.

"My parents are weirdly normal and still together, and still happy together. I should really have turned out better with such a solid upbringing."

Dimitri laughed. "I think you turned out...not *too* bad."

Violet pretended to glower at him. "Well, thanks for that vote of confidence. But, you know, you don't know me that well. I'm very self-absorbed sometimes. I mean, I didn't even think to bring food for lunch today!" She gestured at the now mostly empty containers around them.

"I didn't tell you we were gonna have a picnic, and you don't even have a kitchen to cook in, why would I expect you to bring food?"

Violet shrugged, feeling very conscious that since she'd arrived, Dimitri and her family had given her so much and she wasn't sure what she could offer in return.

"Don't worry," he reassured her, "we Greeks don't give in order to receive. It's not a currency. You don't owe me anything."

Violet laughed quietly, "I know, but I don't like to take and not give back."

"You're giving me your very pleasant company," he assured her.

Violet frowned, "That hardly seems like a fair trade for you."

"Well, I can't help giving you food, it's what happens when you're Greek, you just feed everyone around you."

Violet laughed. The mood had lightened.

"OK then. What's the secret to your delectable dolmades?"

"I can't tell you that, it's a family secret." He smiled mischievously.

"Is it some fancy infused olive oil?"

He shrugged. "Maybe."

"A magic herb?"

"Maybe."

"Oh, come on, you've got to at least answer yes or no!" giggled Violet.

Dimitri shook his head. "I'm not playing this game, I didn't agree to it."

"Dittany!" she said, suddenly remembering the name of a distinctive Cretan herb her mother had told her about.

"My lips are sealed." Dimitri gave nothing away.

Violet smiled and tried to glare at him at the same time and was sure she ended up pulling a ridiculous face.

"I can't tell you, my mother would kill me." He held his hands up, as if to absolve himself of any responsibility.

"Ooh mama's boy, I had no idea you were so under your mother's thumb. *Eisai mamakias!*"[29] teased Violet.

"What? Where did you learn that word?" Dimitri could barely speak he was laughing so hard at hearing the unexpected Greek insult come out of Violet's pretty Canadian mouth. It was a word that meant a spineless mama's boy, and in a culture that extolled the virtues of machismo and strength in its male citizens, it had a particularly biting ring to it.

---

[29] You're a mama's boy!

"I asked Angelo for some useful everyday phrases. He said that one might come in handy." She smiled. "Clearly, he was right."

"Say it again," grinned Dimitri.

"Eisai mamakias!"

He dissolved into fits of laughter once again. "You need to...emphasize the second syllable."

"Eisai maMAkias!" repeated Violet carefully. She looked so focused on the pronunciation of the word, it was strangely endearing. Dimitri's resolve to not kiss Violet that day melted away. He leaned towards her, but then paused, wondering if he shouldn't. She'd been through so much, she probably didn't need him complicating things.

Violet looked into Dimitri's dark eyes, hovering so near hers, a smile still on his lips, and for once didn't need to question anything. She knew which universe she wanted in that moment. Violet leaned forward and felt herself dissolve into the sensation of his lips against hers, and was sure that in the seconds that followed she only existed as this one perfect kiss.

The afternoon passed in a timeless haze of kisses and whispers. If there were other visitors to Aptera that day, Violet and Dimitri didn't notice. They found themselves still in each other's embrace when the slightly embarrassed ticket booth employee, trying to look away, told them in Greek they were closing.

Back in Dimitri's small white car, they headed home towards Sfinari, very much not in a rush, and very much in the heady glow of new love. It was still light, the sun wouldn't set for another two hours.

Even the main road was beautiful in the evening light, the low rays catching the petals of the purple mallow along the roadside, and bouncing off the sea, turning it a deep shade of turquoise.

They reached Sfinari, but Dimitri didn't turn down the road to the bay.

"Where are we going?" asked Violet, pleased the day wasn't over yet.

"It's a surprise," he said, smiling.

Dimitri turned off to the right down a small road that followed along a high ridge, then switch-backed down. It was unpaved and a little rough, and Violet tried not to look nervous. Dimitri's small unassuming car didn't look like it was made for off-roading.

"Don't worry, I know this road well," he reassured her, seeing Violet suddenly tense and grab onto the passenger door. "We're almost there."

The switchbacks thankfully ceased, the road straightened out and the sea came into view. The road bent right and then left and came to a stop in a small bay, next to an abandoned stone cottage. It looked familiar but Violet couldn't place it.

Dimitri turned to her and smiled. "Do you know where we are?"

Violet shook her head.

"Come on, you'll figure it out in a minute," he said, getting out of the car.

As Violet stepped out onto the beach, she noticed Dimitri's cave up to her right. "Oh, we're in the next bay!

Next to Sfinari Bay right? There's your cave." Violet pointed up the headland.

"Yep, Platanakia Beach. We took the long route here."

"I'll say! We could have just walked from Sfinari Bay a lot faster."

"Sure," said Dimitri, "but then everyone would have seen us and you'd be swept away by your aunt and I'd be swept away by my mother and we'd both be having a ton of food shoved down our throats."

Violet laughed. It was very true. Looking out at the dark blue sea with the sun hanging low over the horizon, she couldn't help but think about going for a swim.

"You wanna go for a swim?" she asked Dimitri, who laughed and shook his head.

"Not really."

"Do you mind if I go?"

"I don't think I could stop you if I did mind."

Violet went back to the car and awkwardly changed into her bathing suit, pleased she'd brought it with her, along with a towel. She hadn't been sure where they were going and never wanted to miss an opportunity to swim. Dimitri sat on the beach with his back to the car, being a gentleman but finding it hard not to imagine Violet semi-naked in his car.

Violet emerged in her bathing suit and ran past Dimitri to the sea, dropping her towel near the shore. The pebbly floor dropped away faster than in Sfinari and Violet was under the waves in a matter of seconds. Once again, she heard the soothing sound of the waves caressing the pebbles. She lingered underwater, savouring the quiet movements of the pebbles that were only audible when the waves hit them with the right force.

She stayed underwater so long, Dimitri began to worry as he stood on the shore. He knew she was a strong swimmer and the bay was safe, but the way she'd swum straight under and not re-emerged within a few seconds troubled him. He counted to ten, and then began to take off his t-shirt. He hadn't brought his swimsuit so resolved to just go in in his underwear. Violet emerged to find him topless and in the process of removing his shorts.

"Are you coming in?" she asked, surprised.

Dimitri realized that an explanation at this point would have sounded ridiculous, so he simply said, "Yes," took off his shorts and waded in.

It had been a warm day and the water was marginally less cold than the last time he'd briefly entered the sea with Violet. Still, he found it hard not to swear as he swam out to her.

Violet laughed. "Hey, you screamed less this time. Is the water warmer or have you grown more resilient?"

"I'm very resilient. Almost as resilient as you are cheeky," he said, out of breath from the cold. Violet splashed him and swam away, along the shoreline. Dimitri followed and she slowed so he could catch her. He was a strong swimmer but no match for a water nymph.

When Dimitri kissed Violet in the sea that night, she closed her eyes and felt the milky way around them, she felt every star not quite yet visible appear on his skin and hers, and the water, which were all one. Their limbs tangled and there was nothing else in the world but their love and the sea and the stars.

Searching for Persephone

Beneath the darkened blue
    there is music
Pebbles and stars on the seafloor
    dance in slow perfect circles
    orbiting the space between each wave

Far away
yet in the same place
a warbler calls
    and a flute melody floats
        above the last cypress trees

Listen.
Close your eyes
Cover your ears
    and let your body hear.

A wandering voice sings where the ocean breaks
    nearly free
Drifting through the carob trees
    a hint of warm breath on the breeze
All of these
    tiny pieces of Persephone
    held still in the stones and the sun and the sea.

Chapter 17

In the weeks that followed, Dimitri and Violet spent mornings and evenings together, and most nights in Dimitri's little cottage. They didn't try and hide their romance, there wouldn't have been any point in a place as small as Sfinari. *Theia Maria* initially made her concerns clear to Violet, but Anna had advised Maria to let the couple be.

"They're young and in love, and after everything Violet's been through, maybe we shouldn't rock the boat," Anna urged her sister.

Maria reluctantly agreed to her sister's wishes. In any case, Violet would have to leave soon, and it would be over. Perhaps a little fling was what she needed to heal and move on.

For her part, Dimitri's mother Despoina was similarly unsure of the match, but confident that it would end when Violet left in a few weeks. She'd seen Dimitri have a few brief romances with visiting tourists, and she silenced the voice in her head that noted this one seemed very much different. Violet would leave soon and Dimitri would move on and doubtless marry someone less pale.

In her jewelry store in North Vancouver, Anna sat mulling things over. It was a slow day, with plenty of time to reflect. She knew from her sister that Violet and Dimitri had fallen very quickly in love, and was much less opposed to the match than Maria was. She'd never liked Dimitri's father, Sifi, but she also didn't blame him for what had happened, and certainly didn't blame his son. She'd seen the tragedy first-hand and knew there was nothing anyone could have done to prevent the accident. However, she also knew Violet had been asking questions and wondered what she'd been told.

Anna hadn't been back to Crete since she'd left all those years ago as a teenager. Her sister had visited her here once many years ago. Airfares were expensive and there never seemed to be a good time to go. Anna sighed, knowing she was making excuses for herself. She'd been hiding for a long time and having sent Violet to Crete to face her demons, she wondered if it might be time for her to do the same.

Searching on her phone, she found a last-minute flight to Chania via Montreal and Amsterdam. She took a deep breath, and called Martin, and then Maria. She ensured her two part-time employees could take on some extra hours over the next couple of weeks, then she booked her ticket.

She told Maria she'd like to surprise Violet and keep her planned visit a secret. Maria squealed with delight.

Her sister was finally coming back, after all these years, and she loved a good surprise.

As Anna booked her flight, Violet was just coming in from her evening swim. Dimitri was helping at the taverna still. Violet went back to her room, which she hadn't officially moved out of, though most of her things were now in Dimitri's cottage.

She'd been writing poetry lately, filling the pages of a small notebook she'd found in the mini market. Violet had written a fair bit as a teenager but had stopped in university, her life filled with studies and socializing. And besides, she couldn't really see the use of it. She certainly wasn't going to be a career poet. How many people make a living writing poetry in the modern world? She'd put her enjoyment of writing aside in her adult life, though Persephone had periodically encouraged her to pick up the pen again. She'd always brushed the suggestions aside; there was always an excuse and ultimately Violet hadn't felt that her poems were any good.

But now, on this magical place on the Western shores of an ancient island, she found herself bursting with words, images, feelings, an essence of something she needed to communicate. She didn't worry about whether or not the poems were any good, she simply needed to keep writing them. They flowed out of her pen and onto the pages so easily at times she wondered if she could even claim to be the rightful author.

Violet didn't show anyone the poems, and said she was journalling, if anyone asked. She wanted to keep this little piece of herself private for now.

Sleepless nights still haunted her at times, the darkness turning her mind to Persephone, and in those moments she often felt guilty about her new-found happiness. But in the morning, the heaviness had always lifted, and though she continued to carry her loss, as she always would, she could feel her wounds beginning to heal and Violet mostly allowed herself to be content, for now, with Dimitri in this idyllic place.

Late one evening, the couple laid on the beach looking up at the stars. A few cats slinked around the tavernas in the darkness.

"Do you ever name the cats?" asked Violet.

"Oh no, it's better not to name them," Dimitri replied solemnly.

"Why?"

"Because if you name them, you get attached to them. And they have tough lives, they don't all do well."

"Are you suggesting I shouldn't name any of the cats because I might get attached to them, and then they might die and I'd be sad?" asked Violet, a little amused.

"More or less."

Violet laughed. "By that logic, no one should ever name their children. You know, just in case they die and it's too sad cause they actually had a name."

Dimitri grinned and shook his head. "I think people would still be attached to their children, even if they didn't name them. With the cats, you have a choice."

"I don't feel like I do," said Violet. "I'm already very attached to Zeus."

"Zeus?"

"Yes. The big ginger and white tomcat. He seems to be the leader, and he hangs around me a lot. I feel like he's looking out for me."

Dimitri smiled. "You think a stray cat named Zeus is protecting you?"

"Yes," said Violet, smiling, not even worried that it sounded weird.

"What's he protecting you from?"

"I don't know. Myself?" She wanted to add, "The heartbreak of leaving here, and leaving you," but she couldn't.

Dimitri squeezed her hand and rolled over to kiss her gently.

"Do you know about Cretan-born Zeus?"

"Oh here we go again...go on, fill me in. How was he different from the Greek Zeus?"

Dimitri had been enthusiastically sharing his love of Cretan history and mythology with Violet; he always said he was Cretan first and Greek second, with a bit of American thrown in.

"Well, the original Zeus was from Crete. We call him *'Zeus Cretagenes',* and he was by no means the most important god. He was born in a cave on Mount Dikte, and was nursed by the goddess of the mountain and hunting. The oldest mythologies and religions revolved around mother nature-type goddesses, so Zeus wasn't really the main event. And he lived and died, like a mortal, but rose from the dead again. He represented the cycle of life and death, and rebirth...a bit like Persephone and Demeter I guess, but with a bit of Dionysus thrown in. People used to celebrate his rebirth every year."

"Hmm. There's always a god that dies and comes back to life, like Jesus, in so many religions," Violet mused quietly. "Do you think it's wishful thinking or do you think there's some kind of life or rebirth after death?"

"I have no idea, that's a big question for so late at night."

Violet smiled. "Have you heard from your *yiayia* lately?"

"Yes, she's telling me right now to stop talking and kiss you."

"Whoa, no, it feels weird to kiss you in front of your dead grandma!" Violet pretended to fight Dimitri off as they giggled on the darkened beach. He held her close and kissed her between short bursts of laughter and smiles. Eventually the laughter dissolved into long kisses and Violet pulled him even closer, trying to drown out the voice in her head that was counting down to the end of her time on Crete.

She had ten days left on the island when she finally managed to broach the topic with Dimitri.

They were nestled together in Dimitri's bed late one night, and Violet asked cautiously, "If I was to, in another universe, live in Chania, or somewhere around there, would you come live with me?"

Dimitri looked at her, hopeful but not daring to hope too much. "You want to live in Chania?"

"Maybe," replied Violet. She knew she felt like a better version of herself here. But she also knew there were practical difficulties with her idea.

"I could live with you in the off-season, come here in the summers and help my mom," said Dimitri.

Violet smiled, daring for an instant to imagine this life with Dimitri. "I have to leave in ten days," she said sadly, closing her eyes for a moment to stop them welling up.

"I know," he said softly. "I was hoping you might miss your flight." A sad smile flickered across his lips.

"I'd be lying if I said I hadn't thought about it," admitted Violet. "But I think I need to go back, sort out my life and all that."

"What do you have to sort out?" His tone was gentle.

"Well, I'd need to see if I can get a Greek passport, or a visa of some sort, and there is the tiny detail of learning the language."

"You could learn the language here, I could teach you. And you know all us Greeks know each other, so somebody somewhere could probably get you the paperwork you needed, you'd just have to pay them under the table." He was half-joking but Violet guessed there was a kernel of truth to what he was saying.

She smiled, "But I guess it's also just the personal stuff."

Dimitri waited and stroked her hair. He'd learned that Violet sometimes needed time to decide on whether or not to share certain things.

"This is going to sound strange, and I'm not sure if it makes any sense. But I feel like I'm a different person here than I was back home. I mean, even before Persephone...passed away. I always felt like I was inept, or missing some parts that other people seemed to have. But here, I finally feel like a whole person." Violet paused again briefly. "I think maybe the problem wasn't me, it was just my incompatibility with the world I was living in. I think I belong here. But I also need to reconcile Vancouver Violet with Crete Violet, and figure all that out, and just, take some time to really heal."

Dimitri nodded, understanding enough to know he needed to let Violet leave. At least for now.

"When do you think you'll be back?"

"I was thinking of coming back in a year. And staying."

Dimitri smiled. "I can wait." A year was a long time, but for Violet he would have waited a lifetime.

Violet sighed. "I'm not sure you should wait for me, Dimitri."

Dimitri was surprised. "Why not?"

"A year is a long time. If I feel like you're waiting for me, I'll feel terrible."

"Violet, I don't think I have any choice," frowned Dimitri.

Violet closed her eyes again, willing the tears not to come and trying to find the words to express what she wasn't sure there were words for. "Being here, it's been like a dream. A beautiful dream. It's so disconnected from my life back home. When I'm not in this world anymore, I just don't know if any of this is going to feel real. It's not that I want to be with anyone else, I just need some time to work things out, and if I feel like you're waiting, well, I'm not sure I'll be worth waiting for when I finally come back here." The truth spilled out in the last sentence and caught even Violet off-guard.

Dimitri looked into Violet's blue eyes, with flecks of grey and even tinier flecks of green barely visible. In that moment, the love he felt for her was stronger than anything he'd ever felt or would feel in his lifetime.

"Violet, listen to me." He raised himself onto one elbow and looked at her earnestly. "Don't ever think you're not enough. For anyone, but especially not for me. I'll give you as much time as you want, I can understand you have things to sort out, to deal with. And I'll understand if you decide I'm not the person you want to be with. But don't ask me not to wait because you think you'll disappoint me." He paused and shook his head very slightly. "You can decide what makes you happy, but you don't get to decide what makes me happy, OK?"

Violet nodded, her eyes wet with tears. "OK," she whispered. The warmth of his words wrapped around her and Violet hoped it was enough to keep her demons at bay.

He laid back down. "It's late. Get some sleep, honeybee." He kissed her tenderly on her cheek.

As Violet drifted off to sleep, her mother was flying over the Canadian Rocky Mountains, looking down at the snow-capped peaks and wondering if her daughter was really in love with Sifi's son.

Chapter 18

Anna's plane touched down in Chania exactly three weeks after Violet's. She too felt drained after the long journey, and carried her own trepidation about returning to her homeland. It was strange hearing the chatter of Greek everywhere. Anna found it both comforting and anxiety-provoking. She'd never stopped speaking the language, but hearing it all around her, fragments floating in the air, brought back memories from a distant life.

Maria didn't hold back her joy at seeing her sister for the first time in nearly fifteen years. *"Annoula, yia su!* So happy to have you here again! Welcome home!"

The two of them embraced for a long time. Maria shed a few tears, then pulled away and insisted on taking her younger sister's suitcase. They spoke in Greek.

"You look skinny, Anna. What's wrong with the food in Canada?"

Anna laughed, too tired to respond.

"A shame Martin couldn't come, we'd like to see our ginger in-law again one day."

"He wanted to join me," explained Anna, "but he couldn't get away at such short notice. He'll come another time."

Maria shook her head. "You've been saying that for twenty-seven years, Annoula."

Anna was fed the obligatory *spanokopita* in the car while Maria chatted to her. Unlike Violet, she managed to stay awake; there was too much to catch up on with her sister.

"How is Violet?" asked Anna.

"She's well," answered Maria honestly. "She's much less skinny than when she arrived, she swims all the time and lately she's been scribbling in a notebook, a journal she says. And of course she's very much in love." Maria sighed, "With Dimitris, you know."

"Yes, I know, Maria, you did tell me. Is that really so bad? Dimitris isn't Sifis you know. If Violet's happy, isn't that the main thing?"

"Of course, but it's, you know...Dimitris' mother will want him to marry a nice Greek girl."

"Violet is half-Greek, she's my daughter, Maria, she's hardly a stranger."

"She doesn't look Greek."

Anna couldn't help but laugh. She knew the reason Maria didn't want Violet and Dimitri to be together and it was nothing to do with her fair skin.

"Besides, Violet is leaving soon," continued Maria. She doesn't live here. They're going to both end up with broken hearts."

"Maybe," replied Anna, "but maybe not. And we both know the real reason you don't like her being with Dimitris, Maria."

Maria, for once, was silent.

"It wasn't Sifis' fault," Anna said quietly.

"Ah Anna, I don't wanna talk about it. He was meant to be watching you two."

"It wouldn't have mattered if he was!" Anna's voice rose a little. She was tired of this conversation, they'd had it many times over the years. "Maria, you know I never liked Sifis, he was a womanizing slime-bag. But that's not a reason to blame him for what happened. He was sixteen years old! What teenage boy hasn't been distracted by a pretty girl at some point? How could he have known what was about to happen? He couldn't have prevented it. No one could have. It was just a horrible, horrible accident."

Maria sighed and said nothing.

After some time Anna added, "Sifis left years ago. It doesn't make any sense to hold this grudge against his family. They probably don't think much of him either, I think they've suffered enough at his hands, so why are we making it worse for them?"

Maria shrugged. "It's not worse for them, they do fine."

"You know what I mean, Maria, what is the *point?* Everyone talks so much about community here, but then they feud with neighbours over something a teenager did or didn't do thirty-five years ago. What kind of community is that?"

"OK, OK, calm down, Anna. You know, it's not like we never talk to them, we just keep our distance a little. We're not terrorizing them."

"No, but you still don't want Violet spending time with Dimitris. What does Despoina think?"

"I don't know, I haven't asked her."

Anna sighed and looked out the car window.

Maria was uncharacteristically quiet until they approached Sfinari, when she regained her usual liveliness. "I haven't told Violet about you coming. I'm sure she'll be very happy to see you!" Maria smiled, anticipating the surprise.

"I hope so," said Anna, hoping her daughter didn't see her arrival as an intrusion. She had no plans to interfere with Violet's romance, or to crowd her, but there was a conversation they needed to have, and her own demons to wrestle with.

Anna barely recognized Sfinari. Though it was still a small and unassuming place, there were more restaurants, hotels and villas than she remembered. However, when they turned down the small road down to the bay, she felt her heart swell with long-forgotten joyful childhood memories, though at the same time her stomach tensed with the reminder of long-hidden anxieties.

Arriving at the taverna, Anna got out of the car and looked nervously out to the sea, through her dark sunglasses. The bay was just as she remembered it, though the trees had grown taller and the tables and umbrellas were new, of course. The taverna sign was not the one she remembered, but it still read "*Paradise Fish Taverna*."

Maria gestured to a table. "You sit, I'll go find Violet. She's probably swimming."

Violet indeed had just come out of the water and was sitting next to Dimitri on the shore, just down the beach by his family taverna.

"Vee-o-letta!"

Violet turned around.

"Come see, I have a surprise for you!"

Violet smiled. "A surprise? Is it by any chance edible?" She'd become very accustomed to surprises and gifts being food around here.

Maria laughed. "I wouldn't eat this one."

Violet gestured for Dimitri to join her, and Maria opened her mouth, nearly protesting, but then changed her mind. Anna would have to meet him soon enough anyway, and she might as well see them together.

Anna looked up from her table to see her daughter in her blue bathing suit, still wet from her swim, her green towel wrapped around her waist, trotting towards her, hand-in-hand with Dimitri, with a radiant glow Anna hadn't seen on her daughter since she was a child. She wondered momentarily if she was actually looking at Violet's long-lost twin, such was the difference between this Violet and the one who had left Vancouver only three weeks ago.

Anna surmised within one and a half seconds that the couple were indeed madly in love, and she certainly didn't share her sister's conviction that the romance would end when Violet returned to Canada. After all, she'd had her own experience of recognizing her match very quickly. Sometimes, Anna knew, you just know.

Violet stopped in her tracks when she saw her mother. Dimitri looked over at the olive-skinned dark-haired woman, who, despite the difference in colouring, bore more than a passing resemblance to Violet, and had it figured out even before Violet could catch her breath and exclaim, "Mom!"

She ran excitedly to her mother, her mind racing with questions and mixed emotions. Anna stood up, and the two embraced until Violet's questions found their way to her lips. "What are you doing here? When did you arrive? Is Dad here?"

Anna smiled and stood back to take in her daughter. "I just got here. Your dad couldn't come but he said to give you a big hug."

Violet suddenly remembered Dimitri, standing where she'd let go of his hand when she'd seen her mother. "Oh Mom, this is Dimitri," she said excitedly, gesturing for him to come over.

Dimitri approached a little sheepishly, not having expected to meet the woman he hoped would be his future mother-in-law on this particular morning, wishing he had something to give her, and also wondering nervously if she held the grudge her sister did.

Anna smiled and shook Dimitri's hand, taking in the handsome face that resembled his father's so much, but also noting with relief that he had none of his father's over-confident machismo.

"It's so nice to meet you. Violet's told me so much about you. I'm sorry, I didn't know you were coming, I would have brought you some honey."

"That's OK, I wanted to surprise Violet. I've heard lots about you too. And your honey of course."

Dimitri didn't want to intrude on this family reunion. "I'll leave you ladies to chat," he said, but both Violet and Anna gestured for him to stay and sit with them. He looked around nervously. He hadn't actually ever sat down at the *Paradise Fish Taverna*. It had always been an unwritten rule. He shuffled nervously, not wanting to upset Violet's aunt.

Maria had been watching the scene unfold, and looking at the three of them, suddenly it seemed ridiculous that Dimitri should have to leave. In her mind, she imagined the scene that would play out if she were to tell him he couldn't sit down with Violet and Anna, and it was highly unpleasant. She didn't want this long-awaited visit from her sister to start on a sour note. Maria sighed, defeated, and gestured for Dimitri to sit.

"I bring you some breakfast."

Dimitri sat down cautiously, still nervous and wondering if his mother would mind. The tavernas weren't officially open for breakfast, so his mother wouldn't need his help, and he'd just checked on his bees the day before. Lacking an excuse, he decided he'd have to go along with it and hope for the best. Anyway, he wanted to spend as much time with Violet as he could while she was here.

Violet and her mother chatted animatedly.

"I hear you've been writing again?" Anna asked her daughter curiously.

Violet looked down and shifted in her seat. "A little," she said.

"That's not true," chimed in Dimitri. "She's always writing, but she won't let me read it. I'm hoping she's composing love sonnets to me, but I'm guessing they're love sonnets to the sea."

Anna laughed, "Yes, that sounds about right for my water nymph." She looked proudly at her only child and marveled again at the transformation.

"I bet you're exhausted and just want to sleep, but they're going to force-feed you for hours before they let you rest here," Violet warned her mother.

"Yes I know," replied Anna, "I'll sleep better on a full stomach."

Violet laughed. "And Persephone always said that eating at the new meal times was the best way to combat jet lag."

Anna hadn't heard Violet mention Persephone since the incident and was surprised at the ease with which she spoke of her.

"Persephone was very wise," she commented.

Violet nodded. "How long are you here for?"

"I leave the same day as you, but on a different flight, via London," she said.

"Only ten days? Aw, Mom, that's not long enough, you'll just get over your jet lag and then have to leave again."

"I'll be alright, I need to get back to the shop."

"Ooh I just remembered, I bought you something!"

Violet stood up and ran back to her room to find the little olive wood box she'd bought for her mother in Polyrhinnia. She arrived back at the table and put the intricately-carved item down in front of her mother, who was chatting easily with Dimitri in Greek.

"Oh it's beautiful, Violet! *Efharisto polli!*[30] Is it olive wood?"

"Yes, Dimitri took me to this amazing little shop in Polyrhinnia that's just full of all these handmade treasures. And such beautiful views from the acropolis! Did you ever go there Mom?"

"No, I don't think so," said Anna, inspecting the pretty box. She hadn't explored much of the island, she'd mostly viewed it as a place to escape from. It was refreshing to see it from Violet's point of view, as an exotic land full of riches to be discovered.

Just then, Kosta pulled in to the small parking lot with his in-laws, Christos and Elena. Anna looked up as her parents got out of the car, and drew in her breath quickly. She hadn't seen her mother and father since she'd left as an eighteen-year-old.

Of course, their anger about Anna's marriage twenty-six years ago had fizzled out long ago, but her lack of visits had caused her parents some consternation over the years. They hadn't come with Maria and her family when she'd visited. Flights were expensive, it was true, but Christos and Elena were also not the type to travel far. They'd only left the island a handful of times and had never been outside of Greece. Besides, they felt that as Anna had left, she should be the one to return for visits.

All of this had led to undertones of tension within their relationship. While their phone calls were usually pleasant and polite, Anna had certainly never been close

---

[30] Thank you very much!

with her parents as an adult, and was nervous about seeing them again.

Moreover, there was now the added issue of Dimitri, Sifi's son, sitting with them at the table, holding Violet's hand. For a moment, Anna felt like a naughty child who had disobeyed them, waiting for her punishment to be meted out.

Christos and Elena didn't see Dimitri at first, and to Anna's relief, their joy at seeing her for the first time in twenty-eight years far outweighed any resentment that may have lingered in their hearts. Her mother teared up as she walked towards Anna with open arms; she would have run to her if her legs could still have managed it.

"Annoula Annoula, we missed you so much! So many years! Welcome home!" Anna jumped up, and ran to embrace her mother and then her father in a wave of Greek chatter and intense emotions.

Her father managed to hold his tears in; as a Greek man, he'd had many years of practice. Anna and Elena wept freely, embracing over and over, as if hoping to make up for the many years' worth of hugs they hadn't been able to share.

Violet turned to Dimitri, and was surprised to see him watching the scene intently, his eyes ever so slightly wet with tears. She wondered if he was thinking about his father, about the reunion he would never have. She squeezed his hand. Startled out of his reverie, he turned and smiled a little sadly at Violet, knowing he didn't need to explain anything.

Violet's grandparents were of course aware of the romance that had developed between Dimitri and their granddaughter. Though they weren't pleased, like Maria, they were sure it would end with Violet's departure, and had chosen to mostly ignore the situation. However, they certainly weren't expecting to have to sit down and eat breakfast next to Sifi's son.

Violet wondered if she and Dimitri should leave quietly and avoid a potentially awkward or unpleasant scene. Dimitri was wondering the same thing, but also feared that leaving after being invited to stay by Maria, who was now making them all breakfast, would be rude. The two looked at each other, but before they could say anything or make a decision, Elena turned and noticed Dimitri at the table. She stopped talking very suddenly, causing everyone to pause and follow her gaze over to Dimitri, still holding Violet's hand. The couple sat frozen, acutely aware of every set of eyes on them, unsure of what to do. *Zeus Cretagenes,* as Violet had come to call the ginger and white tomcat, had appeared and was now sitting at her feet, staring defiantly at the suddenly silent crowd. Maria came out of the taverna and quickly assessed the scene.

"Ah, Mom, Dad, you know Dimitris." She spoke in Greek. "I've invited him to join us for breakfast. It's so nice to finally have Anna back here, and to see Violet so happy." She gestured toward the happy couple. "It seemed rude to leave him out of the celebrations."

Elena and Christos hesitated, not sure how to respond. They looked at each other, at Anna, at their granddaughter and her boyfriend, and back at each other again. It seemed so unfortunate to ruin this beautiful reunion with their daughter. And after all, Dimitri wasn't Sifi. Christos shrugged and Elena finally broke the silence.

"Yia su Dimitri. You seem to be making our granddaughter very happy."

"Kalimera sas Kyria Daskalaki, Kyrie Daskalaki. Ti kanete?" [31] Dimitri felt as if he was walking on eggshells. He addressed them as politely as possible.

"Kalla, paidi mou," [32] replied Elena after a short pause.

"Good," said Maria a little too loudly, trying to reinstate the upbeat atmosphere, "I'll bring out breakfast. Everyone please, sit down." She gestured to the two tables that had been pushed together to accommodate the gathering.

The chatter resumed as the family sat down, shuffling through various seating arrangements. Violet, Dimitri, and Anna all breathed a sigh of relief. Maria brought out yogurt with nuts and honey, as well as several huge platters of dakos, and then sat down to join in the celebration.

Everyone spoke spiritedly in Greek, with Anna and Dimitri (and occasionally Maria) doing their best to translate bits of the conversation for Violet. Violet didn't mind, she was enjoying the atmosphere, and was pleased to see the strange rift between Dimitri's family and her own had been bridged, at least for now. She dropped some scraps of food for *Zeus Cretagenes* and his cohorts, and busied her mind with attempting to pick out any Greek words she might recognize. She didn't do very well at this game, they were all talking too fast and there appeared to be at least three conversations going on at

---

[31] Good morning Mr. And Mrs. Daskalaki. How are you both?

[32] I'm well, my child.

176

once. But she was happy. She squeezed Dimitri's hand under the table. He turned and smiled at her.

As they sat drinking coffee (except for Violet, who made do with weak tea with honey), and the conversation had slowed to a less frenzied pace, Violet managed to ask her mother if she'd been to Aptera.

"Shhh don't tell her, it's a secret," joked Dimitri.

Anna laughed. "What's Aptera?"

"It's an archaeological site," explained Dimitri, speaking in English, then in Greek, so no one would feel left out of the conversation. "An ancient city, very atmospheric. There are lots of ruins, and some impressive Roman cisterns, and a theatre."

Maria and Elena had heard of the city, but no one had visited the site.

"And there was a twelfth century monastery," added Violet, "which isn't very old around here, but that would be crazy old in Canada wouldn't it, Mom? And it's the site where the muses defeated the sirens. The name means 'without wings' because the muses plucked out all the siren's feathers, and they threw themselves into the sea and became islands."

"I see you've been teaching my daughter some Greek mythology," Anna said to Dimitri, smiling.

"A little. She knew some from you already of course, but I'd say she still has a lot to learn," he grinned teasingly at Violet, and Anna felt the love overflowing between them. She shivered, though it wasn't cold. A love this strong, she knew, could do powerful things, and she hoped beyond hope that all would be well for them.

Anna managed to stay awake on adrenaline for the duration of breakfast, until, like Violet on the day of her arrival, she felt physically unable to hold herself upright any longer, and asked politely if she might go have a rest.

Maria drove her up to the family home in the village, and Anna slept until dinnertime in the same bed in the same room she'd slept in for the first eighteen years of her life. As she curled up and drifted off, she wondered at how a room and a bed could suddenly make her feel like a teenager again, a young girl who had never left the island of Crete.

Later that day, as the sun moved lower over the calm waters, Anna and Violet went for a walk along the beach, joining the path at the end of the pine trees. They followed it up the headland where Violet had walked that first morning, causing such a stir. It was a warm still evening and the chattering of a few customers at the tavernas hung in the air, along with the gentle lapping of the waves. They ascended slowly and sat at the top of the outcrop.

Anna took a deep breath.

"Violet, there is only one thing I've ever lied to you about, and I'm very sorry." Anna looked straight ahead and Violet held her breath.

"I should have told you a long time ago, but I wanted to protect you, or maybe I was protecting myself."

"What is it?" asked Violet, not enjoying this suspense.

Anna kept her gaze out to the sea. "My brother wasn't ill. He died in the sea. Here. Down near those rocks." She pointed to the rocks off the edge of the headland, where Angelo had told her not to swim.

Violet was silent, not knowing what to say.

"And, he wasn't just my brother, he was my twin," she added.

Violet sat processing this, a million questions competing in her head. "You said he was your younger brother." For some reason this was the first thought she could voice.

"He was younger. By four minutes."

"How old were you?"

"We were ten."

"But, you grew up here, you must have both known how to swim? And the sea here isn't rough. There aren't even any tides." Violet shook her head, knowing there must be more to the story.

Anna took another deep breath and closed her eyes. "It was a windy day. It was just an unexpected wave. It threw him off-balance and he hit his head on the rocks." Anna paused for just a moment. "I saw his head hit and saw him go unconscious. There was... a lot of blood. I couldn't move. I just stood there and screamed until someone pulled us both out of the water."

They sat in silence for a few minutes.

"I'm so sorry, Mom," it was strange to see her mother so vulnerable, she'd always been the epitome of strength to Violet. "But, why didn't you tell me?" Violet asked quietly.

"Lots of reasons. Partly because I didn't want you to be afraid of the sea the way I was after that. I made sure you were a strong swimmer so I wouldn't be worried about anything happening to you in the water." Anna paused again and looked down before continuing. "But I also just couldn't bring myself to talk about it, it was very hard. It was easier just to say he got sick and died. I always thought I'd tell you when you were older, but by then it seemed so irrelevant. It wasn't something I wanted to tell you while we were making *avgolemono*[33] soup you know?"

Violet nodded. "But, why didn't you tell me before I came here? You must have known I'd hear rumours?"

"Yes, but Violet, you were in pieces when you left. You'd just experienced your own traumatic loss. It didn't seem like the time to burden you with mine. Yes, I thought you might hear something, but I didn't know what else to do." Anna paused. "I wanted to tell you when you called that day and asked about the Sfakianakis, but I didn't want to tell you over the phone. And I was worried it might bring back memories for you. You sounded happy again, finally. I didn't want to risk upsetting you all over again."

Violet nodded slowly. Mother and daughter sat in silence for some time.

"So that's why you left? And you've never been back all this time cause it was just too much?"

Anna nodded. She didn't want to cry in front of her daughter but it was taking all her strength not to.

"So, how do you feel now you're here?" Violet asked gently. For the first time in her life, she had the sense she was talking to her mother as a peer, a fellow woman who had also lost someone she loved.

---

[33] Chicken soup made with eggs and lemon

Anna finally looked at her daughter, "You know, I feel alright Violet. I like seeing you happy. It's nice to make some new memories here."

Anna put her arm around her daughter, knowing what she was about to ask.

"So, is this related to the tensions between our family and Dimitri's?"

"Ah, that part is so silly, Violet." Anna shook her head. "Dimitri's father, Sifi, he was sixteen at the time, he used to be responsible for sort of keeping an eye on us while we played on the beach sometimes. Our parents had asked him to watch us, they were busy in the taverna. But Sifi got distracted by a pretty blonde American tourist that day, so he didn't see the accident."

Violet pulled away so she could look at her mother. "But the way you described it, it doesn't sound like Sifi could have done anything. I mean, if he'd seen it and been able to get to the water a few seconds earlier, would that have saved your twin?" Violet realized her mother had never spoken her twin brother's name.

"No," said Anna firmly. "But no one liked Sifi, so he was an easy scapegoat, though that doesn't make it right. Sometimes though, when terrible things happen, finding someone to blame is the only way people can manage the loss."

Violet added all the pieces up in her head, all the tidbits of information she'd collected, and they all fit together now: Maria's panic when Violet couldn't be found that first morning, Angelo's instruction to avoid the rocks by the headland, everyone's reluctance to tell her what her mother could not.

"So," said Violet, wanting to make sure she had it right, "Maria still blames Sifi, and even though he left years ago, she continues to hold the grudge against his wife and son, who he abandoned? That doesn't make any sense." Violet shook her head.

"Maria means well, Violet. She and our parents just, well, it was their way of coping, like I said. Mine was to leave, as soon as I could. I tried to get away from the sea," she paused and smiled, "but then I met your father and ended up right back next to a much bigger, more powerful ocean." Anna smiled at the irony.

"Valley that leads to the sea."

"Yes." Anna had put her arm around her daughter again and they sat in silence until the sun submerged itself in the dark blue waters.

"What was his name?" Violet asked quietly just before they stood up to leave.

"Whose?" asked Anna, though she knew what Violet was asking.

"Your twin's."

Anna was silent so long, Violet started to regret the question and was about to retract it.

Finally Anna sighed. "Ioannis," she said. "Ioannis," she repeated. "I haven't said his name since the day he died."

Standing up, Violet hugged her mother and the two walked slowly back down to the bay in the soft red glow of the twilight sky.

Chapter 19

Violet's final days on Crete were bittersweet. She and Dimitri spent as much time together as possible, going for long walks along the coast, keeping an eye on his bees, trying to pretend they weren't dreading their impending separation, trying to not let it taint the time they had left together.

Anna had been careful to give Violet her space; she knew they'd have plenty of time together back in Vancouver. It was enough for her to see Violet so at ease, perhaps more than she'd ever been.

On her last evening in Crete, Anna sat by the sea, nibbling on pieces of honey-drenched halva. The sun was just setting and the sky had turned electric orange and crimson. The smell of the sea and the pine trees brought back a host of childhood memories, and she was relieved to find that they weren't all bad. Her Greek childhood, so marred by Ioannis' death, had been a contented one for ten years and there were pleasant memories slowly resurfacing, previously buried along with the memories of her twin. She had savoured the time spent with her parents, surprised at how, on the one hand, she felt like a child once again in their presence, but on the other hand, it had felt quite natural to build a new relationship with them as an adult.

And it had been wonderful seeing Maria of course, as well as Kosta and Angelo. She began to wonder if she should, in fact, stay longer. But her flight booking didn't allow any changes, and Anna, always practical, reasoned that she would come back with Martin, maybe next summer, or even over Christmas. He'd always wanted to see Crete. If Violet was set on moving here, as she'd told her she was, there would be more reason and opportunities for future visits. Anna just hoped things would work out between her daughter and Dimitri.

As Anna sat on the beach, Violet and Dimitri sat in his cave in the next bay, holding each other very close and speaking little.

Galaxias

I left when the oleander bloomed
in pink and yellow and twilight
I stole a pebble from the seabed
alive with siren songs
but here, alone,
it sits silent.

I remember the ruins and the myths
where I lingered
in the space where your hand first brushed
    against mine
hiding in the pull of tides too small to measure
hoping it was enough.

But that last night
our nearest star fell into the sea
and in the absence of light we could see
our home
rising and falling,
a river of milky white petals,
a million soft yellow suns
Falling slowly
away,
and one day
back again

Part Two

Chapter 1

Vancouver, May 2019

In Vancouver it rains from November until February. It rains like a cold harsh monsoon under charcoal-black clouds that make 2pm appear like 7pm, for days and even weeks on end. Though Violet arrived back on the last day of May, the weather appeared to have confused spring with winter. An angry torrent poured down from the skies, feeding her trepidation.

Her month in Crete felt like another life in a parallel universe in which she'd been a stronger, more resilient version of herself. She wasn't sure which Violet had arrived back in Vancouver.

With Anna's flight not due in for another six hours, and her father being at work, Violet had planned on taking the skytrain and the seabus to get home from the airport, but the downpour and her usual travel fatigue convinced her that a taxi would be worth the cost. Sitting in the car breathing in the slightly nauseous scent of synthetic pine air freshener, with rain pounding on the windows, Violet couldn't help but feel she should have stayed in Crete. Her eyes welled up as she texted Dimitri to let him know she'd arrived safely. She closed her eyes in the backseat and pretended to be asleep. It was nearly 1am in Greece and she didn't expect to hear back from Dimitri for some time. But half a minute later her phone rang.

"Hello?" said Violet quietly.

"Hey, honeybee."

It was strange hearing his voice over the phone for the first time, and even stranger to think that he was now so far away from her. She choked back the tears and told Dimitri her flights had all been fine, she'd managed to sleep a little, there was a screaming baby on the last leg, thank god for headphones.

"How are you?" She asked. "You're up late."

"I couldn't sleep. I'm down at the beach."

Again, Violet choked back her tears, overwhelmed by the strength of her need to be in Sfinari Bay with the man she loved. She thought back to the night she'd fallen asleep under the stars, and Dimitri, unbeknownst to her, had placed a blanket on her while she slept.

"Are you OK?" asked Dimitri as Violet didn't reply.

"I'm not sure. I'll probably feel better after a sleep."

"And a good meal," added Dimitri.

Violet smiled, "Yes, yes, I'll sleep better on a full stomach."

"Ah good, we've taught you well."

Violet managed to half-giggle through her teary tired eyes.

"Video chat tomorrow?" said Dimitri.

"Yeah OK. Let me know when you're done working."

"OK. I miss you, Violet."

Violet managed to choke out the words, "I miss you too," and hung up the phone. She wished it was sunny so she could have put on sunglasses and hid her tears from the taxi driver. She wiped them away and closed her eyes again while they drove on in silence.

As they approached Lions Gate Bridge, Violet was drawn out of her light slumber by a voice.

"I was in love once."

She opened her eyes, slightly disoriented, and sat up a little. "Sorry?"

"I was in love once," repeated the taxi driver.

"Oh?" said Violet, too sleepy to ask more, and not really wanting to engage in this conversation.

"Her name was Angela. And she was, you know, she was an angel." He paused but Violet remained silent. "She was an artist. She collected feathers and made beautiful wings. Just decorative, you know, you couldn't fly with them or anything."

Violet had no idea what this rather peculiar man was talking about or why he was telling her this, and she was too drained to think of a reply. She couldn't see his face from the backseat, but he had white wispy hair that spread out like a halo around his head, and an unusual accent she couldn't quite place.

"She was from Greece," he continued. "You ever been there?"

"Yes. I was just there," Violet managed to respond.

"Nice place," he nodded, not seeming surprised by the coincidence. "Anyway," he continued, "she started making all these lotions and things, with Greek ingredients. Greek olive oil, honey, herbs. She did so well she didn't need me anymore. Lives on some little paradise island and they sell her fancy lotions all over Greece."

Violet was too confused not to ask questions at this point. "What do you mean she didn't need you anymore?"

"Oh, you know, she was a modern independent woman and all that."

"But even if she didn't *need* you...for money of whatever, didn't she *want* to be with you?"

"Apparently not, otherwise I'd be on that Greek island with her, wouldn't I?"

"He's completely unhinged," thought Violet to herself.

"Anyway," he added, "Just goes to show you can never be sure how things will work out in the end. And who knows, maybe I'll end up back on that island with her one day."

Violet now found herself stifling a giggle in response to the bizarre conversation. She just hoped he was sober enough and sane enough to be driving.

By the time Anna's flight touched down at 10pm, the rain had abated, though clouds still hung over the city. Martin picked her up at the airport, greeting her with a warm embrace and a lingering kiss. He still loved Anna as much as the day he'd met her, and he'd missed her while she was gone. Martin often went away on field studies, but this had been the first time in their married life that he'd been at home without her there, and the house had felt incredibly empty without her chatter and laughter.

"Did Violet get in OK?" asked Anna.

"Yes, she was asleep in the rain room when I left. Guess we should wake her and move her to her bed when we get home. She looked so peaceful, I didn't want to disturb her before I left."

"Did she seem alright?"

"Yes," he said unconvincingly.

"You're a terrible liar," said Anna, leaning her head sleepily on her window.

"Well, you know, she was tired."

"And sad?" asked Anna. Anna had kept him updated from Crete and he'd heard all about Violet's romance.

"Maybe. She'll be OK," said Martin, sounding as if he was trying to convince himself.

"I hope so." Anna closed her eyes.

Morning is always wiser than the evening, especially when the sun is out. Violet woke up in the rain room as the sun rose in the pink sky behind the two tall cedars and the maple tree in the backyard. Both parents had tried to gently wake her the night before but Violet hadn't stirred, so they'd decided there wouldn't be any harm in her sleeping on the couch for one night. Sitting up, she checked her phone to see if there was a message from Dimitri. There was:

I went for a morning swim in your honour. The water is getting warmer. I only swore once under my breath xo

Violet smiled and typed a reply:

Just woke up. The sky is all pink. Wish I could have gone swimming with you xo

Taking a deep breath, Violet told herself it was going to be OK. After all, she had a plan now. She only had to be here for a year. She was going to find a job, apply for a Greek passport, save up her money, learn Greek, and somehow figure out what exactly she was going to do in Crete. She told herself there was time to formulate that part of the plan.

Violet got up and walked slowly to the kitchen. "At least," she thought, "I can finally have a decent cup of tea."

Chapter 2

Like many young people in Vancouver, Violet had continued to live with her parents after graduating. She'd lived on-campus for three of her four years of study, and had planned on moving home only temporarily after graduation. But her work was always sporadic and didn't pay anywhere near enough for her to afford rent in the Vancouver market. So she stayed another year, thinking surely the next year she'd move out.

However, when Persephone was killed, everything had stopped for Violet. She had wanted, more than anything, to just be alone most of the time. And though her parents did their best to respect her wishes, they had also wanted to offer her support, make sure she ate something, and generally take care of her the way parents do. Her mother bought her books on mourning and gently suggested seeing a counsellor, but Violet had refused. She'd skimmed through the books, mostly out of boredom but not found any comfort in them. She'd binge-watched TV shows and movies, barely registering what she was seeing. She'd cried a little, slept a great deal, and endured a pervasive dull sense of numbness, vaguely wondering if she'd ever feel alive again.

But now, living at home for a year didn't seem quite so bad, and a few weeks in, things seemed be falling into place. Violet took a three-month contract doing administrative work for a math institute at the University of British Columbia that ran summer programmes and conferences. She playfully told Dimitri that maybe being surrounded by Greek letters might help her learn the language. She'd purchased several Greek language courses, a mix of textbooks and audio recordings, and spent evenings practicing with her mother.

Violet struggled initially with the alphabet, which appeared as a strange series of unrecognizable symbols, and letters that looked familiar but didn't make the sounds she expected. "Ro" looked like a "p" but sounded like "r." "Chi" looked like "x" but sounded like a Scottish "ch." Some looked familiar from high school math, but "pi" was pronounced "pee" rather than "pie." It made her head swim.

Anna, for her part, wished she'd taught Violet Greek when she was young. Having run from her country when she herself was still young, she'd always wanted Violet to feel Canadian rather than Greek. Of course she'd shared stories from her childhood, a few Greek myths and plenty of recipes, but the language itself had seemed unlikely to ever be of use, so Anna hadn't worried about it.

But now, sitting at the kitchen table, watching Violet struggle with the unfamiliar alphabet, she searched for a way to make it easier.

"OK, let's see, how can we remember that 'ro' looks like 'p' but sounds like 'r'?"

Violet shook her head. She was sure Persephone would have picked this all up so easily, and she was getting frustrated with her ineptitude. "I wonder what Perse would tell me if she were here," she wondered to herself. Then she had a thought. "Could we make a rhyme? Or a song?"

"Ooh yes! How would it go?"

Violet thought and then sang to the tune of *Twinkle Twinkle Little Star*. "The letter 'ro' confuses me, sounds like 'r' but looks like 'p'."

Anna and Violet both laughed.

"OK, now one for 'chi'," said Violet, getting into the spirit. She nibbled on the end of her pen. "If it looks like 'x,' it's really 'chi,' sounds like a loch by the Scottish sea."

Mother and daughter giggled, a little longer this time. Violet was getting into the swing of it now.

"I'm definitely gonna need one for 'ita'," she said, scanning the alphabet.

Anna started this one, " 'Ita' the 'h' is a cheeky monkey—"

She paused and Violet continued, "Sounds like 'ee,' well isn't that funky?"

Anna and Violet erupted into raucous laughter. Martin came in for a cup of tea and said they were having far too much fun to be learning anything.

"Oh no, Dad, that's not true. Studies show that people learn better when they're relaxed and enjoying their learning."

"Is that right?" queried Martin.

"Yes. See, my psychology degree wasn't wasted. I did learn some useful things," said Violet, regaining her confidence.

"Well, thank goodness for that." Martin smiled.

Every weekend Violet had at least one video call with Dimitri, sometimes two. With the time difference and Violet working, it was difficult to talk during the week, though they sent text messages constantly, and sometimes Violet could get through to him on her lunch break. Dimitri laughed when she told him about her Greek letter rhymes.

"Wow, I didn't know you were a songwriter as well as a poet."

Violet had confessed to Dimitri that her notebook in Crete was fully of poetry, though she'd not yet let him read any.

"Well, I'm not going to quit my day job just yet, but I think I might have found my calling," joked Violet.

"Have you got one for 'veeta'?" he asked.

"Not yet, do you have an idea?"

"Hmm," Dimitri thought for a moment. "Veeta looks like a funny 'b,' confusingly it sounds like 'v,' I hope this rhyme will helpful be, to Violet, the honeybee."

Violet laughed. "Bonus points for the extra lines, but minus two for the bad grammar," she said playfully.

Things went on in this way for the first six weeks or so. Violet still missed Dimitri intensely, and Persephone was never far from her thoughts. The commutes to work were long and certainly Violet had difficult days, where she wanted to bury herself in her duvet and hide from the world. Overall, however, she managed. She had a plan and she was in love. The future, for once, looked promising.

But as August approached, despite the warm summer weather, Violet began to find the days more challenging. Her twenty-fifth birthday was coming up, followed quickly by the anniversary of Persephone's death. Violet had no idea how to celebrate her birthday without Persephone, and the link between the two events made her birthday feel more like a day to mourn than to celebrate. Besides, she'd shut out her friends and deleted all her social media accounts following the sudden loss of her closest friend.

Since returning to Vancouver, she'd got back in touch with a couple of acquaintances, but she didn't feel close to any of them anymore. They all knew Persephone and seemed to want to talk about her. Violet found that, strangely, it was harder to talk about Perse to the people who had known her than it had been to talk to Dimitri about her. Maybe because she felt she had to, in effect, share Persephone with these friends, and Violet was terrified of losing the pieces of her she still held. Moreover, hearing about their grieving, rather than comforting her, made her feel she hadn't grieved enough, and if she'd had the audacity to fall in love so soon after the event, perhaps she hadn't cared about Persephone as much as she'd thought.

Violet descended into her tangled labyrinth of thoughts, and began to spend most evenings watching movies on her laptop, rather than working on her Greek.

Her parents, conscious of the situation, and seeing Violet's spirits dwindle, asked her what she'd like to do for her birthday this year. Violet shrugged, not taking her eyes off the murder-mystery series she'd become engrossed in.

Anna's birthday fell on August 12th, and Violet tried her best to be present and make the day special for her mother, but she knew her distraction was obvious. She baked a cake over the weekend, but forgot to add sugar and mis-measured the flour. They drizzled copious amounts of honey on it and Anna assured her it was delicious, but Violet was frustrated and disappointed in herself.

On the following day, the Tuesday before her birthday, Violet found herself unable to move from her bed when she awoke. She hadn't been able to have a video chat with Dimitri the previous weekend. He seemed very busy and she worried she was losing him. Her limbs felt heavy when she tried to move them, and her mind ran in circles, tying knots that pulled tighter and tighter.

She called in sick to work and slipped out of the house quietly, without being seen, grabbing her bathing suit, towel, and her mother's car keys. Violet drove down the quiet residential streets, past the immaculately green lawns and well-kept flowerbeds that defined middle-class suburbia, then through the charming local shops of Edgemont Village, which still held onto its old-fashioned charisma, despite hints of a possible trendy and faceless future.

She turned onto Capilano Road and pulled off into a small hidden parking lot by the river, where the enormous evergreens towered above her, engulfing her in their cool, damp scent. For a moment Violet thought of the subtle scent of pine on Dimitri's pillow.

She sighed and sent her mother a text so she wouldn't worry.

Borrowed your car. Needed to get out. Sorry.

Violet sat in the car with her eyes closed for a moment. She hadn't been here since Persephone had passed away and wasn't sure she wanted to make new memories here that didn't involve her best friend. She also knew, however, that it was a place where she'd always found comfort, and she needed that right now. She got out of the car slowly and took a deep breath before walking over to the path.

A yellow sign warned that the trail was dangerous and visitors were to use it at their own risk. It was indeed rather treacherous, and Violet scrambled rather than walked down it, using tree roots and stones as footholds. Ferns and ivy flanked the rough path, and huge cedars covered in moss soon enveloped her. Violet felt her feet lighten just a little. As she approached the river, she picked up her pace, anticipating the quiet tranquility that awaited her.

Arriving at the edge of the river, she felt her shoulders relax for what felt like the first time in weeks, if not months. She breathed deeply and let out a sigh. The air was damp and fresh here, even in the height of summer, and it was a beautiful sunny morning promising a warm afternoon. Violet looked over to her right, where the two pale logs on the steep bank formed a 'v' shape, nearly meeting at the surface of the still pool. Their reflection created an 'x,' as if marking the location of an unknown treasure. In the past, she'd often seen a kingfisher fish from the logs, and she wondered if the bird had noticed her long absence. She hoped he was still nearby. Violet sat down on a large smooth rock, took off her shoes and quickly changed into her bathing suit. She thought about the evening at Platanakia Beach, when she'd changed awkwardly in Dimitri's car. She missed him so much. She missed Crete. And she missed Persephone.

The water was cold, even in August, and Violet gasped as she waded in. She'd become used to the temperatures of the Cretan Sea, and after having that glorious body of water on her doorstep for a month, driving or busing down to a beach that wasn't Sfinari Beach had somewhat lost its appeal. She'd only been swimming twice since her return several months ago, and she'd put off coming here until she'd felt there was no choice.

Taking a deep breath, Violet plunged under the cool, clear water and swam to her right, past the two logs, and into the deep canyon, where the steep stone walls rose above her, green with moss and ferns that formed mysterious faces, coming into view suddenly, then disappearing as she swam on and her angle changed. Under the water, Violet could hear the quiet sound of the gentle waterfall cascading down the rocks just beyond the canyon, so different to the sounds of the sea, yet with its own haunting beauty. After a few minutes, she turned around, swimming with the current, which was only barely noticeable in this deep open section of the river. As she approached the pool where she'd entered, she saw the kingfisher perched on one of the logs and smiled. "It's going to be OK," she thought to herself.

Violet swam up and down her section of the river until she was exhausted and numb from the cold. She didn't want to have any energy left to fuel her knotted thoughts. Sitting down on a rock beside the river, she wrapped her towel around her and watched the movements of sunlight catching on the water like a mesmerizing dance. She tried to think of nothing but the water and the sunlight for as long as possible.

Back at the house, Martin had gone to work, telling Anna not to worry, Violet would be fine. Anna, of course, worried. She wasn't working today, and had planned to run some errands. But without her car, and needing to keep busy, she decided to surprise Violet with some homemade *dolmades* and *halva*. Her coping mechanisms remained very Greek despite her years in Canada.

Violet eventually returned to her car, feeling tired but calmer. She was dreading going home and explaining to her mom why she'd not gone to work today. It was at times like these that Violet vehemently wished she had her own place. She thought back to her little room in Sfinari Bay and wondered why places like that didn't exist here. There were seaside restaurants and hotels of course, but they tended to be upscale places; there was nothing here with the quaint charm of a Cretan seaside taverna and simple little rooms.

Checking her phone, which she'd purposefully left in the car, Violet saw two missed calls from her mother and a text from Dimitri.

Hey honeybee, sorry I couldn't chat over the weekend. Taverna has been crazy busy. Not sleeping so well. Only 9 more months til you're here. Filakia polla[34] xo

Violet didn't feel able to respond. She knew Dimitri knew her birthday was coming up, but wasn't sure if he'd remember that it corresponded with Persephone's death. She hadn't found the strength, or the right moment, to broach the subject. Though grateful for the existence of video calls, she found that without being able to sit close to Dimitri, to embrace and kiss, hold hands and touch, it was much more difficult to open up about her worries.

Violet drove home the long way and found the house smelling of lemon, herbs and honey. The aromas brought back memories from Crete so strongly, her resolve to put on a brave face for her mother completely dissolved and Violet burst into tears as she walked in the door. Anna hugged her daughter very close and didn't ask the questions that filled her mind. She understood enough.

Violet's birthday fell on a Friday, and her co-workers had kindly brought in a chocolate cake to celebrate. She appreciated the gesture and pretended to enjoy the store-bought over-sugared confection, realizing her time in Greece had turned her into a bit of a food snob. Dimitri had phoned her briefly in the morning, before she left for work, to wish her a happy birthday. He'd asked what she

---

[34]Lots of kisses

was doing, and Violet paused before answering, forcing back the tears that threatened to well up.

"Just going to work, then having a nice dinner with my parents," she said, feeling like the lamest twenty-five-year-old in history.

"That's it?" said Dimitri.

"That's it," replied Violet.

Dimitri could tell all wasn't well, but they didn't have long to talk; Violet had to leave for work very soon. "This is your first birthday without Persephone isn't it?" he asked gently.

"Yes," Violet managed to say.

"And she...passed away a few days later right?"

"I didn't think you'd remember that."

"Of course I remember that. We were at Aptera, by the cisterns when you told me."

"The wingless place," said Violet quietly, feeling very wingless herself at the moment.

"I'm sorry Violet, it must be hard," offered Dimitri, wishing he could pull her close, feeling his words were woefully insufficient given what Violet was going through.

Violet was silent.

"Hey, Violet, don't worry. Just nine more months, then we can be together."

Violet nodded, even though it was only an audio call.

"Are you free tomorrow at 1pm your time?" asked Dimitri "We can have a proper belated birthday chat then, OK?"

"Are you sure you'll be free?"

"I'll make sure I am. And I'll be thinking of you all day, so don't feel lonely."

"OK."

Saturday at 1pm exactly, Dimitri video called Violet from the taverna. Violet answered the call and was surprised to see not just Dimitri, but his mother Despoina, her cousin Angelo, *Theia Maria* and *Theios Kostas*, and even her *yiayia* and *pappous*. Violet's parents joined the call from the living room, Dimitri having arranged for them to be in on the surprise as well.

They all stood around a large table of sweet treats, a large cake in the middle with twenty-five candles, and birthday decorations and balloons all around them. They sang happy birthday gloriously out of key (Violet's grandparents humming along, unsure of the English lyrics), and then all talked at once, yelling *"Chronia polla!"*[35] and inviting her to blow out the candles from Canada. Violet theatrically blew at her laptop screen.

"It worked!" exclaimed *Theia Maria,* after Angelo had surreptitiously blown out the candles himself. They held up each delicious treat and Violet was sure she could taste some of them over the internet. In the midst of the chaos of voices, Dimitri told her he'd also sent her something in the mail.

"I'm sorry I sent it a bit late, but it should get there soon," he said, smiling.

It was overwhelming in all the best ways and Violet shed a few tears, but was thankful these were the happy

---

[35]Many years! A common expression on someone's birthday or name day.

kind for a change. It reinforced her conviction that she belonged in Crete, with these beautiful joyful people who all came together to try and make her birthday memorable.

Dimitri's package was delivered the following Wednesday. Arriving home from work, Violet held the padded envelope in her hands and looked down at her address in Dimitri's writing.

Violet Honeybee Morcomb
370 St. George Rd.
N. Vancouver, BC V7N 3R7
CANADA

It was comforting to think he'd touched the envelope she now held, and had written out her name and address carefully on it. She opened it slowly, and reached inside, pulling out a beautiful hand-carved depiction of two bees. Their heads and abdomens touched, and their bodies curved away from each other to form a circle. Between them they held a round piece of honeycomb. It was about four inches long, with a hook on the back so it could be hung on the wall. She was sure Niko had made it. She smiled, remembering their visit to Polyrhinnia and how annoyed she'd been with him for paying for her things. She still had the necklace and wore it most days. There was also a postcard with a photo of the chapel at Polyrhinnia, Dimitri's scribbly writing on it.

Happy Birthday Honeybee. I got Nikos to make this just for you. It's based on a famous Minoan gold bee pendant found in Malia. We'll be together for your next birthday, and maybe we can even visit the site where the pendant was found.
Filakia polla.
-Dimitri

Violet held the two small items in her hands, feeling grateful and happy but also acutely miserable that she wasn't with the man who had sent them. She was getting tired of holding back tears all the time. Her finger traced Dimitri's writing on the card, then the smooth contours of the wooden bees. She leaned both against the mirror on her dresser, managed a faint smile and texted Dimitri to thank him.

Chapter 3

Persephone's father had never been a particularly sociable man. He had many colleagues, but few friends and very little support after his daughter's death. His partner had left him, his mother had passed away, and now his beloved daughter had been taken from him, so violently and far too soon. Richard had always been awkward when it came to expressing or even understanding his own emotions, so he struggled silently, trying to lose himself in the esoteric books that lined his shelves and confused when his tears fell silently on the pages.

He wasn't the sort to seek out counselling or therapy, so he immersed himself in his work, taking on a contract with the Lascaux International Centre for Cave Art documenting and researching some ancient cave art discovered recently in southern France. It meant relocating for six months, and Richard instinctively felt a change of scenery could only help.

He'd returned to Vancouver in April, half-expecting Persephone to greet him in the little apartment, but of course knowing she wouldn't. He finished writing up his papers, ordered some books on the internet and tried not to notice how quiet his apartment was, every woman he'd ever loved having left him one way or another.

By August, like Violet, Richard's thoughts had turned to Persephone, though they'd never strayed far from her anyway. Her room remained untouched. Occasionally Richard liked to just sit on her bed and look around at her things, still exactly as she'd left them, her favourite sweater slung over her desk chair and her pyjamas folded neatly at the end of her bed. It looked as if she'd just left this morning for work and would be back any minute now. Except she wouldn't.

Richard knew eventually he needed to empty her room, and logically, with a year having gone by, he could see no reason not to. But somehow he couldn't bring himself to start.

On the anniversary of Persephone's death, Richard called Violet. She didn't answer so he left a quiet message asking if she'd like to have a look through Persephone's things.

"There might be something you want to keep," he said, his voice almost a whisper. He was sure if someone could just start the job of moving things around in her room, he'd be able to finish it. As long as it sat untouched, it felt like her essence still hung in the air and he couldn't bear to break the spell.

Violet was once again swimming in the river when Richard called, up and down and back again, trying to exhaust her body and her mind, the only therapy that worked for her. When she saw the missed call, her stomach turned and she had the same feeling of physical illness she'd had on that day with Dimitri in Niko's olive wood gift shop. She hadn't felt it in the past few months; most of the time now it was just a dull ache that waxed and waned like the moon, but without ever disappearing completely.

It was hard to hear Richard's message, he spoke so quietly. Violet wondered how often he spoke to anyone, and suddenly felt guilty for not getting in touch with him and offering some kind of support. But Richard was a socially awkward academic who mostly liked to be left alone to his studies and his reading. Though she'd known him for years, he'd always been a somewhat silent presence, tucked away in his study and only occasionally emerging for food and to use the bathroom. She had no idea what to offer him, especially when she was struggling to manage her own tangled emotions.

Violet sat in her car and imagined herself in Persephone's room. When was the last time she'd been in it? Maybe one evening the week before her death? Or two weeks before? They'd always spent more time at Violet's as her place was larger and Perse always said her dad didn't focus as well with them chatting in the next room. Violet had suspected she just preferred her mom's Greek cooking to her dad's scrambled eggs, or takeaway pizzas.

Violet called Richard back on the landline that was his only phone and said she could come straight over if it was a good time.

"Sure, sure," he said quietly. "See you soon."

Violet hung up and wondered if this was a wise decision. But somehow it felt right to be doing it on the anniversary of Persephone's death.

In Persephone's room, time had stopped when she'd hurried out the door that afternoon to meet Violet for lunch. They'd eaten Indian food at their favourite restaurant on Lonsdale, then the two had walked to the library, and Violet had run to catch her bus, which appeared across the road.

Violet replayed the day in her mind as she sat on Persephone's bed. There was still her faint scent in the room, and like Richard, she marvelled at the way it felt as if she might just walk in at any moment saying something silly like, "What do you mean you thought I was dead? Didn't you know I'm an immortal being, a Greek goddess, to be exact." And Violet would laugh and say, "Excuse me, I think you'll find *I'm* the Greek one here."

Except those playful conversations would never happen again.

Violet stood up and went to the bookcase, perusing the titles but still not daring to touch anything. Books on psychology, counselling, neuroscience, quantum physics, psychoanalytic theory, music therapy and dance movement therapy lined several shelves. A few of her favourite novels stood alone on the top shelf. Persephone got most of her fiction reading from the library, only investing in copies of her most treasured stories. Violet smiled.

Persephone had known how to live well without spending very much. Growing up, Perse's family never had much money but she had a knack for stumbling across gems in thrift stores: cashmere sweaters priced by someone who couldn't tell posh wool from shoddy acrylic, or barely used leather handbags with the decimal in the wrong place on the price tag. As a result, she'd always looked stylish and never felt deprived. She'd used baking soda for everything, from washing her hair to brushing her teeth and cleaning the bathroom. She'd always told Violet that cleaning products were a scam. And the cosmetic industry she'd certainly had nothing good to say about.

"Their whole marketing revolves around making women feel like they're not good enough. And if we buy their product, well then we'll *maybe* be good enough. Except to *really* be good enough, we need to buy another product, and another and another."

"Good enough for what?" Violet had asked.

Persephone shrugged, "Good enough to be worthy of existing, cause you know, as mere women we need to work hard to be worthy. Oh, and if we want to be good enough, worthy enough for a husband, ooh we'd have to buy sooo many more products, expensive ones too, and probably get some botox and a lip injection." She rolled her eyes as far back as they would go.

Persephone had learned to make her own lotions out of simple ingredients. She used to make a lavender-scented one for Violet. It really had been the best lotion.

As Violet had this thought, her eyes fell upon some binders, stacked awkwardly on the bottom shelf of the bookcase as they were too tall to stand up. She ran her hand along them and slowly pulled a red one off the top of the stack. It was full of song lyrics with guitar chords and Violet smiled as she flipped through it briefly. Putting it down, she opened the next binder, a blue one, and was surprised to see Persephone's lotion recipes written out carefully, including the one for her lavender lotion. Excited, Violet stood up and smiled. Then, strangely, she remembered the very odd taxi driver who had told her about his ex-girlfriend who made lotions with Greek ingredients.

"I wonder if I could adapt these," Violet said out loud, nearly jumping up and down. She'd been trying to figure out what to do in Crete, but the answer had so far eluded her. "I could do this! I could sell lotions using our own olive oil, and maybe even have my own shop in Chania eventually!" She was talking out loud, as she often did when she was tired or excited, and Richard, concerned that she was talking to Persephone's ghost, knocked quietly and asked if she was alright. "Yes, sorry Richard, I was just talking to myself. I found Persephone's lotion recipes and I thought I might try and make them."

Richard peeked through the door, slightly disappointed that his daughter's ghost hadn't appeared, but also pleased that Violet might be able to give new life to something of Persephone's.

"That's a good idea," he said in his characteristic soft voice. "Could I, uh, could you make me some?"

Violet looked at Richard, confused for a moment, and then understanding as he added, "It's just they, uh, they might smell like her," he added, his eyes darting around the room.

"Of course, though it might take me a few tries to get it right. I'm not as clever as she was."

"She must have thought you were, or she wouldn't have hung around you all the time." It was the longest sentence Richard had spoken to anyone in months.

Violet smiled, "That's true, she didn't suffer fools did she?"

"No," answered Richard, returning to his usual succinctness.

Violet's phone rang and they both jumped. It was Dimitri. "I'm sorry," Violet said to Richard, "Can I use your wifi for a video call? It's my boyfriend in Crete. I'm sure he'd like to see Perse's room, if that's OK with you? He's heard a lot about her."

"Sure," Richard gave a hint of a smile and walked back to his study, trying not to think back to his own failed romance with Persephone's mother, who was presumably still in Bali becoming one with the universe. No one had been able to get in touch with her about Persephone's death. Richard was certain she'd simply floated away into the ether.

Violet showed Dimitri Persephone's room and he was relieved to see her emotional, but smiling.

"Is it strange to be there?" he asked.

"Yes and no," replied Violet. "It was very strange at first, but now, I feel like it's very healing, you know. Especially being here today. I feel like I'm with her, in a way."

Dimitri smiled.

"Oh, and I've found her book of lotion recipes, I thought I'd try and make some."

"She made lotions?"

"She did *everything*. I thought, when I move back there, I could adapt them and use local ingredients: the olive oil from my *theia* and *theios* and your honey and beeswax? What do you think?"

"I think you might have found your fulfilling career."

Violet laughed. "And have you found your beautiful wife yet?"

"I think I might have." He smiled broadly.

After the call, Violet pulled the next binder, a bright purple one, off the same shelf. It was full of music. Sheet music carefully typed up and printed, all sorts of compositions for various instruments: piano, guitar, guitar and flute, guitar duets. The composer was listed as P. McCullough-Drummond. Violet stared in disbelief. Of course she knew Persephone had *played* music, and occasionally wrote simple songs for her sessions, but she'd never ever mentioned writing music like this.

The binder was comfortably full, there was a sizable collection of work. Violet flipped through it, though it had been years since she'd read music in high school band, squeaking on her clarinet and mostly sitting as far back as possible and pretending to play. She found herself feeling a little hurt that Persephone had kept this part of her life from her. She'd been the one person Violet had shared everything with, while she held back so much from nearly everyone else in her life. She had just assumed it would have been the same for Perse. But it wasn't. What else had she hidden from her?

Violet went through the final two binders. One held recipes and one held Christmas songs. Nothing else unexpected then. As Violet processed her discovery, she knew her hurt was petty. Persephone had every right to keep things private if she wanted to. But there was a nagging voice saying maybe she wasn't as important to her friend as Persephone had been to her.

"Don't be silly, Vi. You know that's not true." Violet heard Persephone's voice in her mind, reprimanding her.

"I know," she answered to the air.

Violet left with Persephone's favourite red cashmere sweater, as well as her binders of music and lotion recipes. She told Richard she'd be happy to come back another time and go through more of her things, but she was sure she had what she wanted to keep. Richard nodded.

Back in her mother's car, Violet realized she hadn't told him about the music, and wondered if he knew. As she drove, her thoughts circled back to the taxi driver. Hadn't he also mentioned that his ex-partner made wings? She felt a tingling sensation down her spine as she remembered Dimitri telling her about the sirens at Aptera.

Violet returned home that day with her spirits restored and her mind clear once again. She immediately ordered the remaining ingredients she needed for Persephone's recipes, having bought olive oil on the way home. She sat down with her Greek textbook and audio recordings. *"Tha ithela ena tsai me gala parakalo,"*[36] she repeated, wishing her mother were home to help her with her pronunciation. "I wonder how you ask for a *decent* cup of tea," Violet said to herself. She thought about the milky way, *galaxia,* and in her mind's eye she saw it hanging over

---

[36] I'd like a cup of tea with milk please.

the headland in Sfinari Bay, and was comforted by the hope that she would, one day, see it again.

Violet was sitting in the sunroom. It was a beautiful day, and Martin was relieved to see her focused and happy once again. He knew what day it was, and had been worried when she'd set out alone this morning, though of course he'd told his wife not to worry as she left for work, assuring her that Violet would be alright. Now he texted Anna to let her know that Violet seemed much better this afternoon and was hard at work on her Greek. Anna was relieved. She had considered taking the day off, but Violet had discouraged her. Both parents were trying very hard to give their adult daughter the space she needed to navigate life's twists and turns, but it was a constant, draining battle.

For now, though, it seemed like everything was going to be alright.

Demeter's Waltz

Guitar Duet

P. McCullough-Drummond

Chapter 4

The months ticked away and Violet and Dimitri counted down excitedly, making plans for all the things they'd do when she finally arrived. Dimitri promised to take her on a trip down to Frangokastello on the southwest coast, with its commanding Venetian castle and beautiful sandy beach, perfect for swimming. They talked about doing a long road-trip one day, exploring eastern Crete, texting each other links to places they found online they wanted to explore together. Violet, surfing the internet on her lunch break, came across the island of Spinalonga. Originally a Venetian fort, it was later used as a leper colony. In the photos, it looked like a wonderful tangle of romantic ruins.

Violet texted, *Have you been here? Can we go can we go? xo*

No and yes! xo Dimitri replied swiftly.

By November, Violet's Greek was improving, and she began to shyly practice with Dimitri on their video calls.

Dimitri, for his part, greatly enjoyed hearing her unusual pronunciations. When Violet tried to pronounce *"perimeno,"*[37] but ended up saying what sounded like "Mary Penny," Dimitri couldn't help but laugh.

"I'm sorry, Violet, it's not you," he apologized. "It's not an easy language to learn. And us Greeks are not really used to hearing non-Greeks speaking our language. But I like your accent, and Mary Penny sounds like a really nice lady. Keep talking in Greek, please! *Mila mou sta Ellenika parakalo."*[38]

Violet glared, pretending to be annoyed with him, though she wasn't really. She was equally bemused at her mistake, and she liked nothing more than hearing him speak Greek, especially now she could understand at least some of it. "No. *Ochi.*[39] I'm not going to speak *Ellenika* ever again to you, if that's how you respond."

"Tell me your favourite sentence again," Dimitri urged.

Violet giggled. *"Poso kanei to peponi?"*[40]

They both burst out laughing. It was a sentence she'd come across in one of her textbooks and she loved the rhythmic sound of it, all the "p's" just popping off her tongue.

"Are you going to buy a honeydew melon when you get here in six months, just so you can ask that question?" Dimitri asked playfully.

"Almost certainly," replied Violet.

---

[37] I wait
[38] Speak to me in Greek please.
[39] No
[40] How much is the honeydew melon?

Violet's lotions had also begun to materialize, after several failed, and very messy, attempts in her mother's kitchen. Anna had come home from work one evening in late August to find her cheese grater caked in sticky beeswax, and several pots and utensils so covered in oil, she was sure they'd never be clean again. But Violet looked so disheartened, Anna's annoyance quickly softened into sympathy.

"It's only your first try, Violet, you knew it might take a few times. I bet Persephone didn't get it right the first time either."

"I bet she did," Violet replied firmly. She was aware her frustration was making her sound like a stroppy, inept child, yet somehow her capable, adult self eluded her.

"Why don't you try again tomorrow? Come on, I'll help you clean up and then we can make *yemista*[41] for dinner."

Violet bought herself a cooking thermometer before trying again, something she'd initially thought she could skip out on. She should have known if Persephone said it was needed, it most definitely was. She wasn't one for unnecessary purchases. She also ordered beeswax in pellet form, saving her mother's cheese grater from death by very hard beeswax. Her second batch was usable, and things improved from there. She dropped off a jar for Richard, and made herself a batch of lavender lotion. It felt like a gift from Persephone, from whatever universe she now inhabited.

Violet's contract at the math institute had been extended; she was well-liked and a good worker, and they

---

[41] Stuffed vegetables, usually peppers and/or tomatoes.

judged that keeping her on would be worthwhile. She'd gained a reputation as the "spreadsheet queen," and colleagues often asked her for advice, or sent their messy spreadsheets to her to be edited into something more presentable. Violet didn't mind. She found it satisfying to create order out of the chaos of an untidy pile of information.

She remembered Persephone telling her about how the universe was inextricably moving towards chaos, maximum entropy, she'd called it, and wondered if the simple act of organizing information in a spreadsheet was somehow a comforting antidote to this, something simple she could control and arrange.

It rained through November and December, as is often the case in Vancouver. Christmas was strange and quiet, without Persephone. Since Perse's mom had left, she and her dad had always come over for Christmas dinner. However, since Persephone's death, Richard had politely declined the invitations that Violet's parents still extended to him. The empty space of his daughter's absence, he felt, would have been unbearable. So Anna and Violet dropped him off a generous helping of turkey, stuffing, mashed potatoes and various vegetables, along with some *melomakarona,*[42] wishing him a very merry Christmas.

Violet hadn't heard back from him about Persephone's room, but Christmas didn't feel like the right time to ask if he'd managed to go through the rest of her things.

---

[42] Christmas cookies made with cinnamon, cloves, honey, and orange.

Violet had a video call with Dimitri on Christmas day. They were working up to more Greek in their conversations.

"Yia su! Kala Christougenna!"[43] said Violet, her confidence growing.

"Kala Christougenna Melissa," replied Dimitri, calling her by her Greek middle name. *"Ti kanis?"*

"Polli kalla. Esi?"[44] replied Violet.

"Kalla," he answered, once again enjoying Violet's accented Greek.

She couldn't resist adding, *"Poso kanei to peponi?"* They laughed.

Anna walked past the sunroom where Violet sat with her laptop, and said Merry Christmas to Dimitri. The two of them spoke in Greek too quickly for Violet to catch anything.

"Thanks Mom, I was just starting to feel confident, but I couldn't understand a word of that! Do I talk that fast in English?"

"Yes," said Anna, "You do. I only asked him how his Christmas was going. He said he had a good day and his mother cooked a delicious dinner, and his sisters are visiting from Iraklion." Violet hadn't even managed to catch the word "Iraklion."

"Don't worry," Dimitri assured her, "you still have four months to learn the rest of the language." Violet was sure that would never be long enough, but she was too excited about her impending move to be particularly worried.

---

[43] Hello! Merry Christmas!

[44] Very well. And you?

She had been carefully saving as much money as possible, which was fairly easy as Violet went out very little these days, didn't pay rent, and only occasionally paid for groceries. She offered to contribute more, but her parents told her to save her money for Greece. Normally Violet would have felt guilty, working so much and giving so little, but somehow knowing it was part of a plan and just a temporary measure before she'd finally spread her wings, made it feel alright. She'd stopped buying most cosmetic products, finally taking the advice Persephone had always given her and using baking soda for most things. She found she needed very little.

In January, Violet finally obtained her Greek passport, after navigating a labyrinth of paperwork and bureaucracy that rivaled the one King Minos built to house the Minotaur. Excited and relieved, she bought a bottle of ouzo (the only Greek drink she could find in the local liquor store; sadly she couldn't find Cretan *raki* anywhere) and opened it on her next chat with Dimitri.

February arrived and Violet booked a one-way flight to Chania, scheduled to arrive on the afternoon of May 2nd. She could hardly believe it when she clicked "confirm" on her browser. Everything was finally happening as she'd planned, and there was a very real momentum carrying her towards her departure date.

Still working through the bottle of ouzo, she and Dimitri had another celebratory drink, though Violet said she much preferred the *rakomelo*.

"In three months, you can have all the *rakomelo* you want." Dimitri smiled.

"Well thank goodness for that," replied Violet, taking another sip of the aniseed liquor. She found herself incapable of drinking even half a shot at once.

By this time, there were whispers in the air of a virus from China, but most people weren't worried, and Violet was no exception. After all, she'd heard similar whispers about MERS and swine flu in the past, and nothing had come of it. She continued practicing her Greek and began to excitedly count down weeks instead of months. It was so close now, Violet couldn't quite believe it and even the February rain didn't dampen her spirits. It was the first time in her life things seemed to be going her way. Having carefully executed her plans, a new life with Dimitri was waiting for her just around the corner. She was sure nothing could change the path that was now so clearly laid out before her.

Back in Crete, Dimitri hoped that the cancellation of all remaining Carnival events in late February was an over-reaction. After all, there had only been one confirmed case of the virus in Greece. When schools, restaurants and bars closed two weeks later, he began to worry, though he put on a brave face for Violet and tried to reassure her that she'd still be able to come in May.

The following day, on March 11, 2020, The World Health Organization declared Covid-19 a global pandemic. Canada declared a state of emergency and Greece went into strict lockdown.

Chapter 5

Violet didn't usually watch the news. She read articles online a little and heard her parents' radio, always tuned to CBC. But now she sat transfixed, anxious and desperately hoping this new virus wouldn't interfere with her move to Crete, but increasingly certain that it would. She listened to Dr. Bonnie Henry, the Provincial Health Officer as she asked that everyone simply, "Be calm, be kind, be safe." She seemed like a trustworthy aunt, a comforting presence on the news. But the numbers and projections looked increasingly worrying.

Her parents tried to reassure her. After all, she had a Greek passport; they would likely let citizens enter, if not by May, then soon after. Probably she'd still be able to go. But in private, Anna and Martin confessed to each other they were worried. They knew how long their daughter had waited and how much this move meant to her.

"Well, at worst it'll probably just be a few more months she has to wait," offered Martin. "Surely she'll be able to go in the fall."

"I hope you're right," said Anna. Her intuition was telling her otherwise and she desperately hoped it was wrong.

In Crete, Dimitri and his mother watched the daily 6pm updates from Sotiris Tsiodras, the doctor in charge of coordinating the country's response to the Covid-19 pandemic. His calm demeanour and quiet confidence were reassuring, and through the spring lockdown, numbers remained low in Greece. There was a sense that they were doing things right, and if they continued, everything would surely return to normal in the coming months.

Still, Dimitri desperately wished he could go on one of his long drives, perhaps to Aptera. He drove slowly when he went out to check on his bees in the mountains, and sometimes risked taking a longer route home. But he couldn't leave Kissamos province.

The tone of Violet's chats with Dimitri was different these days. Both of them were concerned, though Dimitri tried his best to cheer her up, despite the strangeness of the strict new rules he had to abide by. In Greece, everyone now had to send a text message to the authorities every time they left their home, with their name, address, and a number corresponding to the reason they'd gone out. There were seven possible reasons given, and Dimitri had no idea what category checking on his bees came under. He generally called it "work" and sometimes "exercise" if he walked down to his hives by the beach. He was required to carry his passport at all times. All the shops were closed, with the exception of grocery stores and pharmacies. It was a strange and unsettling world, much stricter than what Violet was experiencing in Western Canada.

"Hey, we've waited this long, what's a few more months? You'll have more time to work on your Greek, and plan your honeydew melon purchase," he teased, trying to lighten the mood.

Violet couldn't even smile at his joke. She sighed. "I just can't believe this is happening. I really thought for once things were finally going to work out, and the universe was going to finally let me just...be happy. I miss you so much, and I miss Sfinari Bay. I don't want to be here anymore. I don't think I can do a few more months." Violet's eyes were wet with tears.

"Hey, honeybee, don't worry. You don't even know yet what's going to happen. Maybe you can still come in May. Let's just wait and see."

Violet nodded, but her positivity was waning.

On the last day of March, Violet received a notification that her flight had been cancelled. It now felt very unlikely that she'd be leaving for Crete this spring. The math institute office had closed down the previous week, and all the conferences and summer schools that had been planned were postponed, and then called off. Officially she was working from home until the end of her contract in mid-April, but the reality was that there was very little work to be done right now.

Violet, crestfallen and directionless once again, withdrew into her room and cried. She alternated between feeling incomprehensibly angry at the universe and inconsolably disappointed. She picked up her phone to text Dimitri but found she had no words.

Dimitri, not hearing back from Violet that day, began to worry. He suspected her flight was cancelled. Unable to sleep that night, he tried to call her. Violet couldn't bring herself to answer. She didn't want Dimitri to see or hear her in her current state. She didn't know what to say or how to say it. She turned off her phone.

Violet hoped she would wake up and find this was a horrible nightmare, and she and Dimitri could laugh about it. But she knew it wasn't. She went through an entire box of tissues in a matter of hours that day, then, disgusted with her overflowing garbage bin and feeling guilty about the number of trees that had been cut down in order to soak up her tears, she switched to crying into a towel. The towel lasted about half a day before it was soaked through.

Her parents knocked on her door, but Violet told them in no uncertain terms to go away. Anna left meals outside her door that went untouched, even the *dolmades*.

Violet cried for two days and two nights, soaking a total of three crying towels, then fell asleep, exhausted.

She woke up disoriented, and as the reality of her life, and indeed the world, came flooding back to her, she hid under her duvet and willed the universe to simply disappear.

Dimitri, in the meantime, after not hearing from Violet for two full days, became increasingly distressed.

They usually exchanged texts every day and her lack of replies lately was disconcerting. He'd slept little the past few nights and when he did, he dreamed of swimming against strong currents and woke up thrashing in his bed.

Not sure what else to do, and needing desperately to make sure Violet was alright, he sent the obligatory text saying he was going out to assist someone in need; it seemed the closest available option. Besides, the police were unlikely to be patrolling the sleepy town of Sfinari. He knocked on Maria and Kosta's door, which was still slightly awkward, though less so than it had been before Violet's visit nearly a year ago now. Maria answered the door cautiously and Dimitri asked if she'd heard from Violet.

"No. I thought you two talked every day?" said Maria, surprised, and also worried about Dimitri's haggard appearance.

"Yes, we do. That's why I'm worried. Have you talked to Anna in the past two days?"

Maria hadn't. "I'm sure Violet's OK, she's with her parents. Even if her flight was cancelled, it'll be rescheduled soon. This can't go on forever."

Dimitri had a horrible sinking feeling in his stomach as Maria voiced that last thought.

"Would you mind giving me her mother's phone number? I don't have it. I just...want to make sure she's alright."

Dimitri looked like he was about to cry and Maria felt terrible for him. She wasn't supposed to have visitors right now, they were talking outside her door, and even that was breaking the current rules. But her maternal instincts were strong.

"Why don't you come in? I'll make you some food and we can call Anna together."

Dimitri only hesitated a moment. He was too worried about Violet to be concerned with lockdown regulations.

Maria served Dimitri some *spanakopita* and a leftover stuffed pepper. She made him a calming chamomile tea. Then she called her sister on speakerphone.

"Hello?" Anna's voice sounded hoarse, not like herself at all.

"Annoula, ti kanis? "

Anna paused for much longer than Maria was expecting and eventually said in Greek, "I'm OK Maria but I'm not sure about Violet."

"Dimitri is here," she said quickly, not wanting her sister to say anything about the couple without knowing he was, in fact, sitting beside her.

"Oh?" Anna was surprised. She knew the lockdown rules were strict in Greece.

Dimitri tried to say hello but found he had no voice.

"He hasn't heard from Violet for a few days and he's very worried. Is she alright?"

Again, Anna paused. "I'm not sure if she is," she said carefully.

Dimitri reached a hand up to his forehead, his elbow resting on the table.

"What do you mean? Is she there with you? At home?"

"Yes, she's here. But her flight was cancelled three days ago, and she's been in her room ever since. I...I've tried to go in but she's too upset. I've left food at her door but she just leaves it there, even the dolmades. I even made *halva* for her, with the expensive Greek honey from the deli. The only thing she took was a bottle of water." Anna was clearly crying, trying to sound normal over the phone.

Dimitri rested his forehead in his hand. Thinking of Violet crying alone in her room for days was unbearable, especially after everything she'd been through and how excited she'd been that she'd finally "figured her life out," as she put it. He wanted so badly to be with her, to comfort her and tell her it would all be OK. But he couldn't. There wasn't even a plane flying between their parts of the world.

Maria found her voice and spoke gently, "Annoula, don't cry, don't worry, we'll figure it out." She paused, not sure what the solution was. "Would she talk to Dimitri do you think?"

Dimitri looked up, not sure he could calm his emotions enough to speak. He wanted to be strong for Violet, he didn't want her to see him so upset. He wiped away a tear and tried to collect himself.

"I don't know. She tends to shut everyone out when she gets like this. You know, she was like this after...after Persephone, but she didn't cry so much." Anna paused. "I could knock on her door and tell her Dimitri's on the phone, but Dimitri, if she doesn't want to talk to you, please know it's not personal. I know how much she loves you."

Dimtri wiped away another tear. "OK," he managed to croak.

Anna knocked quietly on Violet's door.

"Violeta, Dimitri's on the phone. He's worried about you," Anna waited but there was no response. "I'm going to put my phone on your dresser, OK, and you can talk if you want to?"

Anna opened the door a crack and peeked in. Violet was completely covered in her duvet and Anna saw her move a little. She put the phone down on the dresser near the door.

Violet lay under her covers debating what to do. She didn't want to talk to anyone. She didn't want Dimitri to see or hear her like this. But she also didn't want him to be worried. Perhaps she was being selfish. Of course she was being selfish.

Maria left the room to give Dimitri some privacy, though she couldn't help but linger by the doorway, trying to pretend she wasn't listening.

Violet pulled back the covers, then pulled them up again, sighed, and threw them off awkwardly. She nearly fell over as she attempted to get out of bed. She hadn't been aware of how weak she'd become.

She walked slowly over to the phone and held it to her ear for a few moments before she managed to whisper, "Hello?"

Dimitri also took a moment before responding. "Hey honeybee," he said quietly, his voice cracking a little.

Violet was taken aback by the emotion in his voice. He'd always been such a calming and strong presence. "I'm sorry," she said.

"For what?"

"For not calling. Or texting."

"It's OK. I just wanted to know you were OK."

"I don't know if I am."

"Me neither." Dimitri took a deep breath. "Look, Violet, this sucks, I know it does. I hate it as much as you do, but I promise you, we will be together soon. As soon as we can. And you'll start your new life here soon. This is just a delay, OK? I'm not going anywhere and neither is Sfinari Bay."

A tiny hint of a smile crossed Violet's lips, "I'm not going anywhere either, which is sort of the problem."

Dimitri also managed a shadow of something resembling a smile. "Look, I know you might need some time, and I don't want to crowd you, Violet, but please, please, over the next little while, can you just send me something, just a text of an emoji, anything, just to say that you're hanging in there, please?"

Violet suddenly felt terrible for what she'd put Dimitri through. He'd always been so supportive to her and she'd completely shut him out in her misery-wallowing. "Dimitri, I'm so sorry. I can send you more than just an emoji. I'm sorry I was so selfish."

"I don't think you're selfish, Violet."

"I think I had a selfish few days of crying into towels. I should have texted you. I just...really didn't think you'd be so worried."

"Your mom is really worried too. We all just want to make sure you're OK." He paused and then added, "You cried into towels?"

"I...felt bad about how many tissues I got through. I thought a towel would be more...ecologically conscious."

She didn't mention there had in fact been three towels of tears.

"It's nice of you to think of the trees," said Dimitri, managing a faint smile.

"Can we video chat tomorrow?" Violet said quietly. "Once my puffy eyes are down a bit?"

Dimitri smiled with relief. "Yes, anytime, even the middle of the night here, just call me. There's not much going on here, or anywhere. And don't worry about how puffy your eyes are, OK?"

"OK."

Anna and Maria, both trying hard to pretend to not be listening, breathed sighs of relief.

Violet hung up and took a deep breath. She looked with disgust at the overflowing garbage bin of tissues and the sopping wet crying towels. She gave herself a pep talk: "Come on Violet, get it together. It's going to be OK. You're not going to lose him, or the life you have planned. It's an annoying delay and there's nothing you can do about it."

Violet finally exited her room and b-lined for the bathroom, where she washed her face with baking soda. The feeling of the water on her face made her realize how thirsty she was, and she drank from the sink for what felt like hours.

Finally, exiting the bathroom, Violet asked her mother if there were any *dolmades* left.

Chapter 6

The weeks that followed felt wholly unreal to Violet, as if the city had become the set of a post-apocalyptic Hollywood movie. The word "unprecedented" quickly became a cliché as people floated uneasily through a strange new world. The streets were quiet. The skies were quiet. The birds sang, perhaps wondering why all the humans suddenly weren't venturing out in their noisy metal transport machines. The weather turned warm and sunny, oblivious to the pandemic. Violet was reminded of how she felt after Persephone's death, as if the world kept on going but she was frozen in time as an observer. Now, it felt like the world was frozen and Violet was desperate to move forward.

The shops ran low on fruit and vegetables and toilet paper. Anna and Martin stocked up on canned and frozen food, pasta and rice. But there was still enough to eat, and life carried on, bringing out the best in some and the worst in others. Neighbours they'd never met shared toilet paper, while other neighbours swept store shelves clean, taking home car-loads of toilet paper they wouldn't have dreamed of sharing.

As summer approached, shops in Vancouver began to re-open, with endless hand sanitizer, mandatory masks, social distancing instructions, and security guards at the doors limiting the number of people allowed inside. Floor decals told people where to stand in the queues, and arrows dictated which way customers should walk down the aisles. Most people gradually went back to work, scowling at any fellow commuter who dared to pull their mask down below their nose. Violet's work contract, however, had ended, and with travel still suspended, there was no further work for her at the math institute. Had she been a permanent employee she might have been furloughed, or given some unnecessary tasks to work on at home, but she suspected it was pointless to ask for a new contract at a time like this.

Still, she remained hopeful that her move to Crete would become a reality in the coming months. She kept practicing her Greek. She went to the river and swam up and down, watching the faces in the rocks, their expressions somewhat sombre of late. The kingfisher kept hunting for fish and a merganser nested nearby, proudly showing Violet her three beautiful chicks. Several times a bald eagle soared overhead.

Violet and Dimitri chatted most days. The taverna had opened on May 25th, and Greece cautiously (or perhaps not cautiously enough) opened its doors to tourists in mid-June, subjecting some to mandatory testing and quarantine.

The rules around travel were confusing and shifted almost daily. The Canadian government still advised against non-essential international travel. But Greece's doors were open. If Violet had been allowed a tiny glimpse of the future, she would have most certainly booked a flight that summer. As it stood, however, it seemed an irresponsible and anxiety-provoking time to move, and surely by the fall things would feel more settled.

Over a video chat in June, they discussed the dilemma.

"Violet, of course I'm gonna say I want you to come. I really want you to come. But...you know, things are OK here right now, everything's open again, but we could go into a strict lockdown again at any time. Lots of people think the government's being too slack with letting in so many tourists, and we might have another spike in cases soon. It's not...a comforting place to be during lockdowns. And it's probably not a good time to start a business. I'd be happy for you to come, very happy, and of course you can live with me and I'll support you. And I'm sure your aunt and uncle would say the same. But...I know how much you want to find your own way, and finding your own way right now in Greece...it's just not the best time."

Violet sighed. "What if it gets worse? What if I don't come now, and then I can't come later? If there is a second wave like everyone says there'll be?"

"We don't know what's going to happen," said Dimitri, also sighing. "But, would you rather be in Canada with your parents for the second wave, or here in Greece with no work and having to send the authorities a text every single time you leave your home?"

"I wouldn't mind that if I was with you," said Violet, tearing up.

It broke his heart to discourage her from coming, but he genuinely wanted what was best for her. He'd found the lockdown in March difficult and unsettling. Despite the feeling that everyone was united in doing their best to curtail the spread of the virus, it had seemed a strange and silent world, shrunken down to the bare minimum of existence, with fear and unrest only just held at bay. And he worried things would get worse in Greece before they'd get better.

They shifted to talking about Violet coming in the fall, arriving in time for Christmas.

Anna, in the meantime, was busy setting up an online jewelry shop. Though her store had re-opened (with reduced hours), many people were now choosing to shop online, and always adaptable, she threw herself into this new endeavour. Violet helped her, but wouldn't let her mother pay her, knowing how much the shop was struggling. Anna figured she'd simply give Violet some extra money when she moved to Crete. She'd sadly laid off her two part-time employees, but assured them she would hire them back as soon as she could.

Violet didn't feel the lack of income as badly as she might have, due to her familial living arrangements and her father's tenured post at the university. As her contract had an end date, she didn't qualify for any of the Canadian government benefits many people gratefully claimed. She'd been thrifty all year, however, and had saved a good chunk of money, enough to make a start, she thought. There was nothing to spend money on at the moment anyway. Except of course baking soda, which was, thankfully, very affordable and not in short supply.

The summer passed in a slow strange dance; Violet felt as if she was on a holiday that had become a prison. She drifted, waiting, on endless standby. Nothing was fine and everything was fine at the same time. She still talked to Dimitri, but gradually their calls and texts became less frequent. They were both running out of things to say.

August came with its usual anxieties for Violet, and somehow the days all felt nearly the same, blurring the differences between months, weeks and days. The disquiet in the air seemed to blend with and dilute her own troubles. She went down to the river and thought about Persephone as she swam up and down, around the corner to the waterfall and back, as many times as she could until she was numb in her body and her mind.

What would Persephone have made of this strange new world they were floating through? Violet was sure she'd have weathered it with her usual practicality, adapted to online sessions and analyzed how different people were managing it all. She missed those conversations, when her best friend had challenged her and questioned the workings of the world and the human mind. Violet tried to find Persephone's voice in her mind but though she could hear the intonation, the colour, and the tones, she couldn't take in the words. She wasn't sure if she was losing her memory of Persephone or indeed, losing herself.

In late August, the province of Chania, just east of Kissamos, experienced an outbreak and restrictions were tightened locally. It felt uncomfortably close to home and Dimitri began to fear the worst.

When the second wave materialized in October, synchronized with the start of the Vancouver rain, Violet's spirits dropped again. The first day of the month had brought a disastrous flood on the Capilano River. The Cleveland Dam broke open with no warning and sent a massive torrent of water downstream, killing one fisherman and injuring several others. As soon as the news broke, Violet received a text from her ex-boyfriend, James. They hadn't been in touch in years, but he knew of her affinity for the river and the news had worried him. The text was followed quickly by a phone call from her mother.

Thankfully, Violet hadn't been there that day; she'd gone for a walk along the shores of Ambleside in West Vancouver, trying to squint hard enough to pretend it was Sfinari Bay. She was safe, but the incident certainly unsettled her. She could easily have been swimming in the river at the time and been swept away. The one place she'd always felt safe suddenly didn't feel safe anymore. It seemed like a bad omen.

Twenty days later, Violet read the news that Canadians were no longer allowed to enter Greece. Though she had a Greek passport, there were very few flights going anywhere in Europe, and she would have had to quarantine on arrival for two weeks. Dimitri had warned her a few weeks ago that he was sure another lockdown was imminent. They stopped talking about spending

Christmas together. Planning anything had ceased to make any sort of sense.

Violet continued to drift through the shapeless days, waiting and wondering and worrying. It had now been sixteen months since she'd seen Dimitri, after only spending a month in Crete. She still loved him, but her love felt increasingly abstract. They'd been apart so much longer than they'd been together, their romance started to feel like a dream to Violet. Their calls took on a slow, sad quality, as even Dimitri's optimism began to fade. Their worlds felt more and more disconnected.

As Dimitri had predicted, The Greek Prime Minister announced a second lockdown on November 5th, after a sudden and alarming rise in cases. There was no Tsiodras this time, and the earlier sense of a country united and well-managed through the pandemic had dissolved into a vague mistrust of the government and disregard for the regulations. Dimitri tried to text Violet about it but couldn't find the words. How on earth could he explain what it all felt like in his world, so far removed from hers, when it had been so long since they'd seen each other?

Violet went down to the river on what would have been Persephone's birthday, November 12th. Strangely, it coincided with the name day for "Melissa," her middle name. Dimitri sent her a text:

Hey honeybee, happy name day xo

That was it. Of course, he couldn't have known it was also Persephone's birthday, but Violet felt his absence from her life more acutely that day than ever. For his name day just two and a half weeks ago, Violet had sent Dimitri a card and a poem she'd written during her stay in

Crete. His reaction, however, had been somewhat muted, and certainly not what Violet had hoped for. It had been her attempt to rekindle their connection, and it had failed.

It was a cold drizzly day and the water was too frigid to swim in, even for a water nymph, so Violet simply sat by the running water in her yellow raincoat, hugging her knees into her chest and watching the river move slowly and freely down towards the sea.

Wingless

Feathers in the sea
and bones in the ground
cisterns painted with the ghosts of water

We watched a bee-eater swoop and call
and remembered when the earth shook
only yesterday and so long ago
again and again

A million wildflowers out of the corpses,
Zeus from the dead,
bees from the oxen.

Time on layers of time,
Jerusalem sage and discarded hymns,
our bones above their bones,
feathers on feathers,
and gravity laid across us all.

Still,
somehow,
here the hard earth crouches
resting, waiting
in the deafening stillness of abandoned memories.

"We are still here,"
I whisper

Wingless
but singing.

Chapter 7

Dimitri

Δημήτριος

Dimitri had always assumed Sifi would never return. After all, he'd been gone for seventeen years. So when he returned from checking on his mountain hives one morning in mid-October, and saw his father in the kitchen, sipping beer and reading the paper, Dimitri was sure he was having a nightmare.

"Kalimera Dimitri," his father said, as if he saw him every morning. Dimitri was silent, struck dumb by shock, which began to shift and rise up inside him as anger. "Aren't you happy to see me?"

Dimitri had no words. The room spun around him and he looked down, trying to regain his balance. The brown and white patterned tiles on the kitchen floor suddenly filled his field of sight, and he remembered looking down at those same tiles many years ago, on the night his father had left. He remembered feeling a flood of anger, not at his father, but at his mother, as his young mind had struggled to grasp the situation. She'd sent his father away. She was the culprit. Only now of course he knew she wasn't. He hadn't thought about that moment in so many years and the flood of rage and despair caught him off-guard.

"Get out," he growled through clenched teeth, still looking at the kitchen floor. His voice was quiet but charged with emotion.

Sifi paused for a moment, taking in his son's response, but then appeared unfazed. "Ah, come on Dimitri, that's not much of a welcome is it? Besides, your mother said I could stay."

Before Dimitri could respond he heard his mother's voice behind him. "Your father is back," she said simply.

Dimitri turned to face her, his eyes wet with tears as the dull ache of old wounds opened up into a torturous fury. *"Why? Why* is he back?" Dimitri spoke in a strange clenched whisper, keeping his back to Sifi.

"Dimitri, he's your father. He's my husband."

"My *father?"* Dimitri's voice began to rise and shake. "No. He is *not* my father! And how the *hell* can you call him your husband? He's been gone for nearly twenty fucking years! He cheated on you, he lied to all of us! Why have you taken him back?" Dimitri hadn't yelled at his mother since he'd been a teenager, and then only a handful of times. But the dam had been broken and the grief he thought he'd moved past years ago now poured out in a violent torrent of words.

"Shhh, Dimitri, calm down, it's OK."

"No! No! It's *not* OK! *I* don't want him here! *You* shouldn't want him here! After everything he's put you through, put us all through!"

"People change, Dimitri. The pandemic, you know, it put things into perspective for lots of people."

Sifi tried to speak. "Dimitri—"

"No! Do *not* talk to me! Ever again. You are dead to me." Dimitri half-turned his head to address his father but couldn't bring himself to look at him. His bitter words were spoken to the kitchen wall. Turning back to his mother, he shook his head and continued. "He hasn't changed. He's only come back now because Crete is safer than America." His volume had lowered but his voice continued to shake. "He's only looking out for himself, like he always has. I just thought you of all people, would know that."

Dimitri stormed past his mother to the front door. He raised a fist, intending to punch the wall, but somehow decided against it. He flung open the door and slammed it behind him, loud enough for the whole village to hear.

In his small white car, he drove on auto-pilot, far too fast down the main road and then the winding gravel track that led to Platanakia beach. He didn't bother to close the car door as he leapt out and ran towards his cave. But something changed his mind, and he stopped, instead stripping down to his underwear in the chilly October air and running into the autumnal sea. Whether from the cold, or his rage, Dimitri screamed as the cold water enveloped him.

He remembered another time in this same place, in another lifetime when he'd made love to Violet in the sea. He dove under the waves and swam along the shoreline, mimicking Violet's movements, which he'd memorized and often replayed in his mind. His face was wet with tears, or sea water, he wasn't sure which.

Things might have gone differently if Dimitri had managed to tell Violet about his father. But he simply couldn't, not on a phone call or even a video call, and the truth was he was running out of fight. In his efforts to be strong for her and protect her from further hurt, Dimitri was aware on some level that he was building a wall between them, but he wasn't sure how to stop it. Telling Violet that Sifi had reappeared felt like placing an impossible burden on her shoulders. Besides, he sensed that she had pulled away, ever so slightly.

When she'd sent him a poem and a card for his name day, only a week after his father had returned, he'd been distracted on their video call. He knew how hard it was for Violet to share her poetry, but the excitement and gratitude he would normally have felt in that moment simply eluded him. It wasn't that he didn't appreciate the poem or the gesture; it was a beautiful poem about Aptera and he'd carried it in his pocket everywhere since he'd received it. Unsurprisingly, however, he found himself unable to be his complete self with her while hiding his demons from her sight.

Dimitri usually spent winters in the family home as the little cottage wasn't properly heated, but with Sifi there now, he bought several small heaters and moved back into his modest abode, where he, like Violet so many miles away, drifted through the nebulous passage of time, trying to find something, anything, to provide a structure or a grounding for his days and nights. He walked the beach and watched the milky way on clear nights. He listened for his *yiayia's* voice in his mind, but she was strangely silent. He listened to his radio. His sisters called him from Iraklion, but he mostly didn't answer. Hearing their anger was too close a reflection of his own feelings and he couldn't bear it. For the first time in his life, his cottage, usually a place of sanctuary, now felt like a prison.

Chapter 8

Sfinari being a small village, everyone soon knew that Sifi had returned, including Maria, who quickly called her sister to pass on the news.

"Anna, Dimitris is living in his cottage down in the bay. It can't be warm there this time of year. He looks like a shadow of himself. I bring him meals sometimes, he looks very skinny."

"You always think everyone's skinny," Anna reminded her.

"Yes, yes, but I mean it Anna, he's not himself. I'm really worried about him."

Anna couldn't help but smile a little at her sister's one hundred-and-eighty-degree turn regarding Dimitri, but she sensed it wasn't the time for teasing. "I don't think he and Violet have been in touch much. I guess it's been so long since they've seen each other, and still no end in sight." Anna sighed. "I'm worried about Violet too. She just sits in her room watching TV."

"Well there's not much else to do at the moment, I suppose."

"Maria, do you think I should tell her? I really don't think Dimitris has told her. She'll be hurt that he didn't tell her, and it's not really any of my business, is it?"

"Anna, if she finds out later we all knew and no one told her, I think she'll be very angry."

"True," replied Anna, already dreading the conversation she knew she'd have to have with her daughter. "It's just I'm trying very hard to give her space and be respectful and not meddle. It's so unbelievably hard, Maria, I just want to fix everything and see her happy again."

"I know, we all want that."

Anna waited a few weeks, hoping Dimitri might tell Violet himself. She asked casually several times if Violet had heard from Dimitri, but her daughter just shook her head and said little.

On Friday, November 13th, as Violet helped her parents clear the dinner table, Anna asked again, sure that Dimitri would have been in touch on her name day.

"He sent me a text," replied Violet, loading her plate and cutlery into the dishwasher.

Anna didn't want to pry but needed to know whether he'd told her about his father. "Did he...say anything? About how he's doing?" she asked cautiously.

Violet shook her head and disappeared into her room. Anna and Martin finished tidying up. Martin knew the situation as well, but had, like Anna, hoped that Dimitri would eventually share the news with Violet. But they were fairly certain he hadn't. Anna took a deep breath, walked down the hallway, and knocked on Violet's door.

"Violeta?"

"Mmm?" came a distracted reply. Violet was sitting on her bed, watching a movie on her laptop that she wasn't really paying attention to. It kept playing as Anna entered and sat down next to her daughter.

"Can you pause that for a moment?" asked Anna gently.

Violet looked up. She could tell from her mother's tone something wasn't right. Anna looked at her daughter, trying to read her thoughts.

"Maria told me something a few weeks ago," Anna began. "I wasn't sure if Dimitri had told you."

"Told me what?" asked Violet flatly, not enjoying the suspense.

"Apparently Sifi is back." Anna paused, watching her daughter carefully. "I know you haven't been in touch much with Dimitri, and you don't need to tell me anything, Violet, but I thought you'd want to know."

Violet was silent and stared at her laptop screen, showing a frozen scene of a man on a ship in a storm, yelling something at someone. Anna sat with her and waited.

"When did he come back?" Violet finally asked quietly.

"In October. I'm not sure exactly when, but it was a few weeks ago now that she called. I didn't tell you right away because I thought Dimitri might tell you, once he'd had a bit of time."

Violet thought back to the video call when he'd opened her poem and hadn't shown the enthusiasm she'd hoped for. Why hadn't he just told her? Did he not want to share things with her? Did he not want her to know?

"Why didn't he tell me?" Violet meant to think it but said it out loud, as she often did.

"I don't know," said Anna honestly. She sighed. "It's been a long time since you've seen each other. Some things are hard to say over a phone call or even a video chat. And he probably is trying to protect you."

"From what? From trusting him? Why would he hide something so big from me?" Violet hadn't meant to show any emotion, but it poured out of her. She knew they'd been drifting apart, but it now felt like he'd pushed her away.

"I know Dimitri is sort of American in lots of ways, but he's very much a Greek man deep down, Violet. He probably wants to be strong all the time for you. A lot of men, they feel they need to hide their vulnerability, especially from the woman they love."

Violet shook her head. "I don't think I'm the woman he loves anymore." She broke down in tears and Anna held her daughter very close.

"Shhh, it's OK," whispered Anna, stroking her daughter's hair as if she were a small child.

After a mostly sleepless night spent deliberating, Violet called Dimitri the next morning. To her surprise, he answered. He sounded sleepy.

"I'm sorry if I woke you. I thought it was 7pm there?"

"Yes, maybe, I don't know." Dimitri had been living in a haze since his father had arrived, sleeping and eating at random intervals. He wasn't sure what day it was, and had answered his phone thinking he was still dreaming. Their last phone call had been a few weeks ago, on his name day and it had been strained and awkward. The last one before that had been a month prior.

"Look, Dimitri, I don't want to bother you. I know we haven't seen each other in ages and you don't have to tell me things if you don't want to. But my mom told me about Sifi yesterday." She paused. Dimitri was silent. "I just want to know that you're OK," her voice broke despite her best efforts to control it.

"Honeybee," Dimitri said, tears falling down his face. He couldn't find his voice to say anything more.

Violet waited. "Are you OK, Dimitri? It's OK if you're not OK you know."

Dimitri tried to collect himself and willed his mind to form a sentence. "I'm so angry, Violet, with my dad for coming back and with my mom for taking him back." He paused and they were silent for some time. "I'm sorry I didn't tell you. I didn't want to burden you, and I just...I couldn't really talk about it."

Violet sighed. "Look, Dimitri, you don't need to protect me, not from everything. I know we're not exactly a couple anymore, but I still care about you and I'm here if you want to talk about anything. You were there for me a lot when I was going through some difficult stuff. And maybe, when I can finally come back, whenever that is, you know, we'll see how we feel?"

Dimitri wasn't sure if Violet was breaking up with him or if they were already broken up, or if she was saying she still wanted to be with him when she could finally move there. "Do you still want to move here?" he managed to ask.

"Yes," said Violet resolutely. "Absolutely."

"I did really love your poem by the way, Violet."

"Oh?" She hadn't expected any mention of her poem.

"I have it in my pocket all the time. And I still have dreams of you in the sea."

Violet teared up but tried to sound strong. "I promise you'll see me in the sea again one day."

"I hope so."

Travel restrictions in British Columbia were tightened in mid-November, with people no longer allowed to even travel within the province. Christmas plans all over the country and were cancelled, if they were ever made at all.

Of course, there were those who chose to ignore the advice, particularly in Violet's part of the world, where rules were rarely enforced. In typical Canadian fashion, the kind-hearted Dr. Bonnie simply asked people nicely not to travel, hoping they'd be sensible and obey. But many people didn't. The retired couple who lived across the street from Violet's family caught the last flight out to Mexico in January, tired of the restrictions and claiming it was essential for their health that they go. Violet was furious with their self-righteousness.

It was true, she could have caught a plane that winter, said she was moving for essential purposes, quarantined on arrival and somehow made it work. But she had no fight left in her, and it definitely didn't feel like the time to set up a business in Greece, a risky endeavour at the best of times. And though she still cared for Dimitri, she wasn't sure how she'd feel if and when she saw him again. Or, for that matter, how he'd feel. So much had changed since their month together.

Violet wondered if there was indeed a universe in the multiverse in which the pandemic had been delayed just a few months, and she and Dimitri were currently together, nestled in his cottage by the sea, helping each other navigate through the strange new world of lockdowns and restrictions.

In Greece, the quarantine eased slightly over Christmas and though there were small cautious family celebrations in Sfinari, Dimitri didn't join any of them. His mother and Maria both came by but he didn't answer the door. They left him parcels of Christmas food: pork, *melomakarona, kourampiedes.*[45] He spent Christmas alone, dreaming of Violet swimming in the sea, but not finding the strength to call her when he woke. The taverna was closed and the bees were quiet this time of year, hunkered down and keeping warm, huddled together. He fed them a paste of icing sugar, water and garlic. And like everyone else, he waited.

---

[45] Butter cookies covered in icing sugar

Chapter 9

Nefeli

Νεφέλη

Nefeli had been in love with Dimitri ever since she could remember. Her family lived in Sfinari, and they'd spent plenty of summer days down at the bay, sampling food and drink from both tavernas. Five years younger than Dimitri, by the time she was fourteen and he was nineteen, she knew she would marry him one day. She just had to wait, she was sure.

Nefeli had watched Dimitri have a handful of flings with visiting tourists over the years, content that when he was ready to settle, he'd finally notice her. She wasn't in a rush. However, the spring that Violet arrived, Nefeli began to worry just a little. She could see in his dark eyes that Dimitri was madly in love with the small pale Canadian girl who swam in the cold sea several times a day. This girl was so completely different from Nefeli, possibly even her opposite, that she began to doubt whether a man who loved this mousy-haired outsider could ever love her.

But still, she watched and waited and kept hoping. She heard rumours the pale girl was planning on moving here. How odd. People didn't move from the Americas over to somewhere like Crete.

Nefeli was the youngest of five children and the only one who wasn't yet married. At twenty eight, her very traditional parents were starting to worry that their pretty but painfully shy youngest daughter might be approaching her sell-by date. In the pre-pandemic days, they'd regularly invited potential suitors over for dinner, but Nefeli turned away each and every one of them, politely but surprisingly firmly. She knew where her destiny lay, and it wasn't with them.

When the pandemic hit, Nefeli felt the same fear and trepidation as many others. However, she also felt a strong sense of relief; relief because she knew the fair-skinned Canadian wouldn't be able to return and steal Dimitri away from her. And also because her parents would now finally have to stop inviting potential husbands over for dinner.

When Nefeli heard Sifi was back in town, she wasn't sure whether this was good or bad news. However, when she heard Dimitri had moved back into his little cottage down in the bay, she spent more and more time walking along the beach and up the headland, sure that eventually he would see her, they could finally speak without anyone else around, and he would see he was meant to marry her, and not the colourless skinny girl.

Chapter 10

Dimitri had been drinking too much, something he wasn't usually prone to. His world had shrunk down to nothing and with restrictions reinstated from early January, he couldn't even go for the long drives that usually were his panacea in difficult times. His bees were wintering in their hives and required little from him this time of year. The days blurred into one another and he wasn't sure if he still slept at night or during the day. He ate the food Maria brought for him and drank coffee. His mother called him periodically but he usually didn't answer. His sisters had stopped trying to get in touch. Sometimes, when the weather wasn't too bad, he sent a text to the authorities saying he was going out for exercise, and walked along the beach, or over the headland to Platanakia Bay. But these walks made him think of Violet, and he usually went home feeling worse than when he'd left.

One cold but sunny day in early February, his mother came down to the cottage with several home-cooked meals and suggested they go for a walk. Dimitri could tell it wasn't a question. Despoina could smell the *raki* on his breath. She was worried.

Sifi had told her to leave Dimitri alone, that he would come round and re-join them in the house in due course. And Sifi wasn't easy to stand up to. But months passed and Dimitri stayed in his cold little cottage, and eventually Despoina told her husband firmly she was going to check on their son. She sent the obligatory text to say she was going out for exercise, or maybe she said was going out to help someone in need. It didn't seem to matter much these days.

They walked along the path behind the beach, where they were sheltered from the worst of the wind by the row of trees, their branches pulled and shaken like the strained limbs of tired dancers.

"Dimitri, we're worried about you. You don't look well."

Dimitri said nothing and kept walking.

Despoina sighed. "I know you're upset about your father, and I understand why, but he does love you, Dimitri."

Dimitri looked straight ahead, not changing his facial expression. "Is that why he hasn't come down here once to check on me? Is that why he left when I was sixteen? Because he *loves* me?"

His sarcasm was biting, the harshness in his voice like a burn on Despoina's skin. It wasn't the son she'd raised speaking to her, it was surely a stranger, a thinner, haggard, angry version of Dimitri.

"He left because I told him to leave. I shouldn't have done that. It was selfish of me."

Dimitri stopped walking and turned to face his mother. "Selfish of you? To send away a man who treated you like shit and lied to his family? Who made promises and then broke them, over and over again? How is that selfish?"

"Because it meant he left all of us. I thought we'd all be better off without him, but it was foolish of me to think I could raise all of you all on my own. I see now you needed him."

"No, mom, that wasn't selfish of you. We were better off without him around. Yes, I needed a father. But not *him.*"

"Dimitri, we don't get to choose our parents. Believe me, I know your father isn't perfect. I'm not a fool, though I know you think I am." Despoina sighed. "You didn't see how things were here after Ioannis died. How horribly he was treated by everyone. For something he couldn't have prevented in a million years. He was made to feel responsible for the death of an innocent child, a family friend. How do you think that felt for him?"

"That's not an excuse," said Dimitri quietly but firmly, as they began walking once again, more slowly than before.

"I never said it was an excuse. It's an explanation, at least part of an explanation, for why he turned out the way he did. When everyone around you thinks you're a rotten person, you start to feel like a rotten person.

He was always running from that blame and never getting away from it."

"So what does that have to do with him cheating on you? Multiple times?" They were standing behind the last pine tree in the row, reluctant to go beyond it and into the cold wind.

Despoina sighed. "I can't pretend to know your father's mind exactly. But people are complicated, and when they're unhappy they do stupid things. Things they think will make them feel better but end up making them feel worse, like drinking too much." She looked accusingly at her son, but he ignored the reference.

Dimitri shook his head. "I don't buy any of this, Mom. You make it sound like he had no control over events, no choice, but he did. He chose to be unfaithful, even when he saw how much it hurt you. How could you possibly forgive him for that and let him back into your life?"

"It takes a lot of energy to hold a grudge, Dimitri, and it will slowly eat away at you. I realize your father may leave again at some point, and I realize he's probably here for the reasons you so eloquently pointed out back in October. But while he's here, and he's my husband, I'm not going to turn him away."

Dimitri was surprised. He'd wrongly assumed his mother was being naive, that she was setting herself up to be hurt once again by Sifi, but he realized now she was much stronger and cannier than he'd given her credit for. She understood the sort of man he was, and she stood by him because he was her husband. Dimitri wasn't sure if he agreed with her decision but at least he could respect it.

"Why didn't you come here sooner?" he asked quietly, looking down at the hard soil.

Despoina sighed. "I did come over Christmas, but you didn't answer your door. And your father thought it would be better to leave you alone. We thought you'd change your mind and come home."

"He doesn't always know best, Mom."

"I know. I'm sorry. I miss you, Dimitri." Dimitri nodded, unable to reply. "Look, why don't you at least try and talk to your father. He's not a monster, and he does want to spend some time with you." She paused, then added, "Don't you remember any of the good times you had with him? In California at the beach? Here, when he showed you how to keep bees?" She pointed over to his hives. "It wasn't all bad. Don't forget that."

Dimitri was silent for a few moments, then said pensively, "I feel like the father I had as a child and the man I see as an adult are two different people. I miss the first one and I despise the second one."

"Everyone is a mix of good and bad, Dimitri. Depending on our point of view, we see more of one or the other."

Two days later, Dimitri called his father.

"Dimitri, *ti kanis?*"

"I'm...not great," he said honestly. Dimitri had stopped drinking after his talk with his mother, but his spirits had no reason to be anything but low.

"Oh?" said his father, feigning surprise.

"Dad, you know I'm not doing well. Why—" Dimitri stopped himself. He'd been going to ask, "Why are you here?" but realized he already knew the answer to the question and it would only make Sifi defensive. "Why did you leave?"

Sifi was silent for a few moments. Dimitri waited.

"Your mother asked me to leave."

"Why did she ask you to leave?"

"You know why."

"I want to hear it from you."

Sifi, again, was silent. But Dimitri had all the time in the world.

"I...had an affair."

"Why did you have an affair?"

"Christ, what is this? Twenty questions?"

"It's not a lot to ask, Dad. In fact, I probably have a lot more than twenty questions for you."

"You want to know why I had an affair?"

"Yes, actually why you had multiple affairs."

"Well, it's complicated. Married life is complicated."

"You know what's complicated? It's complicated when your dad leaves when you're sixteen and no one tells you why, and you find out later he had an affair, and that wasn't his first one, and you ask your dad why and he tells you it's complicated. Just answer the fucking question." Dimitri didn't raise his voice, though it shook with emotion and he spoke through gritted teeth.

Sifi thought for some time. The thing was, he wasn't sure why he'd had affairs. He wasn't the type who tended to reflect on things and untangle his emotions. He just *did* things.

"I don't know," he finally said, which was at least an honest answer.

"You don't know?" Dimitri was exasperated. "How can you not know? You get married in the Orthodox Church, you promise God you'll love and support your wife unconditionally, then you choose to break that promise, to hurt your wife and your children...I mean, *really* hurt your whole family by cheating on your wife, not just once, but over and over, and you don't know *why?*"

"No." Sifi searched for words, feeling very much out of his comfort zone. "I mean, sometimes things seem like a good idea at the time, and you realize later they weren't."

"And then you do it again?" Dimitri was losing his patience.

"Look Dimitri, this stuff had nothing to do with you—"

Dimitri cut him off. "It had *everything* to do with me. And my sisters, your daughters! Would you want them to be treated the way you've treated Mom?" He paused briefly, "When you cheated on her, you betrayed all of us, the whole family. Didn't you think of that?"

"Well, no...it wasn't about you."

Dimitri let out a flat frustrated growl and tried to pull himself together.

"Dimitri, look, I'm sorry. I didn't want to hurt you. I didn't want to leave you or your sisters. But, your mother and I, we couldn't work out our differences. You'll see when you're married, it's complicated sometimes."

"You *made* it complicated! Dad, I'm not an idiot. I might not have been married but I've been in love. The choices you made were yours, you don't get to hide behind the fact that it was complicated."

Sifi voiced a long sigh. He wasn't sure what else to say to Dimitri. "Dimitri, you remember when I showed you how to take care of the bees?"

"Yes, I remember."

"We had some good times didn't we?"

"Yes Dad, which made it harder when you left."

Both men were tired of arguing.

"Your mother says you're in love with a pale Canadian girl." Sifi was trying to bond with his son but it backfired. Dimitri didn't want to talk about Violet with anyone, least of all his father. He hung up the phone and went out into the drizzly afternoon to walk along the beach.

Chapter 11

Despoina

Δέσποινα

D espoina had overheard her husband's phone call with Dimitri, and she could tell it hadn't gone well. As she peeled potatoes in the kitchen she sighed and wondered whether she should in fact have turned Sifi away when he'd returned. After all, she'd sent him away before, and with good reason.

But they were still married, and, despite her years in America, Despoina had retained many traditional Greek values, including a strong sense of duty to her husband. Her independent spirit often battled with her old-fashioned values, and when Sifi re-appeared on her doorstep, she felt this struggle rise up within her. But she also remembered a time many years ago when Sifi had been someone very different, or at least, he'd seemed very different to her.

Despoina had grown up in Kissamos, and her family often went to Sfinari beach at the weekends. Sifi had always been the most handsome man in the surrounding towns and she could hardly believe it when, as a teenager, he began to notice her. Of course, she knew that he was blamed for the death of a child a few years earlier, but having heard the story many times, Despoina was unconvinced that Sifi could have saved the young boy.

There had of course, been other warning signs: namely, his confidence that bordered on egotism and his reputation as a womanizer. Though only eighteen, Despoina was perceptive and certainly wasn't blind to these traits, but she was sure it was all a front to protect himself from the judging eyes and condemnation that seemed to follow him everywhere in the village and even the province. Besides, when his gaze fell on her, she felt like the luckiest and most beautiful woman in the world. He was different with her, she could sense his softer side that he kept hidden from most people.

Despoina couldn't recall what they'd talked about as they began to spend time together, walking along the beaches around Kissamos and Sfinari. But she remembered laughter, so much laughter. She remembered games where he chased her into the waves and then dove underwater, suddenly startling her by grabbing her ankles.

And of course she remembered their first kiss like it was yesterday. It had been a warm August evening. She'd been wearing a red and white dress that trailed almost to the ground. She could recall with striking clarity the nervous exhilaration of the moment he'd turned to her and slowly leaned down to gently press his lips to hers. It had been her first kiss, and the truth was he was the only man she'd ever kissed, and the only man she'd ever thought about kissing. Even after she'd sent him away, many years later, she'd never had any desire for anyone else. She'd only been thirty-six at the time and she could have asked Sifi for a divorce and perhaps remarried. But it simply wasn't in her.

She wasn't sure of the exact moment she'd stopped loving him. But certainly it had been during their time in America. She had never really felt comfortable there; the country seemed to her to be hard and unyielding, open on a superficial level, but underneath that, it expected everyone to fit into its mold. She'd learned English well enough to communicate with customers at the cafe they ran near the beach, and go about her daily tasks, but beyond that, she had no interest in the language. It always felt awkward to her, full of broken rules and strange spellings. She eventually gave up correcting the locals when they pronounced her name "Despoyna," despite the numerous times she'd reiterated that the "o" was silent.

She'd initially included some Greek delicacies on the cafe menu, but quickly realized there was no demand for these in California. People wanted burgers and hot dogs, milkshakes and ice cream and soda. There was no room for expansion in the likes and dislikes of these people who were utterly convinced they lived in the best country in the world, though many had never been abroad at all. Despoina, to be fair, didn't put any effort into making friends; she had no idea how to connect with the people she found herself in the midst of.

Still, she'd tried her best, especially as Sifi seemed to settle in as if he'd always belonged in America. She gave him three children, and for awhile, everything was alright. She watched her children grow up speaking perfect

American English, while making sure they spoke Greek at home, and also teaching them to read and write in the language of her homeland. Her first real fight with Sifi had revolved around this. He'd said there was no point in their children learning Greek; it was one thing to speak it a little at home, but it certainly wasn't worth spending time teaching them to read and write it. English was the language of the future, they wouldn't need Greek. But Despoina refused to budge on this.

"Don't you want them to be able to talk to their grandparents, to write them letters? What if we move back to Crete one day? We might be living in America, but we're still Greek, Sifi."

Sifi had stormed out and returned drunk at 2am. Despoina was sure, in retrospect, that this had been the first night he'd cheated on her. From that moment, she felt the love between them slowly diminish and contort into a sad tolerance of one another, punctuated with painful arguments that she tried to prevent their children from hearing.

Ten years after this first argument, Despoina's loneliness and longing for the island and the culture she'd left behind pushed her to tell Sifi she was moving back to Crete with their children. She knew it was a risky move. And she knew he had as much right to the children as she did, but she felt she had nothing to lose and simply couldn't spend another year in this country with its disproportionate sense of self-importance. She was lonely. Besides, Sifi's parents were getting older and his siblings had moved away; someone should step up and help out at their taverna. Surely her husband would understand that.

Sifi had initially raged at Despoina, yelling every obscenity under the sun. She listened calmly. He'd lost his power over her and she felt nothing anymore when he was angry with her. He stormed out and disappeared for three days. Despoina was unfazed. She booked herself and her children onto a flight in a month's time and began to pack up their things. She told the children vaguely that their father was away for a little while, and that he'd return and join them in Crete, though she had no idea whether he would or not.

Sifi eventually returned looking broken and exhausted. Despoina said little to him, besides asking him to look into selling the cafe. He simply nodded. He knew he'd been defeated. And he didn't want to lose his children.

Returning to Crete had at first felt like the fresh start they'd needed. Despoina had visibly relaxed the moment they stepped off the plane in Chania, and Sifi couldn't help but see a hint of the striking young woman he'd fallen in love with years ago on the island beaches they'd returned to. The children took some time to adapt and settle, of course. It was a very different world for them, and Despoina remembered Dimitri in particular, seeming restless and lost. When Sifi started keeping bees again, she watched them bond, and saw Sifi re-gaining his connection with his childhood in Sfinari.

Life soon settled into a new, quieter rhythm, and while Despoina wouldn't have said she was in love with Sifi at that point, she at least rediscovered some of the traits that had drawn her to him all those years ago. Briefly, there was laughter again. Of course, there remained a certain tension between them and the Daskalakis, but everyone else seemed to have forgotten Sifi's supposed role in the tragedy all those years ago.

Despoina had hoped that things might carry on in this way, and indeed they did for several years. But Sifi, it seemed, began to grow restless. Perhaps he missed America, or perhaps the ever-present blame from their neighbours began to wear away at him. He started drinking just a little too much, and gradually began to disappear for hours and then days.

Despoina, by now, recognized the signs that her husband was having an affair. She knew what was happening long before his bees swarmed and left. Dimitri, now a teenager, did his best to catch the swarms, but managed only to receive several stings for his efforts. Despoina comforted him and applied ice, then honey and thyme to the stings. In response to his questions, she said she knew nothing about bees and why they might suddenly act in such a way. It was a lie of course, but a gentle one meant to protect her son.

She ignored Sifi's behaviour for as long as she could. After all, her heart didn't belong to him anymore; she didn't mind turning a blind eye, but when it began to affect their children, anger and frustration rose up inside of her.

After eight weeks, with Dimitri and his sisters beginning to ask questions she couldn't answer, Despoina finally confronted Sifi when he returned home late one night. Even at that point, though she knew there would be an argument, she hadn't planned on sending him away. All she wanted was for him to see sense and to be a father to their children. But Sifi had had too much to drink to be remotely reasonable. And Despoina, this time, couldn't keep calm, and couldn't hold her resentment at bay. The confrontation escalated and the scene became a blur of tears and suffering.

She couldn't remember exactly what was said, or how she'd told him to leave, or why he'd agreed to it. She only remembered a horrible seething pain so extreme she was sure it eclipsed her very self. She sobbed for hours, even after Sifi left. The children had woken up, though Despoina had confronted him outside, hoping they wouldn't hear. She remembered Dimitri's face, asking what was happening and where his dad had gone, and she couldn't even find a word of a reply through her sobs.

Despoina sighed as she recalled all this in the same house she'd sent him away from all those years ago. She certainly hadn't forgotten the wounds he'd inflicted on her, but, as the years passed, she simply didn't have the energy to focus on the suffering anymore. In fact, she hadn't properly thought about that episode in years. It had drained her at the time, and dwelling on it would have caused her to waste away.

Somehow, as time passed, perhaps out of self-preservation, her daydreams turned more and more to the long-ago joy of their falling in love, and she reflected little on the difficult times that had followed. Gradually, the despair of their lost love faded like an old dress in the sunlight. She hadn't forgotten it, but its intensity had dulled.

So when Sifi turned up at her door that October, Despoina didn't only see the Sifi who had cheated on her and hurt her so many times, the Sifi she'd sent away on the worst night of her life. She also saw a tired middle-aged man, a lonely man, and somewhere behind that, the Sifi who had kissed her tenderly on the beach that night so many years ago.

While she certainly didn't love him anymore, she felt a certain nostalgic tenderness towards him that, coupled with a sense of obligation, had made it impossible for her to simply turn him away. She was wise enough to keep her heart guarded of course; after all, she knew him well and knew that, despite his words of contrition, he hadn't really changed. She was resigned to who he was. But, like Dimitri, she remembered another version of Sifi, a fun-loving and adventurous soul, charming and handsome, a man to whom her younger self had willingly given her mind, body and soul.

Chapter 12

When Dimitri saw Nefeli walking towards him on Sfinari Beach, he actually thought for a moment she was an apparition. He'd just had a frustrating conversation his father, and he wasn't thinking clearly. It was a misty and chilly day, and with the nation in lockdown, who else would be walking along the shore?

As he grew closer, he recognized her. He hoped to just nod and pass her by, but she smiled and walked towards him, as if she'd expected to find him here today.

"*Yia su* Dimitri."

"*Yia su* Nefeli."

Their families knew each other well, they weren't strangers. They usually saw each other at events such as weddings or Carnival celebrations, or Nefeli would come eat at the taverna with her family. They'd never actually had a conversation. Dimitri tried to keep walking but she simply turned and walked with him.

"Do you usually walk on days like this?" she asked quietly. She was shy and small talk didn't come easily to her. But she knew she had to make the most of this chance.

"No," said Dimitri, not in the mood for company at all, yet unsure how to shake off Nefeli without being rude.

They walked on in silence and Dimitri wondered how long she would accompany him. They were allowed to walk in groups of two people, but Nefeli was staying very close beside him and he felt mildly uncomfortable. After a few minutes, the awkward silence became too much for Dimitri and he made an effort at casual conversation. "What brings you down here on such a grey day?"

"I like it here. I like the mist. It makes everything look like a dream-world, like everything is a ghost."

Dimitri didn't reply, still wishing he was on his own.

"Dimitri, do you believe in fate?" she asked suddenly.

"I don't know. Do you?" He was too tired to reflect on things lately, and he had no idea what he believed in anymore.

"Yes. I do."

"Oh?" Dimitri feigned interest.

"I think we were fated to meet on this beach today."

"Were we?"

"Well, what are the chances that we would both be down here on a day like today?"

If Dimitri had known how many times in the past four months Nefeli had walked along the beach and around the bay, he would have known that the chances were indeed very high. But he didn't. And Nefeli had no intention of telling him.

After that day, Nefeli began to knock on Dimitri's door every few days, inviting him out for walks. If he hadn't been so lonely, it would have almost certainly have been annoying.

Nefeli was not at all the type of woman Dimitri was usually attracted to. She was the complete opposite of Violet, demure and dark and gentle, whereas Violet was fiery and full of laughter and surprises. But Dimitri wasn't looking for another Violet; indeed he was sure there wasn't another Violet anywhere in the world.

With his ego bruised from Violet's withdrawal (which he knew on some level he was at least partly responsible for), he couldn't help but be flattered by Nefeli's attentions. And while Violet remained in another distant world, pretty Nefeli inched her way into Dimitri's affections.

As her visits became more frequent, Dimitri began to look forward to seeing her, their walks the only hint of light in his otherwise dark and repetitive world. She had a beautiful smile and large grey eyes, the colour of stone. Her long black hair fell thickly over her shoulders. Their conversations tended to be light and undemanding.

Once she asked Dimitri about his father and he found it impossible to speak to her about him. Sensing his reticence, she changed the subject. Maybe she'd broached it too soon. He'd open up to her in time, she was sure.

Dimitri, for his part, was sure he hadn't meant to kiss Nefeli. It seemed to just happen on its own. He was lonely, she was pretty and she was *there*. She was a nice girl, the kind of girl any mother would be happy for their son to marry, especially if their mother was a Greek mother with traditional values. Nefeli was the sort of woman who would be a standard "good wife;" she'd have babies, cook for them, raise them well, obey her husband. No one in Sfinari would have thought she and Dimitri would ever make a match.

When Nefeli's parents found out that on her long walks, she wasn't alone, but was in fact walking with Dimitri, they were more than a little concerned. Nefeli assured them that Dimitri's intentions were honourable, but her father, Aleksandros, was annoyed.

If Dimitri was spending time with his daughter, holding her hand, kissing her even, then either he was thinking of an engagement, or was simply dishonouring his daughter and their whole family. But Dimitri hadn't come by to ask his permission to marry Nefeli, which didn't bode well. Their families had been friends and neighbours for generations, so it was strange that Dimitri would behave in such a disrespectful way. Confused and irked, he called Dimitri.

"Dimitri, I hear from Nefeli you've been spending time together, walking along the beach. Is that true?"

"Yes," replied Dimitri, his body tensing at Aleksandros' tone. He'd forgotten until now, or perhaps he'd chosen to forget, how his walks with Nefeli would be perceived by her very traditional family.

"And are your intentions toward my daughter honourable?" asked Aleksandros, his voice rising and sounding strained.

Dimitri, of course, couldn't say no. He liked Nefeli and he respected her and her family, so saying his intentions were "dishonourable" didn't feel like an option. "Yes, of course," he replied, feeling as if someone else was talking; it didn't seem to be his own voice at all anymore.

"Good," grunted Aleksandros. "So, of course you want to ask my permission to marry my daughter then?"

Dimitri's head spun. He had no intention of marrying Nefeli. He'd been enjoying her company, it was true. And he had kissed her once or twice. But somehow he'd forgotten what that would mean to her family. He was silent so long Aleksandros repeated the question.

"My permission? My blessing? Why haven't you asked?"

Dimitri took a deep breath. "I'm sorry. I forgot myself." He tried to think of a way out of the situation, but his mind had gone blank. "I...would like to ask your permission...to marry...your daughter." Dimitri barely managed to speak the words. What on earth was he saying? In his mind he saw Violet asleep in his bed, Violet swimming off the same beach he'd walked with Nefeli, Violet huddled against him in his cave the night before she'd left. The memories had mostly turned to dull shadows but for a moment they appeared unexpectedly illuminated.

"Yes, of course," replied Aleksandros, relieved. "We look forward to having you as our son-in-law."

"Thank you," Dimitri managed to say quietly before he hung up the phone. He felt sick to his stomach. It seemed that things were happening, not *for* him, but rather *to* him while he was unable to move or exercise any autonomy. It reminded him of being on a horrible sickly fairground ride as a child in California. He'd waited in a long queue to go on the roller coaster, but, once strapped in and moving, he'd felt unbelievably nauseous and frightened. Yet there was nothing he could do except wait it out until the end.

At first, Dimitri thought he'd simply talk to Nefeli, explain there had been a misunderstanding, and that though he enjoyed their time together, he couldn't possibly be the husband she deserved. But Sfinari being a tiny village, word quickly spread that Dimitri and Nefeli were engaged.

Everyone was surprised. Most people knew that Dimitri had been pining for Violet for the past twenty-two months. A few people might have seen him walking with Nefeli in the bay, but they shook their heads at the thought of a possible romance between the two. They were far too different, and Nefeli was certainly nothing like Violet. Dimitri, having spent twelve years in America was viewed as very modern and liberal in the town, whereas Nefeli's family were very religious and traditional. Dimitri was (or had been) charming and sociable, whereas Nefeli was a shy wallflower, easily not noticed in a room full of people, despite her quiet beauty.

"Oh well," they shrugged. "Who knew, opposites attract. I guess the pale Canadian girl isn't coming back after all."

But Maria of course, didn't shrug. When she heard about the engagement, she protested that it couldn't possibly be true. Everyone knew Dimitri was in love with Violet. Violet still planned on coming back. They'd had a bit of a delay of course, but Dimitri wouldn't do that to her, surely.

Maria marched down to Dimitri's cottage and knocked on the door. They were still in lockdown and she probably should have called instead, but some conversations need to be had in person. Maria didn't waste time with pleasantries.

"Dimitri, what's this I hear about you and Nefeli?" she asked accusingly.

Dimitri took a deep breath and looked away to his left, willing the conversation (and the situation) away. He hadn't even seen Nefeli since the conversation with her father. "Maria, I'm not sure how it happened but it seems to have happened."

"What happened? What do you mean you don't know how it happened? Talk sense, Dimitri!"

Dimitri looked down and shuffled awkwardly from one foot to the other. "We were just going for walks. I was alone here. She's a nice girl. Then before I knew it, her father asked me if my intentions were honourable. I couldn't say no, but when I said yes, he assumed that I wanted to...marry her."

"So, you need to talk to her, call off the engagement. We all know you love Violet, Dimitri. You can't marry Nefeli."

"I've been trying to call Nefeli, she won't answer. And Violet and I...it's been so long since we've seen each other."

"Does she know what's been going on?"

"There wasn't really anything to tell until this morning," said a befuddled Dimitri.

Maria was also bewildered. "Dimitri, you need to sort out this mess. Talk to Nefeli, and talk to Violet. I'm calling Anna tomorrow. I'm sure Violet would rather hear it from you, but hopefully by then there will be nothing to hear." She walked away, cursing herself for thinking Dimitri was any different from his father.

Just after Maria left, Despoina called Dimitri, having heard from her neighbours that her son was engaged. Dimitri found himself having nearly the same conversation with his mother he'd just had with Maria.

"Dimitri, you're not fooling anyone, except maybe Nefeli and her family because they see what they want to see. I won't have you marrying someone you don't love. You need to talk to Nefeli."

Dimitri called Nefeli sixty-eight times that day. Nefeli was busy with her family; they all wanted to come by and wish her congratulations (lockdown restrictions notwithstanding). Even Nefeli was confused by the speed of everything. She'd thought she and Dimitri would at least have a conversation about it before it was common knowledge in the town. Still, it seemed to be working out as she'd planned, so she was pleased. At one point she checked her phone and saw thirty-seven missed calls from Dimitri. She had a horrible sinking feeling and intuited correctly that if she wanted to marry this man, she had to ignore these calls today. And she did want to marry him, more than anything in the world.

By the time Dimitri saw Nefeli again two days later, with her parents of course, their wedding was being planned for September. They were breaking the lockdown rules by walking together, but Dimitri didn't feel he had any say in the situation. He was noticeably distracted, but Nefeli and her parents put it down to nerves. Men often got cold feet before getting married, it was normal. Dimitri tried and failed to figure out how he could break off his accidental engagement. He imagined the scene it would cause if he told Nefeli and her parents that he didn't love her and couldn't marry her. It felt exhausting and he had run out of fight months ago.

Chapter 13

Violet

The wet Vancouver weather dragged on through February, with one snowfall of nearly six inches, which turned to horrible brown slush within twelve hours of falling, pristinely white, from the sky.

Violet hadn't heard much from Dimitri, but she didn't really expect to anymore. She was resigned to the fact that her move to Crete would be primarily for herself, to start her new life. She was sure that once she saw Dimitri again, they'd both understand where they stood and they could go from there. For now, it was all on endless hold, on standby, just like life.

She helped her mother with the jewelry shop, and tried to speak as much Greek with her as she could, though her study sessions in the evenings had ceased. Covid cases had risen following Christmas, with people travelling and visiting family against the government advice. Numbers were going down a little now, but vaccines for most people were still several months away in Canada. It all seemed hopeless.

At least the jewelry shop had recovered well and the new online shop was getting regular sales. Violet helped keep on top of the stock and made sure the website ran smoothly. She wondered about getting a job, but as she still planned to leave, and jobs were few and far between at the moment, she grew discouraged easily after a cursory glance at employment websites.

In March, Violet began to have vivid and upsetting dreams. Sometimes they were about Persephone and sometimes they were about Dimitri. She was usually swimming, though it wasn't clear where she was, trying to catch up with one of them, knowing they were in terrible danger but unable to warn them. Her limbs never moved properly and she could barely make a single stroke in the water. Sometimes she sank, trying desperately to scream and swim. Sometimes there was a trail of blood in the water that she knew led to Persephone.

Once she saw Dimitri, standing on the headland above Sfinari Beach, flying a kite that looked like a large honeybee. It seemed to be alive, flapping its wings and circling through the air. Violet wasn't sure if it was trying to escape from the line or whether it was content to be linked to Dimitri and the earth below. Suddenly the air filled with dark thick clouds that were also the sea, engulfing the kite and the earth in a charcoal-coloured haze that choked at her throat. Dimitri, the only thing still visible, seemed oblivious, continuing to fly the kite he could no longer see. A deafening thunder rose up and roared so loudly Violet felt it vibrate in her bones, and vivid white fingers of lightning lit up the sky in a million impossibly intricate patterns. She tried to call his name, but could only cough and gasp. She tried to run to him but couldn't move her limbs. She watched Dimitri being pulled into the storm, becoming smaller as he receded into the distance, slowly disappearing, still holding onto the end of his kite.

Violet woke up thrashing and sweating, strangled cries emerging from her desperate throat. She usually only had to deal with nightmares in August, and she was finding the past few weeks of disrupted sleep extremely difficult. She got up and made herself a cup of tea. Knowing it was noon in Crete, Violet texted Dimitri, though she left out most of the details of her dream.

Hey, I just had a terrible dream where you got pulled into a huge stormcloud. Just wanted to check if you're OK?

Dimitri received Violet's message on Monday March 15th; it was the day after Maria had spoken to him, and it was also *Kathara Deftera,*[46] the day that marks the end of Carnival and the start of Lent. If the nation hadn't been in lockdown, Sfinari beach would have been dotted with children flying celebratory colourful kites, but today the only kite flying was the one in Violet's dream, and Carnival and Easter celebrations seemed to belong to another world.

Dimitri looked down at his phone and wasn't sure if Maria had told Violet about his engagement, and she was being deliberately cryptic, or if they'd "dream communicated," as she called it. He began to feel panicked. He knew Violet would be worried, and he should

---

[46] Clean Monday

reply. A stronger man would have simply called her and explained the whole situation. But Dimitri had faded into a wretched shadow of himself, and felt he was only a plaything tossed around by forces much stronger than he was. His will had been gently steamrolled to nothing. He decided to reply but keep it short.

Sorry you had a bad dream. I'm OK. Have you talked to your aunt recently?

Violet thought that was a very strange text; she sensed something was amiss and tried to call him. He didn't answer.

Dimitri sat on his couch with his head in his hands, letting his phone ring out, wishing he'd never gone out for a walk on that cold misty February day.

The next morning, Violet felt wretched. She hadn't been able to get back to sleep after her nightmare, and the cryptic text that had followed it. With nothing on her agenda, and Persephone also on her mind, she remembered the binder of music, still untouched. Violet picked out a guitar duet and carefully wrote in the note names of the melody. There was an old piano in their living room that no one ever played. Persephone used to occasionally mess around on it when she came over, always commenting that it needed to be tuned, and that the low F# didn't work. No one else had played it since she'd passed away.

Violet looked down at the keys and found middle C. Counting from there, she slowly and clumsily plunked out the tune. After a few tries, she'd started to make sense of it. It was a beautiful haunting melody, titled "Demeter's

Waltz." Violet was sure it was a reference to Persephone's mother, or perhaps the mother she wished she'd had. It was nice to hear a bit of her friend's music and Violet was pleased she'd managed to play a small part of the piece. She was feeling a little better, pondering whether to give the bass notes a try, when the phone rang.

Her parents were at work, so Violet answered. It was Maria. She was surprised to hear Violet's voice and tried to sound casual.

"I was trying to reach your mother. She didn't answer her cell phone or the shop phone."

"Oh, she's probably just busy there. I'm sure she'll call you back." Violet thought Maria sounded strange. "Is everything OK?" she asked.

"Yes, yes, everything's fine. I'll call back later."

Maria hung up before Violet could reply. It wasn't like her aunt not to chat. Normally she asked Violet a million questions and enthusiastically shared all the local gossip, and Violet was lucky to spend less than an hour on the phone with her.

She frowned. She called Dimitri again. He didn't answer. She didn't want to look desperate, but she was genuinely worried about him. Boyfriend or not, she certainly hadn't stopped caring about him. She sent him a text message.

Dimitri, I don't want to crowd you, but my aunt just called and sounded very strange. And you're not answering your phone. I know it's probably nothing but that dream was really horrible and I'm worried about you. Are you sure you're OK? You can still talk to me about things you know. I still care about you, as your friend.

Dimitri was sitting in his cave drinking *raki* and hiding from his future in-laws and accidental fiancée. When he read Violet's text he barely managed to suppress the urge to throw his phone into the sea.

It wasn't Violet he was angry with of course, it was himself. How could he possibly explain to her this ridiculous mess he'd got himself into? She cared about the Dimitri she'd met nearly two years ago. She couldn't possibly care for the spineless coward he'd somehow become. She was better off without him in her life at all. Dimitri didn't reply.

Violet sat and fretted. She called him one more time. Still no answer.

In Platanakia Bay, Dimitri's phone entered the sea and sunk to the pebbly bottom.

Violet called Maria back, who still hadn't been able to get in touch with Anna. Maria answered, hoping it was Anna calling her back. It was Violet.

"Theia Maria, please tell me what's going on? I'm really worried about Dimitri. I had a horrible dream about him last night, and he's not answering his phone or replying to my texts, and I've never known you to hang up the phone so quickly." Violet was starting to genuinely panic.

Maria wished she'd never called the house. She should have known Anna would be at work on a Monday. It wasn't just that she didn't want to be the one to tell Violet, it was also that she knew this wasn't news that Violet should hear when she was alone at home. Maybe Martin was there. "Is your father home?" she ventured.

"No! He's at work too, with all the people who have lives and jobs and things to do and I'm just sitting here waiting and worrying that Dimitri is dying or something! Tell me what's going on!!"

Maria couldn't see any way out. "Are you sitting down?"

"Jesus Christ, why does that matter? I'm standing on my freaking head OK? Just *tell* me!" She immediately regretted raising her voice to her aunt.

Maria took a deep breath in and said a prayer to the Virgin Mary. "Dimitris is engaged."

Violet thought she'd heard her wrong. Then she thought this must be another nightmare and surely she'd wake up crying and thrashing any moment now.

"Violeta, are you still there?"

Violet managed a whimper. Maria could tell this wasn't going well.

"Everyone knows he's in love with you, Violeta. It's all a horrible mistake. I've tried to talk sense into him but he's completely lost his will, his self. It's all wrong."

"To who?" whispered Violet, responding to Maria's first statement and not having been able to process anything else her aunt had said.

"Nefeli," replied Maria.

"Who?"

"They're old family friends, very traditional, very religious. A strange match for Dimitris. We're all confused, Violeta. It's all a terrible mess."

Violet was silent. She was sure the ground had just been removed from underneath her and she was now spinning through time and space with no idea how to orientate herself. It was true she and Dimitri weren't together, but she realized now that in her heart of hearts she'd never stopped believing they would be together again once she was able to return. She'd also thought that, even as his friend, he would have told her about something this important. She had never felt so utterly betrayed in her life. Maria was talking but Violet couldn't understand what she was saying.

"Violeta? Are you still there?"

Violet couldn't make a sound. She dropped the phone on the floor and walked out the door. She took nothing with her.

Maria made the sign of the cross and called Anna again.

Anna was having her busiest day of the year so far in the shop and wondered who on earth kept calling her cell phone. She could hear it vibrating in her bag and it was extremely distracting when she was trying to help customers. It rang out, only to start ringing once again about five seconds later. Eventually, Anna started to wonder if something was wrong. She excused herself momentarily from the customer who was browsing earrings and checked her phone. Fourteen missed calls from Maria. Anna looked around her shop. She was the only one there today and there were four other customers browsing or waiting to be helped. But fourteen calls wasn't normal. Anna called her sister back.

"Anna, thank God you called. Please, quickly, you need to go home!" Maria spoke so fast Anna could barely catch the words. "I called the house and had to tell Violet that Dimitris is engaged, she hung up and disappeared and

I'm so worried and I'm *so* sorry Annoula, I didn't mean to tell her but she knew something was wrong. I tried—"

"Maria," Anna interrupted her firmly. "You need to slow down. Dimitris is engaged?"

"Yessss!" wailed Maria. "But it's all a horrible mistake, he doesn't love this girl at all."

"And you told Violet this just now?"

"I tried not to, but she could tell something was wrong. She couldn't get in touch with Dimitris either. She called me back. I didn't want to be the one to tell her, Anna, I'm so sorry!"

Anna shook her head and processed this quickly. She knew Violet and Dimitri weren't a couple as such anymore, but she knew her daughter well enough to know she still had hopes of being with Dimitri when she could finally return, and that she would, at the very least, have expected Dimitri to talk to her about this. While she generally trusted her daughter to be sensible, she was also aware that the intensity of her emotions overpowered her common sense at times. "Maria, I have to go. I'll call you back later."

Anna looked desperately around the shop. Martin was at the university. He'd mostly been teaching online from home, but today he'd gone in to get some books and papers from his office. It would take him far too long to get home. She called the one part-time assistant she'd been able to hire back and told her she'd pay her double for today if she could come right now. She said it was a family emergency. Thankfully, her employee arrived within thirty minutes.

Anna called Martin and then drove home too fast, running yellow lights that were virtually red. She arrived home to find the front door wide open, the wireless phone on the kitchen floor, and Violet nowhere to be seen.

"Shit, shit!" She tried to think where her daughter would have gone. She knew Violet had a special spot by the river that she often went to when she was upset, but didn't know where exactly it was. She decided to try anyway.

It was a long walk to the river from Violet's house. But both cars were gone and Violet wasn't capable of pondering a bus route or calling a taxi in her current state. She didn't feel the pavement under her feet, she didn't look before crossing any roads. She didn't feel she existed anymore anyway. The world looked strange, like a bizarre caricature of itself that no longer made any sort of sense. If Dimitri could get engaged without even telling her, had he ever loved her? It was only a few months ago that he'd told her he carried her poem everywhere and dreamed of her. Was that enough time to forget her completely and fall in love with someone else? To plan a whole life together with this person, and not even think to tell her? It didn't make any sense at all. It must have all been a lie from the start, and their love had never been real. How could she have been so blind? Violet's mind raced with angry questions as she walked quickly, eyes dead ahead, for an hour or more until she reached her destination.

The path had never been more than a deerpath, and this time of year, when Violet rarely visited, it was nearly invisible. She picked her way through the mossy cedars and stumbled down muddy tree roots, descending until she reached her usual spot. She stopped briefly and looked down at the cold pool of water, moving slowly down toward the sea. She wasn't going swimming today. She turned and walked uphill to the top of the canyon with the faces on its walls. She wondered how the faces looked today. Were they angry? Confused? Lost? Or perhaps laughing at her naivete. How could she have been so foolish?

She climbed upward, slipping and grappling branches, ivy and foliage until she arrived at the top. She didn't usually come up here. She usually looked up from the water below. Violet stood at the top of the cliffs and walked over to the edge. From this angle, she couldn't make out the faces in the rocks. She knew they were there, but reality is always a question of context and angle. For a moment, in her mind's eye, she glimpsed the milky way in Sfinari Bay, hanging down over the headland, and then she saw Persephone holding the booklet about the Piskies that had disappeared, slowly shrunk away to nothing as people stopped believing in them.

People often say that suicide is selfish. That if people had any concern for the people that loved them, they couldn't possibly choose to put them through the ordeal of losing them. But Violet was no more capable of considering anyone's feelings at that moment than a leaf was capable of solving Fermat's Last Theorem. As far as she was concerned, she didn't exist, and neither did anyone else; the world was blank except for an entirely unbearable pain and confusion that she needed to stop.

She closed her eyes and leaned forward.

At that moment Violet heard the thick, low sound of a feathered wing beating the air, and felt an unexpected breeze on her face. She opened her eyes to see the white tail of a bald eagle moving quickly past her, so close she could have touched it. She took in the sight of its bright yellow talons and the expansive wings that soared effortlessly across the ravine. She stumbled backwards, remembering that she herself had no wings.

Violet looked down and saw her feet on the mossy ground, her shoes muddy and her legs scraped and cut from her ascent. Suddenly her body belonged to her again, and her mind was empty but alive. She looked over at the eagle, sitting in a tall cedar across the river, just downstream from where she stood. He regarded her carefully. Violet's eyes welled up but the tears wouldn't fall.

"Thank you," she mouthed to the eagle who had lent her its wings for just a moment.

She sat down and hugged her knees into her chest. She was too exhausted to cry.

Anna pulled into a small parking lot that she hoped was the right one, parked haphazardly and slammed her door. She looked round, not knowing which way to go.

"Violet?" she yelled into the air. "Violeta!!"

There were two trails, both with yellow signs warning that the path was steep and dangerous. She ran towards one, hoping it was the one Violet took, and scrambled down in her heeled ankle boots, wishing desperately she'd worn flat shoes today. She wasn't religious, but she prayed to whatever god or goddess might listen to her, Zeus or Jesus or Demeter, all the while yelling her daughter's name. She heard an eagle call just above her head. It landed in a tall tree directly above her, called loudly and flew to the left, landing in another tree, watching her and calling again. Anna looked to her left and saw a small path, barely visible. She ran down it, still calling Violet's name, slipping and stumbling in the mud. The path connected with Violet's path near the river.

Violet heard her mother's calls, but found herself unable to make a sound in response. It was like one of her dreams, only this time she wasn't trying to save anyone except herself. Anna finally arrived at the river and recognized the spot from Violet's photos. She looked around, panic-stricken, "Violeta? Violeta!"

Anna and Violet both heard the eagle call as it swooped down near Violet again and landed high in an old cedar next to where she sat. Anna looked up but she couldn't see Violet from her vantage point.

"Violet?" She felt compelled to climb, perhaps because she knew that eagles are messengers of Zeus, or perhaps because she didn't know what else to do. It was an awkward and steep ascent but Anna was running on maternal adrenaline, which has been known to move mountains and rivers.

As she reached the top, out of breath, dirty and hands full of slivers, she saw her only child sitting at the top, and felt a flood of relief surge through her veins and her heart. Violet heard her mother coming but still sat frozen, unable to even turn around and face her.

Anna sat down beside her. "Violet?" she asked gently. Violet leaned into her and finally the tears came. Anna held her daughter close and let her cry for a long time, wishing she could do something, anything, to stop her hurting.

Chapter 14

Violet suffered through the rest of March and most of April, her mother cooking all her favourite foods and her father offering to take her out on hikes when he had a day off. Violet mostly refused, though she did manage to eat small portions of her mother's Greek cooking. She didn't hear anything from Dimitri. She'd overheard he had a new phone number. Maria now couldn't get in touch with him either. Obviously he didn't want her, or her family, contacting him anymore.

In the weeks following Maria's ill-fated phone call, Anna had gently suggested to her daughter that she think about seeing a counsellor or therapist. It was something Violet had resisted after Persephone's death, much as she'd resisted everything and anything at the time. This time, however, she agreed.

She'd been shaken by her own unexpected reaction to Dimitri's engagement, and the past few years felt like a hopeless tangled knot of events that she was unsure how to unstitch. Violet searched online for a counsellor with a creative background. She didn't want to just talk. She'd talked herself in circles in her mind and she wasn't sure how talking in circles to someone else would help her. She found a man called Steven Shore. A mostly bald man in his mid-forties, he looked like someone's pleasant non-threatening uncle, and Violet thought she'd be able to open up to him.

She wouldn't have admitted it, as she thought it sounded silly, but she'd wanted to see a man as she wanted an unbiased male perspective on Dimitri. She had a good relationship with her father, but they didn't talk in-depth about things. Besides, he'd told her often that her mother was the only woman he'd ever loved. He was no help with regards to understanding the nuances of a troubled male mind.

In their first online session, Violet managed to talk about Persephone a little, but not Dimitri. She drew her nightmares, where she searched for Persephone in the river. Steven commented on how the water took up her whole page, there was no surface and no border, she'd coloured the dark blue to the very edges. She nodded. There wasn't anything but the water in those dreams. He asked if she could breathe underwater. She said yes, she could sometimes yell too, but the water always felt heavier than real water, and she couldn't move easily, and she could never find Persephone. He asked about the darkness of the blue. "It keeps getting darker," said Violet, not having noticed until just now that her water-dreams had indeed turned to the colour of the evening sky.

Violet drew the cisterns at Aptera in her second session. Three large black mouths in the hillside, and Dimitri a tiny figure at the entrance to one. She tried, as much as she could, to explain who Dimitri was and where he was. Seeing her struggle, Steven asked if she'd like to write about him, maybe as a poem. Violet hadn't told him that she used to write poetry. She nodded and sat quietly for several minutes while she wrote.

> We met in the wingless world
> Where the sirens fell to the sea
> Mourning the loss
> Of so much more than just a loss
> Everything around us was ruins
> A million years all snuffed out in an instant
> Of movement
> Leaning into you
> Like soaring feathers and wild thyme
> I remember the smell of honey and pine
> That you forgot
> One day by the sea
> Promises shattered like shells on the beach
> Silently breaking
> Tears in the waves
> Eagles soar and swoop
> But the past has no wings
> To arrive at tomorrow

Violet managed to read out the poem, letting the tears fall. When she looked up, she saw Steven wiping away his own tears, and immediately apologized for making him cry. He assured her, as Dimitri had at Aptera nearly two years ago now, that she didn't need to apologize and told her it was a beautiful poem, and that he could feel the strength of the emotions in it.

Somehow, following this, Violet managed to recount, more or less, Dimitri's story. It didn't feel like her own story anymore at all. Steven listened. He nodded.

"I mean, what was really difficult was him not telling me anything. And then not being able to make sense of what happened. I couldn't reconcile my memories of him with this new reality. It didn't fit. I couldn't make it fit in my head. I still can't. Do men...love differently than women?" She looked to Steven, hoping for an enlightened male perspective.

Steven looked thoughtful. "I think love is very personal. Sometimes it can mean different things to different people. But you stayed in touch regularly for over a year after you left Crete right?"

Violet nodded.

"That's a long time when you've only known someone a month."

She nodded again.

"Well, you know Dimitri much better than I do, Violet. What do you think happened?"

Violet was a little annoyed. She'd wanted him to answer questions, not ask them. She thought of Persephone reflecting back questions and managed a half-smile. She sighed. "I don't know. I guess a lot happened after I left. The pandemic, and his Dad came back. There were a lot of things that were out of his control. Maybe, this was one thing that he could control. He could decide to be with someone else, and stop missing me, stop having to think about when I might be able to come back."

Steven nodded. "That may very well have been the case."

Violet couldn't have known that the engagement itself had felt very much out of Dimitri's control. She had told her mother and her aunt she didn't want to hear anything about Dimitri anymore, so she had no knowledge of how events had unfolded. But she was right that he was exhausted from missing her, from waiting for her with no end in sight.

Violet began to slowly untangle the knots that held Dimitri and Persephone together in her bruised heart. The two losses circled each other in her mind like twin stars. She'd felt strange calling Dimitri's engagement a loss; after all, they hadn't really been together for some time.

"There isn't a minimum requirement for trauma or loss, Violet," Steven calmly assured her. "If it felt like a loss, or it felt like a trauma, then it was."

"But how can I even put that on the same level as what happened to Persephone?" asked Violet.

"It's not a contest between events. You experienced two losses, two traumas. They're linked in your mind for many reasons. You don't need to justify those connections."

In her final session, Violet's mind was drawn back to the peaceful dream she had while she slept on Sfinari Beach, the night Dimitri had seen her and placed a blanket over her. She drew herself in the small rowboat, rowing gently through the stars, which floated around her in the calm dark sea which was also the sky. She told Steven the stars were all the people and spirits looking out for her, including Persephone, and described the feeling she'd had of being so completely safe, so secure in an unshakable knowledge that she would be OK.

"And do you feel that way now?" asked Steven gently.

"Not the way I felt it then," Violet replied thoughtfully, "But, I still know that what I felt was real, very real, and is still true on some level even if I can't feel it all the time."

"That sounds like a good thought to hold onto," said Steven as he nodded slowly.

Her new reality wasn't kind or easy, but as the weeks passed, Violet resolved that she still wanted to move to Crete. She didn't feel able to build the life she wanted for herself in Vancouver. On a practical level, there was the disheartening reality that she (like so many others) would never be able to afford to live independently. But it was more than that. She couldn't find a way to connect with the city; it was as if Vancouver were a puzzle and she was a piece from an entirely different jigsaw. No matter how hard she tried, her edges just didn't fit around any of the pieces. Maybe it was the rush hour traffic that seemed to last all day, the heavy rain that fell for days or weeks on end, or the grumpy commuters on over-crowded buses. Something here seemed to make people turn inwards instead of outwards. So many people and yet so little interaction. Violet felt this inward pull on her own being as well, and had no desire to become one more isolated and disenfranchised Vancouverite.

On one level she knew she should, logically, feel grateful to live in such a beautiful place, with her secret spot by the river, the vast ocean, and the towering mountains watching over her, but she also knew in her bones that it wasn't where she belonged. It was only in Crete that she'd felt that elusive sense of belonging for the first time. People seemed to have time for each other, and just being around them had made her feel safe and at ease. She recalled being a lighter, more open version of herself, more comfortable in her own skin. Crete felt like home.

She wanted this new life for herself. She could live somewhere close enough to Sfinari to visit her family, but not so close that she might run into Dimitri and his wife. His wife. She still couldn't really compute it. She clung to her plan. She had her lotion recipes, she kept speaking Greek with her mother whenever she could. Life continued, and she was grateful to Steven for helping her unpack her web of thoughts and feelings. However, there remained a dull ache behind her heart that slowed her laughter and caused too many tears to fall.

She began to dream about Persephone again. But now Perse was angry with her, angrier than she'd ever seen her. Violet couldn't figure out what she was so upset about. Until on May 10th at precisely 2:03am, Persephone hit Violet over the head with a book.

"Ow!" exclaimed Violet's sleeping self. "That hurt! What'd you do that for?"

Persephone rolled her eyes and threw the book into Violet's lap. Violet looked down at it and couldn't make out the title, but she could see her name as the author. Puzzled, Violet looked up at Persephone, who raised her eyebrows as if to say, "Don't you get it?"

Violet opened the book and read the first line: "Persephone and Violet were stuck."

Violet woke up at 2:04 am, sleepily typed the line on her phone so she wouldn't forget it, and went back to sleep.

Waking up the next morning, she couldn't help but smile a little at the dream. She liked seeing Perse in her dreams, even if she was angry and hitting her with books.

"What a strange first line for a book," thought Violet. She remembered telling Persephone, several lifetimes ago now, that she'd maybe write a book for her one day. She hadn't really meant it, but thinking about it now, she certainly had some good material. And time was something she was literally drowning in. Why not give it a try? Two years ago Violet might have feared failure, but failure now seemed an insignificant opponent compared to what she'd been through.

Feeling something akin to motivation for the first time in at least six months, Violet took out her laptop and typed the first line. She was surprised how easily it flowed from there, and she kept typing until her grumbling stomach forced her to leave the bedroom in search of breakfast.

Martin looked up from his tea and thought something was different about Violet today.

"Good sleep?" he asked.

"The best," she answered, smiling to herself. She didn't offer any more information. She wanted to keep the book her little secret for just a little while.

Violet typed furiously in her room for the next few weeks. She searched the internet endlessly and checked out virtual books from the library, researching Greek myths, beekeeping, the history of Crete, and Cornish folklore. She woke up early and stayed up late, leaving her room only to eat and occasionally wash.

Anna and Martin watched their daughter curiously. They could hear the clicking of her laptop keys but when they asked what she was typing, she shrugged.

"It's a secret, for now."

"Will you tell us later?" asked Anna.

"Probably," she replied and disappeared back to her room.

They didn't want to pry, they could see that Violet was feeling something akin to happiness, a state of motivation and focus. And after everything she'd been through in the past few years, this seemed a good enough state to let her linger in. An almost-contentedness.

Violet typed and researched for four weeks straight until the story paused and she ran out of words. She sat frowning at her laptop. Her story was about seventy thousand words and an average novel was ninety thousand words, according to the internet. And besides, it didn't feel finished. There was an ending waiting to happen but, perplexingly, she didn't know it yet, so she sat frowning at her seven-ninths of a draft. Somehow, she knew she couldn't write the ending until she moved to Crete.

"Oh great, *another* thing on hold," she thought to herself.

Chapter 15

While Violet was feverishly typing up her semi-fictional autobiography that May, Dimitri observed the planning of his wedding to a nice girl he didn't love. He had a subdued Easter meal with Nefeli's family. There were no services or celebrations this year. He rarely dreamed at all anymore, but when he did, he was usually swimming in the sea in Platanakia Bay calling Violet's name, though she was nowhere to be found. Once he dreamed he saw his *yiayia* walking away from him. He called out to her but she didn't turn around.

Dimitri might still have found a way out of his engagement if Covid-19 hadn't arrived in Sfinari in late May. Ironically, restrictions had eased just two weeks prior; the strict lockdown had ended, and tavernas and restaurants had re-opened. Greece began to allow in tourists from certain countries, provided they could show a negative test result or proof of two vaccinations. But viruses don't follow logic and regulations. And many people in Sfinari had been lax about the restrictions, especially with an engagement to celebrate.

Sifi was one of the first to show symptoms. On a Thursday evening, his throat began to burn and he developed a cough. He drank some *rakomelo* and went to bed early. Despoina sensibly suggested he sleep in Dimitri's old room. It was probably just a cold, but still, she didn't want to take any chances.

The next morning, he was feverish and his cough had intensified. There were whispers passing through the town that someone from Sfinari had tested positive. Despoina began to worry. For once she was glad that Dimitri was down by the sea in his cottage, seeing hardly anyone. She was still annoyed that he hadn't managed to call off the engagement. She shook her head, she'd have to talk to him again, it wasn't too late to cancel things. Of course it would upset Nefeli and her family, but better to upset them a little now than infuriate them later. She wasn't sure what had become of her handsome confident son. She'd never really approved of Violet, but looking back, she wished she could see Dimitri that happy again. Violet had always made him laugh, and now she couldn't remember the last time she'd seen her son even smile.

Despoina cared for Sifi as best she could, wearing a mask and washing her hands frequently. She put a sign on the door saying they were quarantining. She called the Covid-19 advice line and was told to continue as she had been, isolating and treating Sifi with over-the-counter medications, but she couldn't help but wonder if they should drive to the health centre in Kissamos and get tested. She tried to call her son, but then remembered the fate of his phone, sacrificed on the seabed. She didn't want to risk infecting him, even putting a note through his door seemed unwise.

Dimitri hadn't replaced the phone he threw into the sea in March and the cottage didn't have a landline. With the taverna quieter than usual last summer, money was tight, and there were few people Dimitri wanted to hear from anyway.

The second lockdown, though as strict as the first on paper, was generally treated with much less reverence than the previous one, so he only periodically worried that he hadn't sent out the obligatory text message to the authorities when he went out. For the most part, Dimitri had simply pretended the lockdown wasn't happening through that spring. Initially, he'd sometimes written out a signed statement with his name and address on it, that may or may not have been sufficient. But as the weeks passed, he grew weary of this and mostly tried not to think about what might happen if he were to be stopped and checked by the police. It seemed ridiculous to sign a paper and take his passport every time he wanted to check on his bees, or walk along the beach. He rarely left the bay anyway and the police didn't tend to patrol out-of-the-way villages like Sfinari.

Until recently he'd had regular visits from his mother, as well as Nefeli and her parents. They'd walked outside, masks on, and distanced, breaking the rules but still, they thought, being sensible. So now that the lockdown had eased, it seemed particularly odd to Dimitri that these visits had ceased in late May; he had a sense something was wrong. He had a radio in his cottage, but the general numbers he heard about in Greece and on the island were not concerning; indeed infection rates were declining.

Eventually, with no visits from anyone for nearly a week, Dimitri drove up to his mother's house in Sfinari. He saw the sign on the door and his heart began to race. He knocked anyway. Despoina shuffled to the door but didn't open it.

"Mom, it's me, are you OK?"

"Dimitri?" She spoke through the door, wishing she could open it. "I'm fine. Your father isn't well though." She paused. "I had no way to get in touch." Despoina had given up urging her son to buy a new phone. He seemed determined to cut himself off from everyone.

"I'm sorry. I'll get a new phone," he promised. "Today." Dimitri stood outside the door processing his mother's words, and was surprised to discover that he didn't, after all, want his father to die. He was less surprised to realize that his mother had in fact, been right all along, and he should have replaced his phone months ago.

He thought back to Violet apologizing for not calling him for several days when her flight was cancelled, and recognized that he'd too been selfish to try and make himself unreachable. He'd felt so awful that day that he knocked on Maria's door, so worried, but now he would have given anything to be back there, in those simpler times when he was sure the pandemic would be over by the fall and Violet would be back here in a few months. Dimitri looked down and closed his eyes, trying to will Violet out of his mind. "Is Dad gonna be OK?" he asked.

Despoina hesitated. "Yes," she answered, not very convincingly. "He just needs to rest."

Dimitri could hear the lack of conviction in her voice. "Mom, are you sure,? Does he have a fever?"

"Yes, he has a fever but it's OK, just a little high."

Dimitri desperately wanted to go in but he knew if he got sick as well, it wouldn't help anyone. He stood powerless at the door.

"Let me know if you need help getting him to the hospital, or if you need anything. I can help, Mom."

"OK, OK, go buy yourself a phone. Wear your mask. And don't throw your new phone into the sea because you got engaged to a woman you don't love and couldn't tell the woman you do love about it."

Dimitri wished he hadn't confessed the details of that moment to his mother. He walked away slowly, still trying not to think of Violet, about how she might have heard the news of his engagement. The thought of her suffering on his account filled him with even more self-loathing. He tried to convince himself she probably hadn't minded; she did seem to just want to be friends. But beneath those layers of willful delusion, Dimitri knew beyond a doubt that she would have minded very much.

He drove to Kissamos, where he managed to buy a second-hand cell phone and a SIM card. His mother was the only person he gave the number to. Sfinari was put back in full lockdown the next day due to the outbreak.

Two days later, with Sifi struggling to breathe and his fever at 39.6, Despoina called an ambulance. She didn't want Dimitri to worry, and definitely didn't want him coming to the house, so she waited until the ambulance had pulled away with her husband in the back before she texted her son. She wasn't allowed to go with Sifi, and she had to quarantine for the next two weeks.

Dimitri was out checking on his beehives and had left his phone in the house. He'd lost two colonies the previous winter, which, while not unexpected, always disheartened him. He'd been carefully splitting one of his strongest colonies, moving a number of frames with capped brood into the empty hive, and trusting the bees to make a new queen quickly. There was plenty of food around for them this time of year, so he was hopeful both colonies would do well.

He returned to his cottage feeling the calmness his bees always bestowed on him, but his heart sank when he saw the text from his mother. He wished that, for once, something could go right for him. Life had felt somehow all wrong since Violet's flight had been cancelled a year ago, and their time together two years ago now felt like several lifetimes ago. Briefly, he let himself imagine what it would have been like if she'd stayed. He imagined her living with him in the cottage, swimming in the sea every day, making him laugh and speaking Greek in her thick Canadian accent. He smiled at the memory of her saying, *"Poso kanei to peponi?"* His heart broke all over again.

Dimitri desperately wanted to drive to the hospital, but there were roadblocks between Kissamos and Chania, and he knew he wouldn't be allowed to visit his father anyway. He wanted to go to his mother and comfort her, but he couldn't. He was tormented by a horrible feeling of complete and utter powerlessness, watching the fabric of his life unravel slowly and completely without any way of holding onto a single thread.

He texted his mother, and asked if there was anything he could do.

Just pray for your father, she replied.

He wasn't religious but he prayed anyway; he didn't know what else to do.

Dimitri's father was in the hospital for two weeks. He was given oxygen and a cocktail of medications. Dimitri talked with his mother on the phone every day, eager for updates. Sifi was stable, it looked as if he would pull through. But Dimitri and Despoina still worried. And Despoina was also concerned about her son.

"Dimitri, have you heard from Nefeli?" she asked.

Nefeli. He'd almost forgotten he had a fiancée. *"Ochi,* nothing." He hesitated. "She doesn't have my number, and I don't have hers. I lost all my contacts."

Despoina sighed. "Dimitri, are you going to marry that girl? You need to decide. Don't just marry her because you're going along with what they've planned. It might upset everyone to cancel now, but it will upset them a lot more if you go through with it, and then aren't able to be a good husband to her. No woman wants to be married to a man who doesn't love her. What do *you* want?" She didn't mention Violet, not because she didn't approve of her, but because Dimitri tended to shut down when she mentioned her. Besides, it seemed so unlikely now that he'd ever see her again. Dimitri, for his part, just wanted to feel like a whole person again.

"I don't know what I want," he said honestly. He had no idea how to pick up the broken pieces of himself.

Chapter 16

On June 17th, Dimitri, Despoina, and indeed the entire population of Greece was shaken by a murder confession. For weeks, the country had been waiting with bated breath for the police to charge someone for the murder of a young mother. Her husband, found tied to their baby's cot in their home in Athens, had claimed that a group of foreigners had broken in, stolen cash, and killed his wife in front of him and their child.

It wasn't the sort of thing that happened in Greece; it was surely the plot of a Hollywood crime movie. Only it wasn't. This was their world, this was close to home, and it was real.

Events then took an even more unsettling turn when the widowed husband confessed to the crime. Dimitri, hearing the news alone in his cottage, sat at his little kitchen table with his head in his hands. Like everyone, he'd felt incredibly sorry for the bereaved husband, wondering how it must feel to not only lose your wife, but to watch her murdered in front of your child. He'd thought about Violet's friend Persephone, and then pushed the thought away.

The moment he heard about the confession on his radio, he felt lost, disoriented, and strangely betrayed; the man he'd empathized with, the man he'd felt such strong compassion for, had turned out to be a cold-blooded murderer. He tried to imagine raising a hand against anyone, any woman in his life, but found the thought so despicable it made him sick to his stomach. In a world that felt increasingly unmoored, it was just one more reason not to trust himself, and he began to wonder who indeed he could trust.

At least his father had pulled through. The day after the unexpected confession, Despoina drove to Chania to pick Sifi up from the hospital. She turned off the car radio; she didn't want to hear any more about the murder. Apparently the couple had been fighting, and the husband had murdered his wife in a fit of rage. Despoina shook her head as she thought about it. She had been angry, unfathomably angry with Sifi many times over the years, but their arguments had never progressed to physical blows, though she had to admit she'd often thought about hitting him. Still, she knew it wouldn't have done any good. And Sifi, despite all his flaws (and she knew he had many), had never been a violent man.

When Despoina saw her husband at the hospital, she barely recognized him. He'd grown extremely thin and weak, and his movements were slow and shaky. He was out of breath after just the short walk from the hospital exit to the car. Despoina tried to put on a brave face for Sifi, but inside, she worried that he still had a long road to recovery. He was only fifty-four years old, but he looked and felt at least ten years older.

Despoina, strangely, either hadn't caught the virus or never developed any symptoms.

Sfinari remained in a strict local lockdown for another week due to the outbreak. Dimitri shouldn't have left his house at all, but the authorities were likely unaware of the tiny cottage down in the bay, hidden in the trees with no official address, and sometimes he walked past his hives and over to his cave in Platanakia Bay, looking out to sea and searching for answers.

He wanted to do the right thing. He wanted to feel human again. And he did want to have a family. His father's illness had brought things into focus for him. He didn't want to disappoint his parents or Nefeli's family. He'd disappointed enough people already, including himself. Dimitri called his mother and asked for Nefeli's family's phone number. He would do the right thing and marry the girl he was engaged to. She was a nice girl and would be a good mother, he was sure. Any man would be lucky to have her, with her pretty grey eyes and long dark hair.

He gathered all his memories of Violet, all the plans and hopes and wishes, and packaged them up tightly in his mind, burying them deep underground. He thought of Persephone in the underworld. He thought, one last time, about Violet swimming in the sea, and then shut out the image forever.

321

Chapter 17

Violet spent the summer editing her seven-ninths of a novel, adding in details, rephrasing, researching further, making sure her timelines all added up. She started a spreadsheet with dates and characters.

Still, she couldn't bring herself to share it with anyone, though she did tell her parents she was writing a novel; after all, they needed some sort of explanation as to what she was doing on her laptop for all these weeks, and Violet had never been a good liar. Anna and Martin wanted desperately to read the manuscript of course, but Violet waved away their questions with vague responses and her parents knew better than to push her. They would have to wait.

Covid numbers dropped again in Violet's province and the lockdown was eased a little, with in-province travel opening up for the summer. She helped her mother in the jewelry shop, and took a part-time job in a local gift store, mostly to keep herself busy, rather than for the money. It was low-paying but also low-stress, and she could walk to work. She'd been unemployed for far too long and needed to feel useful again.

Still, the world seemed determined to remain unsettled; a heatwave in late June saw temperatures soar to record highs, and, coupled with a long drought, fueled an early and unusually intense forest fire season across western North America. The town of Lytton, a few hours from Vancouver, reached a temperature of 49.6 degrees Celsius, then abruptly burned to the ground in a matter of minutes. The country gasped in disbelief, and Violet tried to shut out the terrifying pictures that crept into her mind as she imagined how it must have felt for the residents, given minutes to evacuate, not able to take anything with them. They'd lost everything, their lives abruptly and irreversibly changed by a tiny spark from a freight train.

Violet pondered that seemingly insignificant spark and all the loss it had precipitated, as she swam for hours in the river, her only respite from the heat and the tragedies.

But it wasn't the heat or the fires that broke something inside Violet that summer. When she first heard whispers of an unmarked grave containing the remains of two hundred indigenous children, in her own province, on the grounds of a school that had functioned within her father's lifetime, she struggled to compute this new reality. She'd heard about the injustices of residential schools of course, and she certainly knew that her country had a questionable history with regards to the treatment of the indigenous population. But as more and more graves came to light, the word "genocide" was suddenly not hyperbole anymore. Her country, it seemed, was built by murderers. Murderers like the mentally ill man who had killed Persephone nearly two years ago now. Murderers like the Greek man who had murdered his young wife in a fit of rage.

Violet battled an overwhelming urge to flee from this nation where all roads seemed to lead to loss and tragedy. This land, she'd always felt, had never belonged to her. She was the daughter of immigrants, and, on one level, nothing to do with the European colonization of past generations. But who would, or should, take responsibility? And what could anyone possibly say or do that would begin to repair so many layers of grief, loss, and oppression? Violet found she had endless questions that seemed utterly unanswerable.

And though her intentions were pure, as she sat by the river that summer, Violet was sure the trees, the water, the land, all knew she was an interloper and not a rightful inhabitant. She struggled through feelings of guilt and powerlessness, not knowing what she could possibly do to make up for the atrocities of the past. She tried to research the history of the genocide, but reading about it made her feel sick to her stomach, and brought back images of Persephone's death she'd constructed in her mind. She closed her laptop in tears and then felt even more guilty for not reading to the end of the article.

In July she dreamed she was running down the path to the river, but the soil was being pushed up from underneath. Hands emerged from amid the tree roots and grabbed at her feet as she stumbled down. She tried to call out, to say she was a friend and an ally, but she found she could only make strange strangled noises. When she finally arrived at the river, she found the riverbed dry. The kingfisher lay dead in the middle of it. She woke up in tears, feeling more lost and alone than ever before.

Belonging

The earth aches and the sky burns
Voices, buried, begin to rise
Singing slowly
A forgotten chant
from our planet's childhood

This land was different then,
Unscarred and remote
The trees didn't need to grieve
We danced on summer evenings
with the cave nymphs and the Piskies
to the rhythm of the whales in the sea

But the sun shines hotter now
Old trees sigh and burn and fall
Lightning dances like jagged bones across
      the clouds
Our past and our future collide and scatter

And my skin melts

Trying to remember a time
In cool forested shadows

Where we sat untouched,
Belonging to no one but the earth.

Violet spent the following day at the river, needing to reassure herself that it was still there. The soil was drier than she ever remembered and some of the cedars were turning brown. The waterfall at the end of the canyon had nearly dried up. But the kingfisher fished from the pale logs that formed a "v," oblivious to its death in Violet's dream. She took deep breaths and swam in and under the cold clear water until she felt completely numb.

As she sat drying on the rocks, exhausted, she heard a voice behind her.

"You've found the best spot in the park."

Violet turned around to see a man in his thirties, dressed far too warmly for the hot day, holding a thick walking stick.

"I won't keep you long," he said, "but I just found out I'm a torchbearer for the spirit world, and I want to tell you about the zero moments."

He stood beside Violet on the rocks and she wondered for a moment who would hear her scream if he tried to attack her with his large stick. But as he went on, she relaxed; he was clearly not here to hurt anyone. He traced a circle in the pebbles with his stick. "These moments, when you're sitting here by the river, or when you're swimming, when your mind finally stops and is wiped clean, those are important moments, the zero moments. At those times you need to ask the universe, the angels, to show you the way with the least resistance and the most reward." He traced an "x" inside the circle as he continued. "And you need to document those moments, record them, come back to them later, and you'll see that they all make sense in the end. Follow the breadcrumbs, the little signs, and you'll see, it will all work out."

Violet thought about the "breadcrumbs" that had led her to write her book, still unfinished, but documenting so many moments, and the additional "breadcrumbs" that had led to her plans to sell her lotions.

The torchbearer didn't pause long. He spoke quickly but clearly, as if he knew he had only a short time to communicate an important message. "Your motto is 'Play, be light, be bright, create,'" he went on. "The world is changing. But you...you don't need to worry about any of that. You have so much potential, as much potential as Einstein or Schrödinger, and a lot of good things are coming to you. But don't let your humility make you think you don't deserve those good things. Be bold, be big, be brave, be beautiful. Be a peacock."

Violet wasn't sure if he was a madman or a prophet, or indeed, if there was any difference. Still, it was a comforting message at a time when the world seemed full of despair and destruction. She hadn't spoken yet, but as he finally completed his monologue she managed to thank him for the messages. He nodded and asked her if she had any questions. Violet thought for a moment. She wasn't sure if he was really in touch with the angels, but it was a worth a try.

"Do you know an angel named Persephone?" she asked tentatively.

He looked thoughtful and leaned on his stick. "Persephone, the Goddess of the Underworld?"

"Yes, well, she was also a friend of mine," said Violet, looking down at the rocks at the river's edge. The torchbearer stood quietly for a moment, looking thoughtfully at the trees on the opposite bank before replying.

"Well, you know already that she's here. She's in this place and she's in you and she looks out for you all the time. You're entangled, you know. And you're both unicorns."

Violet smiled a little as her eyes welled up. "Thank you," she managed to say quietly, unsure how she could be both a unicorn and a peacock at the same time, but grateful nonetheless for the messages of hope.

The word "entangled" hung in Violet's mind as the torchbearer turned and made his way back up the steep path away from her. She was sure Persephone had told her about quantum entanglement, but all she could draw to mind was an image of the universe as a tiny speck at the beginning of time, everything as one. She tried to imagine herself, everyone she knew, all the animals and the whole planet, the whole solar system, the milky way, and a million other galaxies all existing in that tiny speck, but her imagination fell short. She tried to picture everything exploding, spreading out, becoming distinct, and then moving toward maximum entropy, a state of complete randomness and chaos. Violet wondered if the force of entanglement still held a few things together: herself and Persephone and her family. Just enough to make sense of the chaos in our little worlds.

Violet went home feeling oddly at peace, with a sensation that echoed the way she'd felt in her dream on Sfinari Beach, with all the stars watching over her. She held onto the feeling as much as she could, and somehow, life plodded along, and it wasn't all bad.

Violet ended up selling her lotions in the gift shop where she worked. She'd mentioned them in passing, and Emma, the store owner, asked her to bring in some samples. Emma was impressed and offered to buy a small batch. As Violet hurriedly filed the legal paperwork needed to officially sell her products (there was a lot to go through and it of course required a spreadsheet), Emma was already selling the lotions, recommending them to everyone who came in to her shop. Violet called the brand *Melissa ke Persephone*,[47] M & P for short.

Her lotions sold well. They had quality ingredients and were priced reasonably. Emma took a much smaller cut than she usually would have. She knew Violet was overqualified for her shop assistant job and she wanted to offer something when she couldn't offer a raise. And like most people who knew even a little of Violet's story, Emma wanted to help her out.

Vaccinations rolled out, slowly at first and then faster, and Violet had her first shot in June and was due for the second one in August. She kept herself busy, her family stayed healthy, and most of the world was getting vaccinated. She counted her blessings and took things one day at a time.

Occasionally, against her will, she dreamed of Dimitri. He was usually by the cisterns, sometimes curled up asleep, and sometimes searching for his bees. He called out, "Honeybee?" and she wasn't sure if he was calling for

---

[47]Melissa and Persephone

her or his lost hives. She woke up with her heart aching. But she carried on, that was all she could do.

August came and Violet managed to bake her mother a more successful birthday cake this time. But she still dreaded her own birthday and the anniversary of Persephone's death. She swam in the river for long periods, up and down the canyon, watching the faces, soft yet sunken in the dry August warmth. The waterfall stopped running and the evergreens turned brown, their roots searching the parched soil for moisture as drought still gripped the land. She wondered if she'd see the torchbearer again, but he didn't reappear. Perhaps he'd told her everything she needed to know.

At home, Violet stumbled through more fragments of Persephone's music on her old out-of-tune piano in her parents' living room. She read a book about indigenous reconciliation. She was still waiting.

By the end of August, despite whispers of the delta variant, the post-pandemic world, or at least some kind of "new normal" felt tantalizingly close, and Violet dared to let herself dream once again of her new life on Crete. Her dream didn't include Dimitri anymore, but it was still her dream.

Chapter 18

Greece also burned that summer. Fires ravaged the Peloponnese and suburbs around Athens. But for Dimitri, it was the fiery destruction of the island of Evia that shattered something inside him. Its pine forests had fed vast quantities of honeybees, and the suffering of his fellow beekeepers penetrated his mind and heart, almost as if it was his own. So many like him had lost their colonies, their livelihoods, and their homes. He was beginning to feel that he couldn't manage one more thing going wrong in his world, one more defeat, one more event he was powerless to change.

Still, he told himself, at least Crete remained safe, his father had recovered, and his bees were healthy. The hives he'd split had grown and were flourishing. Dimitri, for once, felt thankful to the Venetians for their ruthless logging of the island all those years ago, now an unexpected protection.

Vaccinations in Greece initially moved at a slower pace, as do most things (for better or for worse) but then gained speed, and to Dimitri's relief, both he and his mother received both vaccines over the summer. Sifi, as he'd had the virus recently, was advised to wait and get vaccinated in November.

After the local lockdown had lifted they met for a walk along the beach, still wearing masks and distancing. He didn't ask his Dad any more difficult questions. He tried to focus on the good times and talked to his father about his bees. Seeing Sifi so weakened and vulnerable had made Dimitri view him differently. He wasn't sure he'd forgiven him, and he knew he'd never understand him, but he wasn't angry anymore. He spoke to his sisters over the phone; their anger and his own had dissipated into relief tinged with pity and a sense of surrender.

The tavernas at Sfinari Beach re-opened once again in late June, for a handful of vaccinated or Covid-tested tourists from specific countries that were deemed "safe." The opened borders were not without controversy; there were debates all over the country about whether the government was prioritizing the economy at the expense of safety. Moreover, after enduring months of strict lockdown, some Greeks felt a strong sense injustice as tourists were now allowed to freely enjoy their country when they themselves hadn't been able to.

But in Sfinari, both family tavernas needed the income badly, so reflecting on what was the right course of action for the country seemed like a luxury they couldn't afford. They opened, followed all the guidelines and did their best. Dimitri made an effort to sell more of his honey in local shops, hoping to supplement the income from the taverna.

Despoina was relieved that her son appeared to relax as the summer progressed. Nefeli and her family began to return. Dimitri no longer dreaded their visits. They talked easily of wedding plans. It was only to be a small "Covid-safe" wedding, unless restrictions eased. They'd decided they didn't want to wait to have a bigger wedding. There would be no telling when that would be possible anyway, and Dimitri had done enough waiting over the past two years. He'd made up his mind, he'd chosen his universe, and he just wanted to start his new life with Nefeli. He was sure he would learn to love her, especially when they had children running around at their feet, chattering and laughing. He looked forward to teaching his little ones about beekeeping. They would be a happy family and he would be a good husband to Nefeli. She deserved nothing less.

The date was set for September 18th.

On the night of September 17th, Dimitri dreamed he was making love to Violet in the sea at Platanakia Beach, under the stars with the milky way behind them. As he slowly awakened and came to the realization that today he was going to marry a woman who was not Violet, his heart and his gut wrenched with pain. He allowed himself a few tears and for a brief moment, considered calling Violet. Maybe he could cancel the wedding, or perhaps just not turn up. But he knew it was impossible. Stopping a Greek Orthodox wedding on the day of the ceremony is no more possible than stopping a freight train with a feather.

So he pushed it all away, back down into the deepest depths of his mind, into Hades' underworld. He'd made his decision. Violet was gone. He was doing the right thing. Nefeli would be his wife.

Chapter 19

Violet also had a dream on the night of September 17th. She dreamed of Aptera, except the cisterns were full of fresh clear water, with high windows sending shafts of bright white light streaming down to the water below. The water was warm and comforting. She was alone, but she could hear someone crying. At first, she thought they were her own sobs, echoing back to her from several years ago, mixed with the sobs of the souls who had died in the earthquake in the distant past, but she slowly realized the cries were Dimitri's.

"Dimitri? Is that you?" she asked the empty air. "Hello? Dimitri?"

He didn't answer and she couldn't find him anywhere. The sobs metamorphosed into the melody of one of Persephone's compositions, played on a flute that sounded like a songbird. She swam all around the cisterns and then climbed out and walked around them, still calling for

Dimitri as she listened to the sweet sad music. But he was nowhere to be found.

Violet woke up unsettled. She knew that by now, due to the time difference, Dimitri was already married. The downside of learning Greek was that she could now understand her mother's conversations with Maria and she'd accidentally overheard the wedding date. She'd known it was coming, and she'd long ago given up hope of being with Dimitri, but somehow it still made her sick to her stomach.

"Persephone, I really wish you were here," she said out loud as she shed a few tears in her bed.

Tremenheere Sculpture Gardens, Penzance, Cornwall
October 2017

Persephone and Violet sat in a large egg-shaped white structure, with a vast oval opening framing the blue sky like a master work of art. And indeed it was a piece of art; they were in a sculpture garden Persephone had discovered in a leaflet, and were sitting in a creation by the artist James Turrell. The garden was beautiful even though most plants were past their prime. There was a cold wind, but the sky was clear and the structure sheltered them. The girls looked up at the stunningly perfect blue oval.

"Funny how just putting a frame around the sky makes you really look at it, changes how you see it," mused Violet.

"Mmm. Context changes everything." Persephone paused. "If you were born drifting through space, with no contact with anything at all—"

"Wouldn't I just explode? And if not, I'd suffocate pretty quickly," said Violet teasingly. She knew this was one of Persephone's philosophical thought experiments and was being deliberately difficult.

Persephone rolled her eyes, "Yes, of course, but just imagine for a minute you could stay physically intact out there and you didn't need to breathe. If you were born, grew up and lived your whole life without seeing anyone or anything—"

"Not even an asteroid?" Violet was feeling cheeky.

Persephone's eyes rolled deep into the back of her head. "God, you're annoying today. You're in deep space, OK? There's *nothing* around you, nothing at all. You just float."

"OK, OK," said Violet. "So what?"

"Well, would you be *you*? Would you have any sense of identity? Could you even ponder what that meant? You'd have no language, no training, no chance to develop and test out your senses. So would you be *you* at all?"

Violet thought for a moment, "Depends what you mean by *me*. I mean, I'd be physically myself, I guess. But, I don't think I'd have much in the way of a personality. If I never interacted with anyone, was never taught anything, I guess I'd be a bit of a blank slate?"

Violet and Persephone were both quiet, thinking for a moment.

"But what if," said Violet, "there were multiple floating people, in different parts of space, so they couldn't see each other, they're just all out there on their own, but they're all different people, different genetics and all. Would they all be the same blank slates?"

Persephone shrugged, "I'm not sure. I feel like they would all have different potentials behind their slates, but their blank slates would all be equally blank."

"So we all need a frame around us? To sort of, contextualize us?" asked Violet, not quite sure she'd followed the point.

"Yeah, but I think our frames are our people. We all need to be surrounded by people who see the best in us. It's our interactions with them that make us want to do better and to grow, and it makes us *be* better, but without any pressure. If you were surrounded by people who thought you were an idiot, you'd turn into an idiot pretty quickly."

"Ouch," said Violet in mock indignance.

"It's not personal," laughed Persephone. "It would be the same for me. I see it when I work with kids with 'behavioural challenges.' Everyone expects them to be 'difficult,' so they are. I expect them to be fun and interesting and kind, and they are...eventually." Persephone paused and smiled. "So, just imagine if this sculpture was made of rotting chicken bones. Would you want to sit here and look at the sky?"

Violet laughed and pictured the pristine white structure as a morbid pile of dead chickens. "Ewww."

"Exactly. But the sky wouldn't have changed, it would still be the same. It would've just been re-framed rather unappealingly."

Violet thought for a moment. "But isn't it also possible that the sky could look even more beautiful in contrast with the rotting chickens?"

"Maybe, for about thirty seconds and then the stench would send you running," smiled Persephone.

Violet thought back to that conversation, from her bed in North Vancouver, and wondered if there were layers of frames, like a matte within a frame, and then another frame around that. And maybe some frames had several smaller frames within them, and all these groups of people just sort of held each other together. Like the frames in Dimitri's hives, all the bees nestled onto them, shuffling and fanning their wings.

Violet knew that Crete had framed her into her best self, but was sure it was the land as well as the people. She hoped it hadn't just been Dimitri.

Chapter 20

Dimitri managed to pretend to enjoy his small wedding by repeating to himself incessantly that he was doing the right thing, Nefeli was a nice girl and they'd have a happy family together. He forced all other thoughts out of his mind.

That night, in their marriage bed, in the little annex behind Nefeli's family home that was their temporary home, Dimitri thrashed and called out Violet's name. Nefeli lay beside him and cried silently. Still, he would learn to love her, she was sure. They were married, her plan had worked. It would get better. It had to get better.

They went on a brief honeymoon to the island of Kythira, northwest of Crete. Their time together was strained at best. They walked along the beach, talking little. Dimitri called out Violet's name in his sleep on each of the four nights they spent there. He didn't remember his dreams when he woke. Nefeli slept little and had no idea what to say to her husband.

A few weeks later a devastating earthquake shook Iraklion and much of eastern Crete. Dimitri called his sisters; they were safe. While Sfinari was too far away to feel any effects of the upheaval, Dimitri couldn't help but think it was yet another sign that his world was still somehow misaligned. He had no idea how to restore it to the life he remembered before the pandemic, when Violet was here with him, and even after that, when he'd been sure she'd return and they'd be together. He tried not to think about it. He tried to think about Nefeli instead but found no feelings attached to her image in his mind. He prepared his bees for the winter and vaguely wished he was one of them, with nothing to worry about but keeping warm and eating honey for the next few months.

Violet, now double-vaccinated and incredibly tired of waiting to start her new life, wanted to leave in October, but her mother and her aunt advised against it. The winters in Crete were quiet and wet, non-essential shops had just reopened in June, after suffering greatly for two years. It wasn't the time to start selling lotions. Spring, they both said, would be a much better season to make a new start.

This was all true, but Maria and Anna also wanted to delay Violet and Dimitri laying eyes on each other again until Dimitri's marriage was more established and Violet had had more time to heal. They both doubted it would make any difference, but they hoped desperately it would be alright.

November came and Violet was sure the universe was mocking her with bizarre weather and rainfall amounts unheard of even for her notoriously wet part of the world. First, a tornado tore through the University of British Columbia, the first one in over fifty years in Vancouver. Then, on the weekend after Persephone's birthday, a poetic-sounding weather pattern called an atmospheric river dropped record amounts of rain across the province, causing floods and landslides that tore apart the highways. The summer fires had destroyed the trees that held the soil, and now it poured onto roads like a deadly brown sea overflowing its shores. People drove through rivers that had once been highways, some abandoned their cars and waded to safety. Others were buried alive in their vehicles, watching helplessly as landslides engulfed them.

Vancouver was cut off from the rest of the country, with every route into the interior of the province blocked or destroyed. Apparently not having learned from experience, many people panicked and once again bought up car-loads of toilet paper, flour, canned goods, and pasta. Violet was sure she was living in a strange nightmarish version of reality. In the city that had never felt like home to her, she now felt trapped, entirely unable to connect to or understand the people around her.

Her parents of course, remained calm and assured her everything would be alright. They always had a pantry full of dried and canned goods, they wouldn't go hungry. Though the brief hysteria proved to be unwarranted, Violet was haunted by a sense that the city, perhaps even the country was pushing her out. And beyond this, and more worryingly perhaps, she wondered if *Gaia,* the earth-mother had had enough of humanity and was attempting to shake herself free of her children.

Violet of course understood that Greece too had endured its own upheavals and instabilities over the past two years, but still, she was sure that life would settle into some sort of normalcy when she was finally in the place where she belonged.

As the omicron variant quickly spread in December (it seemed a cruel joke that the strains of the virus were named after Greek letters), she followed the rules but found she had no energy left for anxiety or worry. As soon as she could, she booked a one-way ticket to Chania.

Part Three

Chapter 1

When Violet arrived in Chania on Thursday March 31, 2022, two years and eleven months later than planned, Nefeli was three months pregnant. Violet, of course, had heard the news before she left, but she was determined not to let Dimitri ruin the plans she'd waited so long to enact. Besides, after everything she'd been through, she felt invincible. She'd made it here, finally, despite everything the universe had thrown at her. Surely she was a Goddess, an Aphrodite or a Hera, ready for absolutely anything.

"I'm Boudica,"[48] she thought, smiling as she pulled her purple suitcase off the carousel with unbridled enthusiasm.

Running towards her *theia,* Violet thought how different this arrival felt compared to the one three years ago. Despite all the challenges and the delays, or maybe

---

[48] Boudica was a British female warrior, revered as a folk hero for leading her tribe in an attempted uprising against the Romans in roughly 60AD.

because of them, she felt like a much stronger version of herself now. She wondered if the things we experience, as well as the people and the places, also serve to frame us. Either way, she finally felt well-framed.

Maria was relieved to see Violet looking so excited.

"Did you bring me *spanakopita* to eat in the car?" she asked in Greek.

"Nai, veveia!" responded Maria. "And *dolmades* too!"

"No!" Violet had been dreaming of the food here. Her mother made delicious *dolmades* it was true, but the fresh Cretan herbs, homemade olive oil and freshly squeezed lemons from the backyard transformed them into something beyond compare.

"Theia Maria, did my mother ever tell you that I don't really eat fish?"

"What? No! We fed you fish everyday when you were here!"

Violet laughed. "It's OK. I didn't have the heart to tell you. But now I've decided it's OK to eat the fish Angelo catches, I trust him to be nice to them."

Maria laughed. Violet seemed so happy, even after her long plane ride. Maybe everything would be OK.

Violet had agreed to spend the first three nights with her aunt and uncle, then she'd booked herself a car rental from Kissamos and a week's stay in a hotel in the town of Maleme, about halfway between Chania and Sfinari. She didn't want to stay in Sfinari for too long, not just because she didn't want to run into Dimitri, but also because she was determined to find her own path. Maleme was cheaper than Chania and bigger than Sfinari; she was sure she could find herself a little studio flat to rent there and make a start on her lotions.

They pulled into Sfinari Bay and Violet could barely wait for the car to stop before she got out and ran towards the sea. Maria thought she might actually run straight in fully clothed, but she stopped at the water line, turned around and yelled, "It's just as beautiful as I remember! Maybe even more beautiful. *Polli oraia!*"

This time she was ready for the onslaught of food that came at her. She told her family she purposely hadn't eaten for a week before arriving, so she'd have space for the giant feast that awaited her. Everyone laughed. They were glad Violet was back. And they tried not to think about Dimitri and his pregnant wife.

On the morning of April 3rd, Violet was getting ready to leave for her hotel in Maleme. She asked Maria for some olive oil, so she could try out her recipes with her "premium" oil, as she called it. Maria took her down to the taverna, saying they had a large box there that she could take. Violet was about to protest that she only needed a couple of bottles to get started, but then remembered she was in Greece and a crate of olive oil was probably considered a meagre offering.

Angelo had just brought out the sizable case and placed it on the table outside, where Violet sat looking out to the sea she'd already swam in six times since arriving. It was April. She had to admit it was a little chilly, but she didn't mind. Angelo disappeared into the taverna, talking to his mom. At that moment, as Violet stared at the giant crate of olive oil, wondering how she'd get it into her car, and from her car into her hotel room, Dimitri and Nefeli walked past on the beach.

Dimitri momentarily wondered if he was dreaming when he glimpsed someone who looked like Violet behind one of the tamarisk trees, half-hidden behind a large box. He stopped dead in his tracks. Nefeli looked up at him, questioningly. She followed his gaze and saw Violet. Her stomach turned and dropped like a stone.

Violet was studying a bottle of olive oil and didn't see the couple straight away. When she finally looked up and saw Dimitri through the branches of the salt cedar, it was as if the past two years and ten months had never happened. Everything fell away and the air between them turned electric.

Angelo came out of the taverna, saw what was happening and quickly went back inside, telling his mother not to go out, which of course meant Maria peeked through the door to watch the scene herself. She made the sign of the cross.

"Kalimera," said Violet, finding her voice before he did.

"Kalimera," Dimitri managed to croak quietly. Neither of them moved. Nefeli tugged gently on her husband's arm. Dimitri turned to look at his wife, standing beside him, holding his hand and carrying his baby, and for a split second he didn't know who she was. He recovered quickly, but that fleeting blank look would haunt Nefeli until her dying day.

"Violet, this is my...this is Nefeli." He spoke in Greek. The word "wife" *(sizigos)* choked him and refused to come out of his mouth.

"Chairo polli,"[49] said Violet, sure her pronunciation was horrible.

Nefeli was silent, not returning the greeting. Her stone-grey eyes bored into Violet. Violet could feel her gaze but she couldn't take her eyes off Dimitri. He stood looking back at her, unable to move, all the layers of their past slowly unfolding in the spot where he'd pressed them down into nothing.

Zeus Cretagenes, the ginger and white tomcat, had appeared at Violet's feet and looked up at her, mewing imploringly. Violet didn't move. He twitched his tail and looked over at Dimitri, then began to lick his paws while still regarding him with caution. Somewhere in his mind Dimitri registered the stray cat, whom he hadn't seen since Violet's departure.

They'd been looking at each other too long and Maria decided enough was enough. Pretending she'd seen nothing, she came out of the taverna.

"Violeta, are you ready to go?" She paused, turned and pretended to suddenly notice the two bystanders on the beach. "Ah, Dimitri, Nefeli, kalimera. Ti kanete?"

Still silence. Eventually Dimitri nodded and managed to whisper, "Kalla."

Maria smiled and continued to ignore the tension. "Angelo, come help us with the olive oil!"

Angelo came out slowly and awkwardly, not wanting to get involved. He tried to avoid Dimitri's eyes. They'd always got along well, despite their families' feuding, but since Dimitri's marriage to Nefeli, things had become

---

[49] Pleased to meet you

strained between them even at the best of times, and this was certainly not the best of times. He picked up the crate with his back to the married couple and put it in Maria's car. She would drive her niece to Kissamos, where Violet would pick up her rental car and carry on to Maleme.

Violet still sat at the table, unable to move. *Zeus Cretagenes* remained at her feet, watching Dimitri. Dimitri still stood on the pebbly beach behind the tamarisk tree, frozen like a statue. Nefeli tugged his arm again, harder this time, and literally had to pull her husband away, back across the beach. She was fuming, humiliated and angry. Dimitri nearly fell over as his feet refused to move from where they were planted. He stumbled and then followed his wife, looking back once at the girl he used to call Honeybee.

Violet sat stunned. With Dimitri and Nefeli gone, Maria went over to Violet to see if she was alright. Before she could say anything, Violet turned to her aunt and spoke.

"He doesn't love her." She was confused.

Maria sighed, looked at the ground, then back at Violet. "No, he doesn't. And everyone knows, including Nefeli."

Violet shook her head. "Why did he marry her if he doesn't love her?" She actually felt sorry for Nefeli.

Maria shook her head. "Violet, it's a long and complicated story. I'll tell you what I know in the car. *Pame.*"[50]

Violet hadn't wanted to hear anything about Dimitri's engagement before, but having seen him with his wife,

---

[50] Let's go

whom he couldn't even bring himself to introduce as his wife, she wanted to understand what on earth had happened. She had always assumed that Dimitri had simply fallen in love with someone else.

The drive to Kissamos wasn't long enough for the whole story, so Maria and Violet stood outside her rental car, finishing their conversation.

Violet tried to put together the pieces.

"So, was he...sort of tricked into getting engaged?"

Maria raised her eyebrows and her shoulders, "Maybe, at first. It's hard to know. But then after his father was ill, he seemed to decide he needed to go through with it, and that was that."

Violet still wasn't satisfied. It didn't quite add up in her mind.

"I still don't get it," Violet frowned and shook her head. She looked questioningly at her aunt. "It doesn't sound like the Dimitri I knew at all."

Maria looked at Violet, unsure how much to say. Dimitri was married now, after all, and was unlikely to get divorced.

"Violet, the whole town knows he never stopped loving you. The only person who doubted that was Dimitris himself. We all told him not to go through with the marriage, and at first, it seemed like he might call it off. I don't know what happened to change his mind."

Violet stood processing this. It all sounded like a horrible mess. She was surprised to find herself feeling sorry for both Dimitri and Nefeli. She thought of Dimitri alone in his cottage over the winter, with Nefeli perhaps devising a plan for their engagement, not out of malice but out of a desperate affection she thought was love. It sounded like the plot of a painful movie, with the hero falling slowly and inevitably towards total collapse.

"What happened to Dimitri's phone?" asked Violet suddenly.

"He threw it into the sea because he couldn't bear to tell you what he'd done."

Violet remembered her panicked phone calls that morning, and then *Theia Maria* breaking the news to her over the phone. She pictured Dimitri throwing his phone into the sea while she waited for him to answer, miles away in Canada, and felt overwhelmingly grief-stricken. A tear escaped her eye, but Violet was surprised that it wasn't for her. After all, she'd surrendered all hope of being with Dimitri a year ago now. But she'd always thought that Dimitri was happy. He'd married his new love and he was happy. The realization that he was miserable filled her with a new and unexpected heartache.

Chapter 2

Nefeli hit Dimitri hard. Dimitri, not ready for the blow, twisted with the impact. They were in his cottage. Tears streamed down her face and she yelled a stream of names at him; every Greek insult she'd been taught never to say suddenly flowed out of her mouth like a toxic river.

Dimitri let her yell. He knew he deserved it. He'd humiliated his wife, who was carrying his child. There was no excuse. He hated himself vehemently in that moment. He'd vowed to be a good husband to Nefeli, but in the first few months of marriage, he'd found they had little in common and even less to say to each other. He'd rarely looked her in the eye over the past few months, and now Nefeli had seen how he looked at Violet, and she realized he'd never look at her that way. She'd married him, yes, just as she'd planned, but it hadn't occurred to Nefeli that marrying a man wouldn't make him love her. She felt everything she held dear slipping away from her and could see no way to claw it back.

She lashed out again and Dimitri let her hit him. She told him to fight back. But Dimitri had stopped fighting the day he got engaged to her.

"Nefeli, I'm not going to fight you. *Please.*"

She came towards him again but changed her mind, turning around instead and hunching over, still sobbing.

"Nefeli, I'm sorry. I deserve all of this. I hate myself right now as much as you do, if not more."

"*Ochi!* If you hated yourself as much as me you'd have drowned yourself in the sea by now!" She launched another torrent of insults at her husband, finally culminating with, "You're just like your bloody father!"

Dimitri tensed. It was the one thing that got to him, the one thing he feared most, being all the worst parts of his father. But he was too drained to take the bait. He'd been through too much and didn't want to argue anymore. His mind circled back to last year's murder, the husband who had killed his wife in a fit of rage. It had seemed so unfathomable at the time, and yet now he found himself wondering if Nefeli was as angry as the murderer had been. How had his life spiraled down to this? He took a deep breath.

"Nefeli, look, please, calm down. Will you let me talk to you? I don't want to go on like this. *Please.*" His face was red where she'd hit him, his eyes were dark wells of grief.

Nefeli glared at him, her hurt and anger still palpable in the air. But she was also exhausted, also running out of fight. She slumped down in a kitchen chair, her grey eyes still on her husband.

Dimitri sat down across from her. "Nefeli, you are my wife, and I don't want to hide anything from you anymore, and I don't want to lie to myself anymore."

Dimitri told Nefeli the whole story, as best he could. He confessed he still loved Violet, which was not news to Nefeli. Dimitri had no idea how often he called out her name in the night. Nefeli sat and listened carefully. It was painful to hear, and a few times she thought she'd ask him to stop. But she could tell her husband was finally being honest with her, and with himself. She realized she'd been a fool as well, to think that marrying a man meant you would learn to love each other, and make each other truly happy.

The next morning, while Violet explored Maleme and made enquiries in her heavily accented Greek about places to rent, Nefeli miscarried. She had gone home to her parents' house to sleep the night before. After her discussion with Dimitri, the couple had decided to give each other some space for the time being. She woke up with the sheets covered in blood and screamed until her parents came into the room.

They rushed her to the hospital, but there was nothing to be done. After checking there were no complications, Nefeli was sent home to rest and instructed to expect the equivalent of a heavy period, with blood clots and bits of tissue, over the next few days. Nefeli thought she must have misheard. She'd just lost her *child* and she was being told it was a period. She was too angry to speak and too broken to cry.

Her parents called Dimitri, who rushed to the hospital, distraught, and with a terrible feeling the loss was his fault. He felt like a murderer.

Nefeli's parents took her home, saying they thought it was best they look after her for now. Dimitri looked at his wife, who hadn't spoken a word yet. He wondered what *she* wanted, but she stared blankly into space and said nothing. Dimitri nodded and said he'd meet them back at their house. They politely told him to call tomorrow. They were aware of what had happened and were not impressed. Dimitri nodded, feeling helpless and guilt-ridden.

Over the next few weeks, Dimitri spent most of his time with Nefeli, sitting with her in her room, trying to will her back to health, but she barely looked at him. He apologized repeatedly, he brought her thyme honey and wildflowers, but she sat in her bed, staring straight ahead, refusing to speak to him.

Dimitri didn't know what to do. He was tired of hurting everyone around him without meaning to. He was worried he was just like his father, in all the wrong ways.

Nefeli, for her part, tried desperately to find a way to mourn her lost child that society and the medical profession wanted to call a heavy period. Even her mother had been matter-of-fact about it, saying it was common to miscarry on the first pregnancy. She was young, she would fall pregnant again, nothing to worry about. Nefeli had no words to express her grief and no one to help her express it. Dimitri tried, it was true, but perhaps it was too little too late. She couldn't bear the thought of hearing Violet's name one more time in the night.

Chapter 3

Violet heard about the miscarriage later that day from Maria, and her heart grew heavy in her chest. She didn't want more pain for Dimitri and his wife, and she also couldn't help but feel partly responsible. She didn't know what had happened between them after they left, but she'd seen the look in Nefeli's eyes, and could imagine what must have followed.

"*Theia Maria,* do you think it was because of what happened the day before? When I saw Dimitri?"

Maria tried to play dumb. "What do you mean?"

"Nefeli saw the way Dimitri and I looked at each other. We didn't mean to—" Violet's voice trailed off and she tried again. "Nefeli was angry, and I don't blame her. Do you think...that could have caused—"

Maria shushed her, not wanting her to say it out loud. "Violet, Nefeli already knew her husband didn't love her. She was only just twelve weeks, it was her first pregnancy, it's not uncommon."

For once, Maria chose not to say what she really thought. She didn't think it would be helpful for anyone, and Violet had been through enough. And after all, it was only a look. Nothing had happened between them and Maria knew neither of them could have done anything differently.

Back in Vancouver, Anna heard the news from her sister and immediately called Violet. Though Maria had assured her that Violet had sounded alright on the phone, Anna couldn't help but be concerned. She remembered what she'd seen between her daughter and Dimitri and she wasn't surprised it was still causing ripples. She couldn't see how it could possibly end well.

"I'm fine, Mom. You don't need to worry about me, OK?" Violet assured her.

"I know, Violet, but I'm your mother and it's my job to worry just a little bit."

Violet smiled. "I know, but really, I know it's not...a great situation, and of course I wish things were different. I feel terrible about what happened." Violet paused and swallowed hard. "But I can't change anything. And at least I'm finally here, and I'm looking at some apartments tomorrow, and I think most people here can just about understand my Greek, so I think it's gonna be OK."

Anna smiled. She was proud of the woman her daughter had become, and though she trusted her, she wasn't sure she trusted what events might unfold around her. Still, there was nothing either of them could do about that.

"OK, Violeta. I'm glad you're alright. Let me know when you find an apartment OK? We can help you with the rent for a bit if you need it."

"Mom, I've got savings and Dad already plunked a bunch of money in my account for no reason."

"That was for all the extra hours you did at the shop during the pandemic. You earned that money."

"I'm not sure I did, but thank you anyway. I'll try not to spend it all on *rakomelo.*"

"Yes, make sure you buy some *dolmades* too."

They both laughed.

A few days later, Violet found a small studio apartment to rent in Maleme. It was a little tired, but bright and airy, up in the eaves above the landlord's garage, with big windows that let the glowing Mediterranean light stream in. She could just about glimpse the Sea of Crete through her front window, between two buildings that stood across the road. She gave the walls a fresh coat of paint in a warm shade of golden yellow that reminded her of honey. She put up fresh white curtains and started to settle in, excited to have her own place for the first time in her life. It felt like a cozy nest and she could hardly believe it was hers.

It hadn't taken long to find a local beekeeper who'd agreed to supply her with honey and beeswax (it didn't seem like a good idea to ask Dimitri right now), and she'd begun some test runs of her lotions.

The local stray cats were enjoying the tins of tuna and leftovers Violet fed them, and she'd begun working on the final section of her novel. Everything was falling into place, and she did her best to keep busy and avoid thinking about Dimitri.

Orthodox Easter came on April 24th, but Violet refused her aunt and uncle's persuasive invitations to come celebrate with them in Sfinari. It would be impossible to take part in the festivities and not see Dimitri, as well as Nefeli's parents. Nefeli, she knew, still hadn't left her bed. Violet didn't want the prying eyes, the judgments, and mostly, the pain of seeing Dimitri and his suffering.

She was still new in Maleme, and though a few locals invited her to their celebrations, Violet felt uncomfortable turning up alone and friendless. She passed Easter in her flat, experimenting with lotions made from olive oil infused with local chamomile and St. John's Wort, while the calming ancient Easter chants wafted through the air from the church.

Chapter 4

When Dimitri showed up at Violet's door on May 2nd, 2022, exactly three years after she'd arrived in Chania the first time, she wrestled through a strange brew of emotions: joy at seeing him, guilt for the joy she still felt when she saw him, sorrow for what his life had become, and a slight trepidation about why he'd come.

"How did you find me?" she asked, knowing it wouldn't have been hard.

"Nice to see you too," he said a little too sarcastically, and then regretted it. He shuffled awkwardly and looked down at his feet. "It's not that hard to find the only pale Canadian in Maleme." He tried to smile but found his mouth refused.

"You want to go for a walk?" Violet sensed this would be safer than inviting Dimitri in. She had no desire to further harm Dimitri's marriage.

They walked along the seafront, passing the promenade of restaurants, most of them not yet open for the busy summer season. The beach was quiet, stretching out before them in a long straight line.

Violet and Dimitri walked slowly, on either side of the pavement, not knowing where to start. Finally Dimitri spoke.

"Violet, I was an idiot and I'm so sorry for hurting you."

Violet hadn't expected an apology. She understood now, to some extent at least, the horrible relentless chain of events that had led to his engagement and marriage.

"Dimitri, I just want you to be happy. When I heard you got engaged, honestly, I was in a pretty dark place. But I thought at least you were in love and you were happy."

Dimitri was silent for a moment. "I thought I'd be happy if I got married, started a new life, had a family. I wanted to do the right thing, but the more I try and do the right thing, the more I seem to hurt everyone around me." He paused before adding. "I'm sorry I didn't tell you I was engaged. I didn't know how to. I was a coward."

Violet looked out at the sea. It was early evening and tiny spots of sunlight twinkled on the water, dancing across the waves. "Well, I'm flattered you thought enough of me that my phone calls caused you to throw your phone into the sea."

"Oh God, Violet, who told you that?" A shadow of a sad smile crossed his face.

"My aunt of course, she knows everything that happens in Sfinari. But I asked her not to tell me anything about you. Until I saw you with Nefeli. I—" Violet wasn't sure how much she should say.

"Go on," said Dimitri quietly.

Violet figured there was no point in holding back now. After all, there was nothing left to lose. "I could tell you didn't love her and I was confused, and just...really unexpectedly sad." Violet stopped walking and looked at Dimitri. "Dimitri, why did you marry her if you don't love her?"

He looked at Violet and had to look away. He was married now. To a wife who sat silent in her room and ignored his daily visits. But then, he knew he deserved it.

He sighed. "I told myself a lot of things but most of them were lies. I'm not here to start anything, Violet. I'm married now. But the moment I saw you in Sfinari, I knew I never stopped loving you. I married Nefeli...so I could forget about you."

Violet's eyes filled with tears and she shook her head. "But I told you I was coming back!"

"Yes, but you also said that we weren't a couple and you were just my friend."

"Dimitri, we were barely talking anymore when I said that. You hadn't even told me about your dad coming back." She paused and shook her head again. "It had been so long since we'd seen each other...everything just felt like it had been a dream. And you seemed distracted. I didn't want to pressure you but I wanted to stay in your life, so I said I still cared about you as your friend. But I guess...I still thought we'd be together...eventually."

Dimitri looked at the ground, then back up at Violet, not knowing what to say and wishing desperately he had answered his phone when she'd called that day instead of throwing it into the sea. They were a full metre apart, the width of the pavement between them, neither daring to move any closer. Through their tears, they simply stood and loved each other, silently and wordlessly for several minutes before Dimitri turned and walked slowly back to his car.

He drove back down to Sfinari Bay and slept in his cave with a bottle of *raki* for company.

Chapter 5

The next morning, Dimitri's bees swarmed suddenly. He heard the low buzzing thrum from his cave and jumped up, panicked. He ran up the rocky slope and back down the other side to his hives. He'd only just checked on them the day before. There had been nothing wrong. The queens had been laying and the brood looked healthy, they weren't overcrowded. But yet, this morning, he watched as one colony after another congregated on a nearby cypress tree, then flew out to sea. He ran to get a box and a sheet, to try and catch at least one of the swarms, but he knew it was hopeless. These were not the usual swarms he'd dealt with in the past. The hives were not dividing, they were leaving.

He stumbled to his car and drove quickly and erratically to his mountain hives, his head pounding, though he knew what he would find. The air was silent and his hives were empty. The farmer across the road told him they'd swarmed at sunrise and disappeared out over the sea in a giant black cloud. Dimitri let out a cry that was more like a howl and crouched down on the ground in front of his hives.

He hadn't cheated on his wife, it was true. Nothing had happened between him and Violet. But the bees, it seems, treat faithfulness as a matter of the heart and not just the body; they understand that the line between the physical and emotional is an imaginary division.

The farmer, seeing Dimitri's distress and not knowing what to do, brought him a small bottle of fresh goat's milk. Dimitri looked up, confused. The farmer walked away as Dimitri tried to say thank you but found his mouth had gone dry and could no longer form words. He picked up the bottle and got back in his car. He realized he was probably still drunk and even by Greek standards, he shouldn't be driving. He drank the goat's milk, thinking it might help, and wondered if the farmer had smelled the *raki* on his breath.

Dimitri rested his head on the steering wheel and willed the world to be different. He willed the pandemic to never have happened, for Violet to have come two years ago, as planned, and for them to be living happily together, he didn't care where. He didn't want to be in this version of his life anymore, in this disastrous universe he'd somehow chosen, which played out as one nightmare after another. He couldn't bear the thought of going home, he couldn't manage seeing Nefeli today. He drove on, not quite sure where he was going, the way he used to drive when his father had first left, following the roads, turning whichever way beckoned.

Word spread through the village quickly that Dimitri's bees had swarmed and left. Everyone assumed he'd cheated on Nefeli with Violet. "Just like his father," some of them clucked disapprovingly. But others, who knew a little bit more of the story, felt quietly sorry for Dimitri.

Nefeli, still unable or unwilling to leave her bed, also heard about her husband's beloved bees. She wasn't surprised, and she probably blamed him less than many people in Sfinari. She understood now that love was something very different than what she'd imagined, and that she and Dimitri would never make each other happy, no matter how hard they might try.

If her family had been less traditional, she would have suggested a divorce, but she knew it was out of the question. So she remained in her bed, and though her body had healed, her heart simply refused to.

When Dimitri called on his wife the next day, her parents refused to let him into the house.

"I'm her *husband!*" Dimitri was angry and pleading at the same time.

"You don't behave like her husband," replied her father.

Dimitri understood what people had assumed, with Violet here and his bees gone. "I swear to you, I haven't been unfaithful to Nefeli," he said honestly. "I've come nearly every day since we lost our child. I'm *trying,* I want to help her. Please, she is my *wife!*" Dimitri's dark eyes shone with grief.

Nefeli's mother, Chrysoula, stood behind her husband, who blocked the half-open door. She would have let Dimitri in. After all, Nefeli hadn't asked them to turn him away. But Nefeli said very little these days. She just sat in her bed and stared, expressionless, out the window, at the buildings beyond, and a tiny glimpse of the Cretan Sea.

For three months, Dimitri returned nearly every day to see his wife but was turned away repeatedly by Aleksandros. The two men yelled and bickered. Dimitri's parents tried to talk to Nefeli's parents. Their discussions went nowhere. Nefeli still sat in her bed, watching it all unfold, wondering what on earth she'd unleashed with her one simple wish to marry Dimitri. She stopped eating.

Chapter 6

Violet continued to stay away from Sfinari as much as possible. She'd heard about Dimitri's bees and knew how heartbroken he'd be. She desperately wanted to reach out and comfort him but she was aware it wasn't her place. He wasn't hers to help. And of course she remembered what Dimitri had told her three years ago, in another lifetime, about bees turning on beekeepers who were unfaithful to their wives. But all they'd done was talk, they hadn't even touched.

Maria had called her the day after and asked her bluntly if she'd been with Dimitri.

"He came to my place, we went for a walk, we only talked," replied Violet, exasperated. "We didn't even stand close to each other! I'm not a home-wrecker, *Theia Maria!*"

"OK, OK, I believe you, Violet, but most of the town doesn't." She paused and sighed. "Nefeli's parents won't even let him in to see her."

Violet felt terrible and powerless. She felt responsible for the way things were unfolding but wasn't sure what she could have possibly done differently. She hadn't come here to cause trouble for Dimitri, but the unrest seemed to follow her like *Zeus Cretagenes* at Sfinari Beach.

So Violet resolved to keep herself busy and tried not to think about the man she loved, and his ailing wife he wasn't allowed to see. She swam whenever she could off the beaches of Maleme, often pushing herself to swim as far away from the shore as possible, ensuring she arrived back on the beach too exhausted to think.

Violet called her mother from the beach one night, following a long evening swim. Anna could tell she was struggling a little, though still trying her best to put on a brave face.

"I just feel like no matter what I do, I make Dimitri's life worse just by being here. And it's hard not to feel like it's kind of my fault that he lost...his bees." She thought about the other loss, the unborn child, but couldn't bring herself to voice this.

"Violet, Dimitri's choices made his life worse. You being there is just a reminder for him of what his life *could* have been."

"Maybe. But it sounded like his choices were made for him in lots of ways." Violet paused and looked out over the sea. It was twilight and the waves were turning a deeper shade of blue. She remembered the drawings she'd made in her therapy sessions with Steven, the pages full of sea, the blues turning darker and the water becoming heavier as she searched for Persephone and Dimitri.

Her eyelids felt suddenly heavy and she wished she was in her bed.

"That might be true, Violet, but you know, sometimes there just isn't anything we can do, and there's no one to blame. It's just...the way things worked out."

"I know," said Violet sleepily, lying back on her towel on the pebbles and closing her eyes. She wondered if she fell asleep here, whether she'd wake up with a blanket on her. But she knew the answer. "I'm gonna go, Mom. I'm really tired and I think sleeping on the beach would be slightly frowned upon here."

Anna laughed quietly. "OK, have a good sleep. I love you."

"Love you too."

A few days after Dimitri's visit, a small black and white cat appeared outside her door, mewing loudly. Violet had been feeding the local stray cats regularly, up near the dumpsters just behind the town where they tended to congregate. However, she didn't recognize this particular cat with its striking markings. One half of her small face was completely black, the other white, giving her the appearance of a feline yin yang. Her body was mainly white, with another black patch near her tail, which then extended in grey and black rings reminiscent of a raccoon. Violet lured the cat over to the road with a tin of tuna and a bowl of water, not wanting to break her agreement with the landlord to refrain from feeding the cats on his property. The cat ate and drank gratefully, and Violet gently shooed away the other cats that came hoping for a bite. She'd feed them later; right now she wanted to make sure this small newcomer had enough to eat.

As Violet returned to her apartment, the cat followed her and mewed forlornly when she went inside. It began to rain, and the thought of her out there alone in the wet world was too much for Violet. She went back out and picked up the cat, who was surprisingly happy to be held, and knocked on the landlord's door with the small stray animal in her arms, the rain soaking both of them. She asked if she could adopt the cat. The landlord, a middle-aged Greek man with a large belly who generally regarded the cats as vermin, was surprised. He shrugged. "If you want," he said in Greek, looking a little distastefully at the small wet creature.

Violet smiled excitedly. *"Efharisto polli!"* she said, as she turned and ran back to her apartment with her new pet.

She already knew the cat's name. With its black and white face, balancing dark and light, she was Persephone, of course.

Chapter 7

Maleme was a small town, and everyone soon knew about the pale Canadian girl who fed the stray cats, and spoke Greek with a thick accent, often getting syllables in the wrong order in long words. Rumours flew that were half-truth, half-invented. Some people said she was here chasing the memory of her Greek lover who had died of Covid-19. Others said she was having an affair with a married man, a goat farmer, who lived in the mountains. Still others, closest to the truth, said simply that she was in love with a man she could never be with.

So, when Violet walked into the small shop by the beach in early May, with a box of sample lotions, Antonia, the shop owner, knew exactly who she was, and wondered curiously which version of her story was true. Her shop sold mainly sunhats, towels and summer clothes, but also carried sunscreen and a handful of cosmetic products. Violet thought she might as well ask. It was daunting and she was nervous, but she'd been through much more harrowing things than selling lotions before. She heard the torch-bearer's voice in her mind, "Be bold, be big, be brave, be beautiful." She tried to channel her inner peacock.

"Kalimera," she said, entering the shop, and hoping she sounded more confident than she felt.

"Kalimera," replied Antonia, eyeing the box in Violet's hands. "How can I help you?"

Violet introduced herself and unpacked her lotions.

Antonia was intrigued. As she rubbed some into her hands, she read the label and asked in Greek, "Who are Melissa and Persephone?"

"Melissa is my middle name, and of course, it means honeybee. I use local honey and beeswax in the lotions." She paused and Antonia waited. "Persephone was my best friend. These are based on her recipes."

Antonia wanted to know more, but had noted the past tense, and the pause between sentences, and decided not to ask. She agreed to purchase a small batch of lotions. The shop had of course, struggled greatly through the pandemic, and she knew she shouldn't be bringing in new stock, but it was only a small purchase and she wanted to help this newcomer with the intriguing story. Besides, the lotions were divine. Antonia purchased one for herself immediately.

When Violet returned a few days later with Antonia's order, the two women began to chat. Antonia was interested to hear that Violet's mother ran a jewelry shop in Canada, and that Violet had helped her mother set up an online shop at the start of the pandemic. Antonia hadn't felt her shop lent itself to being online, and it had seemed far too overwhelming of a project, but talking to Violet, she wondered if there might be scope to pursue something together.

Later that week, they met for drinks at the taverna next door and crafted a business plan. They decided to set up an online shop carrying a range of Cretan handmade products, including of course, Violet's lotions. They would sell directly to customers, and would also distribute the items to shops, connecting craftspeople with appropriate retailers and vice versa. Violet asked her if she knew Niko, in Polyrhinnia, who made olive wood items. Antonia shook her head. Violet showed her the necklace she was wearing, with the olive wood beads. She'd stopped wearing it after she found out Dimitri was engaged, but these days, it felt like a comforting link to a simpler past, though she never wore it on her rare visits to Sfinari. She still had the carved Malia honeybees as well, though she alternated between leaning it up against the mirror on her dresser, and tucking it away, unsure whether looking at it made her feel better or worse.

Violet and Antonia became fast friends and business partners, and Violet spent the summer helping Antonia in the shop and working with her to set up their online shop and distribution company. She'd also very nearly finished her novel, though the final chapters continued to elude her. She was grateful to be busy, and to have a friend in her new hometown.

When August arrived, however, Violet became increasingly agitated and distracted. Her mother called her and texted her more often, conscious of the date that was approaching, but Violet found herself not answering most of her calls, and replying with only short texts, lacking the energy to pretend that she was alright so her mother wouldn't worry. Dark circles began to form under her eyes and she began to make mistakes at work, missing details she would normally have noticed. Antonia asked her several times if she was alright. Violet nodded and said she was just tired. She hadn't been sleeping well; she'd been dreaming of Dimitri and Persephone again.

In one horrible nightmare, she found herself in a dark cave, and she watched Dimitri stab Persephone with the beak of a giant bird. He then flew away down the dark damp corridor with a pair of black feathered wings she knew were stolen from a fallen siren.

On the morning after this particular nightmare, feeling shaken and vulnerable, Violet confessed to her new friend that August was a difficult month for her. They closed the shop early that day and went to the taverna next door for an early dinner. It was a place they'd frequented regularly since Violet's arrival. Over too many *dolmades,* delicious *boureki,* local red wine, and a surprisingly tasty lemon *raki,* Violet recounted, as briefly as she could, what had happened to Persephone, and the doomed romance that had followed with Dimitri. Antonia listened sympathetically, as Violet spoke in half-Greek, half-English, her Greek deteriorating as she consumed the wine. Antonia had heard all the rumours but none of them had come close to the heart-wrenching truth of Violet's story.

Their waiter, whom Antonia knew was named Telis, brought them some more lemon *raki,* unprompted. "On the house," he offered, sensing they needed it. Antonia had noticed him trying to catch Violet's eye the last few times they'd been here, though Violet remained entirely oblivious.

Antonia thanked him and smiled. Violet's gaze remained on the table as Telis glanced at her, trying to look casual, while silently willing her to look up.

When he'd left again, Antonia suggested they think of something to honour the memory of Persephone this August. Violet thought. It was strange to not be at home this time, nowhere near their secret river spot where she usually went to clear her head at times like this. She thought of Persephone's music; she had scans of all the scores on her computer. "Do you know any musicians?" she asked Antonia.

Antonia nodded, though she was becoming increasingly distracted by Telis' attempts to catch Violet's attention.

Chapter 8

Pantelis (Telis)

Παντελής (Τέλης)

Telis' family ran the taverna next door to Antonia's shop, and the families knew each other quite well. Called simply *Taverna Maleme,* it was one of the few in the town that remained open all year, and was a favourite with the locals. It wasn't quite on the beach, but had a charming patio area surrounded by leafy vines and lemon trees. The floor was laid in brick red and golden-yellow hexagon tiles, reminiscent of a honeycomb. The decor was simple, but homely, and the food traditional and hearty.

The youngest of four, Telis had felt it was his duty to stay and help his parents at the taverna. A charming and sociable type, he enjoyed the work, but also secretly wished he could have had the opportunity to spread his wings elsewhere, as his siblings had done. He was twenty-nine, easy on the eyes and quietly confident.

He'd been intrigued by Violet from the start. Like everyone else in the town, he'd heard rumours about her and wondered what the truth was. When she started visiting the taverna regularly with Antonia, he began to hope for a friendship, and possibly more.

Violet, however, appeared completely oblivious to his existence, which only made him increasingly curious and attracted to her. While he wasn't by any means vain, he was used to at least being noticed by women, and was perplexed that this exotic pale creature who often emphasized the wrong syllable when ordering in Greek, had barely looked at him in the several months she'd been coming to the taverna.

That particular evening in early August, he watched Violet and Antonia closely, though subtly, and could see the conversation was charged with emotion. They spoke quietly, in a mix of Greek and English, and though Telis couldn't hear the words, he could see Violet was upset and wondered if Antonia was finally learning her friend's backstory.

Not sure what to do, but wanting to be helpful, he brought them another round of lemon *raki*. Violet didn't look up and he walked away, sighing quietly. He would have to be less subtle if he was going to catch her attention.

When he brought them their bill later, he charged them for much less than they'd ordered and Antonia protested.

He waved away her objections. "You two are here all the time, you get the regulars' discount."

Antonia smiled and thanked him, paid the bill in cash, and said they'd be sure to come back next week. He nodded and looked at Violet, who was still staring blankly at the empty *raki* glasses on the table. She finally glanced up at him.

"Efharisto polli," she said quietly, suddenly self-conscious about her accent as she saw the intensity of his gaze on her.

Telis didn't miss a beat. "Do you like our lemon *raki?"* he asked, now that he had her attention.

"Yes," replied Violet. "It's delicious, thank you so much."

"It's our family recipe. My great-grandfather came up with it for my great-grandmother."

"Oh?" said Violet. "Did she like lemons a lot?"

He shrugged. "Maybe. The story is that she was very difficult, so my great-grandfather had to find a way to make her...relax a little."

"Make her relax?" said Violet, now feeling slightly irked, as well as exhausted. "Why was she so difficult? Did she dare have her own will separate from her husband's? And why did he marry her anyway if she was so 'difficult'?"

Telis sensed he was on shaky ground and wished he'd never mentioned his great-grandparents' relationship dynamics. "Well, he married her because she was very beautiful. And I suspect he didn't have a lot of options at the time. And you know, things were different back then, not like today." He hoped he'd recovered, but feared he'd completely blown his chance with Violet, if indeed he'd ever had one.

Violet looked at him and blinked, not entirely impressed, but noticing he looked suddenly very uncomfortable and a little hurt. She realized she'd probably been too hard on him. "Well, at least something good came out of it all," she offered, in order to make peace and bring the conversation to an end.

Telis nodded, feeling deflated as he said goodbye and walked away from their table.

Antonia raised her eyebrows at Violet.

"What?" said Violet, though she had an idea what was coming.

"I know you're having a rough time of it, Violet, but poor Telis has been trying for weeks to catch your eye. He's completely smitten with you. And when you finally acknowledge him it's only to tear into his great-grandfather for possibly being sexist?"

Antonia had always liked Telis. He'd dated a cousin of hers two years ago, and everyone had assumed they would soon be engaged. But her cousin had ended the relationship suddenly, leaving Telis heart-broken. While he'd since recovered and moved on, Violet's sharp criticisms had stirred up memories for Antonia and she'd found it difficult to watch.

Violet sighed. She'd already regretted her over-reaction, but hadn't registered Telis' attentions at all. She rested her forehead in her palm. She felt awful for all sorts of reasons and this didn't help. And she'd definitely had too much wine and lemon *raki*. "I didn't know he was trying to catch my eye. Anyway, Antonia, I'm not...really able to even think about romance right now. I'll probably just be single forever and have lots of cats, and I'm totally OK with that."

Chapter 9

Not to be deterred, and with a bit of encouragement from Antonia, Telis showed up at Violet's door a few days later with a bottle of red wine, two glasses, and a picnic blanket. Violet was still not accustomed to anyone in the town being able to find her and call on her, and was surprised, but flattered.

"I heard it's your birthday soon. I thought we could have a toast on the beach, and maybe I could make up for upsetting you last week." he said quietly with a nervous smile.

Violet took in Telis properly for the first time, but found herself simply comparing him to Dimitri. He had the same colouring, but with green eyes and slightly smaller stature. His hair was cut shorter. He was younger, nearer to her age. Though he was confident, he lacked Dimitri's quick wit or playfulness. He had a certain charm, but it was a quieter type than Dimitri's. She felt guilty that she couldn't measure Telis against himself, but only against her now-married ex-boyfriend.

However, she appreciated this sweet gesture, and the truth was Violet had begun to feel a little lonely. She'd seen her family far less than she'd planned, and though the locals had always been kind and welcoming, Antonia was the only real friend she had at the moment in Maleme.

"Thank you, that sounds lovely," said Violet, smiling. "But, you know, my birthday's not for a week."

Telis smiled back and relaxed a little. "I know, but the taverna gets really busy around the Feast of the Dormition, so I thought an early celebration might be nice."

Violet's birthday fell on the day after the biggest summer festival in Greece, which made it slightly awkward to properly mark. She couldn't help but be pleased that Telis had planned this small thoughtful gesture.

They walked down to the pebbly beach, which stretched out along the sea and found a quiet spot away from the busy restaurants. Telis laid out the red blanket and poured them each a drink. *"Stin eyia su,"*[51] he said. *"Chronia polla!"*

They clinked glasses and sipped the wine, looking out over the quiet waves in the evening light.

"So how do you like Maleme so far?" he asked.

"It's lovely," replied Violet. "It's nice to be so near to the sea." She gestured at the waves lapping gently on the shore. "And I've got a cat, and I met Antonia, so it seems to be working out." She thought of all the other things she wanted to say: that she'd hoped to see her aunt and

---

[51] "To your health," a common Greek toast

uncle and her grandparents more, and that she'd expected to at least see Dimitri happy. She managed a faint smile.

"Why did you choose Maleme?" he asked curiously. "I mean, it's not exactly a place people move to from overseas."

Violet laughed quietly. "I know. I wanted to live in Chania, but it's cheaper here, and it's closer to Sfinari, where I have family. It seemed to make sense." She paused. "What about you? Are you from here?"

He nodded. "My family's had the taverna for four generations now."

"And will you take it over from your parents?"

He nodded again. "I'm hoping one of my siblings might return at some point and help me out with it. I don't mind doing it, but it's a lot to do on your own."

"All your siblings left then?"

"Yes, my brother went to Iraklion a few years ago, and my two sisters have been in Athens for...six years now I think."

"Why do so many people leave Crete, or at least move to the capital?" wondered Violet out loud. "It's so beautiful here."

"They want opportunities," replied Telis simply. "There aren't a lot of opportunities here, not a lot of options."

Violet recalled Dimitri's story of the plethora of options in the American grocery store, and her own sense of being paralyzed by choice back in Canada.

"Sometimes it's easier having fewer options though," countered Violet.

"Is it?" asked Telis, not sure at all that he agreed.

"I think so. I used to feel paralyzed back home, by so many options. Here, there's only really one shop I could sell my lotions in, so I went in, and I met Antonia. And things kind of just fell into place from there. In Vancouver, there would've been a million stores to choose from. I mean, I sold a few things in a shop I worked in, but to do anything more than that would have been unbelievably daunting and I probably wouldn't have even tried."

"Sure," replied Telis, "but what if you'd gone into Antonia's shop and she didn't want to sell your lotions, and you didn't get along at all. Then what would you have done?"

Violet shrugged. "I don't know. But sometimes you just know when you're on the right path in the right place, and the options...they appear when you need them." She thought of the torchbearer and the "breadcrumbs" she'd followed in order to arrive where she was, but she knew it was too much to explain on a first meeting.

Telis looked out over the sea and wished the magical options Violet spoke of would appear for him at some point. He wasn't unhappy with his lot in life, he just wished he could experience something different, even for a year or two.

They sat in silence sipping the wine for a few minutes. Violet was aware of the romantic nature of the evening but was trying not to think about it. She was enjoying Telis' company but the thought of a relationship, even dating, felt entirely alien and terrifying. She still loved Dimitri and wasn't sure she'd ever stop loving him.

Telis topped up their glasses and moved a little closer. Violet began to feel nervous. She didn't want to lead him on.

"Telis, this is really nice, but I just want you to know...I'm not, I mean, I can't offer anything more than friendship right now."

Telis hadn't expected this sudden confession but wasn't entirely surprised either. Though the rumours varied, they all centred around Violet being in love with someone she couldn't be with.

"That's OK," said Telis. "I just wanted to get to know you a bit."

Violet looked down at the dark red liquid in her glass, suddenly aware that it was nearly the colour of blood.

"Who hurt you?" Telis asked quietly after a pause.

Violet drew in her breath slowly. She wasn't sure she wanted to talk about Dimitri. She paused so long Telis assumed she wasn't going to answer and wished he hadn't asked.

"I met someone when I came here a few years ago. I was supposed to come back the following year, but...the pandemic hit. I kept getting delayed. Eventually...he married someone else." She paused and breathed in deeply again, looking down at the blanket and the pebbles in front of it. "But he doesn't love her," she added.

Telis could feel the pain in Violet's words and wished he could be the one to comfort her, but he sensed she only had room in her heart for this one man.

"Does he still love you?" he asked.

Violet nodded.

"And you still love him," added Telis. It was more of a statement than a question, but Violet nodded anyway.

They sat together as the air cooled and the light began to fade, sipping the wine and speaking little. Telis wished he could think of something to say or do to make Violet feel better, but the silence between them wasn't uncomfortable, it was strangely peaceful. He figured he could play the long game; they could be friends for now and eventually he would win her heart. After all, the man she loved was married and surely she'd eventually have to move on.

The sun sank below the horizon, out of sight from their vantage-point on the north shore of the island. Violet thought of the beautiful sunsets of Sfinari and sighed quietly. They stood up, folded up the blanket and picked up what was left of the wine. Telis walked Violet home slowly.

At her door, he put down the wine and the blanket and offered her a hug. He hadn't been planning on anything more than that, he was resigned to simply being Violet's friend, for now at least. But something happened when he wrapped his arms around her that neither of them expected. Violet found herself unable to let go, the sensation of his body against hers making her feel unexpectedly safe, rather than terrified. All the feelings she'd tucked away deep down for several years seemed to well up inside her and overflow into their embrace. Telis, happily surprised, kissed her softly as she looked up at him. Violet felt everything melt away.

Chapter 10

Violet panicked. She'd woken up next to Telis and as the events of the previous night came back to her, she wondered what on earth she'd been thinking. At some point, she must have invited him upstairs; it was all an unfathomable blur in her mind. Something outside of herself had seemed to take over and propel the situation; she was sure she hadn't chosen to be with Telis. She didn't love Telis, she loved Dimitri. And yet, last night, she'd been completely powerless to resist the attentions of a man who, however, pleasant and attractive, was not the man she loved.

She carefully got out of the bed without waking him, and dressed quickly. Persephone the cat mewed at her imploringly, and Violet, functioning on auto-pilot, fed her quickly. She then stood and fretted, frozen between the bed and her kitchen table, looking at Telis asleep in her bed, then turning away, and hoping that when she looked again, he simply wouldn't be there. She turned towards her dresser and her eyes caught sight of the olive wood honeybees Dimitri had sent her for her birthday several years ago, leaning against her mirror.

At that moment, Telis opened his eyes and took in Violet, frowning at a small wooden object on her dresser, looking distracted and distraught.

"Kalimera," he said quietly.

Violet jumped, as if she'd forgotten he was there, though she was of course all too aware of his presence. She looked over at him in silence.

"Are you OK?" he asked, propping himself up on an elbow.

Violet nodded, knowing her response was entirely unconvincing. She couldn't look him in the eye. Turning her gaze back to the honeybees, she tried to slow her breathing.

Telis found his clothes and dressed quickly. He knew Violet was not OK. He walked over to her and followed her eyes to the olive wood carving. She still hadn't spoken and Telis tried to think of something to say.

"Was that a gift?" he asked carefully.

"Yes." Violet closed her eyes. She wasn't sure if she wanted Telis to leave, or to hug her, maybe even kiss her one more time. But she knew it wasn't Telis she wanted, and it wasn't fair to him.

"I used you," she whispered hoarsely without turning her head.

Telis jerked his head back in shocked bewilderment. *"You* used *me?"* She had spoken in Greek and he was convinced she'd simply confused the pronouns. Telis had been accused of using women once or twice, but he'd certainly never had a woman tell him she'd used him.

Violet, however, nodded. "Yes. I'm so sorry, Telis. I just, I didn't mean for anything to happen between us. I...I love someone else."

Telis shook his head and frowned, trying to process what she was saying.

"OK. I don't love you either. I mean, I didn't expect you to wake up in love with me. But I thought we could just see where things might go?"

Violet shook her head slowly. "I can't. I know I won't ever love you, and it wouldn't be fair to you." She still looked at the honeybees. Persephone the cat had finished her breakfast and approached Violet, rubbing against her legs and meowing loudly.

Telis wasn't used to being rejected; Violet was the first woman in years he'd been drawn to as more than a casual companion. And she didn't want him. His pride and his heart were both bruised.

"But what does he have that I don't? Besides a wife?"

It sounded harsher than Telis had planned and he immediately wished he could take back the second question.

Violet turned away from him and looked sightlessly at her kitchen sink. The question felt like a sting in her chest; she turned slowly back to the honeybees on her dresser. Bees only sting when they're threatened.

"Love isn't a checklist, Telis." She sighed. "You're not missing anything." She shook her head. "I do...like you. But love...it's just not there." Persephone mewed again but Violet didn't move. Unaccustomed to this lack of response from her owner, Persephone turned and looked accusingly at Telis.

Telis looked down at the cat and frowned. He wasn't generally a fan of feline companions. "So, you like me enough to sleep with me, but not enough to give me a chance to be with you?" He was torn between anger and pleading. He wasn't sure he liked the words that were coming out of his mouth but couldn't seem to stop them.

Violet grimaced slightly and turned away again. His questions hurt, but she could tell they were coming from his own wounds, wounds she'd inflicted on him, and she felt awful. The two of them seemed to be swimming through a sea of bruised and confused emotions.

"I'm so sorry. I didn't mean for that to happen." She looked down at the floor. "I guess I was just...lonely. I'm so sorry if I got your hopes up." She managed to glance at him but found him staring at the Malia bees, a look of defeat mingled with anger on his face.

"Gamoto," he muttered under his breath.

Violet remembered the first time she'd heard that word when Dimitri had followed her into the sea, over three years ago now. She closed her eyes and tried to shut out the memory.

Telis sighed. This wasn't the morning he'd hoped to have with Violet. "Should I go then?"

Violet imagined him leaving, and the thought suddenly filled her with an intense loneliness. She didn't want him to stay, but she also didn't want to be alone.

"Tea?" she managed to ask quietly.

"Tea?" echoed a confused Telis. "You want tea?"

"Yes please," answered Violet.

"You want *me* to make tea?"

Violet nodded, her gaze still fixed on the honeybees.

Telis was exasperated. He'd just been told by a woman he desired that she didn't love him, that she'd used him because she was lonely, and now she was asking him to make tea in her home. He was accustomed to cultural differences at work, but this was a whole different playing field. He was about to say that this wasn't the taverna, and if she wanted him to stay for tea, she should make it herself.

But as he watched her wipe away a tear that had escaped, his anger dissipated into a sigh. This wasn't a battle he wanted to fight right now. And despite everything, he was still inexplicably drawn to Violet, and still clung to a hope that one day she might return his affections. After all, how long could she possibly wait for a married man? He walked over to the kitchen and put the kettle on. He searched several cupboards, eventually finding mugs, teabags, and honey.

As he placed their mugs of tea down on Violet's small table, she sat down across from him and finally managed to look up at him as she held the warm cup in her hands. She tried to read his expression. He seemed angry and disappointed, but also somehow begging for something she knew she couldn't give.

"I'm so sorry Telis, I really didn't mean to hurt you." Violet held back the tears.

Telis sighed. "Are you really going to wait for him for...forever?" His tone had softened a little, though his agitation still seeped through.

"I don't know. I really don't know. I know it's ridiculous, Telis, but I can't just turn off my feelings like a...light switch." She looked down into her mug. "I'm so sorry," she repeated yet again.

Telis sipped his tea and tried to put aside his battered ego. He wished vehemently that he didn't fancy Violet so much, and could have just brushed her off and stormed out. But she seemed to cast a strange spell on him. And it was true, she hadn't promised him anything. Sex wasn't a contract.

He sighed. "You did tell me that you loved someone else. You don't need to keep apologizing."

Violet's mind was brought back briefly to Aptera, where she'd told Dimitri about Persephone, and then apologized for making him cry. She lowered her head onto her arm, her other hand grasping the mug handle. She wondered why she was always apologizing for feeling things, or for making other people feel things.

Her black and white cat jumped up onto her lap, awkwardly squeezing in between her legs and the table, purring loudly. Violet thought of her best friend who had seemed to never need anyone, and wished desperately that she could have been similarly self-contained. She was exhausted from the loneliness of loving Dimitri, and ashamed that this very loneliness had caused her to desire a man she didn't love and barely knew.

She thought how much easier things would be if she could simply love Telis instead of Dimitri, and wondered why this wasn't a choice that was hers to make.

Telis drank half of his tea, and then stood up to leave.

Violet tried to stand up from her chair but found that not only had her legs lost their strength, but Persephone stubbornly refused to move. "I guess I'll...see you at the taverna? I mean, if that's OK?" she asked quietly, looking up at him from her chair.

Telis managed a half-smile. "Of course." Unsure what was an appropriate goodbye gesture in the situation, he put his hand on her shoulder for a moment. He remembered how her shoulder, and indeed the rest of her, had looked the night before in the moonlight that streamed in through the curtains. But in the look she gave back to him, he saw only friendly affection mingled with sadness. He tried to silence the voice in his mind that said she would never love him, however much she might want to. Telis walked down the stairs and let himself out, hoping no one would see him leaving.

Chapter 11

Anna and Martin

Anna tapped the kitchen table nervously and Martin looked across at her, raising his eyebrows. He knew she only tapped when she was anxious about something.

"She's OK you know," he said, taking a sip of tea.

Anna sighed. "I know, I know."

It was five days before Violet's birthday, and the two of them were having a quiet cup of tea after dinner. Violet hadn't answered Anna's calls earlier that day. A short text came in yesterday, but nothing today. She'd been in touch with Maria, who also hadn't heard much from Violet in the past few days. Any other time of year, Anna wouldn't have worried so much, but it was August.

"She's probably just busy, which is a good thing," Martin offered. "And she'll call you tomorrow, for your birthday for sure."

Anna nodded and restrained herself from tapping the table yet again. After a pause she said unexpectedly,

"Martin, what do you think would have happened between us if I hadn't gone with you to Vancouver?"

Martin raised his eyebrows again. "Well, surely you would have missed me so terribly you would have come a few weeks or months later." He smiled playfully.

Anna smiled back but continued. "Well of course. But, what if something had happened, something like the pandemic, and I couldn't get to Vancouver. What would have happened between us do you think?"

Martin looked at his wife and tried to imagine his life without her, but found it simply didn't make any sense. "I would have waited until you could come. We would have worked it out somehow," he said simply.

Anna smiled faintly and looked down at her cup of tea. "But I'm sure Dimitri would have said the same thing if we'd asked him, before the pandemic."

Martin looked at her quizzically. "You're not implying I'd have married someone else if you'd taken a few years to come to Vancouver?"

Anna laughed. "Well, we just don't know what would have happened, do we? I saw the two of them together, and honestly Martin, I was certain they were made for each other. And the fact that Violet's presence has caused such disruption to Dimitri's marriage and his life, it only goes to show how strong what they had was...and yet, for whatever reason, he married that poor girl he doesn't love."

Martin sighed. "Anna, I don't know about Dimitri and Violet. But you know, I couldn't possibly have done anything other than wait for you."

Anna looked into her husband's blue eyes and felt overwhelmingly lucky to have found a man so kind and loving and absolutely devoted to her, even after all these years. She only wanted the same for her daughter.

Chapter 12

Violet couldn't bring herself to tell anyone about her brief tryst for several days. She even ignored her mother's phone calls, managing only a short conversation on Anna's birthday on August 12th. She knew she'd sounded distracted, but her night with Telis wasn't something she felt able to talk to her mother about, and besides, she didn't want to cause her any extra worry.

She would have preferred to simply pretend the evening had never happened, but when Antonia suggested they go to the *Taverna Maleme* a few days later, Violet finally told her what had unfolded that night, in as few words as she could.

"We can go back there in a few weeks," sighed Violet. "Just not yet, please."

"OK," said Antonia. "But, can I ask what was so upsetting about it? I mean, Telis is nice, and he's cute. And he seems to really like you. You're both single and you had a fun romantic night together. What's the problem?"

Violet sighed. "I don't know. I just hadn't been with anyone since Dimitri...and I didn't think I would be, or would want to be, certainly not anytime soon. It caught me off guard, I guess."

Violet also had a nagging and illogical feeling that she'd somehow betrayed Dimitri, or perhaps her memory of their love, by being with Telis. She knew it made no sense. Dimitri had married someone else; she owed him nothing. But her heart felt out of place and bruised by the event.

Antonia regarded her friend carefully. "You don't owe Dimitri anything. You know that, right?"

Violet sighed. Antonia was getting far too good at reading her. "I know. Of course I know. But it still feels...wrong." She shrugged, not knowing what else to add.

Antonia shook her head. "Well, I for one, am glad you were with someone new. And you could do a lot worse than Telis. But mostly, I hope you haven't ruined our chances of ever drinking that lemon *raki* again."

Violet laughed. "Don't worry, I wouldn't dream of depriving us of lemon *raki* for long. And believe me, I wish I could fall in love with Telis, it would make things a lot easier. But it's just not going to happen."

Antonia sighed. "Well, Miss heart-breaker, tomorrow is *Dekapentavgoustos*.[52] If you're not going to Sfinari, I was going to invite you for lunch with my family. Not at Telis' taverna, don't worry."

"Thank you, that sounds really nice," replied Violet.

---

[52] The Feast of the Dormition of Mary on August 15th, a major holiday in Greece.

She knew if she went to visit her family during the festivities, she wouldn't be able to avoid running into Dimitri. He'd doubtless be working at the taverna, right next door to where her family would be celebrating and eating. She'd arranged to head over a few days later to celebrate her birthday.

"I was also going to ask if you'd mind coming in a bit early on your birthday," added Antonia. There are some website issues I wanted to look over with you before the shop opens."

Violet didn't mind. She preferred keeping busy, especially in August, and even more so after her unplanned dalliance.

She'd been focused on working through the process of getting licensed to officially sell her lotions in Greece, which was proving complicated. Though Antonia was happy to sell her products, Violet knew she couldn't approach the busier shops in the cities, or sell anything online until she had her license in place. Antonia had put her in touch with a family friend in Chania who had started her own cosmetic line. As far as she could gather from their conversations, she needed to find someone with a chemistry degree to collaborate with and sign off on the ingredients. It seemed oddly strict for a country whose citizens were known for rule-breaking and more than a hint of rebelliousness; but the EU regulations were understandably robust. Still, she'd been given a few leads on suitable contacts and was chasing them up, hopeful she'd find someone willing to help.

Violet arrived at the shop on the morning of her birthday, tired from a late night struggling to make sense of a chain of emails in Greek, between Antonia's friend and a recent chemistry graduate, a potential collaborator. At least she hadn't had any nightmares.

She opened the door to the store, still bleary-eyed, and took in the sound of "Demeter's Waltz" being played from Antonia's phone. Antonia's cousin was a music teacher in Iraklion, and he'd recorded a few of Persephone's pieces on guitar and piano.

Violet stood near the store entrance in disbelief. She recognized the melody, but having never heard the harmonies, the counterpoint, or the bass notes beneath it, she was struck by how much it changed the graceful theme that she'd thought she knew so well. The notes all seemed to be working together, though separate at the same time; they played off each other, interacting, creating expectations that were then broken and redefined. Dissonances were struck and then resolved, questions asked and nearly answered before being swept away back to the main theme where the notes all chimed in consonance once again.

Violet remembered Perse telling her about framing, and how important context was, and she understood now how much the melody needed the notes around it, the *right* notes around it. And though she tried not to, she remembered Dimitri talking about the bees in his hives, and the importance of community. She broke down in tears, but they were mainly happy tears. Antonia rushed over to her, worried she'd upset her friend.

"No, no, it's just so lovely to finally hear it, all of it. *Efharisto polli.*"

Chapter 13

Richard

Four years after his daughter's death, Richard sat alone on her bed. He'd finally managed to clear out her room and now he sat looking at the few things he'd kept and wondered if he should have simply left everything intact and pretended he was expecting Persephone home at any moment. But what was done was done, and he was on his way out now anyway.

Earlier that year, Richard had hit a wall. His work had dried up, there were no contracts in sight, and he'd read all the books on his shelves so many times he knew them by heart. When Harmony had left him, he'd been alright; he still had his mother and Persephone. When his mother had died, it was hard, but again, he'd been alright; he still had Persephone. But when Persephone was taken from him so suddenly and violently, he was left drifting, belonging to no one. He'd buried himself in his work, managing to somehow ignore the pandemic (he didn't go out much anyway), but when he found himself out of work in the strange new post-pandemic world, he simply didn't have any comforts left in his small world. He floated through dull repetitive days and weeks, eating scrambled eggs and toast and cereal, hoping some new cave art might be discovered somewhere soon.

On a dreary April day, as tears fell on his breakfast (or was it lunch?), Richard's eyes wandered over to Persephone's open bedroom door, just visible from the kitchen where he sat. Only a few items, as well as the furniture, remained in it now. One of those items was her old film camera, an Olympus XA she'd found at a garage sale, seemingly barely used. She'd bought it on a whim; she hadn't known what a find it was until she researched it later. It was the camera she'd taken on her trip to Cornwall with Violet.

Richard saw it sitting on her shelf, next to her photo albums and felt compelled to go in and flip through the albums. He picked up the one labelled 'Cornwall', opened it carefully, and tried to see the world through his daughter's eyes by staring hard into the black and white photographs. Inside the album, at the back, was a booklet about Cornish folklore. He flipped through and read about the Piskies. His mother's family had left Cornwall when she was only twelve, and she'd always said she felt mainly Canadian, though remnants of a Cornish accent still infiltrated her speech from time to time. Richard went through the Cornwall photos again, this time searching for Piskies hiding in the background, though he wasn't sure why.

He looked up from the photo album and his eyes fell on Persephone's green suitcase. He had an idea.

On August 18th, 2022, the four-year anniversary of Persephone's death, Richard sat on his daughter's bed for a moment before heading to the airport with her green suitcase packed, including her old film camera and plenty of film in his carry-on. He'd booked a flight to Heathrow, and then a long train journey to Penzance. He'd made a note of all the places Persephone had carefully labelled in her photo album. He would go and see what she saw. Maybe he'd even spot a Piskie.

A few days later, jet-lagged but relieved with the change of scenery, Richard sat in the large white egg-shaped sculpture at Tremenheere sculpture park and looked out at the sky. It was grey today, though it was August. That was British weather for you, even in Cornwall. Still, it was strangely mesmerizing watching the subtle shades of the cloud layers shift and fade within the frame. Richard took out Persephone's camera and snapped a photo of the clouds held in the white oval. He thought about the frame of the photograph and the frame of the sculpture, layers of frames around the sky, usually frameless.

Richard got through his first roll of film in two days and dropped it off at a shop on the high street to be developed. When he picked it up the next morning however, he was disappointed with the results. The photos didn't come out the way he'd expected; the camera hadn't seen all the subtleties his eyes had. The clouds, so alive and varied, appeared as a dull shadeless expanse of grey-white.

He tried again. At Madron Well, he inspected the tree covered in colourful ribbons and charms, the offerings of those hoping for cures or answers. He held up the camera and peered through the viewfinder. He thought about the only thing he really knew about: cave art. He looked at the lines on and around the tree and imagined them as the lines of a drawing in an ancient cave. He moved closer to the tree until he found some pleasing lines around a yellow ribbon and a pink folded note.

He walked on to Men-an-tol. Like Persephone and Violet, he got lost several times but fortunately managed to avoid the field full of cows that the girls had come up against. He looked at the strange stones, standing unassumingly in a farmer's field, the grass around them cut short amidst the longer vegetation of the fields. They seemed lonely to him, nearly forgotten. He glanced around in case there was a Piskie hiding near the edge of the clearing. Everything was quiet. The sun shone in a sky dotted with small white clouds. Richard looked at the shadows cast by the stones and composed a picture out of the lines. He got very close to the stones and captured the markings of the lichens and the subtle imprints carved by ancient stone tools, not unlike the cave art that he knew so well. He looked through the round hole of the central stone, and obscuring the outer edge of the stone, he used the inner circle to frame the view within his frame. He adjusted his angle to frame only a small piece of the standing stone and the grassy horizon beyond. He focused on the frame, then on the horizon. Then, looking around to make sure no one was watching, he crawled through the round stone, a little awkwardly. It had to be done.

By the time Richard reached the village of Morvah he was entirely exhausted. He was accustomed to sitting most of the day, and today he'd walked over six miles. He sat down on a bench in the small cemetery outside St Bridget's church. It was a peaceful spot, and though he'd never been a religious man, he felt a strong sense of tranquility as he sat looking over the silent gravestones and up at the bell tower. "Everything's going to be alright," he thought to himself, though he wasn't sure why. He'd never been much good at decoding the strange physical and mental sensations of his emotions.

Back at his bed and breakfast that evening, he took out his laptop and looked up St. Bridget. This particular St. Bridget, it appeared, was a Christianization of an Irish pagan goddess, who represented poetry, healing, protection, and domestic animals. Richard thought of his daughter's best friend, with her secretive poetry and her less secret love of animals. He pondered the ideas of healing and protection, but they were both a little too abstract for his mind to fully grasp.

When Richard picked up his second roll of film at the small shop on the high street, the young man serving him was interested in his photos. He looked about eighteen, Richard thought, and he had a ring through his lower lip, slightly off-centre to the right. Richard couldn't help but stare at the ring and will it to move to the centre of the youth's lip. His name tag read "Alex." He was, it turned out, a photography student at Falmouth University, working in Penzance for the summer.

"Hey, I really liked your shots," he offered. "Really original framing."

Richard was surprised, but pleased. No one except his mother had ever complimented him on anything besides his paleolithic cave art research.

"Thank you," he said quietly, with a shy smile.

"Are you a trained photographer?" asked Alex.

Richard shook his head, "No, no, just trying out an old film camera I found. I...was looking for drawings in the lines." He was sure what he'd said sounded ridiculous, but Alex nodded, as if it made perfect sense. Indeed, to an art school student, it was a refreshingly down-to-earth description.

"Well, if you're around next week, we have an analogue photography group that meets a couple times a month. It'd be great if you could come on Thursday and show your photos."

Richard had never been invited to anything in his adult life, with the exception of cave art conferences, and Christmas dinner with Violet's family. He managed to nod.

He turned up at the small community hall on Thursday at 6pm, nervous but not terrified, which surprised him. The group were a friendly and diverse bunch of all ages, and from all walks of life. A teenager in skinny jeans sat next to an elderly lady in a floral print dress, looking over her photographs of local wildflowers. Alex was standing chatting to a grey-haired, rather posh-looking middle-aged man, both looking very focused and serious.

When Richard passed his photographs around the circle, his hand shaking and his voice quietly uttering a brief commentary, the group was quiet. He began to worry. Maybe it coming here had been a mistake. Maybe Alex had played a cruel joke on him. Maybe his photos were rubbish after all.

But then the posh-looking man spoke up. "These are really very original, Richard," he said in a regal-sounding accent that didn't sound remotely local. "The way you've framed your subjects," he shook his head. "You've managed to take photos of Men-an-Tol that I actually want to look at."

The group nodded and laughed a little, sharing knowing looks. They'd all seen many photos of the stones and most of them were the same. But Richard, they said, had found something new in them.

He returned to Canada with a new-found passion for film photography. He went out on long walks and daytrips, even taking the ferry to Bowen Island, something that would have seemed hugely daunting just a few short months ago. He started to collect vintage cameras and tried out various types of film. He read books and magazines and scoured the internet for information, tips, tricks and new equipment to try out. Slowly realizing that he now had what people referred to as a "hobby," Richard found a local analogue photography group and became one of their most active members. When a new work contract did come his way, he was almost disappointed to have to take time away from his new passion.

Sometimes Richard still sat on Persephone's bed and looked around her empty room, missing her intensely. But now, at least, he could think back to the day he sat outside St. Bridget's church in Cornwall, and he knew everything would be OK.

Chapter 14

On the day that Richard flew to England, and two days after Antonia had surprised Violet with the recording of "Demeter's Waltz," Violet drove to Sfinari to visit her family. It was on this day, which happened to be the hottest day of the year in Western Crete, that she bumped into Dimitri once again.

Maria and Kosta lived two doors down from Nefeli's family. Violet had purchased a very old, beat-up orange-red car that she called her tomato can. It fulfilled her criteria of being cheap and still running, though the second claim was debatable. Sometimes it took several minutes to start. Sometimes it stalled randomly and sat stubbornly for some time before it would start again. It guzzled oil like an elephant gulping water at an African oasis in the middle of the dry season. But it would do for now. She hung the olive wood bead necklace from her rearview mirror, hoping it would offer some form of protection, though she wasn't really sure why.

Violet had parked her tomato can a few doors down from her aunt and uncle's, where the road widened slightly. Her parallel parking skills had always been questionable at best. It was 10am and already 35 degrees Celsius. She got out of her car, humming "Demeter's Waltz" quietly to herself, and looked up to see Dimitri walking down the steps from the house opposite her, having just been turned away, yet again, from seeing his wife.

Violet was struck by the change in him. He looked haggard and defeated. He seemed to have aged several years since she'd seen him just a few months ago. The dull ache in her heart that she carried all the time intensified almost unbearably.

"Kalimera." This time Dimitri found his voice first.

"Kalimera," replied Violet.

They stood, across the road from each other and not daring to get any closer, with so much to say but nothing to say at the same time. Violet wanted to ask him if he was OK, but it seemed a silly question. She knew he wasn't, and she knew it was none of her business and there was nothing she could do to help him.

From her room upstairs, Nefeli looked out of her window and saw Violet and Dimitri, standing on opposite sides of the road, their love and their hurt pulsing together in the air like a strange twisted soul. Nefeli watched them stand like that for some time, before Violet nodded and walked slowly towards her aunt and uncle's house, turning to look back once at the man she loved completely but could never be with. Dimitri collapsed with his head in his hands on her front steps and this time, Nefeli felt nothing but sadness and regret.

Later that day, Nefeli instructed her parents with uncharacteristic firmness that they were to let Dimitri in the next time he called. Her father protested, but Nefeli, for once, held her ground. Her mother backed her up.

"They're married, Aleksandros! Nefeli wants to see him, and look, she's not well. They can't go on like this forever." Chrysoula had been worried about her daughter for several months, but over the past few weeks her worry had turned to near-despair bordering on panic. Aleksandros seemed determined to ignore his daughter's declining health and refused to call a doctor. Nefeli barely ate anymore, barely spoke and barely moved. She'd grown very thin. They were praying for her, but their God didn't seem to be listening this time.

Two days later, Dimitri sat next to his wife for the first time in nearly four months. She was wafer thin, her cheeks hollow and her large grey eyes, previously beautiful, now only vast empty wells. Her wrists looked like they might snap in the breeze. Dimitri was shaken by her appearance.

"Nefeli, have you seen a doctor? You look very thin."

Nefeli shook her head. "I don't need a doctor, Dimitri. I know what's wrong and it's not something a doctor can fix. It's not something anyone can fix."

Dimitri was silent, knowing he was the thing that was wrong that no one could fix.

But Nefeli continued. "Dimitri, you were honest with me back in May. But I've never been honest with you."

He frowned, confused. He hadn't thought Nefeli would be the type to have anything to hide.

"About what?"

Nefeli looked away, out her window where, just the other day, she'd watched Violet and Dimitri stand frozen, trapped in hurt and longing.

"Dimitri, I've loved you ever since I was a child. When I was fourteen, I made up my mind to marry you. I was sure it was meant to be. I thought I just had to wait." She paused. "But I got tired of waiting. And after I saw you with Violet, that May when she came to visit, I knew I needed to do something if I was going to make it happen. So I walked and walked every day down in the bay that winter, hoping I'd run into you, so I could say it had been fate. And eventually, it happened." Nefeli paused and sighed.

Dimitri waited. Nefeli walking along the beach hoping to run into him was hardly a major confession. He sensed there was more.

"I knew you didn't love me," she continued, "but I was sure, if we could just get married, that I could make you happy. I could give you children, be a good wife and mother, and eventually you'd learn to love me. Eventually you'd look at me the way you looked at Violet. I was sure it would be alright. I didn't mean to cause all this mess."

"Nefeli, you didn't cause the mess. I chose to marry you. I also thought we could be happy, have a family together."

Nefeli shook her head and swallowed. She couldn't look Dimitri in the eye. She turned to the window and said, "Dimitri, I told my mother, that March...I told her not just about us walking on the beach, but that we'd kissed...and more...that we were...intimate. I told her we'd talked about getting married, that you'd effectively already proposed."

Dimitri sat silent, trying to figure out what she was saying and why. He'd only ever kissed Nefeli two or three times before they were married, and as kisses go they were as chaste as they came. There had certainly been no talk of marriage.

She went on, "I knew if I told her that, she'd say enough to my father that he'd make sure we got engaged."

Dimitri sat stunned.

"So that was why he called you that day and asked why you hadn't asked his permission to marry me." Nefeli sighed with the relief of the confession, but was terrified to look at Dimitri, who sat silent, trying to reconcile the woman he thought he'd married with the woman talking to him now.

He'd underestimated Nefeli, or perhaps overestimated her, he wasn't sure which.

Nefeli eventually glanced at Dimitri, whose blank gaze had moved from his emaciated wife to the window behind her. She decided she might as well lay everything out.

"I saw you called so many times that day, but I knew if I called you back, you'd call off the engagement, and I...I just couldn't bear the thought of that." She closed her eyes. "But I had no idea, Dimitri, what all that would lead to. I thought, I mean, I *really* truly thought, I could make you happy, and once we were married, you'd love me as your wife and the mother of your children. I had no idea how selfish I was being." She shook her head and continued, "I made sure my parents were always with us after that, so you couldn't talk to me on your own. I was so scared you'd call off the wedding. I was so naive, I can see now it was ridiculous and childish, but I was so sure of everything then." Nefeli paused again. "I'm so sorry, Dimitri."

She turned to look at her husband, who was looking at the ground between his feet, trying and failing to find words. Nefeli waited. After several minutes that felt like forever, she added, "I don't expect you to forgive me, Dimitri. I will never forgive myself. But please, say something."

Dimitri finally looked at his once beautiful olive-skinned wife, whom he'd thought was a pure and innocent being. He felt betrayed and disappointed.

"I used to respect you Nefeli. I might not have loved you, but I did respect you." He frowned and shook his head. "Now, I don't even know who you are. I married a lie."

Nefeli wasn't surprised at his reaction but she was too far gone for tears.

"I did love you Dimitri, I did everything out of love," she offered.

Dimitri shook his head. "That isn't love." He was saddened that Nefeli's idea of love had been so childish and callow.

Nefeli nodded. "Yes, I can see that now, Dimitri, I can see it was a selfish and immature kind of love, but I couldn't see it then."

The two sat in silence for a minute or so. Dimitri would have been angry, but Nefeli's physical state was so frail he couldn't see her as anything but a small scared child.

"My parents would never let us divorce," stated Nefeli matter-of-factly, "but I think you should be with Violet."

Dimitri looked at her, not sure what she was saying. "But, you're still my wife, Nefeli. Despite everything, we are still married. How can I be with Violet?"

"Ah, Dimitri. I saw you the other day, outside. You saw her again, by accident. She was getting out of that ugly red car as you left. I could see how badly you both wanted to be together, I could see how much you both loved each other, but you couldn't even cross the road to say a proper hello...because of me and everything I put you through. Dimitri, I don't want to be the reason you're not with the woman you love. Just go to her, I give you my permission. No one will blame you. The whole town knows you love her."

"Nefeli, I'm not going to do that. I made a promise, I can't go back on my word."

"Your heart has already broken all your promises." Nefeli turned her head to look out the window, away from Dimitri. "Besides, as my husband, your responsibility is to look after me. The only thing I want from you now, is for you to allow yourself to be happy."

"Nefeli, I *can't.*" Dimitri paused and looked down again. "I can't do what my father did to my mother."

"Ah, Dimitri, it's not the same. I'm giving you my permission, my encouragement even. Just go, be with her, be happy."

"Nefeli, I'm telling you I *can't*. I know half the town thinks I already have, but I haven't and I won't and it doesn't matter how many times you tell me to."

Nefeli sighed. She hadn't expected such a fight. She'd thought he'd be pleased to be free.

"We're still married," he repeated. He looked at the small shrunken young woman in the bed that used to be Nefeli. He searched for the pretty girl with big grey eyes who had walked with him on the beach, and couldn't see her. Lies or not, it was awful seeing her wasting away like this, all because he couldn't love her like he loved Violet.

"Nefeli, I'm very worried about you. You look like a ghost of yourself."

"Yes, I feel like a ghost most of the time."

"I'm going to call a doctor."

"I don't need a doctor."

"So what are we going to do, Nefeli?" asked Dimitri, looking into his wife's large stone-grey eyes.

Nefeli sighed. "I don't know." The truth was, she had an idea, but it wasn't one she could share.

Dimitri left Nefeli's place and called for a doctor. He was horrified that her parents hadn't done so already. The doctor came the next day and Nefeli's father tried to turn him away. Dimitri fought with his words one last time and won. He knew Nefeli's life depended on it. God wasn't going to save her.

The doctor reported that Nefeli was severely malnourished. There was no physical cause that he could see, but he said he'd like to run some blood tests, just to be sure and asked if someone could bring her to the health centre in Kissamos over the next few days. Dimitri nodded. Aleksandros didn't reply and Chrysoula looked at the floor.

The doctor asked if Nefeli had been under stress recently. Dimitri, Aleksandros and Chrysoula all looked at each other and around the room and wondered where to start.

"A little," said her father.

"More than a little," added Chrysoula.

"We've had some challenges in our marriage," offered Dimitri, "and she had a miscarriage a few months ago."

The doctor could sense the tension in the house and was keen to leave. He nodded.

"See if you can get some food into her, some soup, protein shakes, a bit of fruit and vegetables. And definitely fluids: water and herbal teas, no coffee. I'll be back in a week to check on her. If she hasn't improved, she may need to be hospitalized."

Dimitri wasn't surprised, but Nefeli's parents both gasped.

Aleksandros glared at Dimitri. "This is your fault," he scowled.

Dimitri didn't want to argue. Blame seemed a silly game when Nefeli's life was on the line. Besides, in a way, he felt it was indeed his fault. He ignored the comment and stood up to leave.

The anxious doctor stood up as well, but Nefeli's parents appeared frozen.

"Shall I show the doctor out?" asked Dimitri, not wanting to overstep his place in their house.

Chrysoula nodded almost imperceptibly, as Aleksandros appeared unable to move or respond.

Nefeli lay awake until 1:45am that night, then carefully slid out of her bed and got dressed very slowly. She was extremely weak and this simple task required all her energy. Then, she moved silently down the stairs for the last time. She opened the front door slowly, and stepped out resolutely into the warm August night, closing the door quietly behind her. She turned down the road, towards the sea, and kept walking when the road ended. The ground turned steep. Nefeli began to stumble and she didn't fight gravity when it caught her and rolled her tired wasted body down to the sea below. She felt no pain.

Later, someone claimed they'd seen a golden ram swoop down and take her up into the sky, through the clouds and into the milky way. Nefeli held on and didn't look back.

Chapter 15

The next morning, Nefeli's parents panicked. She wasn't in her room. They called Dimitri. She wasn't with him. Dimitri rushed to the house. They called the police. No one in the town had seen her. Someone in the house nearest the sea said they'd heard strange noises late last night, but they'd thought it was an animal, a goat perhaps, losing its footing on the steep bank.

At 11:52am they pulled Nefeli's body out of the sea.

Sfinari was in shock. There hadn't been a death in the sea here since Ioannis many years ago.

"This is your fault!" Aleksandros screamed repeatedly at Dimitri. "You did this to her! You killed Nefeli, my beautiful, beautiful Nefeli."

Dimitri didn't defend himself. Several men held Aleksandros back when he lunged at Dimitri.

The police questioned Dimitri and questioned Nefeli's parents. They questioned the doctor who had seen her the day before. She had clearly been unwell and in a weakened state. She'd gone for a walk late at night and lost her footing. It was ruled an accidental death.

Victims of suicide cannot be given funerals in the Orthodox Church and cannot be buried on consecrated ground. Their souls, it is claimed, cannot enter the kingdom of heaven. Nefeli knew better than to leave a note.

Dimitri got in his car and drove. He drove for hours and wasn't sure where he was anymore. He drove in circles, back and forth along the old coast road and the new highway, up through the mountains and back down again. The roads, the fields, the trees and buildings all blurred into abstract meaningless shapes around him. He thought of Violet and then felt guilty for thinking of Violet when his wife had just been found dead. He thought of the last time he saw Nefeli, only yesterday, and his refusal to be with Violet while he was married to her. Had she thought this was the only way she could make him happy? Aleksandros was right, he'd killed Nefeli. He hadn't meant to, but he had.

Violet drove to Sfinari as soon as she heard what had happened. Everyone had congregated in the square, anxious and upset. For her aunt and grandparents, it brought back long-ago memories of little Ioannis' horrible accident in the sea. Violet wanted to be with her family that day, but she also worried her presence might be upsetting to Dimitri. And while she tried to ignore the gossip, she knew there were those in Sfinari who held both her and Dimitri responsible for Nefeli's decline. She wasn't expecting an easy time of it.

By the time she arrived, Dimitri had left and was driving aimlessly around the island trying to calm his desperate thoughts. No one knew where he'd gone, and Despoina and Sifi were understandably concerned.

Despoina found Violet in the crowd and asked if she knew where her son might be. Violet felt awkward that his mother was asking her, Dimitri's ex-lover, to help find him. Being able to answer the question almost felt like an admission of guilt.

"Did you check his cave?" asked Violet.

"His cave?" replied Despoina. Violet's discomfort levels rose once again. She wasn't sure if it was meant to be kept a secret. "Where is it? Can you check?" pleaded Despoina.

Violet drove down to the bay, which was eerily quiet. The tavernas hadn't opened today. She parked quickly and ran towards Dimitri's hives. It was strange to feel the air hang silent and still around them, and Violet felt a pang of emptiness as she passed. She remembered the first time he'd brought her here and she'd tried to hide her tears under the mesh hood. She ran on, over the hill, and scrambled down the rocks on the other side, then across the ledge to the cave. It was empty. Violet texted Despoina to say he wasn't there.

Violet walked back to her car a little more slowly, pausing briefly at the beehives and at Dimitri's cottage. *Zeus Cretagenes* had joined her, walking very close beside her and watching her carefully. She walked past the room she'd stayed in that first time she visited, and a million memories of a previous version of herself flooded back. Memories of Dimitri, smiling and confident, so different to the Dimitri she was looking for now, congregated in her mind. But Violet collected herself and held back her tears. Dimitri had just lost his wife. Surely it was inappropriate to reminisce about their romance at a time like this.

She drove back up to Sfinari and sat in her car for a few minutes before rejoining the crowd. Dimitri was still nowhere to be found. She didn't know where else to look. She wrapped the olive wood necklace around her wrist.

Maria called Anna at 5pm, as soon as it was morning in Vancouver. She explained quickly to her barely-awake sister what had transpired. Anna was silent for a long time, trying to take it all in. Memories of Ioannis circled this new sadness in her mind, and of course, she was worried about Violet.

"Are you still there, Annoula?" Maria asked.

Violet was sitting nearby, and felt suddenly guilty that she hadn't been in touch with her mother more over the previous week. They'd talked on her birthday of course, but since then she'd sent only a few short texts and hadn't answered her mother's calls. She just hadn't known what to say or how to say it.

Anna and Maria spoke in Greek for several minutes. The words sounded strange and foreign to Violet, as if she'd suddenly forgotten the language she'd worked so hard to learn. She remembered the way it had sounded on her her first visit here, how she'd liked to hear the words roll off Dimitri's tongue, not knowing what any of them meant.

"Yes, Violet's here, she's OK," Violet heard her aunt say. She closed her eyes, trying to will her surroundings and her situation into something other than what it was.

"Your mother wants to talk to you," said Maria, holding out her phone to Violet. Violet opened her eyes and looked at Maria's phone. Somehow her hand refused to move and take the phone. "Your mother," Maria repeated. "She just wants to make sure you're OK."

Violet nodded and took the phone from her aunt. "Hello," she managed to say quietly.

"Violet, Maria just told me everything. I just wanted to hear your voice and check that you're doing alright."

Violet was silent. She searched for words but couldn't find any.

"Violeta?" Anna's voice was gentle.

"I'm here. I'm sorry, Mom. I'm sorry I've been so quiet. I was just trying to get through some stuff. And now it all seems really unimportant in comparison."

"It's OK Violeta, you know you don't have to tell me everything, but sometimes your parents just need to know that you're alright, even if you're struggling a bit. We don't mind if you don't tell us the details., but...especially when you're so far away...it's just nice to hear your voice."

"I know. I'm sorry." Violet wiped a tear from her cheek.

"It's alright," said Anna tenderly. She sighed. "What an awful, awful mess." The words felt inadequate; it was hard to know what to say. "But are you OK, Violeta?"

"I think" said Violet quietly, "I'm as OK as I can be, given the situation." She paused. "And I'll call you tomorrow, I promise."

"OK." Anna paused, wondering whether she should mention the man she knew her daughter still loved.

"I...hope you find Dimitri," she eventually added cautiously.

"Me too. I mean, I just hope he's alright."

"I'm sure he's fine. He probably just needed to get away from everyone for a bit." Anna hoped she sounded more sure of herself than she felt.

"I hope you're right."

Anna hung up the phone and thought about her twin brother, taken so suddenly, so long ago now. She wondered what sort of life she might have had if the accident hadn't happened. If they hadn't been playing in the sea that day, if it hadn't been windy, if they'd just moved away from the rocks a little. Would she have ever even left Crete? Was there another version of herself, living in Sfinari or nearby, maybe running a shop for tourists. No Martin, no Violet. Would she have married someone else, had other children? It was strange to think about. Her mind drifted to Persephone and she wondered how Violet's life might have been changed if Persephone's life had been spared. Would she have ever moved to Crete?

"So much life from all this death," she thought to herself. "Bees from the oxen." She just hoped there were no more tragedies waiting to happen. She made the sign of the cross and begged a God she only half-believed in to keep Dimitri safe.

By nightfall, Despoina and Sifi were panicking. They'd called their son a hundred times, they'd sent him dozens of text messages. But he hadn't responded. They sat in the square with the light fading: Violet, Maria, Kosta, Angelo,

Despoina and Sifi. Despoina suggested Violet try calling him. Violet felt awkward. She was sure if Dimitri wouldn't talk to his mother, he wouldn't answer her call.

"Ah, it doesn't matter," said Sifi. "His phone is going straight to voicemail, it must have died." They debated whether they should call the police, but decided to wait until morning.

Violet stayed with her aunt and uncle that night. Nobody slept.

Chapter 16

Violet got up before the sun rose over Sfinari, before the otherworldly music of the dawn chorus enveloped the town. It was at 6:15am. She couldn't wait any longer. She drove down to the bay once more and ran over to Dimitri's cottage. She called his name, she knocked, she peeked inside. It was empty. She ran past the lifeless beehives, and over to his cave, again calling his name. Empty. It felt like one of the nightmares she used to have back in Canada.

"Shit, shit, shit," she said out loud, her eyes tearing up. She knew Dimitri well enough to know that he would blame himself for this, and she was worried about what he might do. But where would he have gone?

The pale morning light began to seep into the sky above her, and a few birds began to sing shyly, the sound quickly growing into a natural symphony that filled the air and blanketed the small bay. She looked around frantically, as if hoping the sheltered beach might have an answer.

Zeus Cretagenes was, strangely, nowhere to be seen this morning, but a golden eagle soared overhead, and Violet watched it circle and fly away to the east. "If only I had a pair of wings, to find him," she thought, "like the sirens when they were searching for Persephone." Something clicked. Persephone. Sirens. Wings. Wingless. Aptera.

It was a long-shot, she knew, but it had been one of his favourite places. If he'd wanted to be further from Sfinari, where no one would find him, maybe he would be there.

She ran back to her car, stumbling up over the rough rocks and sailing down the other side of the hill. She jumped into her tomato can, which thankfully started quickly, as if sensing the urgency of the situation, and drove it as fast as it would go. She wasn't sure if she could remember the way, but she knew there would be a brown sign directing her there from the main road. Violet prayed to a God she didn't believe in, she asked Persephone, wherever she was, to help her. She tried to remember to breathe. She watched the *kandilakia* pass by on the roadside and tried not to drive too fast.

As she approached the small parking lot at 7:40 that morning, she saw Dimitri's white car and breathed a sigh of relief. He was here. She just hoped he was safe.

Aptera wasn't open yet, but the fences were largely ornamental. In her hurry, she cut herself sliding under the barbed wire.

"Shit, shit, shit," she said again. "Dimitri!" she called as she ran through the silent ruins in the dry yellow grass, through the monastery and over to the cisterns. "Dimitri?"

He wasn't there. Her finger was bleeding badly. Violet swore again. She ran over to the theatre.

"Dimitri?" she called, tears and panic building up inside her. Somehow she felt that if he wasn't there, he was nowhere.

And then she saw him. A dark shape, curled up on the second step from the top.

"Dimitri!" she called as she ran towards him.

Dimitri had found himself at Aptera the previous afternoon, though he couldn't remember taking the turn-off from the main road, parking his car, or even paying his entry fee. He wandered the ruins aimlessly, not sure what he was looking for. He sat at the entrance to the cisterns and remembered the day that Violet had told him about Persephone. A bee-eater swooped low and he flinched, then shivered, though it wasn't cold. He wandered over to the theatre, where he'd kissed Violet for the first time, or maybe she'd kissed him. He remembered telling her about the sirens, Persephone's companions, asking for wings and singing to find her. About the muses defeating them here and plucking out the sirens' feathers. If only Nefeli had had wings, she wouldn't have tumbled into the sea. She could have flown away.

He didn't know that, as far as Nefeli was concerned, she had.

When the site closed for the evening, Dimitri hid in a grove of trees. His car was still in the parking lot, but the unenthusiastic ticket booth employee simply shrugged and left.

Dimitri didn't expect to sleep, but he laid down under the stars in the ancient theatre. He watched the milky way until it blurred, his eyes closed and he slipped into a sleep too dense for dreams.

Now, in the quiet morning light, Dimitri heard Violet's voice penetrating his deep slumber. He expected to be pulled into a dream about her, but instead found himself half-awake, with heavy-lidded eyes looking up at her standing over him.

"Dimitri, are you OK? Are you OK?"

Dimitri stirred and tried to answer. He remembered as he awoke, why he was here, and his body felt unbearably heavy.

"Dimitri, are you OK?" Violet asked again, tears of relief falling down her face, still not quite believing that she'd found him.

"Violet," he croaked as he sat up slowly.

"I've...we've all been so worried about you," Violet was out of breath and spoke with difficulty through her tears.

Dimitri noticed her finger was bleeding badly. He also noticed the olive beads wrapped around her wrist.

"What happened to your finger?"

Violet had forgotten it was bleeding and she'd managed to get blood all over her shorts.

"Shit," she said again. "It doesn't matter, Dimitri. I'm sure it'll heal."

She sat down beside him, careful to leave some space between them. Dimitri reached into his pocket and handed her a tissue for her injured finger. A small piece of folded paper fell out of his pocket. He picked it up quickly and held it tightly in his hand for a moment before putting it back into his pocket. Violet knew it was her poem, she didn't need to ask. She began to calm down and catch her breath.

"Dimitri, I'm so, so sorry about what happened."

Dimitri looked at the ground, then out toward the sea. He wasn't yet ready to look at Violet.

"How did you find me?" he asked.

"Lucky guess," said Violet. "I was down at your cave looking for you, and I saw an eagle, a golden eagle, and I wished I had wings. And then I thought of the sirens searching for Persephone, which made me think of Aptera."

"Golden eagles are rare here these days."

"I know," said Violet, remembering the eagle that had saved her life back in Canada.

"You know they're meant to be messengers of Zeus."

Violet nodded. "That makes sense then. It was Zeus who eventually found Persephone, wasn't it?"

Dimitri nodded. "But, in some versions of the myth he also consented to her abduction."

Violet looked at Dimitri. She'd forgotten that detail. "Maybe he didn't know how much pain it would cause." She remembered that Zeus was Persephone's father, and thought about Dimitri's own troubled relationship with his father.

"Anyway," said Dimitri, still staring out over Souda Bay, "you know I'm not Persephone."

"Yes, but—" she wasn't quite sure how to explain that he and Persephone had become linked losses in her mind.

"You're a follower of Demeter, Persephone's mother." It was easier to talk about the myths than the reality.

Dimitri sat silent for a moment. "Violet, do you ever think about what our lives might have been like if the pandemic hadn't hit, or if you'd just stayed in Crete that first time?"

"I try not to." Violet swallowed hard to avoid crying once again. "But yes, sometimes, but...it hurts too much."

Dimitri nodded. "Does it hurt as much as this?"

Violet didn't reply straight away. She wasn't sure if he was referring to the pain he was feeling from his wife's suicide, or the pain of not being with her, or both, or everything that had happened since she'd left.

"I...can't imagine what you're feeling right now, Dimitri. But you know, I lost someone too. And I know how broken I felt, for such a long time." She paused, remembering those eight months in her room, before her mother sent her to Crete. "But I promise you, it does get easier."

Dimitri was silent for a minute or so before he said slowly, "You didn't kill Persephone."

Violet frowned. "Did you kill Nefeli?"

"Not literally, no. But she...she did it because I didn't love her. I wanted to love her. I really tried." He shook his head and looked back down at the ground.

"Do you remember when we sat in the cisterns and I told you about Persephone?"

Dimitri nodded.

"And do you remember when I said that if Persephone hadn't met me, she wouldn't have been at the library at that time, and she wouldn't have been killed?"

434

He shook his head. "But it's not the same, Violet."

"Yes it is. It might be messier and more complicated, but ultimately, what you told me still stands true."

"What did I tell you?"

"You said that it's not up to us to choose how things play out. That yes, maybe if Perse and I hadn't met, she'd still be alive now doing wonderful things, but equally maybe she would have died years earlier. We can't know how every decision we make is going to affect everything and everyone. You said we had to trust ourselves...and trust the universe, God, or whatever we believe in."

Dimitri sat thinking for a moment. "I shouldn't have married her. How can I trust myself again if I made such a stupid decision?"

"You did the best you could at the time. I mean, there was a pandemic, and then your dad came back." Violet paused. "Nobody makes all the right choices all the time. And what does it even mean for a choice to be 'right' or 'wrong?' Even my decisions...I thought I was being responsible, going back to Canada to save and plan, and then waiting out the pandemic. But, looking back now, maybe I should have just stayed here." Violet looked out over the bay as she continued. "My choices affected your choices too. If I'd stayed—" Her voice trailed off. It felt too disrespectful to Nefeli's memory to say that if she'd stayed, Dimitri wouldn't have married her. And who knew what might have happened in that universe anyway. "I mean," Violet found her voice again and continued, "I couldn't have known how things would play out, and neither could you. So that's why we trust in...something beyond ourselves. We trust in the process that unfolds that we can't always understand, but somehow, it all falls into place. And sometimes we wish the pieces fell differently, but...it's not always up to us."

They sat in silence for a few minutes. Dimitri mulled over Violet's words before he spoke again.

"Nefeli told me some things, the day before she died. I guess she wanted to confess." He swallowed. He didn't have the energy to tell the whole story right now. "She admitted she'd been dishonest, in order to get me to marry her. I didn't expect that." He paused, shifting his gaze from the sea to the ground and back to the sea. "Then she told me we couldn't divorce but she wanted me to go and be with you."

Violet sat suddenly upright. "She said that?"

"Yes. But I told her I couldn't. We were still married and I didn't want to do what my father had done. But now...somehow I've managed to do worse." He kicked at a small stone on the ground at his feet. "If I'd said to her we'd just separate, and I'd go and be with you, I don't think she would have...done what she did."

Violet was silent. She hadn't expected this at all. "I...don't understand. Why did your wife want you to cheat on her?"

Dimitri sighed. "She realized that the way she'd loved me, the way she'd tricked me into marrying her, was selfish. It wasn't really love. When she saw us...just looking at each other, she knew that was love, and she knew I'd never love her. She wanted me to be happy, or so she said. She thought I wouldn't be happy unless I was with you. And when there was no way for that to happen while we were married, and no chance of divorce...she just...made herself disappear."

Violet sat reeling, trying to take in what Dimitri was saying.

"This is all from her seeing me at the taverna that day?" she asked.

"That was the start of it. We had some...conversations after that. And she also saw us a few days ago, the day you were arriving at your aunt and uncle's, and I was leaving. Do you remember?"

Violet nodded. Of course she remembered. She hadn't realized that moment was being watched, and would ultimately contribute to Nefeli's downfall. It was hard not to feel the guilt she'd just told Dimitri not to feel. She sighed and wondered what had happened to their love during their time apart.

"Did I ever tell you about the Piskies?" she asked.

"Don't you mean pixies?" asked Dimitri, a little confused at the sudden change of topic.

"Nope. The pixies are in Devon. In Cornwall, they have Piskies. Or at least they used to. They're the little people, you know, a bit like fairies, but Piskies are usually quite mischievous. Some of them are helpful, but some of them are awful little things. Anyway, people used to see them all the time, up until about two hundred years ago."

"What happened to them?" asked Dimitri.

"Well, when people stopped believing in them, apparently they shrunk down smaller and smaller, until they just disappeared."

Dimitri thought of Nefeli, wasting away, getting smaller and smaller, and disappearing. Was it because he hadn't believed in her? Maybe, he thought, it was because she'd stopped believing in herself, and in the love she thought would one day bloom between the two of them.

"So, maybe when we didn't see each other for so long," continued Violet, "it was hard to keep believing in the love we had. And it just sort of...shrunk down until it was like a tiny beautiful dream, too small to see clearly. And we both had to sort of tuck it away, because the dream didn't fit in with the reality either of us found ourselves in."

Dimitri finally turned and looked at Violet. "Violet, I'm not the person you fell in love with anymore. I've been a coward and a spineless idiot. I've hurt everyone around me, including you. I'm not...ever going to be able to make you happy, or make anyone happy."

"Dimitri, I'm not here expecting anything. You just lost your wife...and however complicated that relationship was, I'm not so disrespectful or naive to think that we're going to just...kiss and make love here and live happily ever after."

Dimitri almost smiled, remembering how Violet had always made him laugh.

"I'm here as someone who cares about you, who is not going to stop caring about you, no matter what you say. You helped me through a horrible time, when I'd just lost my best friend, and I just want to be here for you through all this, OK?"

Dimitri managed to nod very slowly.

"And anyway," added Violet, "do you remember what you told me, in your cottage that night, when I told you not to wait for me?"

Dimitri thought. He remembered the conversation and suddenly felt guilty all over again because he hadn't kept his promise. "I'm sorry I didn't wait for you in the end," he said solemnly.

Violet shook her head. All those promises felt so irrelevant now. "That's not what I meant. You said that I didn't get to decide what made you happy. And you said to never think that I wasn't enough. So, if you asked me to do those things for you, then it seems only fair that I can ask you to do them for me."

Dimitri closed his eyes and dared to feel just a tiny hint of hope, like a timid star appearing in a dark sky. He held out his hand and Violet held it in hers, though she didn't dare move any closer. For now, it was enough.

Chapter 17

Dimitri attended Nefeli's funeral a few days later, still broken and in shock. He avoided eye contact with Aleksandros. The event went by in a blur; the passage of time seemed strange lately, slow and fast at the same time, and often disorienting. He felt guilty every time he thought about Violet, but those thoughts were the only comforting thing in his world, so he held them close anyway. Her poem still sat in his pocket, folded carefully.

Violet felt it would be best to stay away from the funeral. The following day, she went to Nefeli's grave to pay her respects. As she laid down the flowers she'd brought, she had the feeling that the gesture was hopelessly inadequate. It reminded her of the discovery of mass graves of indigenous children back in Canada, and how she'd done her best to learn and to educate herself about the history and the current situation. It didn't feel like nearly enough. How on earth does one begin to make amends for the tragedies that we're connected to, yet powerless to prevent?

Violet pulled a small notebook out of her pocket and wrote a poem as she stood at Nefeli's grave.

Seeds

Once in a dream
I seeded a small cloud
and watched it float across the blue
I kept it on a string,
let it out for shade and pulled it in for warmth.

It took many shapes: a warbler, a honeybee,
      the sea
It danced to the music I played
and sang only my poems.

Until suddenly
It began to grow,
To pull and twist,
Soft edges turning to jagged horns
Shapes shifting and slowly emerging
Medea the witch, a curse,
Aries in the sky,
A tortured golden ram
Sweeping down
Bellowing
String snapped
Upon me

Scarring me and every thought, every belief,
      every word I'd spoken,
Destroying what I thought was the truth.

It was only a dream
it was only a cloud
but it swept you away
and left us all broken.

And what good is it to say
I'll never dream again
(We all know that's a lie)
To say "I'm sorry" a thousand times
When the words fall
Too late and far too small
But somehow all I have

My hands try to rebuild the ancient palaces
    that a million warriors destroyed
Every day
Just a little
Is all I have

She folded the pages carefully and left them on Nefeli's grave with her flowers. She wasn't sure what else to do.

Two days after the funeral Aleksandros and Chrysoula went to stay with their second youngest daughter and her family, on the outskirts of Chania. They came back to Sfinari only occasionally over the next year, and never stayed for long.

In the weeks that followed, Violet and Dimitri spent most of their time together, between Maleme and Sfinari, as best friends who often held hands. Dimitri met Persephone the cat, who immediately curled up on his lap and refused to move. He helped Violet and Antonia set up their new website, and promised to recolonize his beehives in the spring, so he could supply Violet with honey and beeswax.

In Sfinari, everyone simply assumed the two were a couple again by October, and most people didn't blame them. Only a few people knew they did no more than hold hands. They hadn't kissed since Violet left at the end of May over three years ago, in the pre-pandemic world that felt like a distant dream. Still, they were happy. Or at least, they were finally moving towards happiness.

In Maleme, somewhat predictably, word soon spread about Violet and Dimitri, and the woman who had drowned in the sea. Violet was aware of the whispers when she passed, and the many eyes that silently cast blame on her, but after everything she'd been through, it hardly seemed to matter. Besides, she knew people would soon lose interest and cast their glares elsewhere. However, she was worried about what Telis might hear.

Chapter 18

Telis

Τέλης

Telis wasn't terribly surprised that he didn't see Violet at the taverna in the days immediately following their night together. He had planned on playing the long game, backing off for a little while, making her miss him perhaps, and then he was sure she'd soon come looking for lemon *raki* and *dolmades*. He'd texted her on her birthday of course, and she'd sent a friendly but short reply. Five days later, he finally put his pride aside and called her. He couldn't have known it was the day she found Dimitri at Aptera. He only knew he hadn't heard back from her, and it hurt.

A few days later, he heard about a drowning, a possible suicide in Sfinari, and he wondered if it was someone Violet knew. He thought about texting her, but decided against it. But when he overheard some locals in the taverna speaking of how Violet had finally settled down with the man she loved, he felt like he'd been hit in the stomach with a bowling ball. He lingered at the next table, moving much more slowly than he needed to, but ensuring he didn't appear to be eavesdropping. He heard them tell the tragic story of a beautiful woman who had thrown herself into the sea when she'd realized that her husband was desperately in love with Violet. She'd sacrificed herself, they said, so that the two could be together, or so the story went.

Telis swallowed hard and took a deep breath. It was a busy evening, and, always professional, he hid his worries behind his charming grin and lively banter with his customers. But by the end of the evening, he was exhausted and his face hurt from the effort of smiling while his heart ached silently.

After closing up the taverna, he half-walked and half-ran down to the beach. Despite his fatigue, he felt the need to move quickly, trying to calm his thoughts with the motions of his body. He stood on the spot he'd sat with Violet that evening, just over two weeks ago now. He picked up a stone and threw it as far as he could, out into the waves. It was strangely cathartic, and he stood there for some time, throwing pebbles aimlessly into the Cretan Sea. At 3am he finally wandered home and slumped into bed. He wasn't sure if he slept at all.

The next morning, Telis went into Antonia's shop, pretending he needed sunscreen. Violet wasn't there, which was both a disappointment and a relief. Antonia greeted him warmly, though she was dreading the conversation she knew was coming. Telis tried to make casual small talk until Antonia rescued him from his ruse.

"Telis, I know you're probably looking for Violet." Telis furrowed his brow slightly, trying to feign confusion.

"She's...had a lot going on. You've probably heard the story by now." Telis managed to nod. Antonia sighed. "I know she wanted to tell you herself, but she just wasn't able to, not just yet."

"So, it's true then?" He'd hoped, somehow, to find that the rumours were false, though he'd known this was unlikely. He swore under his breath as he leaned on the counter and looked down at his hands. They looked odd and disconnected, as if they didn't belong to him at all. Hands, he recalled, that had touched Violet once, but now never would again. He leaned on his elbows and rested his head in his hands.

"Are you alright, Telis?" Antonia asked gently.

He looked up and Antonia was sure she saw tears in his eyes, though Telis would never have admitted it.

"Yes," he looked up, cleared his throat, and straightened his posture, regaining some semblance of composure. "God...what a mess." He shook his head and looked down at the dark countertop by the till. He wanted to ask Antonia if Dimitri was a decent man, if he would treat Violet well. But he also wanted to punch Dimitri, though the truth was he wasn't a violent man and he knew it wasn't really Dimitri he was angry with; he'd come second place and his pride was hurt. He wondered again what Dimitri had to offer that he didn't. He thought of Violet's smooth pale skin in the dark. "Is she...is Violet OK?" he managed to ask.

Antonia nodded. "I think so. I mean, it's been a lot...for both of them. But I think she's doing OK." She paused, pondering whether to say more. "And you know, I wanted to hate Dimitri, after what he put Violet through, but the fact is, he seems like a good guy." Antonia opted not to add how in love the couple the clearly were, how they fit together in a way that she couldn't quite explain, as if they'd already been together for years, or lifetimes. Of course, they were officially just good friends, but it was clear to her that they belonged to each other.

Telis nodded. He was out of words and felt as if the life had been sucked out of him. He'd allowed himself to dream just a little, about running the taverna with Violet, about having blue-eyed, fair-skinned children at their feet. But then, he shouldn't have. She'd told him she was in love with someone else. He felt like a fool.

He walked back down to the beach. It was early and still quiet. He threw another stone into the sea but it didn't bring him any satisfaction this time. Violet belonged to another man and there was nothing he could do about it. He wished he'd never turned up at her apartment that evening, never had that one perfect night with her that had made him dare to dream of a life with her. He sighed. She'd told him from the start that she loved Dimitri. He should have listened to Violet instead of his ego and his wishful thinking.

Chapter 19

It was an unusually warm evening in late September, about a month later, when Violet and Dimitri walked past the *Taverna Maleme*. Dimitri had met up with Violet as she closed the shop with Antonia, and had suggested a walk along the beach. Violet agreed before she remembered that it was impossible to avoid walking past Telis' taverna on the way. While she did want to talk to Telis eventually, she wasn't sure she was ready, and she was also fairly certain that Telis had no desire to meet Dimitri. So she simply hoped they could walk by quickly without being noticed.

Telis, however, was outside on the patio, clearing a table that had been laid for two. He looked up and saw Violet with a man he knew must be Dimitri. He'd had some time to come to terms with the situation, but he still felt an unpleasant pang of jealousy and sadness seeing her hand in his. He debated pretending he hadn't seen them, but decided it was impossible.

"Violet, *kalispera!*" he said smiling, trying his best to sound casual. *"Kalispera* Telis," Violet managed to smile.

Despite the awkwardness of the situation, she found she was pleased to see him, and relieved that he didn't seem to be holding a grudge. She knew Antonia had spoken to him. However, she desperately wished she could have had a conversation with him before introducing him to Dimitri. Yet here they were.

"Dimitri, this is Telis. Telis, this is Dimitri." She tried to sound relaxed. She watched Telis' face carefully, to see if it changed when she mentioned Dimitri's name. It didn't. Violet breathed a quiet sigh of relief. Telis, through necessity, had mastered the art of not showing emotion.

"Nice to meet you," Telis said politely to Dimitri. "Are you coming in?" he asked Violet. "I have a bottle of lemon *raki* with your name on it. And some *dolmades."* He knew he couldn't avoid Violet and Dimitri forever in a town the size of Maleme, and besides, he was curious to observe Dimitri himself.

"Shall we go in for a bit?" Violet asked Dimitri. Like Telis, she knew they couldn't avoid each other forever and it seemed as good a time as any to re-enter the taverna. Dimitri wondered vaguely what the slight tension in the air was about, but was happy to comply.

As they sat nibbling on *dolmades,* Dimitri noticed Telis regarding him cautiously, and stealing frequent glances at Violet, who appeared just slightly on edge.

"Are you alright?" he asked Violet quietly.

"Yes." Violet knew Dimitri knew her too well to be fooled. "I'll explain later." She knew she didn't need to tell him anything, but she didn't want there to be any secrets between them.

Telis, for his part, had been sure he'd despise Dimitri, who had functioned as an imaginary punching bag in his wounded mind over the past few weeks. However, when he met him, he was almost disappointed to find little to dislike. Telis prided himself on being able to read people; years of interacting with customers at the taverna had made him adept at this. But where he searched for malevolence in Dimitri, he found only hurt.

Though his pride still demanded to know why Violet loved Dimitri instead of him, he could now see the question was a pointless one to keep asking. Like Antonia, he could sense something palpable in the air between them, a sort of entangled connection. The two of them sat talking softly at their table, the ache of past miseries hanging heavy over them, but tempered by a sense of slow healing and quiet comfort. Telis, finally, surrendered fully to the defeat. He heard Violet's voice in his mind: "Love isn't a checklist, Telis." Seeing them together now, he finally understood what she'd meant.

He wondered wistfully if he'd ever meet anyone else like Violet. He glanced over at her, and noticed Dimitri noticing him looking at her, but without malice. He wondered if he knew. He took a deep breath and went to greet the group that had just entered the taverna.

Back in Violet's apartment later that night, she and Dimitri sat on opposite ends of her couch. She struggled to tell him about Telis, pulling awkwardly at her shorts and avoiding his eyes. When she finally managed to confess,

Dimitri smiled ever so slightly, and looked at her sadly and affectionately. After everything they'd been through, the event hardly seemed worth mentioning, but he could see it was important to her to share it.

"Violet, I'm happy you want to be so honest with me, but, you know I was married. You could have been with a thousand men if you wanted to be. It really doesn't matter and isn't even any of my business."

Violet met his gaze but then looked back down at her shorts, tugging at a loose thread.

Dimitri couldn't help but wonder if there was more that Violet wasn't telling him. He couldn't understand why she seemed so upset about one night with another man, when she'd been single and free to do as she pleased. "Do you still like him? Or...love him?" he asked cautiously, a little worried that his new-found hope for their future might be about to crumble.

Violet laughed, caught off guard by the question. "No, no. I mean, I like him of course, as a friend."

Dimitri visibly relaxed.

"He's a nice guy," Violet continued. "But I think I hurt him. I didn't mean to lead him on." She took a deep breath. "But besides that, I think the other reason I felt guilty about it was that I didn't love him. I didn't think I would, or maybe I didn't think I *should* want to be with someone I didn't love. I just...hated the idea that I'd needed someone, in that way, who wasn't you." She looked down.

Dimitri looked at her wistfully. "I know what it's like to be lonely, Violet. And I made far more of a mess of things out of my loneliness than you did. You're allowed to be human, you know." He squeezed her hand.

Violet looked up at him and smiled just a little, feeling a weight had been lifted off her shoulders.

Dimitri slept on Violet's couch, as he'd continue to do for most nights that fall and winter.

Chapter 20

As time passed, Dimitri found that Violet was right, he did start to heal, and crucially, he began to forgive himself. Occasionally he found himself smiling, cautiously at first, though guilt and shame still haunted him.

On his name day on the 12th of October, they spent the day with his family in Sfinari. Violet went for a rather bracing swim and declared sadly that would be her last one for the year.

She texted her mother before she went to bed that night in Dimitri's cottage, the heater beside her as the evening air had grown cool.

Had a nice day with Dimitri and his family.

Ate too much and drank too much, in a good way.

So sleepy. Night night. Love you.

By the time Anna replied five minutes later, her daughter was already fast asleep.

Violet had begun to dream again. That night, she dreamed she was swimming in the cisterns once more, with a glass ceiling and cool clean water. Everything was the colour of the sky on a warm summer's day. When she looked back to the entrance, she could see a dark archway and brown murky waters, but she couldn't remember swimming through it to get to where she was. She worried a little that she'd have to pass back through it eventually, to leave the cistern, but then she dove down deep into the water, and found herself swimming just above the seabed, dotted with seaweed in a million shades of green. Around her a thousand tiny multicoloured fish floated and darted. She kept swimming underwater, moving towards a bright white light, and when she eventually resurfaced, she found herself on Sfinari beach, with Dimitri waiting for her, her towel beside him on the pebbles.

Christmas came and Violet experienced the twelve-day Greek Christmas season for the first time. She ate far too many *melomakarona* biscuits and drank just a little too much *rakomelo* and red wine, or maybe it was just the right amount.

On January 6th, on the Feast of the Epiphany, Dimitri announced he was going to dive for the cross today. Violet looked blankly at him. This wasn't a tradition her mother had ever mentioned. They were eating breakfast at his parents' house; they'd been staying between here and Violet's family's place over the festive season.

"There's going to be a procession down to the harbour from the church, he explained. Then the priest will bless the crucifix, and throw it into the water, and a few men, mostly much younger than me, will dive into the water and try and get to it first."

Violet blinked. "You're going to jump into the sea *today?* You used to tell me I was crazy for swimming in May!"

Dimitri smiled. "Yes, but this is a tradition."

Violet was still baffled. "But it's like, ten degrees out there today!"

Dimitri was amused by her indignation. "Didn't your mother ever tell you about Greek Christmas?" he teased.

"Yes," said Violet, "but she never mentioned a bunch of crazy men diving into the sea in January." As she said it she wondered if her mother had avoided the topic as it reminded her too much of the painful loss of her twin brother. Dimitri had the same thought but neither of them voiced it.

After a pause, Violet asked, "So, why exactly are you trying to find the cross?"

"Because, whoever finds it will be blessed with good luck for the next year."

"Ah, OK," Violet nodded, finally understanding. She and Dimitri were both overdue for a good year.

Despoina had come into the kitchen and overheard his plans.

"Dimitri, don't you think you're a bit old for that? You should leave it to the younger men. The cold water is hard on your heart, you know."

"My heart's been through worse," he replied, looking tenderly at Violet. "Anyway, this will be my last year Mom, I promise."

At thirty-five, Dimitri was certainly at the upper limit of the "young men" who took part, but, he reasoned, he'd missed a few years due to the pandemic. And anyway, there weren't very many young men in Sfinari these days. If he didn't dive, it might just be Angelo and a couple of teenagers.

Clouds obscured the blue of the sky, but the day was bright and mild as they all walked down towards the harbour, just north of the village. Violet held Dimitri's hand and felt a sense of calmness come over her. Her aunt and uncle and her grandparents, as well as Dimitri's parents, were all walking together, sharing in the day's festivities.

When they arrived, Dimitri and six other men lined the pier, standing stoically in only their swimming trunks. The priest stood at the end of the pier and blessed the small wooden cross. He dipped it into the sea three times, and threw it into the waves.

Dimitri watched the cross hit the water and dove in quickly. He felt the coldness envelop him and, while focused intently on the cross, he was also flooded with memories of Violet in the sea, of swimming towards her. He remembered her strong graceful movements, and how her skin had felt against his in the cool salty water. He swam for the cross like it was Violet and no one stood a chance against him.

When he came out of the water back onto the dock, holding his prize, cold but elated, he looked for Violet on the shore and smiled proudly at her. Violet saw his dimples appear fully for the first time since she'd left the island nearly four years ago now. She smiled back and waved to him. Somehow she'd known he'd be the one to find the cross today.

She felt so safe and at ease in that moment, she was reminded of her dream on Sfinari beach several years ago, where she'd floated effortlessly in her little boat, protected by countless souls all around her. She remembered the torch-bearer at the river telling her not to feel unworthy of the good things that were to come. She smiled and breathed deeply.

Someone handed Dimitri a towel, but he didn't take his eyes off Violet, standing on the shore, watching him intently. He dried himself off, picked his way through the small crowd and embraced Violet triumphantly. If anyone in Sfinari had any thoughts, it was only to wonder why they didn't kiss. But Violet was thrilled to feel his arms around her again, just for a few moments.

Chapter 21

As spring approached, they began spending more time in Dimitri's cottage. Violet was pleased to be back at beautiful Sfinari Beach. She slept in his bed while he slept on his couch. He always insisted she have the bed. Violet could smell him on the sheets, a scent like honey and herbs and pine. She wouldn't have stopped him if he'd joined her, but still, she was content and didn't want to rush anything. She knew things were complicated. Besides, waiting was something she'd had a lot of practice at.

On March 13th, Violet asked Dimitri if he was free the following day. "There are some places I'd like to show you," she said in a mock American accent, echoing his invitation years ago.

Dimitri smiled. "Sure, but if it's a road trip, I think we should take my car. No offense, but I don't think your tomato can is safe for long distances."

"You're just biased against tomato cans because of your traumatic American shopping experiences," shot back Violet, still in her exaggerated accent.

Dimitri laughed. He'd only started laughing again in the last few weeks. It felt liberating.

"We can take your car, but I'm driving this time," said Violet firmly.

Violet and Dimitri drove his little white car down to Frangokastello, on the south coast. It was one of the places they'd talked about visiting together when she came back. The seaside tavernas and villas were still sleeping for the winter, lending an air of peacefulness akin to a slow waking after a long restful slumber. They walked around the old Venetian castle and along the deserted beach. The Libyan Sea stretched out before them, its waves breaking gently on the pale sand. Behind them, the White Mountains rose up dramatically, like ancient stewards of the shores.

"Do you know about the *drosoulites?*" Dimitri asked her as they wandered out along a sandy peninsula.

"The what?" asked Violet. It was a cool morning and she was wearing Persephone's favourite sweater. She knew it didn't suit her; it was too big and red wasn't her colour. But wearing it always made her feel that Persephone was by her side.

"Drosoulites. It means 'dew shadows.' People say they've seen processions of figures here, some on horseback, and some carrying weapons. They start off at the church over there." He pointed to a small building to the east, a bell tower and cross barely visible from where they stood. "And they walk towards the castle." He

460

nodded in the direction of the imposing structure. "It happens in late May or early June, around the anniversary of the battle here in 1828. Some people say they're the ghosts of Greek fighters who died in the battle against the Turks. Other people say it's just a mirage from Africa."

"What do you think they are?" asked Violet curiously.

Dimitri shrugged. "I don't know. I'd have to see them myself I guess. But they looked real enough to deter a Turkish army sixty years later, and apparently the Germans opened fire on them in the Second World War."

Violet thought for a moment and remembered the double-slit experiment Persephone had told her about. "Maybe they're both," she suggested.

"Ghosts and a mirage?"

"Well, maybe they're whatever the person who sees them believes they are." She paused, unsure whether she could explain the double-slit experiment clearly. "Did you know light is both particles and waves? Persephone once told me about this 'double-slit experiment,' it's a quantum mechanics thing. I don't know if I can remember all the details, but basically, depending how you look at light, how you measure it, it behaves either like particles or like waves. If we look for particles, we find particles, not waves. But if we look for waves, we find waves instead of particles. So, we sort of...create and change reality just by observing it."

Dimitri thought this over, feeling the science was slightly over his head. "So, you think people make the *drosoulites* whatever they look for? They see ghosts if they want, and a mirage if they want? And both are...valid?"

"Something like that," said Violet, wishing Persephone were here to explain it all more clearly. She smiled as she imagined her walking on the beach beside them, her eyes lighting up and her hands moving wildly as she described the experiment excitedly.

"So, what do you think the *drosoulites* are? I mean, if you had to choose one option." Dimitri asked.

"You know, I think a mirage from North Africa is pretty amazing in itself. But I'm gonna go with ghosts. Mainly because I want there to still be people who believe in ghosts and spirits. I don't want all the magic in the world to disappear like the Piskies did."

"Well, maybe we should come back here, in late May and stay for a night or two," suggested Dimitri. "We could look for the *drosoulites* at dawn, and turn them into ghosts just by looking at them." He smiled at Violet. "And you know the south coast of Crete is supposed to be one of the best places in the world to see the milky way."

"I remember, you told me that years ago. I still don't know if it could possibly look more amazing than it does over the headland at Sfinari Beach," said Violet, remembering the night she fell asleep on the beach nearly four years ago now.

"Well, I guess we'll have to see."

"OK, but let's not wait four years this time."

"No," said Dimitri, squeezing her hand.

As they drove back north through the mountains, the wildflowers not quite yet in bloom, but the promise of spring in the air, Violet watched the scenery pass as she drove and felt so full of happiness she thought she might burst.

After exploring the beach, they'd wandered around the pretty nearby town of Chora Sfakion and sat in a cafe, sharing a *sfakianopita* and sipping *zesti sokolata*.[53] It had felt like they were just an ordinary couple, on a pleasant day out.

Violet turned and smiled at Dimitri, sitting next to her in the car. He smiled back and put his hand on her knee, without thinking, because it felt like the most natural thing in the world. But the feeling of her leg under his hand brought back a flood of memories of Violet's legs, and none of them were exactly chaste. He pulled his hand away. He was still conflicted.

Nefeli had passed away seven months ago, and he felt he should wait a year before starting anything romantic. Every time Violet made him laugh, a hint of guilt still crept up in the back of his mind. But then, Nefeli had told him to go and be with Violet, to allow himself to be happy. He wasn't sure whether being with Violet or not being with Violet was more disrespectful to Nefeli's memory.

"I'm sorry," he said.

"For what?" said Violet, who, for her part, was thrilled he'd touched her for just a moment.

"For not...you know...for only holding your hand." He looked out the window and then at her.

"Well, technically you just touched my leg so I'm calling that a step in the right direction," she turned and smiled at him.

---

[53] Hot chocolate

He grinned and looked out ahead at the road stretching out through the mountains.

"Honestly, Dimitri, it's OK. You don't need to explain anything to me, and you definitely don't need to apologize. I'm just happy to be spending time with you. If you want to just hold hands for ten years, really, I'm OK with that."

"Is that what you want?" asked Dimitri.

"To hold hands for ten years?"

"Yes."

"Well, no. I suppose I'd like to hold hands for many *many* years. And ideally I'd also like to make crazy passionate love in the sea again, but you know, I'm not in a rush."

Dimitri laughed out loud and blushed slightly. He wasn't used to talking so openly about these things.

"The sea is a bit cold this time of year," he managed to respond.

"Yeah, but I bet we could warm it up," joked Violet.

Dimitri laughed and shook his head.

"But you know, no rush," added Violet.

They drove in comfortable silence for several minutes until Violet asked him in Greek if later in the year, they could visit Spinalonga. Dimitri's dimples appeared as she spoke. They usually spoke English together, but he still loved hearing her speak Greek. She spoke fairly well now, but with an accent that he found utterly beguiling.

"Nai," he replied, "but only if you speak Greek to me the whole time."

"Sure, as long as I don't have to explain the double-slit experiment to you again." She spoke in Greek, with the exception of "double-slit experiment," which she had no idea how to translate. To be fair, Dimitri didn't either. They smiled at each other, and the space between them in Dimitri's little car was saturated with their pure and undemanding love.

Back in Maleme, Violet pulled into the grocery store parking lot. "I just remembered I need a few things," she said, still in Greek. She gestured for him to come with her. "I might need some help," she said, smiling mischievously.

Dimitri was suspicious. "You sound like you're plotting something."

"Me? Plotting? I don't know *what* you're talking about."

They walked into the store and Violet led Dimitri over to the produce section and picked up a large honeydew melon. Dimitri laughed. Now he could see where this was going. They walked to the checkout, where Violet barely managed to sputter, *"Poso kanei to peponi?"* before she and Dimitri collapsed in hysterical laughter.

The confused store clerk smiled awkwardly and wondered what drug the couple were on and where he could get it. They paid and left with the giant melon, stumbling out through the door in fits of laughter. Dimitri put his arm around her and kissed her forehead. Violet thought she might explode with happiness then and there.

Dimitri laid awake on Violet's couch that night, watching her sleep and remembering the night he'd found her sleeping on Sfinari Beach. At one point Violet thrashed and called out in her sleep. He went over and laid a hand on her shoulder to calm her.

"Shhh honeybee, it's OK," he whispered. He stroked her arm and kissed her on the cheek. Violet didn't wake up.

The end of March brought an explosion of wildflowers, and Violet's dreams turned vivid and intense once again. On the last night of March, asleep in Dimitri's cottage, Violet dreamed she'd stepped out of a cave and was walking steadily up a mountainside in the dark. She began to realize that there were others around her, on the same path, forming a procession heading upwards. As she neared a man in front of her, he turned around and she recognized the torchbearer from the river. Indeed, he was holding a torch, which he passed to her as he nodded a silent acknowledgment. Violet nodded back and he handed her some crumbs of barley rusk. She instinctively dropped the crumbs into the flame of her torch, knowing they were not gone, but merely transformed.

She turned around to pass the torch on to a tall woman behind her in a simple white gown carrying a basket with a single blood-red poppy. The woman handed Violet the flower, but Violet hesitated, not wanting to take her last bloom. The woman stood and waited, patiently holding out the flower. Violet knew she had to concede, and traded the torch for the flower.

As she turned around again, she was aware that her feet were bare and the grass was soft and cool under them. She continued walking for what seemed like hours, the procession sometimes seeming to dwindle and nearly disappear, then reappearing with a series of torches, passed up and down. Her limbs began to ache but she had no desire to stop walking. She knew the destination would be worthwhile.

Finally, at the top of the mountain, a walled building appeared, the colour of the summer sky. It seemed to glow, as if the sun shone on this one building, though it was surrounded by darkness. The Greek word for light blue, "*galazio,*" echoed through her mind. As Violet drew nearer, she could see that the walls were made of millions of pebbles and small stones, all the same striking blue and perfectly fitted together like a flawless intricate puzzle.

She walked through the archway, down a corridor, and through another archway into a large circular room, the walls composed of the same pebbles as the outside. A grand domed ceiling sat high above her, and as she looked up at it, she wasn't sure if it was the sky she could see, or more blue stones. As she looked down again, she saw that her feet had left the ground. The walls had disappeared and she found herself floating in a perfect endless blue space, moving effortlessly and freely, still holding the red poppy.

Looking closely at the flower, she saw that its dark centre was actually made of tiny intricate peacock feathers, all shades of teal, green, turquoise and black. She couldn't see anyone else, but she knew she wasn't alone; the air vibrated with the energy of a million souls and endless possibilities.

Violet woke up slowly in Dimitri's bedroom, savouring the last remnants of the dream, letting her mind continue floating in the peaceful *galazio.* She could smell Dimitri's coffee and heard the kettle boiling for her tea. Propping up the pillows behind her, Violet reached for her notebook and pen on the bedside table. She wrote feverishly for several minutes.

Lost and Found

It started with an ending
After all, healing dances with loss
and growth moves in valleys

I searched for my twin star
on the mountainside,
The snow-capped peaks and the flowering slopes
above the olive groves
Into the night sky and out beyond the planets
then down to the bottom of the sea
Where a million golden fish became the sun
and grains of sand waited like tiny fallen asteroids

I began to find unexpected things:
A small flame
A rusk
A perfect song
Your heart

But still I searched
lifting every delicate poppy petal,
every prickly wild artichoke leaf,
the soft translucent wings of honeybees

Until the strength of my longing to find
outgrew the object I sought
and I forgot, even while I looked,
        what I had so ardently desired

I laid the petals down,
Put the barley in the fire
and whispered to the water and the air
words both sacred and profane

I reached through the tiny cracks
    in my carefully constructed walls
Until I felt the shapes of the stars
    around my fingers,
Until my eyes closed and I could see with my mind
    the perfect blue world:
The fish, the fossils, the ruined temples,
A billion galaxies racing, floating,
Time falling and twisting,
Gravity bending the fabric of ourselves
into the unspoken calmness of knowing,
while red petals unfold neatly within me.

Pebbles to sand and sea to air
Breath into flight
Feathers blooming in the clouds
Everywhere is here,
where I am
where you are,
Free to be lost
Searching
To be found

Poem completed, Violet slipped out of bed and through the half-open bedroom door. Dimitri didn't see her right away and Violet watched him for a moment as he poured his coffee.

"Kalimera," she said smiling.

Dimitri turned around. *"Kalimera*, honeybee."

Violet still stood in the bedroom doorway, smiling and watching the man she loved.

"You OK?" he asked.

"I'm very OK. I had the most amazing dream."

"Really? Was I in it?" he asked teasingly.

"Well, not exactly, but I sort of knew you were there." Violet walked through the living area over to the small kitchen.

"How did you know?"

"It's a bit hard to explain. But everyone was there, all around me. I could sort of just...feel you in the air." Violet paused and took a sip of the tea that Dimitri had made for her. She could taste the generous dose of thyme honey. "Anyway," she continued, "I'm going to go for my first swim of the year this morning."

Dimitri raised his eyebrows. "Is this an April Fool's joke?"

"Nope. You coming?" she teased, knowing he wouldn't dare.

Dimitri shook his head, but a few minutes later, he went with Violet down to the beach. After all, she had promised him he'd see her swim in the sea again, one day.

It was a beautiful early spring day under a cloudless sky. Gentle waves lapped the pebbly shore. The sun wasn't yet hot but there was a promise of warmth in the air.

Dimitri watched Violet run into the sea and dive under the waves. He smiled. She re-emerged with a slight gasp. "OK," she said, "I admit it's a little bit chilly." Then she dove under again, came back up, and swam along the shoreline.

Dimitri watched her and wondered why on earth he'd waited so long to allow himself to be truly happy. He took off his shirt and waded in. If the water was cold that day, Dimitri didn't feel it. He swam towards Violet. She slowed so he could catch her.

When Dimitri kissed Violet in the sea that morning, all the years they'd spent apart simply disappeared like the stars in the blue sky, eclipsed by the strength of their love, so pure and complete that it warmed the sea and the air around them.

Coda

Violet finally finished her book that summer, with Dimitri and Antonia helping her with some final edits. It was published the following year to great critical acclaim and became an international bestseller. She is currently working on a Greek translation and has plans for a screenplay, as well as a book of poetry.

Dimitri reestablished his hives that spring, with the help of his father, who didn't leave this time. Their relationship remains complicated, and their conversations tend to be restricted to bees.

Antonia and Violet launched their website in June and their business has been growing steadily. Violet did finally succeed in obtaining a license to sell her lotions, and began using Dimitri's honey and beeswax. Her products have been selling well both online and in a handful of shops on Crete, including Antonia's store in Maleme.

Anna and Martin came to visit the following spring. Martin managed to burn while wearing SPF 55 sunscreen, while bird watching in the mountains. He didn't let it ruin their trip. They plan on returning for yearly visits.

Despoina finally told Violet the secret to their family *dolmades,* but she is sworn to secrecy and cannot reveal anything in the pages of this book.

Violet and Dimitri are contemplating a wedding, but Violet is unsure whether the Orthodox Church would allow such a pale member to join their congregation. Either way, they do plan on starting a family but currently are simply enjoying being together.

She and Dimitri (and Persephone the cat) still live between Maleme and Sfinari, spending most of their summers in Dimitri's cottage and winters in Maleme. *Zeus Cretagenes* still looks out for Violet, and she still feeds the stray cats wherever she goes, swims whenever she can, and continues to enjoy asking, *"Poso kanei to peponi?"*

~the end~

Glossary of Greek Terms, Phrases, and Places

To keep things simple for the reader, I've described the Greek words and phrases as they are used in the novel, which may mean in some cases that certain subtleties or alternative forms of the words are left out.

I have endeavoured to spell the Greek words in a way that will be clear to English-speaking readers. Some sounds are of course approximated to the nearest English equivalent. One sound that is difficult to spell with the Latin alphabet is the Greek letter "chi," which I've usually spelled with "ch." This letter combination should be pronounced like the "ch" in the Scottish word "loch."

Aptera / Άπτερα An ancient city, now an archaelogical site located near the bay of Souda, east of Chania. In Greek mythology, it is the site of the contest between the sirens and the muses.

avgolemono / αυγολέμονο A tangy sauce made with eggs and lemon. It may also refer to chicken soup made with this sauce, and rice (kotosoupa avgolemono).

avronies / αυρονιές Wild asparagus, harvested from the mountains in the Spring.

bougatsa / μπουγάτσα A dessert made with phyllo pastry filled with sweet custard and dusted with cinnamon and icing sugar. It may also be made with a savoury cheese filling.

boureki / μπουρέκι Cretan roasted vegetables. This particular dish usually includes potatoes, zucchini, and onions, as well as cheese. Note that this is a Chania specialty; in other parts of Greece, and even other parts of Crete, the same word refers to baked or fried pastries, a very different dish.

briam / μπριάμ Another variation on roasted vegetables, similar to ratatouille. The exact contents may vary, but it often include potatoes, eggplant, tomatoes, peppers and zucchini.

chairo polli / χαίρω πολύ Pleased to meet you.

Chania / Χανιά A city on the northwest coast of Crete, with a striking Venetian port. It is the capital of the Chania regional unit and is on the same site as the Minoan city of Kydonia.

choriatiki / χωριάτικη Greek salad, usually composed of tomato, cucumber, green pepper and feta cheese. It literally translates to "village salad."

chortopita / χορτόπιτα Local wild greens (chorta) and mizithra cheese in phyllo pastry.

Chronia polla! / Χρόνια πολλά! Many years! A common expression on someone's birthday or name day.

Demeter / Δήμητρα The Greek Goddess of agriculture and the harvest, and the mother of Persephone.

dolma (singular), dolmades (plural) / ντολμά, ντολμάδες Vine leaves stuffed with rice and herbs, cooked in lemon juice and often drizzled with avgolemono sauce. They can also include meat, usually ground beef.

dakos / ντάκος A Cretan breakfast dish consisting of barley rusk topped with tomatoes and cheese. It may also include peppers and olives.

Dekapentavgoustos / Δεκαπενταύγουστος The fifteenth of August. It is the Feast of the Dormition of Mary, and a major holiday in Greece.

drosoulites / δροσουλίτες Dew people. The word refers to the ghostly figures reportedly seen at Frangokastello, thought by some to be spirits of the deceased soldiers who fought there against the Turks in 1828.

efharisto / ευχαριστώ Thank you

efharisto polli / ευχαριστώ πολύ Thank you very much.

ekklisakia /εκκλησάκια Tiny churches. Another word for kandilakia (see below).

Ellenika / Ελληνικά The Greek language

Eisai mamakias / Είσαι μαμάκιας You are a mama's boy.

eseis? / **εσείς;** And you? Commonly asked after answering "Ti Kanis?/How are you?". This form is used when you are speaking to more than one person, or are addressing someone formally.

Esi? / **εσύ** And you? This is the informal form.

feta / **φέτα** A Greek brined curd white cheese made from sheep's milk and/or goat's milk

filakia polla / **φιλάκια πολλά** many kisses

Gaia / **Γαία** One of the primordial goddesses in Greek mythology, considered the ancestral mother. Gaia was the embodiment of the earth, and gave birth to the sky (Ouranos) and the sea (Pontus).

gala / **γάλα** milk

galaxias / **γαλαξίας** galaxy

galazio / **γαλάζιο** light blue

gamoto / **γαμώτο** fuck

Hades / **Άδης** Zeus' brother, and the god of the underworld. He fell in love with Persephone and abducted her to be his wife.

halva / **χαλβάς** A sticky cake made with semolina, honey, cinnamon and cloves. Note that this is a different type of halva than the Middle-Eastern tamari-based dessert.

Iraklion / **Ηράκλειο** The capital of Crete, and the largest city on the island. It is a port city located on the north central coast. It is also commonly spelled "Heraklion" when written in English.

Kala Christougenna! / **καλά Χριστούγεννα!** Merry Christmas!

kalimera / **καλημέρα** Good morning

kalimera sas / **καλημέρα σας** Good morning to you

kalispera / **καλησπέρα** Good evening

kalitsounia / **καλιτσούνια** Sweet cheese pastries made with fresh mizithra.

kalla / **καλά** Good. A common response to the question, "Ti kanis?"

kandilakia / καντηλάκια A roadside shrine, set up to commemorate someone who died in a fatal road accident, or to give thanks for surviving a serious accident. Also called ekklisakia (see above).

Kathara Deftera / Καθαρά Δευτέρα Clean Monday. The first day of Lent in the Orthodox Church, and the start of the fasting season. It is often marked by the flying of kites, and signifies the beginning of spring.

Kissamos / Κίσσαμος A port town in the province of Chania, located about 40km west of the city of Chania.

Knossos / Κνωσός A very large and popular bronze age archaeological site located near Iraklion on the north central coast of Crete. It is often said to be the site of the oldest city in Europe.

kourampiedes / κουραμπιέδες Butter cookies covered in icing sugar, usually served at Christmas.

kria sokolata (singular), kries sokolates (plural) / κρύα σοκολάτα, κρύες σοκολάτες A cold chocolate drink.

Kronos / Κρόνος The son of Gaia and Uranos, and the leader of the first generation of Titans. He ruled during the Golden Age until he was overthrown by his son Zeus.

Kyria / Κυρία Mrs.

Kyrie / Κύριε Mr.

Maleme / Μάλεμε A village about 16km west of Chania. Its military airport was the site of an important battle in the Second World War.

melissa / μέλισσα Honeybee. It also means lemon balm.

melomakarona / μελομακάρονα Christmas cookies made with cinnamon, cloves, honey and orange

Mila mou sta Ellenika parakalo / Μίλα μου στα Ελληνικά παρακαλώ Speak to me in Greek please.

mitera / μητέρα Mother

mizithra / μυζήθρα A Greek whey cheese made from sheep or goat milk

477

Muses / Μούσες - The mythical sources of inspiration for the arts and knowledge.

nai / ναι Yes

ochi / όχι No

Ouranos / Ουρανός One of the Greek primordial deities and the personification of the sky. Ouranos was the son and husband of Gaia, as well as the father of Kronos.

paidi mou / παιδί μου My child. Often used by any older person addressing a young person.

pame / πάμε Let's go

pappous / παππούς Grandfather

Persephone / Περσεφόνη The Greek goddess of the underworld, and the daughter of Demeter and Zeus. She was abducted by Hades but was permitted to return above ground for half the year. She is also referred to as "Kore," meaning girl.

perimeno / περιμένω I wait

Platanakia Beach / Παραλία Πλατανάκια A small secluded beach just south of Sfinari beach.

polli kalla / πολύ καλά Very good

polli oraia / πολύ ωραία Very beautiful

portokalopita / πορτοκαλόπιτα A dessert made with layered phyllo sheets soaked in sweet orange syrup.

Poso kanei to peponi? / πόσο κάνει το πεπόνι; How much is the honeydew melon?

rakomelo / ρακόμελο Raki that has been flavoured with honey and spices, often cinnamon and cardamom.

raki / ρακή A distillate of pomace, what remains in grape presses after wine-making. Also called Tsikoudia, it is often served in Crete as a complimentary digestif after a meal.

sfakianopita / σφακιανόπιτα Cheese pie with nuts and honey. It is named after the Sfakia region, which is located next to Chania.

Sfinari / Σφηνάρι A village on the west coast of Crete, about 60km west of Chania. Sfinari beach is a lovely swimming spot, in the bay just below the village.

sirens / σειρήνες Creatures that were half-bird and half-women, renowned for their beautiful singing. They were originally Persephone's companions, but were thrown into the sea by the muses, where they became known for luring sailors into the rocks with their songs.

sizigos / σύζυγος Wife or husband.

skaros / σκάρος Parrotfish

spanakopita / σπανακόπιτα Spinach pie

Spinalonga / Σπιναλόγκα An uninhabited islet just off the coast of Crete near Elounda. It was previously a Venetian fort and was also a leper colony. Currently it is a popular tourist destination.

Stin eyia su / Στην υγειά σου To your health, a common Greek toast

Tha ithela ena chai me yala parakalo. / θα ήθελα ένα τσάϊ με γάλα παρακαλώ. I'd like a cup of tea with milk please.

theia / θεία Aunt

theios / θείος Uncle

Ti kanete? / Τι κάνετε; How are you? Used in formal situations, or when addressing more than one person.

Ti kanis? / Τι κάνεις; How are you? Used in casual or familiar circumstances, when addressing one person.

tragodia / τραγωδία Tragedy

veveia / βέβαια Of course, certainly

yemista / γεμιστά Stuffed vegetables, usually peppers and/or tomatoes. They may be stuffed with rice, meat, or cheese.

yemistes piperies / γεμιστές πιπεριές Stuffed peppers

yia sas / γεια σας Hello. Used in formal situation, or when addressing multiple people.

yia su / γεια σου Hello. Used in informal situations, when addressing only one person.

yiayia / γιαγιά Grandmother

zesti sokolada / ζεστή σοκολάτα Hot chocolate

Zeus / Ζευς The king of the Greek gods, and the god of the sky and weather. His most prominent symbols are the thunderbolt and the eagle.

Zeus Cretagenes / Ζευς Κρεταγενής Cretan-born Zeus, an earlier version of the Olympian Zeus (see above). According to a Cretan myth that emerged in Mycenean times (though it may have roots in earlier Minoan mythology), Zeus was a minor god, a mortal, who was born, lived, and died a violent death as a young man, but came back from the dead. His resurrection was celebrated every year in Crete.

Acknowledgments

My first thanks must go to my very understanding husband, for tolerating being a "writing widow" over the past year or so, but particularly in the weeks I was feverishly completing my initial draft. I'm afraid I rather neglected to contribute to any household tasks during this time, and he was remarkably patient. He was my first and last reader, helping with every step along the way, from proofreading to logo design.

I'd also like to extend a huge thank you to Anna Doxastaki, dramatherapist and general fount of knowledge, for her invaluable Cretan perspective. Beyond just correcting my very basic Greek, Anna gave me much-needed insight into the food, festivals, and nuances of Cretan culture.

I am also grateful to Natasa Cecez-Sekulic, author, content creator, and self-publisher, for her insightful feedback and suggestions, especially in regards to the psychology of Balkan men, as well as the self-publishing process.

Thanks also goes out to Natasha Pashchenko, musician and linguistic wizard, for her very thorough proofreading, and removal of unnecessary pronouns.

I also owe a debt of gratitude to the very talented Jessica Lichon of Lichon Photography, for reading the full text of this novel and generously working with me to come up with a stunning cover photo.

And, finally, thank you to my sister Emily Perkins, for agreeing to model for the aforementioned photo, which meant standing waist-deep in the frigid Pacific Ocean in February, a feat I think even Violet would have struggled with.

I'd also like to mention the books and online resources I referred to while researching for this novel. My education in beekeeping began with *Bee Time* by Mark L. Winston, an intriguing read for novices and experts alike. Very informative but much less entertaining was *The BBKA Guide to Beekeeping (2nd ed.),* by Ivor Davis NDB and Roger Cullum-Kenyon. The online resource *Beekeeping in the Mediterranean from Antiquity to the Present* (ed. F. Hatjina, G. Mavrofridis, R. Jones) was also invaluable in understanding the history of beekeeping on Crete.

A History of Crete by Chris Moorey was my main reference for (you guessed it) the history of Crete, and I highly recommend this book to anyone interested in learning more about this beautiful island. I also referred to *The Civilization of Ancient Crete* by R.F. Willetts, a somewhat more esoteric read, but full of fascinating facts nonetheless.

I discovered the wonderful book *Mythos* by Stephen Fry a little late in the game, but did use it to update some of my descriptions of various myths. My initial research on Greek myths referred to many websites, but mainly https://www.theoi.com/ and the online Oxford Research Encyclopedias: https://oxfordre.com/. In addition, I took inspiration from Dudley Wright's 1919 text, *Eleusinian Mysteries and Rites,* describing the cult of Demeter and Persephone, recently reprinted by the Lost Library.

Besides drawing on my own experiences exploring the island of Crete, I referred to many websites for information, including https://www.explorecrete.com/, which also informed my descriptions and reflections on Cretan myths, specifically *Zeus Cretagenes.*

My ongoing learning of the Greek language has been through the *BBC Greek Language and People (new edition)* textbook and audio recordings. I am especially thankful for the very pleasing phrase, *"Poso kanei to peponi?"* which, like Violet, I hope to be able to use in Greece one day.

When writing about Cornwall, I drew on my own visits to the region, but also referred to several websites, mainly https://www.atlasobscura.com, and for folklore: https://faeryfolklorist.blogspot.com. W.Y. Evans-Wentz's 1911 text, *The Fairy Faith in Celtic Countries* (also reprinted by the Lost Library) contained a fascinating section on Cornish folklore and beliefs, which also informed my writings and reflections on the Piskies.

ACKNOWLEDGMENTS

This is a work of fiction. While it references existing locations, institutions, and global events, the characters and their lives are wholly imaginary. Any resemblance to actual persons, living or dead, or actual personal events is purely coincidental. In addition, details of geography have sometimes been altered in order to better fit the storyline.

Thank you so much to everyone involved in making this book a reality. I am eternally grateful for all the hours of hard work that so many of my friends willingly contributed. Without all of this help and support, this book would never have become a reality.

Ευχαριστώ πολύ!

About the Author

Shannon Perkins Carr is a certified music therapist and emerging writer. Born and raised in North Vancouver, Canada, she completed a Bachelor of Music degree at the University of British Columbia in 2005. She then worked for several years as a guitar teacher, administrator, and rock musician. Shannon moved to London, England in 2008, where she continued working as a musician and administrator. In 2013, she graduated with distinction, earning an MA in music therapy at Anglia Ruskin University, Cambridge.

Shannon has written articles on music and movement, as well as inter-cultural adaptations, and has presented at music therapy conferences in both Canada and the UK. She currently runs Connecting Through Music, offering music therapy, education, and classical guitar performance in Victoria, BC, where she has lived since 2019. *Searching for Persephone* is her debut novel.